W9-AVS-288

THE MANDARIN CLUB

A Novel

THE MANDARIN CLUB

A Novel

To DIANE —

Hope you enjoy
the story!
Cheers, *[signature]*
5/13/06

GERALD
FELIX
WARBURG

**bancroft
press**

Published by Bancroft Press ("Books that enlighten")
P.O. Box 65360, Baltimore, MD 21209
800-637-7377
410-764-1967 (fax)
www.bancroftpress.com

Cover and interior design: Tammy Sneath Grimes, Crescent Communications
www.tsgcrescent.com • 814.941.7447

ISBN 1890862-45-2
LCCN 2005934850

Printed in the United States of America

First Edition

1 3 5 7 9 10 8 6 4 2

FOR SANDOL MILLIKEN STODDARD
Prolific author, wise teacher, true friend

✳

What is precious is never to forget,
    Never to allow gradually the traffic to smother
With noise and fog the flowering of the spirit . . .
The names of those who in their lives fought for life
Who wore at their hearts the fire's center
Born of the sun they traveled a short while towards the sun
And left the vivid air signed with their honor.

—STEPHEN SPENDER

1

THE LAST DANCE

They were an eccentric bunch, self-selected and cocksure. They scorned pretense. They shared a passion for debate and dialectic, for the dynamic of intellectual competition as a blood sport. They were subversives, eager to reject the rules of the day, pledged in countless toasts to live freely and fully.

In the beginning, as Rachel remembered it, there was simply the "Gang of Five"—Mickey Dooley, Branko Rosza, Alexander Bonner, Martin Booth, and Barry Lavin. They had been drawn to each other from among the intimidating blend of braniacs and athletes, valedictorians and 4-H Club presidents who peopled the Stanford campus. The feeling of obligation was burdensome, the Spanish mission-style walls of Serra House—home to the university's China Studies Center—thick and imposing. But under Mickey's guiding hand, they had found each other for inspiration and mirth. They had bonded together to take on the world, somehow sensing already that their lives would become entangled.

They were public school kids, products of those Jimmy Carter years, the ideological wasteland of the post-Vietnam War era. The Sixties and their passion-driven cause-politics were over. For the young, nothing had risen to replace them.

Each of them had harbored a vision on that New Year's Eve—that last night of celebration before 1979 and their new lives arrived. They had shared a distant dream, a dream of China that had for so long seemed remote and unattainable.

Tonight, their sense of possibility was electric. Only two weeks had passed since the stunning White House announcement: Washington was abandoning Taiwan and recognizing the communist government in Beijing. Diplomatic relations with the People's Republic would commence with the new year.

China's vast interior was now accessible to Americans and American commerce. The forbidden door that had stood before them, threatening to

1

render irrelevant their studies of language and bureaucracy, had swung open. Opportunity loomed before them in the China of their imaginings. China, the infinitely large consumer market. China, the morally superior Middle Kingdom. China, the anti-Soviet counterweight.

Tomorrow, their years of speculative theories would be challenged. Their academic idyll would be over and a new reality at hand. The news from Washington had transformed them. Suddenly, they were hot properties, their knowledge valued, their skills in great demand.

"It's too damn hysterical!" Mickey had chortled one day in the lunchroom as he waved a stack of pink phone message slips. "I've got a bunch of banks in a bidding war—for me!"

Immediately after President Carter's speech, the first corporate calls had begun. Bechtel Construction was looking for a translator for a trade mission. Chevron Oil needed a bilingual office manager. Could Serra House recommend anybody? Within forty-eight hours, the telephone queries had become more urgent. Advanced Micro Devices needed an expert on the Science and Technology Ministry, fast, and they would pay top dollar. United Airlines wanted to build an Asia sales force fluent in Mandarin and knowledgeable about Chinese contract law. Even the Central Intelligence Agency contacted the Serra House head, trolling anxiously for brains to beef up their analysis capabilities.

One of the campus' sleepiest backwaters—where scholars pored over translations of Chinese bureaucratese and theorized about Politburo decision-making—became the prime hunting ground for frantic recruiters. To the delight of all, the handful of adventurers who had taken a flier on the obscure field of China studies—while mastering Mandarin on the side—were suddenly being offered signing bonuses, if only they would join up tomorrow.

They could reinvent themselves. On the streets of Beijing, or among Washington's new elite of China experts, each could adopt a new persona. They would be shorn of the heavy definition of past lives in small towns and school cliques. With their new purpose came the freedom to transform themselves as the world changed about them. Like the very remoteness of China, this promise of liberation was itself a compelling attraction.

The guys in the Club faced the future with a confidence that Rachel, the latecomer and the sole female, could only envy. They prodded each other, striving for accomplishment and a happiness they could not quite define. They challenged each other from library to tutorial, from the drinking contests in the bar to alleged conquests in the bedroom. Yet, with all their quirks, they seemed an unlikely mix.

Mickey Dooley was the most calculating of the originals, a flip womanizer whose charm lay in his appearance of utter directness. He had been blessed with a skill in presentation that endeared him to his elders—part Puck, part Daniel Boone, part Donald Trump. Mickey loved his campus years; nevertheless, he was the one most eager to leave the security of the familiar. He was an Army brat, an outdoorsman who knew the western desert from a childhood passed in such mischief as hunting prairie dogs with firecrackers and a pocketknife. He was ingenious, seemingly able to talk his way through anything.

Booth—"Martin" to his late father, but simply "Booth" to the rest—was clumsy and earnest, burdened with the guilt of a minister's son. His Iowa roots were deep: the Dust Bowl privations of preceding generations had somehow been mainstreamed through the family DNA. When the car tire went flat on one of their road trips, Booth instinctively quoted Scripture. He expected life to be hard; his Swedish ancestors had never known a life of privilege. He gave thanks for the camaraderie of the gang, their capacity for intense study broken by weekends of amusement in which, otherwise, he might never have indulged. He remained righteous to a fault, a crusader at heart.

Then there was Alexander Bonner, their skeptical Steinbeck. Alexander retained an air of remove that could have been mistaken for aloofness. It was almost otherworldly, this ability of his to sit silent and bemused, to observe their manic play from the fringe. He saw things, though. He saw humanity in all its frailties, savoring the idiosyncrasies of others. Where Mickey was the big talker, eager to fill any silences, Alexander always seemed possessed of some private wisdom. Long before life nearly crushed him, Alexander's reflective presence offered Rachel comfort. He listened. He gave a sense that he knew where she was going before she got there, all while he waited patiently, with those penetrating eyes, for her to arrive.

Branko Rosza was the fourth of the original quintet, serious and fatalistic.

Branko was a Slav, dark in his outlook, expecting the worst from people left to their own base instincts. He was remarkably insightful about individuals and motives, a genius really, if there was one among them. "The Cipher," his classmates called him; he was a chess master who hated to lose. He was first and foremost Hungarian, just one generation removed from the Displaced Person camps of World War II. He remained resolute in his anti-communism; ideology afforded him a clear mission in morally ambiguous times. Even then, his destiny was clear to all: Branko was an operative, born to spy.

Barry Lavin was painfully handsome, a bronzed swimmer with a self-image that brought certitude to his every task. That he was the type of guy who had mapped out a life plan in some Eagle Scout essay did not bother Rachel in those days. He was a Florida bank president's son; his was a world of precision, of absolutes, of targets to be met. He made her feel wanted, his irrepressible optimism winning her trust despite the air of inevitability he brought to his courtship. He succeeded at everything. There was a safety in their coupled status that allowed Rachel to venture out from a secure base, comforted that she had a solicitous big brother nearby. She welcomed the sense of security, however smothering. She tolerated it for years until her self-confidence grew and she finally came to see how he relished the control, keeping his secrets to himself, fearing always where they might lead.

It all came back to Mickey, their ringleader and master of ceremonies— Mickey, who seemed to manipulate developments with a deft hand. It was Mickey who had located the professor on sabbatical whose Menlo Park house was for rent. Mickey first brought the five together under one roof, decreeing that they should set up house together. Mickey orchestrated their madcap road trips; to smoke joints and cheer mindlessly for the Giants at Candlestick Park; to bar-hop on Union Street and holler into the night as they rode cable cars down to the Buena Vista Café; to camp out and skinny-dip along the Pacific coastline at Point Reyes, north of San Francisco. He was the one who insisted on adopting Li Jianjun and shoe-horning him into the studio above the garage on Plum Street. They took pity on "Lee," one of the first exchange students Beijing authorities permitted to study in America, a clever companion who had wearied of his vagabond existence when Stanford locked the stuccoed dorms each holiday break.

Reaching back through the fog of remembrance, Rachel could recall that last December night in 1978 when they had celebrated with gusto. Mickey had billed his grandiose vision "The Last Dance." Branko and Booth had created elaborate place cards with Chinese characters. Barry insisted they dig out what passed for their formal wear, and produced a camera with tripod and flash to memorialize the occasion.

"I feel ridiculous," Rachel had whispered to Barry as they dressed beforehand at the boys' place. The cleavage on her black cocktail dress was overdone. It would bring disapproving clucks from the other guys' dates, she feared.

"You look naughty!" Barry muttered conspiratorially. He relished it a bit too much, she thought—the ritual, the knowing glances at her objectification. He liked it when notice was taken that his girlfriend had removed her granny glasses and curled her hair, playing the role as she took his arm and they made a formal entrance. Barry was in full tuxedo and crisply starched shirt; she looked quite dishy even as she teetered on her heels.

Branko tended the makeshift bar in a room cramped with packing boxes. He puttered with the glasses amidst the cans of soda pop and a bottle of Seagram's scattered on a sticky counter-top. Branko was the most sober of the lot that night, having signed on with the CIA and already begun the security clearance process. He was destined to continue his Jesuit-scholar type work in Washington, helping decipher the captured messages from behind the high walls of Zhongnanhai, the Beijing compound for China's elite government officials. His mission was clear: to unravel the mysteries of Communist power and deploy the insights as a weapon in the struggle against them.

Booth was nursing his drink on the sofa, a party hat on his red hair and a goofy grin on his face. Having taken a job with the Senate Foreign Relations Committee, he would be the first of them to arrive in China. He would head out the very next day with a trade delegation coordinated by his new boss, California's freshman senator, Jake Smithson. Booth's sense of duty was fulfilled as he drank deep and, for this one night, nearly guilt-free.

Mickey Dooley was pumping Marvin Gaye on the communal stereo as he hopped about, ever the host and provocateur. His ponytail swung incongruously behind his baseball cap, a red "A" for Albuquerque stitched above the black bill. He was facing the radical change ahead with cool aplomb as he danced one by one with all the guys' dates, fueled by the energy of the party he had launched. Mickey floated above the pedestrian concerns of others, but then, things always seemed to fall into his lap. He had closed a sweetheart deal with American Express, to assist the marketing director in establishing a new Beijing office. Mickey with an expense account—it was a frightening concept.

Barry, Rachel's Almost-Perfect-Boyfriend, was dancing to a tune of his own, working methodically at some kind of fox trot, alone with his drink. He would pause periodically to admire his form in the long mirror fronting the hall closet, humming to himself, lost in his private reverie. He had signed on with IBM to develop Chinese sales opportunities. It was an ideal set-up for a man intent on playing the sharpest poker hand and cornering the largest stack of chips.

The plan had been for Rachel to follow in June, once she finished her bachelor's degree. They would get married at some point—either at her folks' place in Wyoming or in Stanford's Memorial Chapel. Her hopes for a history doctorate would have to be put on hold. She was just trying to keep up, ignoring her intuition, doing the expected. So deep was her hunger for acceptance that she had mastered a capacity for dismissing self-doubt.

From the start, Rachel had been uneasy with her role in their little fraternity, the only female Mandarin language specialist and the sole undergraduate in the China program at Serra House. The several years age difference that separated her from most of the scholars seemed at times an entire generation as she struggled to project a tough exterior, fearful of being found wanting. She liked surrounding herself with the more certain guys, whose depths and contradictions were left less explored. She liked men's clothes, still preferring the feel of denim and corduroy, the smells of leather and a dusty kerchief, over soft linens or silk. She kept her thick blonde hair in a knot, wanting desperately, as in her Wyoming ranch days, to be accepted as just one of the gang.

She was nagged by a sense that she had missed out on something, that she was just a little late to the party, not privy to the inside joke, laughing too anxiously with the older boys. The "Summer of Love" had never made it to Cody High. By the time she arrived in Palo Alto, LBJ and Nixon were history. The Vietnam experience and Watergate had already become loaded metaphors, no longer current events. She had missed all the excitement the older students had lived, the satisfying clarity derived from the contest of good and evil.

She bonded with the troupe, though, through many months of shared seminars and common dreams. There was established a tribal commitment to each other that seemed certain to endure. For Rachel, this family provided emotional context, making her feel, even while romanced by Barry, that she had found another set of brothers, as solid as her own flesh and blood.

Right on time, Alexander had appeared, rumpled as ever in his chinos, sporting a tacky orange tie. Now sitting on the couch, he was tossing a football from hand to hand. He, too, was departing soon, off to chronicle the American landings in Beijing as a special correspondent for the *San Francisco Chronicle*. Rachel had been secretly disappointed. She noticed even then how she lived vicariously through others, how her hopes had been higher for Alexander. She expected he would be the first in the bunch to actually get that Ph. D.; his ability to discern the nuances in *People's Daily* was remarkable. But he, too, was determined not to be left behind when the adventure began.

They could not be certain what Li Jianjun really made of them all. Acneed and shy, Lee was ever so serious when sober. He drank little that night as he watched their antics with a look of sorrow. He had brought no date to witness their rite of passage, and spent much of the evening on the back porch, deep in conversation with the equally earnest Branko.

Lee was, they had belatedly discovered, the most genuine intellectual of them all, the one who most revered ideas for their own sake, endlessly questioning premises and implications. He pressed far beyond what was safe and acceptable, willing to test the gods. A product of great hardships, Lee savored the freedoms the others often took for granted. His patriotic vision was clear. His very foreignness—and his capacity for self-criticism—enabled him to see the contradictions in their lives to which the others were then oblivious.

It was Lee who harbored the most dangerous desire to challenge the status quo, the one true revolutionary among them. Soon, he would be forced home by events, home to duty and country, home to witness the American invasion, the hordes of capitalist missionaries whose gaudy individualism and raucous style so riled his father and China's old guard. Lee, alone, was burdened with the foresight to fear the events to come.

To the rest, it seemed their moment had arrived. Barry was finally going to make some money. Branko would have a real job confronting a formidable adversary. Booth would answer the call to public service, with a decent salary to boot. Mickey would have to get a haircut. Now, it was all to begin.

So they drank that sentimental New Year's Eve—rum and scotch and sweet soda pop, a volatile mix that would only prolong wicked hangovers. Rachel could remember the toasts still.

They pledged to honor each other always, to treasure the time of shared lives lived fully. They swore never to forget. They drank to the future, to the kaleidoscope of possibilities that beguile the young. They toasted to peace, and to prosperity. They drank to each other, to the familial bonds that united them for a time against the forces of chance and change certain to scatter them.

Just before midnight, Mickey roared his parting shot: "China here we come! And may it someday be said that we Mandarins came to do good . . . and did well!"

She could hear him still, his voice quavering with an energy that charged the proceedings with danger. Booth had begun to rise in protest. But Mickey, in his tux top, boots, and blue jeans, had waved him off, barreling ahead, Seven-and-Seven in hand.

"Watch out, or that'll be our epitaph!" Mickey said, giddy with drink. "Just like those old-time missionaries out to convert the native Hawaiians. 'They came to harvest souls. Ended up owning all the land!'"

The challenge implicit in Mickey's benedictory toast spoke to Rachel for years whenever she questioned her purpose. To change the world for the better? Or just to find a comfortable niche within it? To do good, or simply to live well? Mickey's riddle remained, a vivid and haunting memory of an otherwise blurry night.

Years would pass before their once parallel paths would collide and their core principles would be tested: love and honor, duty and country. They would struggle mightily to fulfill their promises, clinging always to visions of how simple things had once seemed so very long ago. ✳

APRIL

2

OPENING DAY

Rachel survived. Buried beneath the tangle of tubes and a bandage wrap that muffled the disembodied hospital voices, she was nearly certain of one fact—she *was* alive. Through her pain, she felt uplifted. The prospect of renewal seemed strangely euphoric.

Drifting in a morphine haze on that day of violence and disintegration, she began to reconstruct the events of the morning. It was Monday, April Fool's Day—the beginning of a new week, a new season. She had been running late again, Rachel recalled, a recurrent tardiness that set her on edge. It seemed she was late to everything in her life. She hated this fault, the Sysiphusian futility with which she tried to perform too many deeds and was left feeling she had not done one thing well.

Routine had steeled her since dawn. It was the routine, the familiar—the packing of the school lunch, the signing of a field trip permission slip—that gave her comfort through the tense years after the 9/11 attacks. She had not done the solo mom part well, however, and she knew it.

Cornflakes and backpacks for Jamie had been a blur. She had failed to be sufficiently amused by the salt-in-the-sugar-jar April Fool's jokes. The ten-year-old gave her one of those sullen, off-to-the-assembly-line looks as he trudged onto the school bus. His innocence made his modest attempts at mischief all the more endearing: Adam before the Fall. She could not protect him and feared for his vulnerability.

Rachel was mired in the past, her thoughts stuck in that extended time of communal loss. She was weary of the holy wars in Baghdad and Kabul, in Leeds and London, of living in al-Qaida's crosshairs and trying to explain it all to her fourth grader. Her mind still replayed the horrific assaults on the nearby Pentagon and New York, recalling the smoke that had hung over Jamie's soccer field for days, the unending stream of funerals at the crowded National Cemetery. She still avoided the Metro and

Amtrak. She still worried about anthrax and the water supply. She took little comfort from all the bio-weapons defense drills held at the local elementary schools; she knew how well "orderly" evacuations had worked in New Orleans.

The streets of her Arlington neighborhood retained some of the gung ho boosterism from those long months of recovery. Rachel had found some solace in the return of worthy values—that old-fashioned community feeling. But the intoxicating wave of Yuppie patriotism—and the righteous certitude it had brought to her many friends in government—had grown old. Now, when she eyed one of those faded "Let's Roll!" bumper stickers, it only fed her disquiet.

As Rachel walked the three blocks back from Jamie's bus stop, she summoned resources for her daily transition from nurturer to business woman. A swirl of inconvenient emotions weighed upon her.

It was a bright world all about her, a world of scrubbed faces and lumbering Rockwellian school buses pulling relentlessly forward. There were the neighbors plowing defiantly down the hills and onto the George Washington Parkway in their gargantuan Expeditions and Humvees, red-white-and-blue flags snapping crisply on their antennae.

Yet she gazed skeptically at the tidy flowerbeds amidst the oaks and whitewashed picket fences. She sensed silent fears lurking behind the cheerful facades, worries of dying parents and moody children, troubled marriages and floundering careers. Fissures, she was sure, ran deep beneath the placid beauty of the suburban idyll.

Barry was away once more, meeting with some corporate board in L.A., or with some honey in New York. Or maybe he had embarked on his umpteenth IPO tour from Hell, selling Shanghai-produced chips in Vancouver, or Illinois tractors in China. She could picture the land drifting by below the corporate Gulfstream while Barry surfed his e-mail, disposing of little items in his annoyingly precise manner as he pecked at his keyboard.

Slogging over the Roosevelt Bridge in traffic, Rachel longed for a home in the countryside, away from the constant perils of the capital. She envied the ease of Barry's escape. He was the man of one thousand exits, the master at avoiding intimacy. Riding in the cool distant blue, that was Barry, all suit, no soul. With whom did he really share his heart? She no longer knew. Once again, she had slept poorly, yearning to be touched.

She regarded herself dispassionately in the mirror; she felt rushed for the one appointment of the day she looked forward to—breakfast with Alexander. In her haste, she had overdone the rouge on her cheeks. Her dark blonde curls were a bit askew, though the recent highlights were holding. Thick welcoming lips. Strong chin and bright eyes. But a neck that betrayed her. The beginning of long wrinkles undeniably placed her in her forties. She felt pretty enough—the compliments still came, the admiring manly looks that uplifted her as she strode by. She was morning-fatigued already, however, and she was running late, again.

She would have to drop her car at the garage and go straight to the Willard without checking in upstairs at her Talbott, Porter and Blow office across F Street. She'd have to rush back from breakfast for her partners' nine o'clock weekly. Mickey Dooley and Lee were supposed to be in town for a ten o'clock meeting on export licenses with their man from the Chinese Embassy. She chaired the firm-wide review of lobbying projects at eleven. Then Senator Jake Smithson was down for a private lunch Talbott had asked her to sit in on—fundraising for his presidential campaign, no doubt.

Worse yet, it was starting to snow, the spitting seeds of moisture perversely blossoming white. They danced defiantly through the cherry trees along Constitution Avenue, where Rachel sat in her red convertible, punching the program buttons in a vain search for tranquility. *Whose wicked sense of contradiction was designing this day?* She would ponder the thought many times before she could finally rest.

Alexander Bonner would be early. But then Alexander, the first-born, was always early. He savored the dawn hours, country or city; something in the sense of possibility inspired him. "Mornings are like an empty baseball diamond," he had once explained. "Lines chalked, infield dragged, grass cut, with a clean white ball waiting on the pitcher's mound."

He would begin his days with classical music, preferring the calm of Brahms to the passion of Beethoven, then amble through the newspapers, in no particular hurry. Alexander never rushed things. He was a born observer, Rachel believed, a man who could truly hear you without that annoyingly patronizing smirk effected by so many modern males—the one that said, "*OK, this is the part where I pretend to listen so we can then do it my way.*"

Alexander had finished with the serious news and was deep into the day's special baseball coverage when Rachel finally arrived at the high-ceilinged dining room of the Willard Hotel. She gathered herself at the threshold, watching him in his corduroys and rumpled broadcloth shirt as he chewed his waffle. To her, Alexander seemed very much the bachelor, marked by his loss, sixteen months since his wife Anita had died of ovarian cancer. He sat strong-shouldered, with strands of thinning yellow hair and a gaze still vibrant in its intensity.

"Happy Opening Day!" She gave him a hasty peck on the cheek and a one-armed hug. "I'm glad you've eaten."

"Happy April Fool's Day," he offered as she sighed and sat, at 8:22 a.m., breathing hard.

"I'm so sorry. The traffic was a bear."

"Hey, I'm the optimist . . . I figured you'd make it. Even ordered breakfast for you." He gestured smoothly at her plate. "Bran muffin and cranberry juice, right?"

"Bless you!"

She pulled at her oversized muffin and the conversation flowed easily, sliding from the personal to the professional.

Alexander asked first about Jamie.

"As usual, he's lost in his daydreams," Rachel said with a smile. "He creates a whole fantasy world where he hardly hears me when I call."

"The boy needs a kid brother—or sister."

Rachel grimaced. "It's hard to explain things to kids these days. Bombs in the subway, anthrax in the mail. Freak dancing. Heck, I was reading to him the other night, that Paul Simon book, *At the Zoo*. You know, with the lyrics of the old Simon and Garfunkel song? Anyway, he says, 'Why would a hamster turn on frequently?'"

"So what did you say?" She had Alexander laughing, wondering at his own lack of parenting skills.

"What *can* you say? I just hugged him and changed the subject."

As Rachel ate, Alexander sidled up to the work part of their meal. A background interview was ostensibly part of his agenda this day. It was to be off-the-record, yet promised to be perversely stilted for old friends. Alexander's *Los Angeles Times* was doing a big series on K Street power brokers, and he had been assigned a sidebar on lawyer-lobbyists with international clients. It was only natural for Rachel, as one of the top lobbyists in the city, to offer some guidance.

He waited for her to settle in before beginning his queries. "So, I looked up your registrations last night, the Lobbying Disclosure Act forms. Impressive list of foreign clients there."

"Sleuthing on-line again, huh?"

"It's remarkable what you can access."

"Pisses me off what they make me put on the public record. It's like being on view-cam—having to list every meeting you ever have on Capitol Hill. One sleazeball like Abramoff gets exposed and we all get treated like ex-convicts."

"And every campaign donation you ever make. Didn't realize you had so much extra dough to spread around."

"I feel violated when I see all my personal affairs out there. We're the most regulated industry in America."

"Worse than lawyers?" Alexander tested her.

"Most people think we are."

"Speaking of which, how do you work out conflicts at the firm? You know, competing client interests?"

"They don't exist." She smirked, swiping one of his berries, then smacking her lips. "We don't allow ourselves to get put in that box."

"How can you avoid it? Look at your Turkey contract. TPB gets a million a year working for the Turkish Embassy. So what happens when your aerospace clients want to sell fighter planes to Greece?"

"We just field a different team."

"A different team?"

"Different team, same firm. No big deal. Besides, it's the *Armenian* lobby that really goes crazy about our Turkey work. We're 'stra-te-gic coun-se-lors.'" She stretched the phrase out as if it offered some special legitimacy. "We advise them on how to put forward their best argument, how to most effectively advocate their cause."

"I see. But even such morally neutral work has consequences."

"A little judgmental today, aren't we, Mr. Reporter?" She was eyeing Alexander carefully now. "Actually, I won't work for just anybody. Wouldn't work for the Saudis, for one—they treat their women like chattel."

Alexander reflected for a moment before pressing. "So, what about conflicts in your Asia business? You've registered for the big Hong Kong construction consortium, Mitsubishi, and the Taiwan representatives' office here. But then you lobby for a bunch of the U.S. corporations selling in Beijing—"

"That's mostly on export licensing."

"Right. With Mickey Dooley's company, Telstar." Alexander was picking at the last of his berries, spearing them carefully with his fork. His fingers were long and nimble, she observed once again, like those of a cellist. "Selling space launch stuff. Pretty sensitive hardware."

"Mickey's been a hero—the guy holds Telstar's whole China operation together."

"He just nailed that enormous satellite contract. Must have made a killer bonus for pulling off that deal."

"He earns every dime he gets. Mickey's been a real pal to me. Never forgets a favor. I'm supposed to see him today, actually. And Alexander, you know, those overlaps—your so-called 'conflicts'—are not that difficult to manage."

The waiters were hovering now, fussing with crumbs on the starched linen. One was scraping with a silver tool, another refilling the water glasses with an awkward splash. Rachel was flustered to look around at their fellow diners and to realize they had gotten a bit intense. With its heavy drapes, oversized flower pots, and dark formality, the Willard felt more like London or New York than Washington.

"Obviously, the Chinese know you do some work for Taiwan," Alexander said. "And Beijing doesn't object?"

"The Chinese *like* it that we're working with competing interests—that we're playing in the big leagues. Besides, they've got parallel interests on trade stuff: Taiwan is the biggest investor on the Mainland today. They've sunk almost a hundred billion dollars there. Taiwan has got so many people in Shanghai and Guangzhou that Taipei can't cross the Communists on anything. It's like when you think you're buying a house, but it ends up owning you. So, it's copacetic."

"And if it wasn't?"

"We would build a 'Chinese wall,' or something," she offered, smiling demurely. "That's what lawyers are for."

Alexander rolled his eyes. "Don't you ever feel like you're selling the same information twice?"

"What do you do with your *Times* web sites and your Sunday TV talk show gigs? You guys recycle the same stuff over and over, only in different places. So, you can't play holier-than-thou with me."

"That's . . . well . . . different." He could only laugh.

"If I'm the first to know that Senator Smithson is going to pull a flip-flop on the China trade agreement, there's no reason I can't use that information all over town. My job is to be my client's eyes and ears. I'm not going to apologize for being good at it."

They fenced on, Rachel amused, Alexander increasingly uneasy. She was too close a friend for him to play *60 Minutes* interrogator, and there was a limit to where he wanted to go with the reporter/source game. So, as he sipped his tea and carefully regarded this lacquered part of her personality, he tried to turn the conversation away from her affairs at TPB.

It was Rachel who persisted. "Let me tell you something about Mr. Talbott. Do you know what he does on weekends?"

"What?"

"While your caricature of a K Street lawyer has him quail hunting with senators, he's in some inner city church basement helping with programs he sponsors. He supports about a dozen charities in this town—most of them anonymously. The man is like Ebenezer Scrooge—*after* he sees the ghost."

"Wasn't there something peculiar about your Mr. Porter, the bank lawyer who makes all those acquisitions?"

"Alan Porter does all the investment deals, sure."

"So half your shop lobbies and the other half works with Porter investing the profits?"

"Alexander, this is totally off the record, right? Your paper is just doing a case study, an abstract—"

"Of course."

"I'll come after you, you know, Bonner. I'll climb in your window at night and beat you about the head and shoulders if you burn me."

"Remind me to check the locks." He found himself amused at the thought of Rachel paying him a nocturnal visit. "Actually, I believe you would."

"Damn right, I would." She stared him down a moment before continuing. "Well, Mr. Talbott is rather indifferent to wealth. Money is just a way of keeping score for him. It's Porter who runs the books and does the investment deals on the side. So there is your Chinese wall—right down the middle of the firm."

They turned briefly to the headlines of the day—the administration's latest judicial confirmation battle with the filibustering Senate and the endless hearings on the Katrina response. This was just obligatory, though; here they danced to separate tunes. There was an altogether predictable Red State/True Blue chasm dividing their views on all things political. Iraq they had agreed to stop discussing altogether—Rachel backed the unpopular mission to take the fight against terrorism overseas; Alexander condemned the politicized intelligence he insisted had led Washington to prosecute "the wrong war in the wrong place at the wrong time." Rachel was a libertarian Republican, committed to small government, low taxes, and support for the commander in chief. Alexander remained a hopelessly pure, Howard Dean kind of Democrat, the only guy she knew *still* whining about the butterfly ballot, the hanging chads, and the Florida recount.

They shared a bit of gossip about their Stanford friends. Branko's wife had given birth to a fifth child. Mickey was facing a nasty custody fight with his Beijing-born wife, divorce Chinese style. Booth was gearing up for

Senator Smithson's long anticipated presidential primary campaign. Lee was riding herd on North American affairs at Beijing's Foreign Ministry, trying to keep China's bitterly divided factions in line.

There were few surprises. They were all living the lives they had charted so many years ago. Their prophecies were being fulfilled, their talents applied, their dreams realized—or so it seemed.

Alexander spoke of his latest writing project: an essay for the *Sunday Books* section about a recent work on the 1970's legacy, of all things. "I'm trying to find some deeper meaning in a decade everybody files under 'vapid.' "

"It's true," Rachel chuckled. "I always felt ripped off. Came of age in a time without a purpose. Kind of embarrassing. I mean, Disco Fever, indeed."

"You aren't alone," Alexander continued. "People think of the Seventies as some leftover decade. Formless, without transcendent meaning. After the Cultural Revolution. Before Reagan."

"They got teach-ins and free love and birth control pills. We got Watergate and sexually transmitted diseases."

"Seriously, we came of age surrounded by kitsch. Like the author says: 'How does one connect the dots from *Jonathan Livingston Seagull* to Jimmy Carter to the Captain and Tennille?'"

"Vapid!" She was giggling now. "You've got that right; the word is inescapable."

"So I'm playing with this thesis," Alexander continued. "I argue that this whole anti-ideological swing colored Washington's foreign policy. Take our relations with China. Suddenly, it didn't matter if they're Maoists, if only they'd buy our Treasury bonds. I mean, today Home Depot and WalMart are bigger in Beijing than they are in Little Rock. We're starting to believe they're all just like us."

"You're right." Rachel was nodding in agreement. "We just don't want them buying Unocal or Maytag!"

"Anyway, it's blinded us to all the contradictions," said Alexander, barreling ahead, jabbing the air with his fork for emphasis, "and now we're going to pay for it."

"Pay for it?"

"Yep," Alexander insisted. "Sorry to darken your morning, but I see real danger ahead."

"You sound like we're going off to war against the godless Commies. Seems to me we've still got our hands full draining the swamp in Baghdad."

"You can dismiss it all as war-gaming theory. You forget that a lot of those guys in Beijing actually *believe* their own rhetoric—you know, kinda like Wolfowitz and all his former Pentagon pals. That's what the whole fight is still about inside all the Chinese government factions."

"Alexander, it is *not* going to happen."

"When did your capacity to be surprised hit its limit?"

"What do you mean?"

"I don't mean to be alarmist, but look: in the last decade and a half, the Berlin Wall falls. The Soviet empire evaporates. A president gets impeached for lying about a blow job. The race for the White House ends in a *tie*. We see a million refugees flooded out of an American city. Not to mention 9/11, the holy wars with al-Quaida, and tracking Saddam down into some rat hole. What's next—your guys gonna try to make Iraq the fifty-first state?"

Alexander was on a roll.

"So, you'd better be prepared to suspend disbelief all over again."

"C'mon, you bleeding heart," Rachel sighed, recalling all the anxious disappointments of those years. "I've got to make my nine o'clock, or I'll be running late all day."

As she stood, her cell phone rang: her secretary with an update. Mickey Dooley had just called in belatedly from San Francisco to cancel their morning meeting. Lee had bailed on his D.C. trip just last night—stuck in Beijing on some urgent matter, she said. A welcome hole now loomed in Rachel's schedule and she breathed a bit more easily as they rose to leave.

Alexander walked her down Peacock Alley, the long mirrored hallway where, a century before, couples had once paraded in their elegant gowns. Neither Barry nor Alexander's late wife, Anita, had ever been threatened by the friendship between their respective spouses. But then Anita had adored Alexander. She had nourished him, encouraging anything that brought forth his dry wit. Rachel assumed that Golden Boy Barry, the self-absorbed one, would never have noticed if another man had been sweet on his wife.

They reached the sidewalk behind the Willard Hotel and emerged into the sleet. Alexander was to turn right, to the Press Building on Fourteeth Street, Rachel to cross past the Borders Bookstore and the garage, into the beckoning oversized chrome and glass doors lettered "TPB."

He offered a chaste one-armed hug again. But Rachel lingered, chin on his shoulder, her breath warm on his neck.

"You don't like me as a lobbyist, do you?"

"It is not your best side, Rachel. But it's a part of you."

She pushed back, holding him at arm's length.

"It's all me, Alexander. The same old Wyoming cowgirl." Then she kissed him in the center of his forehead, her fingertips soft and soothing at his temples. She kissed him so deliberately that he could feel both lips, moist and lingering.

A roar of sound erupted at that instant, accompanied by a flash of yellow light. The walls of the buildings shed a layer of brick and glass that began to cascade down from a darkening sky.

The concussive pulse staggered them. Shielded by Rachel's frame, it felt to Alexander as if someone had blown out the windows of a car they had been racing. The force intensified, buckling their knees, shuddering all in its wake, like the earthquakes that used to rattle beneath his office high-rise in Taipei.

The FBI agent would later explain that the bomb was relatively small and amateurish. The poorly packed explosives, similar to those used at many construction sites, were consistent with the theory of a lone perpetrator—some disgruntled employee, some random anarchist with a cause.

Alexander remembered hearing a resonant series of thuds as he watched a wave of debris wafting above the avenue. From over Rachel's shoulder, he viewed a riotous mix of yellow Post-Its and paper shreds suspended, icicles of glass and the casual vinyl flotsam of gravity-defying interiors, settling ever so slowly to the ground. The office detritus seemed herded in slow motion by the smoke, until hurtling at them south over F Street came a random section of window frame, striking Rachel squarely, slamming her on top of Alexander and pinning him to the ground.

3

DECIPHERING THE HUMINT

While Rachel was giving Alexander a good bye kiss, Branko Rosza was settling into his chair at the head of an oblong conference table on the seventh floor of the CIA headquarters building in suburban Virginia. Branko, the National Intelligence Officer for East Asia, was uncharacteristically jumpy this Monday, having begun his workday in Langley with a modest hangover of domestic irritation.

The First of April started disagreeably for Branko. Spontaneity did not come easily to him. Branko and his wife Erika shared a passion for ritual. Though not a particularly religious couple, they had an accumulation of modest ceremonies that brought rhythm and order to their family life. Their McLean home was a cheerful place; their kitchen refrigerator was decorated with a magnetic calendar highlighting future causes for celebration. Such days had come to provide the anchors for the busy household of seven, a certain center amidst the blizzard of after-school lessons and sports activities. Everything from obscure European saints' days to Hallmark holidays yielded cards and special meals.

With five children under sixteen—and the twelve-year-old an especially creative prankster—breakfast this day had been an adventure. The milk was green. The orange juice had been spiked with Sprite. The car keys were hidden under the ice in the automatic dispenser. Branko was a notoriously deliberate person. The early games of the day proved burdensome, challenging his compulsion for control.

A squat, dark-haired man with a wizened face, Branko moved forward with a sense of mission. He was playing a role that honored the brutal hardships his parents had endured. They were both Hungarian refugees and had met in a displaced persons camp in Europe in 1946. It was many years before they possessed enough faith in the future to start a family. Shortly thereafter, in 1956, Soviet tanks of occupation rolled past the

Roszas' Budapest apartment block, and the family fled across the border to Austria, then on to Liverpool, England, finally making it to Cleveland in the early 1960's.

Branko was an infant when the Soviets invaded, and, ultimately, an only child. He was raised in an anxious home where frivolity was suspect, loyalty exalted. Branko, with his incongruous green eyes, would play chess for hours with his silent father, plotting elaborate stratagies, trained from a young age to think many moves ahead.

That the quiet boy had tested as a genius was no great surprise. His uncanny ability to assess motive and intent made him a brilliant analyst of information. He excelled, winning numerous academic scholarships and flourishing as a Chinese language specialist in Palo Alto, before moving seamlessly into his first government job in the intelligence business. He mailed in his thesis on Beijing decision-making, becoming the first of the Mandarin boys to secure his doctorate. Branko was a rarity, having worked his way through every significant Asia job at the Agency—in both analysis and operations. Now he sat, literally, at the head of the table for the intelligence community's Asia work.

He ran this particular Monday morning 0900 exercise—still held in Langley pending a move to new facilities at Bolling AFB—like a refined tutorial. All opinions were welcome. Debate and dissent were expected. Sucking up to the professor—beyond the formalism of addressing him as "Doctor" Rosza (a vain indulgence he had subtly encouraged over the years)—would be punished. Blinding glimpses of the obvious were ruthlessly skewered. They earned taxpayer dollars for providing fresh thinking. He demanded no less from each of the staffers reporting to him, pressing them relentlessly for new insight.

"What do we make of the Nanping expansion?" Branko skipped the pleasantries, calling the meeting to order on the central issue of the day. "And what are the implications of this Chinese military move for U.S. and Taiwan response? James, let's begin with NGA."

James, a tall African-American official from the National Geospatial-Intelligence Agency, responded, his hands gripping a thick red file of photographs. "The Nanping missile base in China's Fujian Province has shown a significant increase in activity over the last three days. We believe this is beyond routine maintenance and suggests a further expansion of capabilities."

"*Significant increase* defined by what standard?" Branko inquired.

"An additional deployment of phased array radar and site preparations for another two batteries of the CSS-6 missiles."

"Which would bring total deployment to . . . "

"Nearly five hundred CSS-6's and 7's at the Nanping base. That would be a virtual doubling in size there." James paused before anticipating. "You will recall, Dr. Rosza, that the first PRC medium range missile deployment during the 1996 Taiwan Strait crisis was accompanied by Chinese live-fire military drills."

"Yes, I recall that the deployment attracted some interest here." Branko allowed just a hint of a smirk. They all knew he had been the head of the Taiwan listening post at that time, closely following developments at the U.S. intelligence community's signals intercept facility, Yangminshan, burrowed deep into the suburban hills outside Taipei. It had appeared then that China's provocative move—deploying missiles for the first time along the Fujian Province coastline opposite Taiwan—might lead to a shooting war.

"My point being, sir, that we have been focusing our satellite photo work the last forty-eight hours on depots and roads which might confirm a third and fourth battery, another two hundred and fifty missiles."

"Is the work at the Chinese base transparent?"

"Yes and no. It's exclusively night-time activity. But they know when our birds fly over, and they know our satellites can pick up certain night-time activities. So they must assume we're getting some good pictures." The folks at NGA were quite proud of their high-resolution photographs. "Telstar's satellites even give us the Caterpillar logo on top of the back-hoe."

"NSA, what's SIGINT allowing us to pick up from communications?"

"Our listening stations in the region do not report anything unusual, sir." A demure blond woman with oversized horn rim glasses responded without missing a beat. "The usual Chinese phone and fax traffic back to headquarters. Their e-mail volume is routine, though we did pick up some complaining about quality control."

"Can we get more specific on that?" Branko pressed.

"Dr. Rosza, the transcripts suggest something beyond the usual complaints about the quality of the hardware. Apparently, the Fujian base is pushing for delivery of systems at a pace the production folks—this is all indigenous now, no longer Russian import—consider a little surprising. They seem to be shipping stuff to Nanping without requisite spare parts."

"What is military intelligence saying about the haste?" It pained Branko to lean on the armed services. But the recent shake-ups in the U.S. intelligence community placed a premium on sharing nicely. Besides, Branko believed, it was better to find out what the competition had than learn it later, at some White House showdown with the Pentagon boys.

"Their conclusion parallels ours, sir." It was Arthur Moffitt, his deputy. "It clearly suggests a hurry-up under orders from Beijing."

"Arthur, what do we make of their failure to obscure these developments? They trying to send us a message?"

"Unclear, sir. Beijing has made some diplomatic commitments the deployments would appear to contradict."

"Any evidence this might be a Second Directorate gambit? You know, provoke the Americans again and let the diplomats and the Politburo deal with the consequences?

"No, sir. Human Intelligence captures suggest that the military-civilian tensions continue to run high in Beijing. But HUMINT hasn't turned up anything on the Nanping developments that suggest these don't have top-down Party support."

Branko pondered the implications a moment. "But they've still got deniability?"

"Right. And it is consistent with recent doctrine to challenge Taipei and Washington by presenting some new reality on the ground."

"Indeed. Military threats don't work unless people know they are being threatened," Branko said, lapsing into pedantry—it was the instructor within who never passed up a teaching moment. Then he continued with his inquiry. "Anything we see in their haste to suggest it is all a mirage, a Potemkin Village made for satellite detection?"

"No sir. This looks like the real deal. With a two hundred kilometer range on the missiles, the latest move could push Taipei right over the edge."

Branko started to ask a question, but paused to think. It was a measure of the group's regard for their leader and his vaunted analytical skills that no one stirred while Branko fiddled with his pen. Another series of questions ensued to each intelligence division represented—fully twenty minutes of asked-and-answered—before he began to make valedictory remarks on the morning's gathering, artfully employing the royal "we."

"So the Nanping base is hot again—in contravention of explicit diplomatic pledges. The deployment of still more CSS-6's means that Taipei's margin of safety in the Taiwan Strait will soon disappear completely." He had his colleagues' undivided attention.

"We have good news for Beijing. Once again, they've rattled Taipei's cage. The Taiwans will be under intense pressure to talk peace, love, and reunification with the Communists, starting tomorrow.

"The bad news," he continued, "is that, with the Politburo politicians agreeing to more missiles, the generals will agitate even more to finally use a few of them. Furthermore, Taiwan's friends in Congress will be apoplectic over the White House reluctance to sell Taipei more sophisticated weapons for deterrence."

"If Senator Smithson gets this . . ." Here, Branko paused to correct himself. His respect for the Senate Foreign Relations Committee's chairman was well known to the group. "*When* he gets this, corralling Jake Smithson is going to keep the folks in Congressional Relations rather busy."

"Of course, the Agency has no obligation to inform Congress," said his deputy, Moffitt, who was quick to reassure him. "That threshold hasn't been crossed."

"Yes, Arthur, this is still preliminary," Branko agreed. "And CSS-6 missiles aren't new. The Chinese have had some for several years. But they deploy the missiles for effect. They push them to the seacoast just like pushing a pawn. Well, now there will be an effect in this town as well. We need to anticipate what the policymakers will be demanding from us.

"I want NGA to double our satellite surveillance of Taiwan's air fields. See how the Taiwans will respond," Branko continued. "Let our station chief in Taipei know we need capture on what kind of response they are planning in Taiwan—both political and military. And we may need to alert the Pacific Command team in Honolulu, in case the White House calls for them to crank up the engines for another U.S. carrier cruise through the Taiwan Strait. Anything else?"

Branko had wrapped things up thoroughly; there were no questions.

As the staff stood to file out, Branko pointed casually towards James. "Leave me those satellite photos, would you please? I'd like to have my own look. And Brownell, may I see you for a moment?"

James silently handed his two thick files to Branko. James was the last to slip by Gabriel Brownell, the representative from the CIA's operations directorate, an assistant to the man who ran the Agency's agents on the ground in China.

"Sit down for a minute, Gabe." Branko seemed distracted as he hunched over to peer at the photos. "You know, I used to do some of this photo analysis."

"Yes, sir."

"In fact, I held most of the posts represented in the room this morning. I have carried many of your portfolios."

"Yes, sir."

"Used to find these photos pretty interesting. Missiles. Troop deployments. We'd sit in a dark room looking at enlargements of a bunch of party hacks playing at the beach. Once had a satellite shot of one of the Politburo members humping a lady at the Party retreats they used to have at Beidaihe. My assistant used to call them a sort of 'poor man's porno.' Made you feel like a bunch of high tech peeping Toms. Rather creepy."

"These *can* be disturbing photos."

"I've seen it all, buddy. Raw data. Pre-analysis. Stuff fresh out of the darkroom."

"I'm sure you have. Your coverage is legend—"

"Brownell," Branko cut him off sharply, "one question. Exactly *when* did you intend to get around to sharing the take we've gotten from the Bravo Compartment?"

Brownell blanched. He pushed heavy glasses back up his nose. "The, uh—Bravo."

"The Bravo Compartment—the electronic collection operation your directorate has been running at Zhongnanhai. You know the place—cozy little compound inside the Forbidden City in Beijing, where all the ruling bureaucrats live." Rosza's eyes had a way of shrinking, his visage pinched and narrow, when he was angry.

"The Bravo take? Right. Well, we haven't . . . they haven't prepared edited transcripts that are ready."

"Ready? Ready for *whom*?"

"With all due respect, sir, the Deputy Director of Operations said that, that until we had some confirm on the, uh, the reliability of the speakers . . . they had a 'No-Dis' slapped on them."

"*No-Dis*?"

"Not For Dissemination, sir. The Deputy Director said th—"

"I know what No-Dis means." Branko tapped his pen methodically, prolonging the moment, underscoring his disgust. "Listen, we may be working together for some time. I want you to remember one thing. Don't you *ever* hold out on me."

"Sir, the DDO said that—"

"*I* am the National Intelligence Officer for East Asia. I require information from the Bravo Compartment to help discern Beijing's intentions. I don't give a crap whether anyone tells you otherwise, unless it is the Director of National Intelligence or the President of the United States. Don't you ever hold out on me again, or I'll have your butt shipped to Lagos."

"Sir, I never—"

"We are finished." Branko pushed his chair back and swept up the photo files.

He was at the door and Brownell was just beginning to find his footing, when Branko turned in a final fury.

"Do you even *know* who launched the Bravo Compartment? Who

recruited the source who facilitates this operation in the first place? Who planted the seed once upon a time? Who courted him? Who pleaded with him—at the greatest possible risk—to work with us during the darkest hours after Tiananmen? Do you?"

Branko's disgust was on full display as he answered his own question: "He was *my* fucking agent."

4

ON TOP OF THE WORLD

While Rachel and Alexander were embracing outside the Willard, Mickey Dooley was chewing breakfast in his suite at the St. Francis Hotel, twenty-five hundred miles to the west in San Francisco. He savored the bacon grease as he licked his thick fingers.

On the brink of his fifties, Mickey was proud of his ability to keep secrets. The fact was, he had become an exceptionally good liar.

As he perused the sports pages in his morning paper, Mickey once again compartmentalized his life with great facility. There was China business, there was American stuff. There was his wife, Mei Mei, of whom he was ever wary. There was his Hong Kong mistress and her growing demands for attention. There were the Mandarins, his old Stanford Club brethren, who had known him in more innocent times. And there were the spooks hanging at the bar of his favorite Beijing watering hole, looking to see if he might run them another shady errand. Each had their distinct places, years of private confidences tucked safely in their respective drawers.

He lived in dread of the day they would all inevitably collide, when his separate lives would merge and he would be carried away in the flood of contradictions. At that fateful hour, he told himself, he would bear his cross stoically. In the interim, he managed the balancing act deftly. Only in rare moments of solitude would he peer into himself to examine the mess he had made of his life, a candor best treated with a heavy dose of scotch.

Tanned and a bit heavy, he sat motionless in his terrycloth robe bearing the hotel's "SF" script. Today, he would indulge himself. He would rally his spirits and reward his many successes as a man of international business.

He deserved it, he assured himself. It was hard-earned comp time, a reward to self for his latest deal-making wizardry, an international soldier's R&R, just like Dad's Army pals always used to laugh about into their beers. There would be no burdensome Catholic guilt to restrain him. He had left behind his religious indoctrination—and all those years of his father's stern drilling—the day he left Albuquerque for Palo Alto.

He had finally slept after the third whiskey. It had been an ugly, drunken sleep, though. His dreams were black and twisted. Mei Mei's father, the air force general, had been hollering at him in Mandarin about his tardiness in delivering some gizmo to the old man's comrades in the Chinese rocketry business. The patriarch was squinting and angry, his lecture rambling on, seemingly for hours. "You make yourself suspect," his father-in-law seethed. "Maybe you are working for CIA to sabotage the people!" He blathered on, quoting Chinese fables and expressing disappointment that his little princess had married such a heathen slouch.

When awake, at home, in the Beijing neighborhood of the foreign compound, Mickey could speak better Chinese than most. His language skills had aided his ascendancy in the China business. But "Dream Mickey" was flustered, a failing kid back in New Mexico, shuddering under his father's glare. Mickey felt better to be alert, safe from the hectoring Chinese voices.

Mickey gazed about his suite as he cleared his brain, anticipating the day to come. He made a habit of requesting the '09-numbered rooms, especially 1009 and 1109 near the top of the old St. Francis tower. The corner suites in the original brick-faced portion of the hotel looked over Union Square. Mickey could stand at the windows and see the Berkeley hills, the Bay Bridge, and the old San Francisco industrial waterfront. He watched in the Square below as the sidewalks were hosed down, the sprinklers misting beds of yellow and orange tulips. The pleasant racket from the cable cars rolling down Powell Street was softened by distance. The Bear Republic flag on the façade fluttered in the morning breeze.

He strained to summon the old rhythms of Mickey the Ringleader, the guy who always brought the party with him. He searched for the taproot of energy that had driven him to overcome so many challenges. He missed the States and hungered for the familiar, the carefree.

His life as an expatriate in the People's Republic of China was the ultimate paradox of fulfillment and fear. He labored to maintain his public image amidst the emptiness of marriage to a frigid foreigner. Mickey played the homespun cowboy role to the hilt—even wore his alligator-skin boots to most of his business meetings. He was the master of the import-export game in Beijing, a leader of the American community in town, the garrulous go-to-guy for his corporate allies. He had just engineered another lucrative satellite deal, providing the Chinese access to a new generation of U.S. space launch technology, Telstar's finest. All the execs back at Houston headquarters thought Mickey was a brilliant success.

His career was a credit to his cleverness—and his connections. With the help of his powerful father-in-law, he got it all done for Telstar in an intensely competitive market. He had just finished serving a term on the board of the American Chamber of Commerce in Beijing, the consummate wheeler-dealer who could fix any nettlesome trade problem.

In darker moments of introspection, he came to bear his professional success as a private shame, peddling satellite cargoes and high-performance supercomputers like so many knock-off watches. He ran errands for the Defense Ministry and worked a shopping list pushed by Mei Mei's father. He saw to it that the Customs guys and mid-level bureaucrats were covered with generous bribes. In the process, he hoarded tidbits of information with which to someday entice Branko, hoping that Branko might overcome his disdain and favor him in a pinch. Like a poker shark, he built mental files on all parties to his games, tucking away little insights for the reckoning day when he might need them.

The silent resignations of middle age were now weighing upon his life of compromise. The accumulated burden had gotten old—the settling for less, the entrapment in his warren of obligations. The China game had lost its charm and, during increasingly frequent moments of reflection, he saw the caricature his life was becoming as once noble goals were betrayed.

He peered out the window, across the west tower of the Bay Bridge. The sun was making its first appearance, a promise of pure light through purples and grays. The rays spread beyond the steel frames, catching windows of other high-rise hotels, illuminating the placid bay, and pointing silvery fingers at cargo ships stalled in the flat water below. For a moment, Mickey was transfixed. He ignored the paper in hand and the silent sports figures hurtling ghostlike across the television screen.

There was a stillness in which Mickey could sense the movement of the earth, exaggerating the arc of the first rays of sunlight. As he reflected on his heavy load, he saw a simple fact with a new clarity: he wanted out.

He yearned to confess his many sins against God and country. He yearned to confess and be done with it all, to be free of his tangled web of collaborations—all his "special friends" at Beijing's Ministry of Defense, his two martini lunch pals from the political dumping ground in Washington's Commerce Department.

He wished to be done with his Hong Kong mistress, the sharp-nailed German woman who demanded silks and liked to ride on top. He longed to be out from under the sheer weight of his deceits, from the serial maneuvering and stream of tales that made his brain ache. He was weary of sex without love, and love without sex. He wanted to quit the game—the *baksheesh* for trade licenses, the envelopes of cash for Port Authority guys, and all the petty misdemeanors and squirrelly crimes that marked his life of international salesmanship.

He began to construct a new vision. He imagined coming home to America, sipping scotch in a Barcalounger, snug inside a New Mexico rancher. His mom and pop, now mellowed with age, would live down the street. Grandma would bake and fuss over the kids. Grandpa would teach them to fish. Mickey would wrestle cheerfully with his boys, betting the over-under on the Lakers, socking away some cash for their college tuition. He'd clean up his act.

Never again would he miss a Little League game for some stupid staff meeting. Maybe he could even hook up with one of his old high school sweethearts who had stayed home in Albuquerque and long since divorced. They could make an American home for the boys. They could cruise beyond middle age and build a future together. He would hike the John Muir Trail along the Sierra ridge before he got too old. He'd find an inner calm. He'd begin to integrate his life into one coherent whole. He'd slow down and finish growing up. Maybe, just maybe, he could finally become the model citizen he had always aspired to be. Maybe he could do good instead of just living like some Gatsby swell. Noble deeds—that is what he aspired to—noble deeds and simple peace. He could realize his vision. He could be released.

But at this moment, he could see no escape from his own intricately designed Hell. He was a hostage, trapped in his web of Beijing favor-banking. He could see no hope of ever recreating some American Wonder Years for his boys. His two Chinese-American kids would not clear the Communists' exit controls—not since he'd had the temerity to utter the word "divorce" in Mei Mei's presence. Her father was viciously effective; he could surely block their departure.

So Mickey looked to San Francisco for a day of release. He was energized, recalling familiar scents that triggered memories from his college days. The eucalyptus harkened back to the slow drive up to Stanford's Memorial Chapel. The dry fields of grass and laurel recalled drinking chardonnay on the headlands just north of the Golden Gate Bridge. The smell of hot dogs and java roast brought back cold nights at Candlestick, roaring the Giants on in air thick with cannabis. The salty ocean smells beckoned him back to Point Reyes and a bracing hike along the shoreline cliffs. His brain surfed through the sensual recollections as he tried to rally.

He had received a last-minute reprieve from the need to fly the red-eye back to Washington to take a meeting at the Talbott firm with Lee and Rachel. The Chinese Embassy trade guy was all worked up about a series of export licenses in the new satellite deal. But the meeting had been scrubbed. Now, miraculously, at the breakfast hour, he had nearly finished his work for the day.

He had risen at 5:30 a.m. to dispose of his calls—to Beijing, Taipei, New York, and Virginia, in that order. His last call was local, using a secure line to contact an export agent helping him complete his secondary business in San Francisco. It was his Singapore-based middleman's peculiar request for krytrons—high-speed electrical switching devices of little use to his satellite customers. But he was beyond caring about such things. He was quite willing to follow the explicit instructions his Beijing contacts had given him. His buyer had secured the contract, and executed the peculiar routing, shipping via Vancouver, thence to Taipei, Taiwan, of all places. *Bizarre*, he thought. But Mickey had learned long ago not to ask too many questions. It was easier that way.

His thoughts were interrupted by the phone, ringing loudly in the high-ceilinged room. It was the scrambled cell line again, the secure one the Ministry had issued him in Beijing.

"Yes?" he answered, before adding, as a quick afterthought, "Baker here."

"Good morning. This is Rashid. The check is in the mail."

"Everything OK with the postman?"

"Everything went fine. You were right. The little station is looser than the big one." They'd begun using the smaller San Jose airport instead of SFO for international shipments: fewer Customs personnel to hassle them for some of their more sensitive dual use cargoes. "It was even smoother than the satellite stuff we sent last month. The TSA boys still are more interested in people coming in than hardware headed out."

"Any more hassles from the sellers—the guys up in the factory in Fairfield?"

"No, but I did not feel so comfortable with all these questions about end use."

"No sweat."

"Just rather strange having to answer three times these questions about destination." The smuggler's accent was rather precise, conjuring for Mickey the image of a South Asian clerk. "So, my friend, I am just as pleased to be taking my leave from all these questions about end use. I don't think they entirely bought that business about timing strobes for music video shoots."

"Hey," said Mickey, "half of Hollywood has moved to Vancouver. Stupid unions drove 'em there."

"Certainly."

"So, where are you headed?"

"Caribbean, I think—maybe a Club Med. Some place warm and sleepy, until you call again." Mickey chuckled under his breath. He could make better use of such a destination than his rather prim export man.

"Well, happy trails, my friend. And don't forget to call in next month. I may have a components thing I need help moving out of Germany."

"Certainly, Baker. So long for now."

Mickey flipped the line dead, and tossed the phone back onto the rumpled bed. The transaction seemed too easy.

What's the end use for this stuff? he wondered. *What's the deal with the Taipei routing? Somebody back in Beijing have a brother-in-law across the Strait he's doing favors for?*

He pushed the remainder of his meal aside as he reached for his yellow pad. Carefully, he checked his shopping list for the day, crossing off "ketchup shipment" for the krytrons, and lining over "rash ointment" for Rashid. He'd put in his call to his Albuquerque attorney to answer the immigration questions. But he still needed divine inspiration on how he might possibly get free of Mei Mei's clutches and bring his kids home to America. Booth might have some insights there—righteous Booth, the straight arrow who wore his conscience on his sleeve.

Mickey added Booth's name to the phone list. He'd already put in a call to Rachel's secretary at TPB with yesterday's good news from Beijing that they could cancel their ten o'clock meeting.

Good old Rachel—his Stanford comrade who had become Telstar's Girl Friday in Washington, staffing their every American need. Talbott's firm had covered it all, from lobbying for China's trade agenda to convincing the Commerce Department to waive satellite export license restrictions. Rachel had been the best of them all; he saw that now. She had the truest heart, and was a far better person than he. He missed her—that grinding determination, the sparkle, the reverence for the small kindnesses in life, no birthday ever forgotten. He wished he had been the one to marry her years ago. Too bad her husband Barry had turned out to be such a flake. *How had they all misjudged him?*

His work done, Mickey reminded himself that the day now held considerable promise. He was headed to the fitness center to lift and jog on the treadmill, day one of his new resolution to firm up. Then he would head over to Berkeley to hook up with a favorite Swedish masseuse, beatific Bettina. She worked in the nude, her modest artist's studio filled with incense and meditative sitar music. Invariably, she restored him with the perfect blend of Nordic firmness and sensual release, delightfully free of entangling words and complications. There was a simplicity in the shallow exchange he rarely found wanting.

He'd have a drink on Telegraph Avenue—or maybe just a caramel latté today, if his resolve held. Then, after a little souvenir shopping for the boys in Union Square, back to the hotel for a book and a nap. Finally, the Giants' Opening Day game: from her clients at Coke, Rachel had secured him a box seat on the third base line.

It might turn out to be a fine day, after all.

He rolled the breakfast trolley aside, reaching for the television clicker. Surfing channels, he jumped from the ESPN scoreboard onto a live C-SPAN telecast from Washington. There on the screen behind Senator Smithson was a disgusted looking Martin Booth. Some Administration blowhard was testifying before the Senate Foreign Relations Committee on Asia policy, rambling on about human rights in Myanmar.

"Fuckin' wuss!" Mickey hollered at the screen as the Assistant Secretary droned forth. "Same old State Department bullshit."

Mickey clicked to NBC. *The Today Show* was not yet screening on the West Coast. Doubtless, a crowd had already gathered outside the studio—caffeine-overdosed citizens screaming for the cameras at dawn, rapturous for two seconds of on-air fame.

Mickey was bouncing his right knee nervously. He flipped to CNN, where the highlights from the late basketball games proved to be more lively. His Lakers were revived and rolling.

The secure phone rang again. Mickey shook his head, wondering what brand of scramblers they used to keep the satellite signals one step ahead of the FBI and the NSA and whoever else liked to listen to international businessmen talk. This time it was his man at Telstar, calling from down in Silicon Valley.

"Mickey? We need you to drop by today and go over the plan for the licenses on the jammers. You know, the electronic counter-measures kits."

"Aw, shit." There went the coveted hole in his schedule. "You guys still sweating that? I told you, I got that stuff all worked out back in Washington. I didn't even have to go back there."

"Yeah, but the boss is getting heat from the customer. Seems like they got ants in their pants on this one."

Mickey did not welcome this. "I told you, it's wired. We've got clearance from the Commerce Department. And State isn't even in the loop. They get no interagency sign-off any more."

"I hear you. We just gotta make sure this gets Fed Ex-ed in time."

"*In time?* What's the rush on a bunch of jammer payloads?" Even as he said the words, Mickey was sorry. He had made a lot of money over the years by not blurting out such thoughts.

"I don't know, probably some kinda war-gaming. Making sure they won't be blind if somebody starts jamming them. Just be here by noon. We'll do one more walk through."

"OK, OK," Mickey grumbled before he calculated. "But listen, how about two o'clock?"

He could see things getting worse. If they were so anxious for him to baby-sit the next shipment, he probably would have to go back to Washington after all. He would be responsible for making sure the TPB team delivered an export license in a timely fashion. His visions of California leisure were crashing and burning.

"Good, then—whoa! Mickey? You still there?"

He was struggling to cling to his plan now.

"Check out CNN! A bomb's gone off by the White House!"

It took a moment to register as Mickey's eyes darted back to the picture. And then, there it was, in his suite, as well. There were the images before him, marching along as if in a macabre Bourbon Street dream parade.

He saw drifting smoke on the TV, just over a reporter's head. A crawler at the bottom of the screen warned of "Graphic Footage." He couldn't find the damn remote. It was better without the sound anyway.

There was the TPB building, with shredded white curtains wafting gently through skeletal window frames—the very same TPB building where, according to the original schedule, he was to have been arriving within the hour. To Mickey, in his momentary horror, it came as no surprise that Alexander Bonner was on camera, too. There was Alexander, dazed and muttering.

It was the sight of Rachel Paulson's inert body, her face caked in blood, that slapped Mickey back to reality.

5

DANGEROUS GAMES

Li Jianjun sat on the darkened porch, sipping green tea, waiting for the moon to rise.

It was a cold night in Beijing, unusually bitter for the beginning of April, although the heavy layer of pollution backing up south from the mountains kept an edge off the chill. The resulting blanket tasted of diesel fuel, exhaust from buses, and industrial plants still encircling the northern capital despite the vaunted efforts of Beijing's city planners.

Lee needed the moment of stillness away from the angry voices of his colleagues. He could hear them arguing even now as they lingered in the compound's conference room. He was eager for reflection, struggling to find context for the third long day of debate over options he considered risky. *Were they truly prepared for the confrontations ahead?* He doubted it. In disgust, he flicked the ashes of his cigarette, watching them fall slowly like dying petals letting go.

They were in a recess on the last night of an extended spring policy planning exercise. His boss, the foreign minister, had left the Zhongnanhai compound to share a dessert toast to his elderly mother celebrating her birthday at a restaurant not far from the senior government employees' enclosure. But he would be back to see his deputy Lee, the head of the North American Section, and to wrap up the session.

Lee had expected to be arriving in Washington at this hour, tending to Ministry business with his Chinese Embassy counterparts. He had abruptly aborted the trip, though, intercepted en route to the airport by a call from an anxious colleague. He had been tipped off to some mischief the boys at Defense were planning to spring at the conclusive policy session.

The call had proved prescient. The hotheads working under the old generals were pushing the envelope once more, proposing to launch another in a series of provocations, to test Taiwan and its vacillating American protectors. Taiwan, again. Lee had grown weary of the dangerous games the army boys were ever so eager to play.

Now he was drained, his bones stiff in the sharp night air. He stood and stretched, eyes closed. Gingerly, he executed a few toe touches. His hamstrings clutched. He thought of his father exercising amiably with the day nurse, Xu An, whose services Lee had procured. They were both a bit sweet on the middle-aged woman.

Parkinson's was slowly shutting the old man down. His knuckles were curling, his shoulders hunching, and his feet increasingly deaf to the brain's insistent commands. Yet the smile of the aging engineer grew ever gentler and child-like as the disease took hold. The irony tore at Lee, deepening his dread of the impending loss. As dementia set in and death approached, the old man's rough edges were fading. The bullying commands were forgotten, the authoritarian voice having melted. What remained, underneath the layers of a life of trial, was an unexpected tenderness. It made Lee even sadder for the void looming beyond his father's imminent passage into darkness.

Lee had taken to scrawling awkward verses in his journal. His attempts at poetry and short stories left him even emptier, though. He had fallen into idealizing his American days, especially those first weeks of freedom in Palo Alto. He allowed his mind to float, to think heretically once again. He would fantasize, and the revolutionary within would emerge briefly on paper. But then he would set his pen down and come back to earth, to the unsavory choices before him. One night, he burned the journal, feeding sheet by sheet into the blue flames of the coal burner.

In the end, he would be orphaned. He saw it now. At forty-eight, he gazed at an empty future—no parents, no children. It was too late for him; he would be left alone with his stubborn ideals and his rancorous countrymen.

In his father's face the previous Sunday, he had seen a vision of his own demise. There would be no gentle hand to ease his passing. There would be no witness for him—no one to come to his rescue. He recognized now that his run had peaked, that his patriotism was misplaced, that he was sliding down from some precipice of experience, into his own inevitable decline.

He stood in the shadows, finishing his Camel, the cigarette tip the only light on the porch. It sparkled whenever he inhaled, pulsing like a firefly, illuminating his jet-black hair and severe eyes. Lee toyed with the smoke, attempting a picket line of rings by contorting his mouth in a brief moment of play. The nicotine and the air combined for a stimulating kick before he crushed the butt on the railing. Flicking it into the bushes, he hitched up his slacks before turning back to the policy wars.

A solitary figure remained in the conference room. It was Chen, making notes intently on a red file folder. The defense ministry's global strategist, Chen was Lee's foil in these interagency sessions. They clashed predictably, like an old couple familiar with each other's pronouncements. They would measure themselves against one another, testing the limits of candor and dissent, sharpening their minds, playing devil's advocate. Lee wondered if their set-piece encounters amused their colleagues, like the rancorous talk shows on CNN International with those jowly journalists trying to shout over each other.

Theirs was a clash grounded in mutual respect. Chen was the most reasonable of the brains at Defense, a modern man with a graduate degree from M.I.T., a man for whom the excesses of the Cultural Revolution were a horror never to be repeated. Chen had slowed down the faction that saw modernization merely as a way to restore a neo-Maoist purity to state control. Chen could see through the older military men, soldiers trapped in their web of rhetoric and fabricated deadlines for progress on Taiwan's "reunification" with the Mainland. Yet, Chen also could still outmaneuver the clever young comrades who were so eager to manipulate their doctrinaire elders.

Then, again, Chen's bureaucratic colleagues would instantly betray Lee if evidence of his past transgressions were ever uncovered—those dark times after Tiananmen when his struggle to honor the martyrs had led him to cross his own government. They would send Lee to a quick death by pistol shot. *Whom would they bill for the bullet?*

For Lee, it sometimes seemed a question of when, not if, his stubborn idealism would prove fatal. He fancied himself a genuine patriot, determined to stand and fight to the end. Yet, in his private moments, he questioned his flirtations with discovery and death. He could anticipate no brighter future. Seeing no other way, he grew more daring with each passing challenge.

Chen, leaning over the long rectangular table, was holding his tea when Lee entered.

"Cable traffic?" Lee's question seemed to startle his colleague.

"Yeah, same old crap. Guys in the field trying to suck up to the boss."

"But the boss eats it up, right?"

Chen set his papers down and sighed. "Yes, Lee, just like your foreign affairs boys. The ministers always welcome such loyalty."

He was only a few years younger than Chen. But Chen's wife—who fussed affectionately over Lee, the divorced bachelor—insisted the burden of the Defense Ministry post had aged Chen prematurely. Chen was almost bald, with thick white eyebrows and John Lennon granny glasses, giving the appearance of a Chinese leprechaun.

"I'm sure this makes your contrarian views even more valuable."

"Valuable? At present, I am not certain what value is placed on caution."

"Deliberation has served us well on the Taiwan question. Bought us time. "

"Our leadership needs some results," Chen said as he reached across the table for a cigarette from Lee's pack. "May I?"

"Sure," Lee said, noticing for the first time a slight tremor in his colleague's hand.

"Results?" Lee made no effort to hide his skepticism. "Right."

"It is real this time," Chen warned. "We're ratcheting things up, my friend. Finally going to kick Taiwan in the ass."

"Really?"

"And you know what I think Washington is going to do about it? Nothing. Just like when our brave pilot rammed the American spy plane out of the sky over Hainan."

"Now wait. They didn't sit when the Taliban in Afghanistan let that Saudi madman attack their—"

"That wasn't about Afghanistan. That was about New York, and the Pentagon. The fact is, most Americans can't even find Taipei on a map. Besides, their military is already over-extended. If they make too big a stink, we can crash their stock market in a day just by sitting out their Treasury bond auctions."

"Why now?" Lee turned his head sharply towards the door, but they were alone in the room, the others drinking tea and watching CNN.

"Because our fearless leaders have been farting around on the Taiwan issue for decades. How many Party Congresses can they make the same empty pledge to?"

"We've got plenty to show." Lee's voice shot up. "Hong Kong's return. The trade agreement. We've come quite a ways since Tiananmen."

"Why should our generals forget the promises to bring Taiwan back to the Motherland?"

"Generals always overestimate the utility of force."

"So do politicians. But this isn't a grad school seminar, my friend. You have military men here. They spend a generation building bases and missiles, they eventually want to use their toys."

"You can't—"

"It's like the Americans' Manhattan Project. Imagine the grief Truman would have caught if they'd spent all that money and effort, and then he didn't drop the bomb?"

"But that is illogical."

"It is inevitable," Chen insisted. "Every year that goes by, Taiwan drifts farther away from us. Their kids have no memory of the Mainland. They sit there with all the treasures they stole from our National Museum. They are Chinese, yet they show us no respect. Problem is, they believe all that Star Wars stuff—that they'll be able to sit for generations taunting us from behind some impregnable missile shield. Just like that corrupt old dog, Chiang Kai-Shek, hiding behind Eisenhower's knees and the Seventh Fleet. Time is not on our side; that is where you make your fatal miscalculation."

Lee tipped back in his chair, regarding his colleague carefully, searching for an opening. "Time. Yes, time. The damn political calendar seems to dictate everything. I mean, we've got to get the new missiles in Nanping before the Seattle summit meeting. We've got to have some Taiwan trophies before the next big Party Congress."

"It's true," Chen chuckled. "We've become like the Americans. We even have WalMarts and suburban sprawl. There's your convergence!"

"And what if it is our politicians who have miscalculated? What if their schemes for pressuring Taiwan blow up?" Lee's tone grew harsh. "Are we ready for war over a goddamn island we never governed?"

"So you would do nothing?" Chen crushed his cigarette. "Typical Foreign Ministry bullshit."

"Not nothing."

"Admit it! You'd do nothing while twenty-five million countrymen on Taiwan drift away."

Lee glared. *Where was this going?* He thought the wild boys in the Second Directorate were still checked by moderate forces over at Defense—that China's modernization would not be hijacked by ideologues intent on a neo-Maoist restoration. At best, Chen sounded defeatist, and at worst, approving of the next round of provocations.

"There is a difference between cautious forward movement and acting precipitously. In chess, you don't—"

"*Precipitously?* After almost sixty years of occupation of Taiwan by Chiang's generals and their American military pals?"

"Time can be on our side, too. Taiwan's moneymen are up to their ears in Mainland investments. We can crash their markets in an hour with one belligerent statement from our Foreign Ministry. We'll end up owning them without firing a shot."

"It's true," said Chen, again chuckling. "Throw in a few of our live missile drills, and half of Taiwan's money will be wired to Switzerland overnight. We can knock out their whole electrical grid. Shut down every single computer on the island."

Lee nodded in silent admiration.

A sudden commotion erupted in the next room, shouts followed by excited chatter. Anxious American voices could be heard booming from the television. The door flew open and a head shot in, calling to them.

"Hey, comrades! Come look at the news. Something's hot in Washington!"

Lee and Chen rushed into the lounge, where a dozen aides were huddled. The air was thick with unfiltered cigarette smoke. A bottle of bai jiu wine was on the counter, waiting to share a ceremonial *ganbei* toast with the minister when he returned to close the conference. The shots had already been poured; they stood waiting, cloudy and yellow, in old cut glasses.

Posted on the big screen was a familiar American conceit. "Breaking News," it read. Lee had seen the same crawler the first time when the fugitive football player had driven his white truck up and down the California freeway. The same with that interminable farce of a presidential election, when for weeks CNN had aired footage of dazed U.S. citizens hand-counting ballots. It had become a fixture again for the so-called anti-terrorist campaign and the New Orleans flood.

This time, an over-excited journalist was shouting through the sleet in Washington about some street-corner explosion. Lee waved his hand and began to turn away in disgust. Then he caught a glance of the picture, over the reporter's shoulder. There was a smoking office building and beyond it, the side of the U.S. Treasury Department.

"That's Telstar's—" said Lee, catching himself as he strode forward, peering nervously, until he was almost on top of the screen.

Sure enough, it was the building where Telstar's lobbyists worked— Rachel Paulson's firm. The office where the American corporations had coordinated China's defense during the recent trade debates. The office Mickey Dooley used as his Washington base of operations.

The office where I was supposed to be sitting . . . right about now. Lee's mind was careening. *Whose bomb? What was the target?*

He started for the door. He needed to get a call through to his own guys in intelligence back at the Foreign Ministry, and his eyes darted about frantically as he considered his next move.

Then the television microphones picked up the curses of a man on his knees, leaning over a body. It looked like that old footage he'd seen at Stanford from the Kent State riot, or some of the pirated police film he'd viewed from that horrible 1989 night in Tiananmen Square, when the PLA had been sent to crush the democracy activists under their tank treads.

The camera zoomed in for a tighter shot and Lee was immobilized. He was sickened by a sense of the familiar as some long-imagined scene played out before him. He could see it coming now, that final moment of discovery, when disparate events would inevitably collide and burst upon him.

It was Alexander—Alexander Bonner—slowly turning as he bled, muttering oaths as the howl of approaching sirens grew louder.

Lee drew back, afraid for himself, afraid for his past and for his barren future. His colleagues were indifferent to his private terrors, busy wisecracking as they began to speculate about motive. Just then, the Minister of Defense strode in. He stopped to watch a few moments before he let out a low whistle.

"Who the fuck's guys pulled this one off?" the Minister chortled.

His was the line most fascinating to Branko's team when they began to pore over the Bravo Compartment transcripts in Langley the next afternoon.

6

CORRALLING JAKE

Martin Booth was an amiable soul. Life had granted him more than his share of blessings, he believed—a loving wife and kids, a happy home, and good health. He approached each day fulfilled, driven still to do his good works. The onset of middle age helped him accept his failings and those of his fellow humans. Time had taken an edge off his righteousness, soothing the occasional disappointment. But as Booth sat that April Fool's Monday in room number 419 of the Dirksen Senate Office Building, his irritation with the boss was growing.

Jake Smithson was behind schedule again, and nowhere to be found. Three senators were milling about the dais and General Arno Hollandsworth, the Assistant Secretary of State for East Asia and Pacific Affairs, was sitting ramrod straight at the felt-covered witness table, his hands folded neatly on his papers. The klieg lights were on, warming a cavernous room that already felt stuffy. Senator Landle of Iowa, the committee's ranking minority member and a man of impeccable manners, was stalling.

"The committee will come to order," Landle said, gently rapping the base of the wooden gavel. "Good morning, Mr. Secretary. We are pleased to have you with us. I just wanted you to know we will have a brief recess as we await the Chairman, who seems, uh, to have been caught in traffic."

Landle smiled vacantly, then turned back to Booth in the small staff chair behind him, offering his arched eyebrows in a theatrical scowl.

Booth had spent longer than usual preparing for this Monday morning session, held unusually early to accommodate the administration witness' flight schedule. Booth was rather proud of Smithson's opening statement, the intricate traps it laid, the irresistible bait it offered to the press. It was to be a key salvo for the California senator's new campaign refrain, assailing "an administration adrift." He'd designed it to underscore a theme Smithson was to use later in the week at the Los Angeles World Affairs Council, and then with the *New York Times* editorial board.

The goal was to land a punch on the White House during the appearance of the circumspect Hollandsworth. Smithson would have edited the line of questioning by now, absorbed it, made it his own. Barreling in late and rushing through the questioning would take the edge off the ambush.

Typical Smithson. Booth's loyalty to the man extended beyond the issues, a filial faith from one ever hoping for the best from his adopted hero. Booth had long been the indispensable aide, a surrogate political son to the California senator. Booth had been there for Smithson—from the days of the Iran-contra arms scandals to his recent pointed questioning of the intelligence community about WMD-tracking failures before the invasion of Iraq.

The senator had blistered the White House for "kissing up to China" after Tiananmen; Booth had been the architect of the whole media campaign. The rhetoric was striking in its virulent anti-communist strain, coming as it did from the left. But then China and Taiwan Strait issues always made for strange political bedfellows. The media had loved the counterpoint: a liberal legislator moving to the right of a conservative White House—a senior politician with a high tech constituency who had the balls to put principles ahead of politics. Reporters wrote fawning stories about him with the same cynical subtext: "Honest Man Found in Washington."

Silicon Valley and the aerospace interests had frowned on Smithson's human rights crusade, and subsequently played hard-to-get with campaign funds. Then Booth organized the home state trade delegation to the Asian economic summit. That had worked, too. After the release of seven survivors of Tiananmen, Smithson brought all the California high tech execs back to his side through a dramatic switch to support the trade agreement with China. Booth had brokered the prisoner release, a master stroke that enjoyed the quiet cooperation of both Li Jianjun and Mickey Dooley. They had all played their hands brilliantly, as in the Club days of old.

Through it all, Booth had fiercely defended his boss. Booth was the consummate insider who drew great pleasure from his vocation, relishing the exercise of reflected power. But Booth remained troubled by

Smithson's recklessness; the senator's relentless philandering offended him. Booth's moralist upbringing, his absolutist sense of right and wrong, made him view Smithson's flexible version of marital obligation as shallow and distasteful.

Booth's own very harmonious marriage was a genuine union of spirit. His partnership with Amy stood in such a stark contrast to the private mess of Smithson's life that the senator's escapades became an issue for the staffer. Amy was a full-time homemaker, a magna cum laude Penn graduate who had given up her curator's work with the Smithsonian because she had chosen to be there each day when the school buses rolled up. Late at night, as Booth and Amy talked, both began to dread the coming presidential campaign. Booth confessed to growing doubts he could endure the endless compromises required by the circus ahead.

Booth was a loyalist. But he had such an intimate view of the moral fissure in his boss that, at times, he often wanted to avert his gaze. *How could a leader so brilliant, so gifted at rallying the political center to the justness of a cause, risk so much?* Every time the media sex police exposed and brought down another of the high and mighty, Smithson's aide cringed, fearing his boss was living on borrowed time.

Then, there he was—the effervescent legislator himself—striding through the public entrance, a retinue of press and public swirling about him like moths drawn to light. Only the anxious Booth was troubled by the senator's wet hair, and the amorous morning detour it suggested to him.

"Good morning. Good morning." The senator patted each of his colleagues on the shoulder as he slid by their chairs at the dais. "Martin, may I see you a moment?"

He beckoned for his legislative director to follow him through the brass-plated door into the anteroom tucked just behind the senators' chairs. Here was their inner sanctum, where several committee staffers were discussing in hushed tones the business of their day.

"Senator," Booth whispered firmly. "You need to get the show on the road."

"Just one sec here." Smithson was calmly steering them into a corner now, fellow staffers amused as they shuffled out through the impossibly heavy door, leaving the two of them alone. "Just want to make sure we're all on the same page with this proliferation hit."

"Senator," said Booth, "it's a two-fer. You get news—above the fold, maybe—about the Iranian nuclear program. And you stick it to the Administration for being blind to promiscuous Chinese exports."

"Now Martin, I'm with you." (Except for Booth's spouse, only the senator used his given name.) "I'm just wondering about the time and place you've chosen for the hit. You certain this is the best forum?"

"Sure," Booth replied. "It tees up your Los Angeles speech. We may get a two-day bounce on the West Coast. And it sets the agenda for when you do the *New York Times* editorial board."

"You're comfortable with sourcing?"

"None of it is U.S. government origin," Booth said. "So you're not divulging any classified matter."

"But if you did get it from Langley, it would be?" Smithson asked.

Booth tried not to be defensive as he struggled with the senator's point. "They can't just classify any fact that's in the public domain, and then say nobody can discuss it."

Smithson paused to reflect as a head peered back in at the two of them from the doorway. It was Senator Landle's aide, hesitant to interrupt, but clearly sent to prod.

"Coming right now," Smithson said, then pressed his last questions to Booth. "Where does Hollandsworth go with this? What's his come-back?"

"It doesn't matter what he comes back with, Senator."

"Doesn't matter?"

"Once you've made the charge, you've made the news," Booth insisted. "The facts will be out there. They'll be tied up for days responding at the State Department. You can broaden the nuclear nonproliferation theme while they're backing and filling."

Smithson tapped the papers in his hand with his pencil. "OK, my friend. Let's rock and roll."

They strode out into the lights together, a bit of an odd couple. Smithson, the former astronaut, had the trustworthy face of a TV anchorman. Soft, ruddy features. Friendly, good neighbor eyes. He wore his warm chestnut hair long, seasoned with just enough gray to give balance to his sturdy frame kept trim through days of jogging and weekend 10k races.

By contrast, Booth was short and heavy. His frame bespoke too many expense account lunches, too many hours behind a desk. He often appeared out of breath, as if he was a quarterback calling plays in an anxious last-minute huddle. In his graying hair, he had retained an arresting shock of red running from cowlick to forehead—a dagger-like line that hinted at his boundless energy. Amy called it his Harry Potter streak, caressing it admiringly as part of their foreplay.

Smithson's assault began with a disarming opening, a polished but predictable tour d'horizon. Using his best more-in-sorrow-than-in-anger tone, he surveyed the state of U.S.-Asian affairs, from Korea to Indonesia, lamenting the "lost opportunities" of unilateralist administration policies he alleged had "left the U.S. hated, and no longer respected."

"One is left wondering precisely which American values we stand for other than opposing terrorism. We have a growing democracy, and long time ally, in Taiwan. Yet, this administration refuses to significantly assist their defense against a Communist neighbor bent on intimidation. What if Taiwan's deterrent fails? Then we will be forced to place American military forces in harm's way to defend freedom."

In the armless chair behind Smithson, Booth was waiting to enjoy the senator's hit.

"And what of China's recent export practices, aiding in the development of sophisticated weapons delivery systems by rogue nations near and far. Will this administration continue to turn a blind eye to China as it arms our sworn enemies?"

Then, to Booth's amazement, Smithson bailed. The senator cut Booth's prepared text abruptly, wrapping up the statement without mentioning evidence of renewed Iranian missile imports from Beijing, then calling on Hollandsworth. The soldier-turned-diplomat began to serve up pablum, reciting what he maintained was a string of White House successes in Asia.

"Why did you kill it?" Booth whispered into Smithson's ear. "The Iran stuff is solid."

Smithson rocked back in his thick leather chair, whispering to Booth: "I decided to punt. It was just too hot, too soon. Better in the Q&A."

Booth sat and stewed, watching the press corps as they followed the text of Hollandsworth's prepared statement. It was milquetoast, deliberately long enough to limit time and energy that might remain for critical questioning. Of the twenty or so reporters at the rectangular press tables, at least two-thirds were Asian. The hearing was probably news back home for some, Booth reflected. But, without the Iran missile hit, it wouldn't even make filler in the *Post*.

The room was still as Hollandsworth's monologue rolled on. The ceilings were far too high for an office building. Harsh shafts of light leaked between forty-foot tall curtains. In the distance, Booth could hear a wailing siren. To his right, a couple of Republican staffers were sharing a private joke, oblivious to the set piece being performed before them. Another morning of fruitless toil in the United States Senate.

Smithson pulled his punch once again in his opening question round, using his five minutes on some queries about the Japanese economy before reserving the balance of his time. Then, finally, at the very conclusion of the hearing, he had his inning.

"Mr. Secretary, I have one last line of questioning before we adjourn," Smithson said. There were only two senators left in the room now. The balance had been chased by a series of bells, beepers, and anxious aides summoning them to other business. "It relates to Chinese export practices."

"Yes, sir." Hollandsworth's voice betrayed no reaction, though he pulled forward just a bit in his chair.

"Am I correct in my understanding that, while the Chinese have not formally acceded to the minutes of the Missile Technology Control Regime, China has nevertheless committed to abide by these 'MTCR' standards in its export practices?"

"There have been certain diplomatic assurances in that regard." Hollandsworth shifted in his chair, eyes narrowing suspiciously.

"I can interpret that as a *yes*?"

"Affirmative."

"These MTCR assurances coincided with American approval of the trade agreement with China?" Smithson pressed.

"Yes."

"Actually, it was how the Senate came to approve their joining the World Trade Organization, was it not?" Smithson was looking up pointedly from his reading glasses. Booth was motionless behind him, waiting for the hook.

"Well, to be precise, Senator," Hollandsworth began to reply, "there were a number of conditions both sides mutually agreed to."

"But MTCR export standards were the central issue, Mr. Secretary—the quid pro quo, if you will. The point was that China would get the trade deal only if they stopped spreading missile technology around to the so-called 'Axis of Evil.'" Smithson smirked ever so slightly in a gentle dig at the shopworn phrase.

"Well, Mr. Chairman, there was no explicit linkage. Thus, some could argue otherwise."

"For this senator, that was the central reason." Booth noticed Hollandsworth stealing a glance down at his watch as Smithson continued. "These Missile Control standards bar assistance in the development of delivery systems for weapons of mass destruction to nations outside the nuclear nonproliferation treaty—so-called 'rogue nations' like North Korea, Cuba, Iran. Is my understanding correct?"

"Well, Mr. Chairman, these are technical issues. I think you really would have to ask the Defense Department."

"With all due respect, General, upholding these standards is a key goal of American foreign policy. Last time I checked, foreign policy was conducted by the Department of State. My last question, in fact, relates to diplomatic policy. What is our government's response to the recent delivery to Iran of M-70 missiles by the Chinese?"

"M-70 missiles?" Hollandsworth said, unflinching as he held Smithson in a prolonged stare. His military training served him well.

"M-70's, yes." Smithson was intent upon his target now.

"M-70 missiles."

"Yes, Mr. Secretary. M-70 missiles. To Iran."

An aide was whispering in Hollandsworth's ear from the first row of chairs behind him. Smithson was infinitely patient. Senator Landle darted back in through the doorway to the anteroom. He stood just behind Smithson at the dais now, engaged in a hasty conference with his legislative assistant.

Hollandsworth spoke with deliberation: "Senator, some of these matters might best be briefed to the committee by others. These matters are quite sensitive."

"My question relates to diplomatic response. China is helping an unstable nation, a nation still in a state of declared war with the United States, to acquire delivery systems for weapons of mass destruction. What is to be our response?"

"Mr. Chairman, if I may." It was Landle, playing defense for the administration as he leaned down into his mike from a standing position. "Perhaps, if we're going to deal with classified matters, this might be a subject for a closed session."

"Tom, there's a legitimate policy issue here," Smithson insisted. He knew it was the question—and the evidence now out in the general public—that mattered far more than the response. "China is in bed with Iran's weapons program. Again. There's been no refutation of the evidence by the administration witness here. Let's see . . ."

Smithson peered over his glasses at his notes before he continued. "Thirty missiles delivered in port last March the twenty-fourth, wasn't it? My question is really quite simple. How is the administration going to respond to this latest Chinese outrage?"

Hollandsworth and Landle were unmoved. Once more now in the silence, Booth could detect the wail of distant sirens growing louder. *Was the president's motorcade due on Capitol Hill for some meeting?*

"Mis-ter Chair-man," the Assistant Secretary finally began, the twang of his Carolina accent prolonging the honorific. "The development of options in response to a hypothetical threat to U.S. national interests is a complicated matter. The allegation you are making in this public forum raises serious considerations. Let us examine them carefully one by one . . ."

Thus, the filibuster was launched. Chairman Smithson had already pressed the limits of decorum. Now, he would be paid back in kind. He received a response so long and obtuse that, even as Hollandsworth ploughed forward, the timing lights governing Smithson's five-minute question round shifted from green to yellow.

A sharp commotion erupted in the back room, heard through the now open doorway. Within moments, aides and senators alike were chattering and passing notes, then disappearing into the anteroom. Smithson remained intent on his stare-down with Hollandsworth. The State Department official showed no signs of wrapping up, even as the disturbance spread to the press tables behind him and to his left. Few were still paying any attention to Hollandsworth's remarks.

"What the hell is going on?" Smithson muttered to Booth, who had just been handed a pink phone message slip he was beginning to read.

"An explosion. There was . . . was some type of explosion across from the Treasury Department." Booth spoke in an anxious whisper, his voice catching. "Senator, they say Jonathan Talbott was killed."

Hollandsworth brought his monologue to a merciful close just as Smithson's light flashed to red.

7

Dreams of Whiteness

There was an intimate calm inside the ambulance as Rachel was rolled along. She lay with a Mona Lisa smile, wincing only when they cornered. The siren's call seemed so very far away, in some other world. She felt the pulse of the drugs coursing through her veins. For the moment, she could rest secure.

"Who? Who is . . ." she finally said, struggling to move her lips, almost choking on the taste of dust. "Who's going to meet Jamie's bus?" Then she fell back into a smothered dream of whiteness, unconscious once more.

She was drifting, tumbling backwards in time, past work and men and motherhood, past Stanford and the Last Dance, back to childhood days on the ranch north of Cody. The remembered bits and pieces of her past seemed to flow magically into a coherent whole. She could discern the pattern now.

She saw vividly the mosaic of her years, assembled like the pottery shards at the old Indian campground in Sunlight Basin. She heard again the thunderheads of her youth, booming off the high Absaroka canyons east of Yellowstone. The battering storms would gather quickly, soaring clouds moving to cover the sky. Then they would strike, flattening the blues and greens of mid-afternoon, bringing dark into the main cabin.

At age twelve, Rachel used to sit cross-legged on the Navajo rug, ruing the fact that she, the youngest, had been left behind. Father smoked Marlboros on the porch, waiting for the storm to pass. Mother snuck gin in the pantry, her private ritual of escape. The brothers were already gone, away to State U. in Laramie, headed to Denver and Portland, to city jobs and city wives. At such times, Rachel had sat alone, watched over by the silent, impassive grizzly head above the stone hearth.

She recalled a moment when her journey had begun. She would close her eyes and spin the Rand-McNally globe, round and round and round again. She dreamt even then of fleeing, of finding an anonymous place to discover herself. While the globe spun, she would try to cheat, as an unobserved child will. She would hover her finger near tropical latitudes as the earth traversed her hands, feeling the topographical bumps flit by like Braille messages. As she chanted "I am going to live in . . . ", she would try to stop the spinning planet with her finger near the sea—on Hawaii, Tahiti, or the Philippines.

She longed for the sea, for the sensation of cleansing waves washing over her, salty and strong. She had never seen the ocean, though. No matter how hard she tried to trick the gods, it seemed her finger always came to point on that enormous pink land mass farthest from home, off in faraway Asia.

China. From the start, she had been aware of some predestination. Even before she had devoured *The Good Earth* and Stilwell's memoirs, she had imagined China awaiting her, mysterious, alluring, and utterly foreign. That danger—the very foreignness of it all—had been the attraction. Now, as she stirred from her dreams on her hospital gurney, she could see that for the first time.

It was almost noon when her mind began to ground itself back in the present and she felt she could speak once more. She was in the intensive care unit at George Washington Hospital, goofy from the painkillers and hours of disembodied remembrances. The medics had cleaned her up and stitched her scalp. Alexander Bonner was at her side, holding her left hand gently, peering over the back of a doctor reading x-rays.

"Nothing there," she said, startling them with her attempt at humor, her voice gravelly and hoarse. The doctor turned and spoke firmly to her. She had a concussion, several nasty cuts, and a shoulder fracture.

Two serious looking men stood at the foot of her bed, she could see now, just to the left of where Alexander sat. Beyond them, she noticed a uniformed Washington cop.

"Ms. Paulson. Hello. I'm James Hickman with the FBI. This is Detective Bryant from D.C. Police. If you feel up to it, ma'am, we'd like a few words with you."

They looked like a matching pair, thick and sorrowful. But the policeman had a longer face, his eyes sloping downward like a basset hound. Hickman from the FBI appeared more hospitable, a dusting of white in his Burt Reynolds moustache.

"Ma'am," Rachel repeated vacantly. "Ma'am. Wow. You know, Mr. Hickman, nobody calls me *ma'am*, except one of my ten year-old's playmates, a British kid. Doesn't know any better, I suppose."

She started up on her right side, then gasped. "Oh, Alexander. Have you called Jamie? The school. What about picking him up?"

"Rachel, I got it covered." Alexander grabbed her good arm, steering her back to her pillow. "Don't worry. I already talked to the principal. I'm going out to meet him before the extended day release."

"The snow. What about the snowstorm?"

"It's OK. No snow.

"Another AccuWeather false alarm," she said, giggling a bit, then began to drift.

"Mr. Paulson, we really need to ask your wife a few—"

"Sergeant, I'm not Mr. Paulson," Alexander said, looking down at Rachel, who was settled now. "I mean, Detective. Whatever."

"Just a friend," she said absently, "friend of the family."

"I haven't been able to reach Barry yet by phone or by email," Alexander explained to Rachel. "He's on the company plane, on the way to Seattle. They're trying to raise the pilot through the FAA or something."

"But weren't you staying with Ms. Paulson at the Willard Hotel?"

He felt the cops' eyes on him. For some reason, he felt sheepish, like he had something to hide.

"We just had breakfast. In the Main Dining Room."

"And you were walking on—"

"F Street."

"F Street."

"Behind the hotel?" Hickman and Bryant were both taking notes. At the periphery of the scene, Alexander noticed Rachel seeming to float, like a helium balloon released from a child's hand.

"Uh, right, in front of her office. I mean, we were just crossing the street to the, the TPB headquarters, crossing F right by Fifteenth Street."

"The Talbott, Porter, Blodge—what's that?" The FBI man was turning again to the detective, who gave him "Blow."

"Oh, God!" Rachel was moaning now. "Mr. Talbott!"

Alexander had her arm again, as he, too, flashed back to the fluttering of the curtains from the shattered TPB windows. Mr. Talbott, indeed.

Now it all started to flow back over him. He could see the funereal curtains, the shattered SUV, the severed leg, still in pin stripes and a shoe. He staggered to his feet, about to retch, needing fresh air.

"Whoa there." The detective steadied Alexander, sympathetic under the circumstances. "Have you had a CAT scan?"

The FBI guy was very much the doctor now, standing by as he added, "You might have a concussion there, too."

"No, I didn't get a direct hit. Just banged up a bit." Alexander stood in the doorway breathing more heavily. The uniformed cop was pacing in the doorway, as jumpy as that policeman with the drawn revolver he'd seen on F Street.

"What was it?" Rachel was crying softly. "A bomb?"

"We think so, ma'am."

"The TPB garage?" asked Alexander, cocking his head now, elbows on knees as he straightened.

"Yeah. The TPB building."

"How many people were injured?"

"We're still trying to ascertain casualties, sir. Can we get your name?"

"Alexander Bonner. *Los Angeles Times*." Reflexively, he started to offer a handshake, then just shook his head.

Rachel was watching, her face ashen as she pulled herself just a bit higher on the mattress. She bore a look of animal fear, her eyes sliding towards the cops in the doorway. "Who would . . . why would anybody do this?"

"Ma'am, we know you've had a bad blow. We do need to try to get some information from you." It was the FBI man again, very tentatively. "Others could be in danger."

"Yes." She lay back, her eyes closed tight.

"What did you see?"

"We were just walking out of the hotel together . . . the restaurant. I was just . . . I was just saying goodbye to Alexander. I . . . I had my back to the, uh, TPB . . ." Ripples of fatigue were spreading, eroding her efforts at coherent thought. Rachel could hear anxious hospital voices in the distance. But she was unanchored, her thoughts drifting away on some unseen tide.

"What did you see at the building? Did you see any people on the street? Any particular vehicles?"

Rachel's eyes were closed, her face blank. But then she spoke with a sigh of resignation.

"I was just kissing Alexander." She began to weep again, a low wailing sound. The men looked at their shoes. "A good bye kiss."

Alexander was close by. He took a deep breath, calling up the image, taking control. "I was looking right at the building, talking with Rachel. It was, just, normal. You know, a bunch of cars trying to get into the garage. Nine a.m. rush and all that. There was a big gas guzzler, a black SUV trying to get in off F Street. A blue car in the chute. Parking attendant. A panhandler. A gray taxicab. Not that many people, really."

"The building! What happened to the people inside?" Rachel searched their faces for clues. She tried to sit up again, to get on a level with them. But the sheets and the lights and the weight of the pain in her shoulder pressed back against her.

"I'm sorry, ma'am," the detective said. "We really don't know yet. Don't know definitively about the casualties. We're trying to put it all together, to figure out who was where and who is OK."

"You work there, right?" The FBI man again.

"At TPB. Yeah. I'm the, uh, in charge of the Congressional work and a director on our board."

"Law firm?"

"Yeah. I mean, mostly lawyers. But we, uh, do a lot of lobbying work."

"You're lobbyists?" He said it like *proctologists*. "Who do you lobby for?"

"We, uh, I mean, we have, oh, more than a hundred clients. A lot of corporations and cities, and . . . " She slowed as another wave of confusion rolled through her brain. ". . . governments."

"Governments? You lobby the federal government for state governments?"

"No. We, uh, yeah. We help cities get federal dollars for construction projects. Like the Seattle airport expansion. And, you know, when military bases close and they need conversion funds . . . El Toro, California, the old Marine air field in Orange County."

She began to ramble. How to explain? It was hard, like one of those old, inane SAT analogy tests. The drugs they had given her made everything pitch and roll. She couldn't find her footing. The questioning seemed like it would never end, even though it was just beginning.

A cell phone rang. The detective regarded the number. "I gotta take this one," he said apologetically. "Try to gather yourself for a few minutes while I deal with this."

As he walked beyond her vision, she began thinking hard, more clearly, composing her own personal Talbott obituary. She knew the story line too well. He was such an odd duck—a gentle man with peculiar vanities.

Jonathan Talbott was a shy Episcopalian, distinguished by a series of touchstones like the green bow ties he wore daily. The awkward 1950's-style plaid suits. The limo and driver who called at his Georgetown residence on P Street each morning at eight. But he would walk, sometimes for blocks, to take the air. The black Lincoln would trail discreetly before Talbott climbed in and rode the balance of the distance to his office.

Jonathan had been an unhappy securities attorney in New York before he and his law partners invested in a Washington outpost. This was around the mid-seventies time of the Lockheed and Chrysler loan bailouts. Porter and Blow had joined him in the enterprise. To their surprise, they masterfully navigated the political pitfalls and secured everything their clients needed from Congress. The three senior partners enjoyed the exercise and began to develop an extensive book of legal business in Washington. Ultimately, they established their own D.C. venture, divorcing their New York firm and starting their own.

Over the years, Porter had drifted away from the government relations side of the practice, dabbling in merchant banking. He leveraged his D.C. insider position to broker investments with some of the corporations and foreign enterprises that formed their client base, anything from purchases of East European pollution control equipment to Hong Kong real estate deals. Then, during a legislative strategy session on saving the B-2 bomber funding, Blow had keeled over with a massive heart attack. He was a board room casualty, DOA at George Washington Hospital.

Talbott continued to build the business, delegating the management functions to Rachel and a handful of driven colleagues. As revenues climbed, he placed the TPB imprimatur on everything, from the heavy brass doors of their Fifteenth & F Street building to the linen hand towels in their bathrooms. In the flashy, make-a-quick-buck world of influence peddling, Talbott was unique. The older he got and the more successful the government relations side of the firm became, the more he came to view himself as a trustee of the public interest, with a remarkably high load of pro bono clients. The Protestant ethic hard at work within drove him to harvest wealth from his clients, then use TPB's considerable influence to secure funds for everything from Head Start programs to breast cancer research.

Painfully awkward with colleagues, he led a quiet private life. His spacey patrician wife, a recluse from the Washington social scene, painted an endless series of enormous, muddy brown canvases. His only child, a daughter, lived on a vegan commune in New Mexico, meditating and making turquoise jewelry.

Central to the image of openness Talbott had created for the firm was his personal office design. He sat at the very center of the firm's second floor perch, a line of oversized windows front and back. When the elevators opened on the firm's reception, there, behind a wall of mahogany-framed glass, was Talbott himself, writing in longhand at his desk or speaking on an antique black telephone.

Talbott had been determined that lobbyists leave behind forever the days of hookers and cigar smoke, the times when winks to committee chairs were accompanied by envelopes of cash that got business done. He insisted that TPB advocates be professional advocates. They would shape policy on the public record, no longer second-class citizens like the stepchildren lobbyists in most of their competitors' K Street law firms. They would comport themselves like officers of the court. Their objective was honest victory in the political arena. Talbott was known to detest the scores of cocky youngsters who came to town only to make money, punching their public service ticket in Congress for a matter of months before hanging out a shingle on K Street—as if they had years of experience to sell.

Talbott's latent sense of public purpose endeared him to Rachel. No one, it seemed, was as pure of motive as Jonathan Talbott, the old Eli, Yale Class of '61. Perhaps his greatest fault, Rachel recalled, was his sentimental assumption that others shared his noble intentions.

"Ma'am, sorry about that," said the sad-faced FBI man after he returned. "If you're feeling stronger, can we try some more?"

"Sure."

"Who are your biggest corporate clients?"

"Drug companies. Coca-Cola. Bechtel. Ag companies like ADM. Tobacco."

"What's ADM?"

"Archer Daniels Midland," the policeman interjected helpfully. "The big grain conglomerate that makes ethanol gasoline."

"Oh, really." Mr. Hickman nodded, impressed, then turned back to Rachel. "Anybody controversial?"

"Officer," Rachel said, managing a weak grin, "they're all kind of controversial."

"I think he wants to know if you have any clients somebody might want to kill," said Alexander, trying to help.

"Kill our clients?" Rachel was trying to shake her head, but it just rolled sloppily. "Or kill us?"

"Ma'am, we need you to focus on this if you possibly can."

"You really think it was me they were trying to blow up?" It was a new concept, and a repugnant one. She struggled to comprehend the implications. "Who would want to kill me?"

She thought first of Jamie. How to shield him in a world full of crazies? Then other faces paraded by: Talbott, Barry, Mickey, and Lee. Next came the twisted ones—the World Bank protesters, anarchists, and environmental whackos. There was a horde of caustic voices circling about her now, like the flying monkey-men in the *Wizard of Oz* horror scene.

"To be safe," said the FBI man, "gotta assume any of you is a target. We don't know yet. You've got twenty-four hour uniformed protection until we do."

"Oh, I don't know. We've got all kinds of people pissed at us on any given day," Rachel continued. "We've got mayors who are furious because they want more dollars than we can get. We've got desperate dot-com executives about to go under if they don't get their Pentagon contract. We've got corporate attorneys demanding bigger tax breaks for their employers."

Bryant and Hickman were both taking copious notes.

"I mean, there's foreign governments that want Uncle Sam to sell them more arms. There was a Save the Earth group in Seattle that opposed the new airport. They dumped a bunch of dead seagulls on our lobby. Smelly things. Then there was the Armenian guy who poured blood on our carpets—"

"Foreign governments?" They both wanted to know.

She paused, fighting hard to clear her head now, to maintain her brief burst of energy, survival instincts kicking in. She was thinking about day care and car pool, about a better lock for the sliding glass door in back. She was thinking about how she would explain all this to Jamie. His nightmares about bombs on the Metro were already bad enough.

She stared at the men before her: two gray men in suits off the rack, working their note pads like some B-movie news reporters. Alexander was still holding her hand. It felt warm and strong, and, strange as it seemed, she wanted to take him under the hospital covers with her, to kiss him again.

"Foreign governments." She repeated herself. "Yes. Turkey. The Jordanians. The Swiss on that Jewish reparations thing. A number of state-owned enterprises in the PRC—you know, mainland China. A lot of different interests."

Rachel turned back to both her inquisitors. "Officer," she asked, "do you really think I was the target of the bomb?"

"Well, you were supposed to be there."

"Right! I was supposed to be in Jonathan's office at nine o'clock. We had clients due there at . . . at ten. A senator at noon. Canadian Ambassador later. Chinese Embassy guys, too. I mean, it's going to—it was going to be a long day. You think somebody was trying to kill us all?"

The men conferred briefly in a whisper. The cop spoke first, with a sigh. "Mind if we sit down, ma'am. This is gonna take awhile."

Then they started all over again, at the very beginning.

It was nearly three hours later before Alexander learned of Jonathan Talbott's fate. Alexander was sitting behind the wheel of his green Saab in the parking lot of Thomas Jefferson Elementary School, listening to local updates on all-news radio, when he heard.

Five or six people had died, the WTOP reporter said. They included a garage attendant, a pedestrian, two or three people in a taxicab, and one person in Talbott's office. Alan Porter had been sitting in the open room, opposite Talbott's desk, and was killed instantly. Talbott, who had been in the mahogany-lined private bathroom, was trapped by debris for ninety minutes, but the D.C. fire squad brought him out, virtually unscathed.

This was the information Alexander took with him as he entered Jamie's school building. Alexander was envious as he walked the hallways. It was like another planet, a place of primary colors and bright-faced, tousle-haired kids giggling in the corners. Bulletin boards were covered with cheery projects. The linoleum floors and lime colored tiles on the walls felt like the 1950's. It had been many years since Alexander had been inside a public school. In this wholesome world, so near a city full of self-absorbed grown-ups, he felt like an intruder.

When he reached the principal's office, Jamie was waiting, quite still and serious in a straight-backed chair. He was calm, as if this was an altogether familiar routine, as if Alexander picked him up every Monday. They chatted quietly as they rode home, talking of baseball, the Nationals, and the beginning of Little League season. Alexander tried to be chipper for the boy's benefit.

At home in Rachel's kitchen, Alexander poured a bowl of Fritos and two root beers while Jamie curled up in an oversized chair in the living room to watch the end of the Opening Day broadcast on Channel 20. It was the sixth inning. The Nationals were down 7-2. Shadows reached into all corners of the decrepit Robert F. Kennedy Stadium. Alexander found himself turning on lights and checking doors. An Arlington police car was parked across the street now; Alexander walked out and spoke briefly with the officer. He would have to explain things to Jamie, and soon.

Alexander procrastinated before he resumed his solitary patrol of the house. He was snooping now, going far beyond a basic security check.

What the hell am I doing? he wondered as he nosed into the private closets and upstairs corridors. He was looking for some clue, though he knew not about what. He peered into intimate spaces—in drawers and medicine cabinets. He checked the showers, ran his hands down an elegant blue silk nightgown trimmed in white lace hanging on the back of the master bath door. It smelled of Rachel—her hair, her perfume—arousing his senses with an electric wave.

Gradually, he discerned a schizophrenia about the interior. There were two different homes here, or so it appeared upon closer inspection. The design was all smooth surfaces and chrome, IKEA furniture with not enough cushions. But the hallway tables and the master bedroom upstairs were cluttered with photographs of Jamie on a horse in the Wyoming mountains, grandparents and grinning uncles in cowboy hats. Rachel's bedside table was busy with books and catalogues, with stacks of pictures back from the photo shop. An unworn dress, still on the hanger, had been tossed over a rocking chair already piled high with clothes.

By contrast, Barry's private study was like an airplane cockpit, a table full of computer gadgetry, a color printer, a large shredder, and not a single book. There was a large sharp-edged filing cabinet with a combination lock. An immaculate desk held nothing but a matching set of gold scissors and letter opener set placed just so. A black leather couch with a bedroom pillow was at one end, a light on in the guest bath. An FM radio station, chatting away from hidden speakers, was the only human touch in Barry's inner sanctum.

The common spaces in the house were white and tiled, the dining room too fancy for a kid, the table polished and evidently unused. The kitchen was messy, with items on the counter from breakfast, notes, lists, and the weekend newspapers. The finished basement was similarly segregated. The playroom was pleasant chaos—stacks of shoe boxes filled with K'nex, Lego towers, stuffed animals, old puzzles. But the workroom was too neat, with tidy compartments for every screw and nail, tools all hung on labeled hooks, and a bolt lock on the interior door.

Alexander went back up to the second floor, finally entering Jamie's room to pull the shade down and turn on a light against the falling dusk. There, on Jamie's hastily-made bed, was his baseball glove, a Nationals logo ball in the pocket. By his bed was a tiny framed photograph of just Barry and Jamie—Barry wearing a suit and a shiny grin, Jamie looking serious in his team jersey and cap.

It seemed almost as if Barry was deceased, memories of his dutiful fatherhood reverently kept intact, a shrine to his perpetual absence. Barry was a gentle and kind father; Alexander had seen it. Rachel was quick to defend his parenting, his most endearing attribute. But Barry was such an absentee, Alexander knew, flighty and secretive in his world of business travel, inaccessible even to his oldest friends. Rachel had confided her fears of late that Barry had some secret life, "another wife and kids tucked away in Jersey like that guy Charles Kuralt had." She'd said she felt marooned, despairing of the wait for the return of a once amiable stranger.

Alexander lay back and thought of Barry flying on that corporate plane to nowhere. Peddling technology to the Chinese, brokering some Korean telecom deal. He was angry now—angry with Barry, angry that he still hadn't heard from the man seven hours after his wife had nearly been killed. He was angry at the shadowy figures exacting vengeance, making some idiotic statement by blowing people up on a Washington street corner. Mostly, as he lay there on his ten-year-old godson's pillow, Alexander was angry with himself. He was angry for the reserve he had allowed to grow thick like a hedge about him.

Why should a simple walk down an elementary school hallway make me feel like an alien? He wondered how he had come to feel so estranged from such a normal family routine.

As Alexander ruminated on Barry's failings—and his own—his thoughts drifted to his father. His father, tossing the ball with him by the outfield fence amidst the soft morning promise of a Sunday game. His father the grinder. His father, sweaty in the tunnel of the Fresno stadium, spitting tobacco juice, toweling off after a shower and another loss. His father, ever stoic, never cursing, as he laced up his spikes for another game played in the minor leagues.

The rhythms of trial and failure were so much a part of his memories. With Mom at his side, driving, and his three sisters in back of the old Chevy station wagon, Alexander had ridden up and down Highway 99 year after year to watch Dad. Through Fresno and Modesto, Stockton and Sacramento, Pop had shuffled, from the Oaks to the Kings, to the Bees and the River Pilots. They would eat peanut butter and jelly sandwiches and sing Motown songs on the radio, driving the potholed route his father had followed in the vain effort to make it to the big leagues, before a dead arm and a fondness for Gallo jug wine extinguished the dream.

It was after dark when Alexander awoke with a start. Jamie, quite motionless, regarded him with sad eyes as he stood over him. Evidently, he had been there for some time.

"We lost." It was all the boy said.

8

EVENING AT THE OASIS

There was a series of calming eddies in Rachel's memories, gently swirling pools into which the flow of time became diverted. Once immersed pieces floated to the surface, presented for re-evaluation. These recollections held clues from a past that had seemed too rushed. She could examine them, as a geologist would a slice of sedimentary rock, experiencing the moments once more, learning anew. Invariably during these reflections, she returned to that last fall together at Stanford, to that shared life before things became so terribly complicated.

It was late in the evening, she recalled this time, and they had been blowing off steam with one of their Friday drinking games. They were settled in at a gritty little beer and burger joint on El Camino Real, just over the Menlo Park line, called The Oasis.

They had made it into a sort of clubhouse for their group. There was a familiarity about the place that gave them comfort, something unpretentious about the garish green martini glass on the neon sign out front and the rotund waitresses inside. The floor was covered with a thick layer of sawdust, creating a roadhouse feel. Juicy burgers arrived at tables in red plastic baskets, color-coded toothpicks marking the cheese. The fries were crisp and hot, the pitchers of beer frosty and cheap. There was a scruffy crowd, a mix of deliverymen and the local bowlers who tolerated the students in their midst.

With Alexander, she had ridden over to the guys' house, rolling on their bikes down streets with bucolic names like Lemon and Orchard. Alexander had produced some pungent Mendocino buds and they had gotten high along the creek bed at dusk, savoring the smoke and the easy talk it brought forth.

Later in the evening, they were all gathered in the bar. Barry was impressively drunk, his hands gripping Booth's shoulders as he egged the others on and called for another round. Branko was holding his own, working on a late burger, deep in conversation with Lee. They drank from their mugs, soaking in the welcome camaraderie. It had been another long week running tutorials and composing thesis chapters in the student carrels lining the Serra House hallways.

Rachel, her back turned to Barry, was ensconced in the corner booth, engaging Mickey. Their conversation had started as light banter, in keeping with the mood of the evening. She remained gracefully buzzed from the sunset joint. She had felt provocative ever since, unconcerned about the sense she was, or wasn't, making. She was pleased to suspend her insecurities and assume everything came out sounding profound.

Mickey was retelling stories from one of his adventures in the Colorado mountains. Rachel was amused and curious. She wondered, as she often did, at the components of his kaleidoscopic personality that flashed through his beery grin. She was seeing Mickey in a new light this night. She was fascinated by his ability to be all things to all people. He was a consummate performer. Here was a guy who could track bear on horseback, but also ace the college boards. Here was a guy who could sweet-talk the hard-bodied California beach girls, but who also spoke fluent Mandarin.

For some reason that night, she had probed deeper. Mickey had been teasing her about her primal fears, snakes and spiders, and asking about her phobias. She had suddenly turned toward him and leaned right into his face. Holding him with her eyes, she asked him directly: "Simple question: name that which you fear most."

Mickey shucked and jived a bit. His shoulders would actually drop as he rolled back from the hips, maneuvering to laugh it off. Rachel just held her pose, prodding. "Give it up, Dooley."

"You're really serious?" he asked after a while.

"Dead serious. No dodging this time."

He stroked his chin, throwing her yet another sideways grin, then peered beyond her, searching for one of the gang to rescue him. It was to no avail.

He smiled cautiously as he began. "That which I most fear . . . "

"Yep."

"Sheesh, got me there. I mean, just between you and me?"

"My lips are sealed."

"The truth is," he said, "I've always been afraid of dying young."

"Dying young?"

"Yeah."

"Bullshit. You push the edge all the time. Cliff-diving, hang gliding out at Point Reyes, all that survivalist stuff you guys do out in the desert."

"No, Rachel. I mean, I think that's why I do it. The waste of dying without having fully lived. Scares the hell out of me."

"I've never seen you afraid," Rachel countered, regarding him skeptically. "I've never even seen you flinch."

"That's the point," Mickey said. "It's probably death defiance. I just think it would be fucking tragic to pass some mundane existence in the 'burbs, only to get run down in some shopping mall parking lot."

"Tragic?"

"Sure. In some ways, I've always thought I'd die young. Half expected it even. Something I saw in the desert once. Maybe it was the peyote or the Budweiser. It made me want to do it all. To cheat death, to outrace my demons. I wanted to see every continent. Taste every dish. Seduce every pretty girl."

"Every one?"

"Present company excluded, of course."

"I should be flattered?"

"Roomies' girl." He was flirting with his eyes now, his trademark "aw shucks" look. "Hell, Rachel. You're like a sister."

"Story of my life!" She was laughing now, but exasperated. There was something simple and pure that rang true in his confession. "I wonder if you ever had—"

"Hey! What's this heavy tête-a-tête? Gotta share!" It was Barry, leaning in to break up the private moment he'd spied out. Before Mickey or Rachel could respond, Barry was shouting over them at their comrade. "C'mon, Lee! Rejoin the party! Gotta keep up, my man."

Lee appeared sullen, a bit far gone. He gazed warily at the shot glass in his right hand as Branko tried to explain something he wasn't following.

"Truth or Dare!" A shout erupted. It had been Barry's idea. Truth or Dare, the guys' adaptation of a game of self-revelation—a game where they threatened to expose their deepest secrets.

Barry was circling now, grinning, a bit too eager as he roared: "Branko goes first!"

Branko regarded him coolly for a moment, thinking as he chewed, a bit of onion caught in his brown moustache. The others had gathered, so Branko played along, turning first to Alexander.

"OK, let's start with you, Alexander," Branko began matter-of-factly.

"What the hell are you doing living here in academic nirvana with a bunch of engineers and business whizzes? Shouldn't you be off writing novels somewhere? Don't writers need to go suffer for a while before they have anything to say?"

Alexander smirked, but did not miss a beat. "I'm a plant," he said. "I'm spying for *Reader's Digest*, collecting material on how The Chosen Ones live."

He reached and sampled one of Branko's fries before continuing. "My assignment is to chronicle the rise of an entire generation devoid of ideology. You'll all end up as characters in my first bad novel."

He raised his glass and gave a slight bow.

"Pretty weak, Bonner," Mickey said, moving to reclaim the lead. "Barry, you're next. Your question is for Booth."

Booth was grinning, his thick red curls splayed in several directions. "Martin B., OK," Barry hesitated. "Would you sell out your country for a million bucks, or—"

"Or a babe!" Mickey added.

"Yeah, a hot one," Barry parroted.

Booth pressed forward, ever earnest, struggling to play against type, emboldened by the whiskey shooters Mickey and Barry had been pushing. "I won't need to. I will be Secretary of State, preaching democracy to the developing world, and bringing freedom to the godless Communists. Then I'll step down and tour the nation giving inspirational speeches with Billy Graham."

"For a fee, of course," Mickey interjected.

"Of course. A big fee. I will have a limo and driver, and run diplomatic errands for the UN before I retire home to Iowa to raise thoroughbreds. I'll be livin' the dream, guys."

Next, Booth threw a lob to Rachel, something about describing "perfect foreplay."

"A kiss," she offered, swigging her beer. "A good kiss."

But the boys leaned in, wanting more. "C'mon, girl," Mickey demanded. "Give it up!"

"It's that simple. That's all you need, really. A kiss that communicates. Mischief. Intimacy. Desire. An invitation to an unveiling."

Mickey let out a long whistle of admiration to break the awkward silence that followed. Rachel had captivated her male audience, as usual.

Then, a bit sobered, she turned to Branko and asked him why, if his parents were European, he seemed obsessed with studying all things Chinese.

"I'm so sick of reading Kissinger and Brzezinski and all those Euro-centric academics. Back east, all those Kremlinologists yammer on and on about the Soviets. Well, you know what?"

Branko had their attention.

"The fucking Soviets will sink under the weight of their own corruption, their own internal contradictions. They don't believe any of that Marxist-Leninist crap they spout. But the Asian dictators—they are true believers. The Communists in Beijing will have far greater staying power. They have refined the ability to dominate the masses. They exploit the Asian tradition of sacrificing individual will to communal need. They will prove to be far more efficient tyrants."

He looked sternly at Lee as he concluded. "The Chinese are the Orwells to come."

Way too serious. But that was Branko, and his fellow Mandarins just let it pass.

Mickey drew an easy question—to describe errors he had made the first time he had sex. His response was droll, if uninspiring. Rachel thought for a moment that she actually detected some embarrassment, a private place he was protecting beneath all his bluff and bluster.

Barry was asked about Rachel: Would he or would he not marry her after depriving her of her innocence? He bobbed and weaved effectively, caveating, temporizing, throwing in a couple of glib lines. Ultimately, he said, they all would dance at the wedding. It was a welcome declaration for Rachel, never quite sure where she stood as she struggled to keep up with her chosen man.

The last question of the night was directed at Lee by Mickey.

Mickey was on his feet, squeezing his palms in that almost annoying display of energy he could barely contain. It was his moment, the conductor center stage to orchestrate the night's grand finale.

He paced a bit for dramatic effect, then suddenly slid into the banquette right next to Lee. Mickey was enjoying it all almost too much, stalking his weakened quarry, closing for the kill.

"My old friend, Lee. Ah, yes." He began to lightly massage Lee's shoulders. "It nears midnight at The Oasis. Tonight you must tell the truth."

Mickey milked the scene, relishing the spotlight. Then he pulled back to confront his target.

"Why, of all the students in China, did the Party choose you to lead the first big student exchange with Stanford?" Mickey's words came ever slower now as he drove home the query. "And what the hell will they expect of you when you return?"

Here it was—the question Lee had been waiting for, the one he'd been dreading since he first arrived twenty-two months earlier. He'd practiced the response countless times back in Beijing. He'd continued to rehearse it with his security chaperones at the Chinese consulate up in San Francisco, to whom he reported every month.

Lee knew what he was supposed to say. He knew well the price of his ticket to the West. He'd prepared to mouth the safe lines, to obscure his fears and fantasies beneath the fog of the Party line.

That was all before, though. It was before the intoxicating flirtations with freedom. Now, after he'd tasted the forbidden fruits, his resolve was weakening. He'd witnessed brilliant young minds—teenagers in seminars—challenging the conventional wisdom of their elders. He'd shared the irreverent debates of their after-hours Club. He'd ridden the cable cars, laughing and hollering in the fog. He'd walked the Pacific cliffs, smoking marijuana, arguing history. He'd been to the wild art galleries and X-rated movies. He'd witnessed the cornucopia of choices in the supermarkets, the malls full of plenty, the shiny cars full of rambunctious children and grinning parents. He'd read the free press and watched the uncensored television news. He'd even dabbled in his own private journals, writing verse and short stories with an imagination he'd never known. He'd seen the world with new eyes. He'd grown to question all he'd ever learned.

He had become the very subversive he'd been warned to avoid.

Now, when the moment he'd most feared finally arrived, it was too late. Wading through the evening tide of liquor, he was unwilling to play back the properly filed response. So, like some faraway tune recovered, he embraced the truth. It seemed the simplest thing to do.

"My father was a mechanic," he began, breathing deep. "He fixed stuff during the Long March. He was still just a kid, really. He could make anything work again: guns, trucks, whatever they could get their hands on. The old guys loved him. He married during the Japanese occupation, and had two daughters. His first wife and children were killed by Chiang's troops, the counter-revolutionaries, in 1948, just before the end of the war. He came to Beijing and became a top cadre, an Army engineer.

"Several years later, he married again. A teacher, my mother was. He started another family—me." Lee was averting his eyes, gathering himself as he rolled ahead.

"My mother was killed during the Cultural Revolution, in 1966, after we were forced to leave Beijing. My father could barely go on. He was ashamed at what had happened to the country under those cannibals, the Red Guards, the wild-eyed ideologues who thought life was so cheap. He was ashamed that his own people could cause so much suffering, and that Mao, our great leader, our revolutionary hero, had inspired it all.

"But then my father came back again. His friends were rehabilitated under Comrade Deng. The country seemed to have a brighter future. My father had all the benefits of the Party. He could take care of me. His friends were big shots once more. I was sent to university in Beijing to study the enemy, America, to learn everything about you, your business, your pro-paganda techniques. I was trained to speak slang English, to sing Elvis and Beatles songs. They sent us to infiltrate, to learn your ways, to identify your weaknesses."

He paused again, longer this time, and steadied himself, fighting back the flood of emotions that threatened to overwhelm him. Then he summoned all his strength as, desperately, he tried to make them believe.

"When I return, when I go back to China, they will find ways to make me betray you all." ✸

✳

MAY

✳

9

THE RED DRAGONS

"**I** need you," Alexander said, pleading with Branko.

"I am likely to disappoint you."

"See me. Talk to me."

"No harm in listening, I suppose," Branko relented.

"Gimme some markers, at least."

"Don't expect me to fill in all the blanks," Branko said. "Besides, you fly solo quite well."

"Yeah. Too many years of practice."

As he replayed in his head the conversation on that most public of lines, a reporter's cell phone query to the CIA, Alexander understood. He'd developed some sensitive information he was close to publishing. Could the Agency provide some guidance? Branko had implicitly acknowledged he would. The McLean Family Restaurant was a virtual second cafeteria for CIA veterans; its selection confirmed that this would be, in fact, a business meeting. Still, Alexander's hopes were quite modest as he rolled north above the Virginia cliffs on the George Washington Parkway, struck by the beauty of the late day sun reflected in the river below.

As he took the Route 123 exit west, Alexander appreciated the irony of the setting, a relic of the Cold War. When it was first recognized that the White House and Congress rested in the cross hairs of a single nuclear strike, federal planners dispersed the security bureaucracy. The nascent Central Intelligence Agency was banished to Virginia farmland, far beyond Washington's downtown.

Over the years, the suburbs crowded around, ringing the Agency fortress with a civilian moat of pricey housing developments and retail centers. Just down the road, past Potomac School and Langley High, sat remnants of an old shopping mall, with a barbershop sporting an old red-and-white revolving pole. A whimsical pet store specializing in birdhouses and seed sat alongside an unimposing local eatery, which Alexander, the inveterate urbanite, almost overlooked.

The diner smelled to Alexander of another place and time. The red leather seats were sticky. The noisy kitchen churned out burgers and milkshakes, but also moussaka and a touch of feta in the house salads. The waitresses had tiara-like hats on their heads. The line of waiting families extended past the cash register, a pleasant mix of Little Leaguers in uniform and elderly couples out for an early supper, and added to the decibel level. The clamor was so great, Alexander realized, that even one of Telstar's latest directional mikes could not sort a private conversation out of the background clatter. Here, a most public venue afforded considerable privacy to converse.

Branko was waiting at a table in the back when Alexander arrived.

"Greetings, my friend," Alexander said, offering a strong hand and an easy smile. Branko had already lost his tie—a good sign. "Congratulations on number five. Pretty impressive for an old fart."

"Thanks. You still got a couple in you."

"Right," Alexander nodded. "I just need to find a child bride."

"Hey, c'mon. Erika is going on forty-three, and isn't necessarily ready to quit. And I'm already facing the prospect of being in a wheelchair before the youngest gets to college."

"You're a lucky man."

"I tell Erika that every night."

They both ordered cheeseburgers and fries. Branko had a chocolate shake, Alexander a Miller Lite.

"So, how's Rachel doing?" Branko asked after a time. "She sounded rather disoriented when I telephoned her at the hospital."

"Yeah. She's mending OK. The shoulder turned out to be just a hairline fracture. But her head is sure in a different place."

"I'm certain that was quite a life changing experience—near death, and all that. You went through it yourself, I'm sure."

Alexander was sipping the tap water from an old Coca-Cola glass. "It's been much tougher on her. I was in Sarajevo, remember."

"Yes. And after what you went through with Anita the past few years

. . . you know all about loss."

Alexander thought to respond, but Branko's bluntness was disarming. "Anyway, given that this was her office, and her people, it was like having her home violated."

"Is she now back at work?"

"Just part-time, for now," Alexander replied. "She's spending a lot more hours at the house with Jamie. Motherhood still centers her. Helps her see things more clearly."

"Any Barry sightings?"

"Oh, he's trying to do the right thing, I guess. He's been spending a lot of time with Jamie. Taking him to after-school stuff, even going down to Colonial Williamsburg. But it's weird, Branko. When Barry takes Jamie away, Rachel just seems even more anxious, more out of sorts. It's tough. She's lousy at putting her own needs first."

"Most mothers are, I've observed."

"Then he just disappears—for days at a time. Mumbles something about the New York markets, and some trade deal. I figure he's off selling warheads to Osama. Barry's just so . . . distant."

"Been that way ever since Stanford."

"Anyway, it's tough on Rachel. And now she's heading back into the work routine, too soon in my opinion."

"I'm sure there will be some ghosts there, though the Talbott firm just keeps grinding out those billable hours in temporary quarters, right?"

"Yeah, they knocked out a wall, moved a bunch of people up to their penthouse suite, and went back to work. I guess they got to eat."

"Well, I'm certain they have competent security now."

"It's like an airport, Rachel says. A lot of rent-a-cops and metal detectors. Not too good for people in the PR business."

Alexander paused as the beer and milkshake arrived. He drank eagerly from the frosted mug, letting the chill wash over his tongue, waiting to ask what he had wanted to ask for weeks.

"Do you think she was the target, Branko?"

"No."

"How about Talbott?"

"I don't really know."

"What about all the foreigners who were due in that day? And Senator Smithson, even Mickey Dooley? Any evidence who else this guy might have been after?"

"Far as I know, it's still not clear. It's all with the D.C. Police and the FBI anyway. It's domestic. Homeland Security. Not CIA business."

"Hey, after all the screw-ups tracking Bin Laden, I thought you guys didn't hold out on each other any more. Under the new system, aren't the FBI and CIA supposed to share everything?"

"It takes some time to end decades-old rivalries."

"But they must touch base with you, right? I mean, half the TPB clients are overseas. They must have a lot of enemies."

"Alexander, you know I can't go there. I don't even have a solid hunch myself. Sounds like they are close to ID'ing the last of the bodies at the garage entrance. But I couldn't help you even if I did know."

"I recognize that. But that isn't why I called. Still it bugs me they haven't figured out the 'who' or the 'why.' And it's Rachel, too, you know. I worry about her. And Jamie. I feel as if they're really vulnerable."

They were gazing past each other, both a bit embarrassed at where the conversation was taking them. Alexander let the silence linger. This was hard; he so admired Branko, the one guy whose sense of mission had not diminished over time.

Branko, like Alexander, was clumsy with fellowship. Yet, they had retained their mutual respect. Branko found Alexander's insistence on getting the facts right highly admirable. Alexander, the solitary plodder, bereft of family, was a figure familiar to Branko from his own childhood.

It was Branko who spoke first this time, meandering again around the subject at hand. "You know what is so remarkable about aging? It strikes me whenever I'm in contact with any of our Stanford compatriots."

"What's that?"

"How unchanging people actually are as they mature. I saw it once again at my high school reunion a few years back, my thirtieth, in Cleveland. The jocks are still jocks—same with the nerdy guys. The good people from those days—the guys and girls you could see even then had heart, who knew their soul—haven't changed. And the assholes, the worms, just got fatter."

"Seems to me you warned me about that once."

"Did I? But anyway, I digress. You called about the other matter."

"Right." Alexander was thrown off by Branko's ruminations. "China."

"What is it you think you've got?"

"I've been following up on Senator Smithson's ambush of Hollandsworth. You know, when he did that little hit on the Chinese missile exports to Iran."

"That's hardly a new story."

"I know, the Chinese getting promiscuous on exports again. Missiles to Syria, missiles to Iran. It's just that I'm getting a lot more detail this time. I'm trying to explain the pattern to our readers. What's a friend of the United States doing selling such dangerous stuff to our—"

"You mean, a 'strategic competitor' of the United States."

"OK. A friendly strategic competitor whose ass has been kissed by six consecutive American presidents. I mean, what's China trying to accomplish?"

"Make some money. It's probably not any more complicated than that." Branko was munching his cheeseburger. "Rarely is."

"Well, I've got all the usual stuff about how Chinese exports fund their military technology base. And I've got some good quotes about their zero sum approach. You know, how they think that helping America's adversaries lessens our ability to dominate the Third World."

"Anything to fuck with our heads," said Branko, agreeing. "It's the same old foreign policy theory they have followed for centuries. Play the barbarians off against each other and pick up the spoils."

"Sure," said Alexander. "I hear the effectiveness of the U.S. bombing in Iraq and Afghanistan freaked their generals out. Made them rethink their whole approach to warfare."

"No doubt," said Branko. "Probably figured out they wouldn't need to do amphibious landings to capture Taiwan. Just need to push a few buttons."

"I mean, can you imagine what the Chinese military guys felt seeing all that precision-guided ordnance hitting home?" Alexander asked. "Well, anyway, I've been working this angle. Even got a Pentagon guy on record, though the White House folks will probably clip his wings. I'm just not sure I believe that kind of empty ideology really is still at work in Beijing in the twenty-first century. This isn't Mao and the Cultural Revolutionaries we're talking about any more."

"Remember Lee's Lesson Number One: they are not like us," Branko said, smiling as he wiped ketchup from his moustache, again deflecting the subject at hand. "Funny, I went to a lecture a while back by Gaddis, the Cold War historian."

"Great researcher."

"He lectured about his recent book. Spent five years looking through old Soviet documents. Know what was the scariest thing he found?"

"What?"

"How many of the old Communist ideologues actually came to believe their own propaganda. They convinced themselves by repeating the catechism so many times. So don't underestimate Communists' capacity for self-delusion just because the Chinese are doing IPO's for their Internet companies and trying to buy our oil companies."

"Right," said Alexander, nodding. "Where does the aggressiveness at home with missile deployments fit in?"

"Huh?"

"You know, the new stuff I'm hearing about Nanping activity." This was the fishing part. But Branko was slow to bite, so Alexander continued. "My view is that it goes beyond routine. I understand this is the same base they used to rattle Taipei in 1996. Nanping. Fujian Province."

"I seem to remember the incident."

"You were on the ground at the time, weren't you? In Taiwan?"

"Sabbatical," Branko deadpanned. "Field research."

"If I remember correctly, you almost got to witness the outbreak of WW III when the Chinese started to bracket Taiwan with missile test launches. Anyway, I'm trying to figure out China's motives in pushing the missile thing again. Why would they go hot at the Nanping base now in violation of their private pledges to Washington? "

Alexander affected a casual air, but Branko remained silent.

Alexander tried another tack. "A buddy of mine out at RAND has been doing research on Chinese decision-making. He's got this theory—"

"Everybody's got their favorite theory on Chinese decision-making, Alexander. Probably a thousand Ph. D. theses on the topic. Most of them are clueless. We still don't know how it all works."

"Anyway, he's got this theory about factions in their Politburo. Remember during the Cuban Missile Crisis, when Washington figured out there were a bunch of Soviet military hard-liners getting the upper hand on Khruschev?"

"Sure."

"They were a bunch of provocateurs. They kept escalating even while Nikita was trying to back away from the brink of nuclear war. They were shooting at our U-2's, running Soviet ships right up to the U.S. blockade, deliberately making it harder for the civilians in the Politburo to secure an endgame deal with Kennedy."

"If I recall, the Director of Central Intelligence even told President Kennedy at one point that he thought there had been a coup in Moscow."

"Exactly."

"So?"

"What if there was a similar rogue group in the Chinese military now? Some cell trying to force the new leadership's hand? Ramming our spy planes? Arresting priests and dual nationals? Proliferating nuclear hardware to a bunch of trouble spots? Lining the Taiwan Strait with missiles?"

"You're suggesting there's been some kind of coup in Beijing?" said Branko, sounding skeptical.

"No. The technocrats think they're still calling the shots. But they feel compelled to appease the hard-liners more and more often in recent months."

"That's certainly true. The technocrats are trying to act like populists—make sure they take care of those left behind by all the economic growth. But they're not opening up the economy in order to liberalize their politics. In fact, they are rebuilding central control, restricting information access, and rounding up intellectuals, just like the old days."

"Exactly. Well, what if some of the old guard—say a bunch of defense ministry folks—were systematically trying to screw up U.S.-China relations?"

"For what purpose?"

"To keep us from getting along too well? To foment a crisis so they'd have an excuse to impose their agenda? You know, it's the conventional wisdom in Washington these days that the Chinese are such rational actors in these matters. But look how far into the deep end they went in '96 when they bracketed Taiwan with missile tests. Or how nutso they went when the U.S. accidentally hit their embassy in Belgrade. Or the whole Hainan episode, when their field commanders lied to Beijing and then chopped up our plane and sent it home in boxes. I mean, going back to the Cultural Revolution, they've done some pretty bizarre things."

"Hell, we've got our own right-wingers here in Washington—the China haters. Some of them are Booth's buddies. What do they call themselves?"

"The 'Blue Team.'"

"Right. I even got asked to one of their brown bag lunches. Anything to make holy war on what they call the 'panda huggers,' the get-along-with-China-at-any-cost folks at the State Department. The Blue Team guys see foreign policy as another ideological crusade. They are just looking for any excuse to thwart China's modernization."

"My source thinks the guys in their Defense Ministry are pushing hard for the Nanping missile deployments. He says our intelligence community even has a name for this little cell in Beijing, somewhere in one of the People's Liberation Army's intelligence departments . . ."

Alexander paused to sample another french fry, dangling it casually between them.

"Calls them 'The Red Dragons.'"

Branko, green eyes still intent upon him, gave him nothing.

Alexander waited. It was an extended silence, too long to bear much promise of insight. He chewed slowly, holding Branko with his gaze. Then, after considerable deliberation, Branko finally responded with a sigh.

"You're asking about a riddle we've been trying to solve for more than sixty years." He sounded like an academic again. "It's very much in the nature of Leninist systems to have little cells operating secretly—sometimes even at cross purposes. But this business of thinking there are Good Chinese and Bad Chinese is bullshit. They're a great and ancient civilization with thousands more years of experience than we have. They can play good cop-bad cop with the best of them. The fact is, the Chinese like to play chess. Seems almost like they invented the game."

"Chess is *your* game."

"Once upon a time. The Chinese always like to push a pawn. Shove it in your face."

"To what end?"

"To provoke, to test. To sit back and watch, and learn from your reaction. Generations of careful observation have convinced them that Americans are so fucking impatient that they can wait us out on almost anything."

"They're right, of course."

"Sure they are. Combine that with our reverence for the almighty dollar, and they believe we're truly easy pickings."

"So, how far do you think they're going in Fujian?"

"Hard to say."

"Is this definitely new construction?"

"Alexander, I can't be your source on that."

"Is it solid?"

"Is *what* solid?"

"The stuff I'm getting on new construction at Nanping," said Alexander, pressing. "More CSS-6 missiles deployed opposite Taiwan."

"Alexander, I . . ." Branko began to retreat, "This is sort of 'high policy' these days. We've got a White House intent on a hunky-dory summit this summer. A number of photo opportunities with smiling presidents commanding the world stage. Nice bounce in the polls. The stuff you're digging up runs counter to message. Nobody wants to get into a public pissing match with China right now. We're way too distracted fighting terrorism and mopping up in Iraq and Kabul."

"Screw the message. Isn't the intelligence community supposed to just go with the facts?"

"We serve at the pleasure of the president. Hell, the CIA Director doesn't even get face time any more. We pass along what we see to the new DNI czar. And then the White House is free to set policy."

"And spin the facts."

"Yes, and spin the facts," Branko conceded. "Every president does that to a certain degree to make his case."

"And if the facts are that China's shoving missiles in an ally's face? That we are headed for a showdown in the Taiwan Strait? Another U.S. military deployment that the American people are completely unprepared to support?"

"Don't be so certain."

"All our war games, all our Taiwan Strait simulations, show that escalation happens real fast. Standing orders drive it. The military guys will mix it up damn quick. Before the civilians can get a handle on things, we could be in a shooting war with a nuclear power."

"Read Lao-Tzu, Alexander. The Chinese are pretty cautious."

"Yeah. And read Clausewitz. 'War is the natural extension of politics.' The Chinese are damn good at politics, too. They think we're tired, overextended. They're looking for an opening, probing for our vulnerabilities. They're ready to force some hard choices on the U.S. government."

"Yes," said Branko, folding his hands as he sighed again. "You're probably right on that."

Their meal was finished. Alexander remained dissatisfied. Around them, the clamor continued unabated. A kid wearing a Cubs uniform had knocked a strawberry milkshake into the aisle. The mess was oozing between the cracked floor tiles even as a busboy chased it with a rag, foaming pink as he swabbed.

"Damn it, Branko! You're playing the Sphinx today."

"I will take that as a compliment."

"Shit," said Alexander as he flopped back on his seat. "Thanks a lot."

"What exactly do you expect from me?" Branko darkened. "I know where you are going with this rogue cell stuff."

"But you won't help."

"It goes into the deep end."

"It's about facts, about whether—"

"It's about policy. It's about decisions that elected officials will have to make. Not intelligence analysts. And not speculating reporters."

"It should be about informed judgments, about getting the facts out there, so citizens and their elected representatives can have an informed say."

"It's about your story, too. Admit it, Alexander. Your headline. Your ego gratification. You're too close to it."

"It would be nice if you were there with me. I mean, am I off base here? How 'bout a little guidance for an old member of the Club?"

Branko sat back, measuring him. Alexander could see him reading the situation, weighing the options—ever the chess master, playing the board ahead.

"Want to know what I think?" Branko smirked.

"Yeah."

"I think you've carried a torch for Rachel for twenty-five years, and I think—"

"The missiles, Branko! Nanping! Don't change the subject."

"And I think you should rescue her from that schmuck."

Alexander grimaced, then put his hands to his head, defeated. "He *is* a schmuck, isn't he?" he muttered. "Why?"

"Why *what*? Why won't I help you? Or why is Barry a schmuck?"

"Both."

"I won't help you any further because you don't have hard evidence for your assertions. And Barry is a schmuck because he is so fucking evasive, so ready to dodge with that calculating shine. He is married to a bright, energetic woman." Branko stood now, picking up the check. "Yet I suspect that when all is said and done, the dark secret is Barry doesn't really *like* women."

Alexander was still sitting, carefully regarding a friend of three decades, the parade of riddles marching between them. China and the Agency.

Rachel and Barry. Suddenly, it clicked. Elusive Barry, with his private den. Wistful Rachel trying to maintain appearances.

Alexander felt like an idiot. He was supposed to be the sage observer. But when it came to matters of the heart, he was always the last to know.

10

MASTERING THE MATRIX

I t was a zoning quirk that drove the Secret Service crazy. This twelfth floor conference room, with the ultimate high-rise conceit, had windows that looked down on the White House and the South Lawn. The TPB atrium above Fifteenth Street, towering over the Treasury Building, was all glass and steel, undamaged by the recent troubles below. On the rooftops of nearby government building, agents perched anxiously with binoculars, searching the skies, Stinger missiles at the ready.

Power. That's what the penthouse view said to Rachel, providing an uplifting charge on her first full day back. She took comfort in the strength as her heels clicked purposefully down the long marble corridor towards the beckoning conference room doors, the reassuring tapping sound of the secretaries' keyboards flowing from tidy cubicles.

"Good morning, Ms. Paulson." The trademark TPB formality from the staff. "Good morning, Ms. Paulson. So good to have you back."

Her colleagues were gathering to check her out, to weigh her ability to absorb and rebound. Entering the room, she saw tight smiles and thin lips. Ladies in Nancy Reagan red and Bruno Maglis. Guys in white collared shirts and pin stripes, Blackberries strapped like armaments on their shiny leather belts. They all clapped carefully.

Rachel walked to the head of the oval table, which was designed to mimic the one used across the way in the Cabinet Room. She cast a quick glance over the Treasury Building at the limp flag hanging above the East Wing. She *needed* this meeting. She needed to play the role: the field general back in the saddle.

It was time for Rachel to run them through the client matrix, to roll down the monthly review of dozens of initiatives they were pursuing within the federal bureaucracy. The charts were at hand: reams of TPB computer printouts, each page stamped CONFIDENTIAL. Here, their trade secrets were reduced to code. A series of hieroglyphics adorned the documents—asterisks and parentheses containing dozens of symbols, all captured for partners to review. They stood for promises and pledges—commitments made that would be secured down the legislative road. This was her play-book, and it was ready for the returning coach.

Mastering the matrix offered Rachel the illusion of control. As she struggled to begin her transition back into the Washington work world, she required this grounding. She was desperate to get her arms around the challenges that floated about her in a life that suddenly lacked any apparent order.

"I'm dangerous," she'd warned Alexander the night before in a phone call. "I feel like I'm pregnant or something. My skin is incredibly sensitive. I get these intense cravings for a particular food. I feel like running off to conquer Pike's Peak, or going wind surfing in Tahiti."

"Rather inconvenient," Alexander said, laughing as she rambled.

"I have no time for a goddamn mid-life crisis," she groaned.

She had become hopelessly overprotective of Jamie, she knew. She suspected danger lurked around each corner. She was reluctant to let him play at friends' houses. She stood sentinel on the sidewalk, arms crossed, as he rode his scooter up and down the driveway, waving to the ever-present Arlington County police car.

Her mind exercised a will of its own, slithering past the topic at hand. She developed a voracious appetite for fiction, savoring the perorations of Ian McEwan, and losing herself in the moody World War II works of Alan Furst. Her thoughts dallied with the surreal and the religious. Her sleep was heavy and irresolute.

In vain, she tried to ride the waves of emotion as they welled up from deep within. She wished to be done with artifice. She became a threat to all that was pretentious. She felt a new reverence for life, a respect anchored by the very fact of her narrow escape. She felt the rekindled appreciation of sense and sensibility, the eagerness to share any small kindness, the desire for fulfillment. She was alive and renewed. She was a survivor.

On that first morning back, she felt perilously flip, even as dozens of eyes watched her. The standing ovation was nice, but just that—nice. Polite smiles all around.

They might excuse her stumbles for a day or two. Then they would blow right by her—especially some of the more ambitious ladies in the firm, professional jealousy being what it was. Her competitive instincts kicked in. She had no choice. Clients were lining up for Capitol Hill visits. "So very sorry about your partner getting blown up," she imagined them saying. "But where is my tax break?"

Congress was grinding away, marking up bills in committee, moving appropriations to the floor. She had no choice. Business marched on. It was time to dance.

"Let's start with Energy and Water," she began, breathing deeply. "Always the first appropriations subcommittee to report out a bill. Let's see . . . Phil. The City of Tacoma has been in to see Congressman Myers. The chairman is on board to support the riverbed improvements, a $7.5 million earmark. The chart says your Senate-side strategy is in place with Mr. Kerr. Need any help?"

She looked up from her papers sprightly, smiling like a schoolmarm managing her brood, struggling mightily not to betray her difficulty in staying on the lesson plan. *If they're listening so intently*, she worked to convince herself, *I must have something important to say.*

"Nope. May need to get some extra local juice with Bingham once we get to conference. I've got some VIP calls lined up, in case. But we look solid so far."

"OK, then, to the University of Missouri. Liz, we look good for the earmark for their agricultural research building. Nice to have Senator Guerin chairing the subcommittee. Looks like a slam dunk. Will we get the full three million?"

"Can't say for sure yet, but we're pressing to get the whole amount when the subcommittee votes. Depends on the allocation they get from the full committee pot, but I think we're good for the three mil."

"Sounds great. OK, next up is Telstar. Tom, would you like to walk us through our strategy for the R&D grant."

Tom Bacigalupi, her deputy on this, her biggest account, updated their colleagues smoothly. They were on target for ten million dollars in funding for Telstar's photovoltaic system for ships at sea—a barnacle they were trying to attach to the Department of Energy's appropriations bill. She pressed to ensure that the vaunted TPB template was being followed. "Fallbacks? Media strategy? Client visit with stakeholders? Plans to circle back with champions and Congressional leadership? Follow-up letters from local VIPs?"

All seemed in order. With Rachel's firm hand back at the helm, the good ship TPB was under sail once again. They'd disposed of the bodies, swabbed the decks, and sailed on with the wind. The carnage seemed hardly to slow them. The dead man who had perpetrated the April Fool's Day crime had still not been identified. Yet, Jonathan Talbott had brought construction teams on site in revolving shifts, night and day, to make their physical plant whole again. Weeks after Porter's funeral, TPB had gained more new business than they had lost.

Rachel was reassured by the morning's exercise. She could still ride point in a storm. She could still get the job done. The more her colleagues spoke, however, the more she felt staggered under the weight of the mundane. *What if I hadn't been late coming over from the Willard that morning? You would all be here marching onward without me, talking business and making lunch reservations.*

She moved on to the education bill, but her mind was drifting. She was thinking of other people and places. She was thinking of Jamie's quizzical stare that first evening at the hospital. She was thinking of Iceman Barry, checking the home alarm system, briefing the cops. She was thinking of the ocean, yearning once more for the cleansing foam to wash over her. She was fighting an overwhelming desire to flee, to strip off her heels and stockings, to toss her scarf and run free—to be done with it all.

"Rachel? May I see you a moment?" It was Talbott, in a gray suit at the doorway. *How long had he been watching?*

"Certainly. Karen, will you take over?" She slid her charts to a colleague on her right and stood, relieved to have been rescued from her dangerous daydreams.

The walk down the hall to Mr. Talbott's temporary office on the other side of the suite was awkward. After some time, her boss spoke.

"It's the FBI again, Rachel." Talbott, ever the proper Brahmin, pronounced the word "again" with a formal long "A." "They requested the opportunity to see just the two of us first."

Then, as they approached the Fourteenth Street corner of the floor, there was Mr. Hickman, he of the sad eyes and neighborly smile, standing with an assistant. Hickman reached to greet her, a firm shake offered with a bracing left hand and a steadying gaze. She fancied him, and was embarrassed to find herself checking for a wedding ring.

"I have some good news," Hickman began after they were seated. "As you know, we've shared your frustration trying to solve this one."

"We know you have been making every effort," Talbott said. "But it has been several weeks now. And the perpetrators are still at large."

"Yes. And we know your personal loss has been compounded by the disruptions and the need for added security."

"It has been a terrible loss. And a terrible uncertainty."

"Sir, as you know, there were no claims of responsibility. It's been a lot harder given the number of possible suspects. I mean, there have been a number of sensitive areas we have had to get into, the need to coordinate with FBI, CIA, Homeland Security."

"Sensitive areas?" Talbott asked.

"Just all the different folks—foreign interests and all—that you do business with. So many people coming and going from your offices that day, too."

"Mr. Hickman, is this not a murder investigation? This isn't CIA work. I don't understand."

"Certainly, sir. And that is how we've treated it. It's just that we had a lot of ways to go trying to establish motive. We've had to analyze a certain amount of circumstantial evidence on who the real targets were. The Canadian Ambassador. Senator Smithson. Mr. Dooley."

What does this have to do with Mickey? Rachel was confused as she listened to them parry like attorneys. *Where was this going?*

"And your conclusions?" Talbott cut short the speculation with his own question.

"We think we've got it resolved."

"Resolved?"

"We think we know who it was that day with the bomb."

"Indeed. Who?"

"We have no positive ID. The bomb was apparently in the perpetrator's lap. Didn't leave much intact to work with, I mean, on DNA." The FBI man pivoted as he got to the point. "Mr. Talbott, what more can you tell us about the New World Land Company?"

"The Hong Kong investment consortium?"

"Yeah. The real estate outfit."

"That was one of Mr. Porter's ventures with the Hightower Fund."

"And how much do you know about his partners in this venture?"

"Actually, very little. You see, Mr. Hickman, as we have explained to you several times, I run the government relations shop. Mr. Porter managed our international investments. But how does this relate to the bombing?"

"Mr. Talbott, Ms. Paulson." Rachel started a bit at the mention. She had begun to think the two of them had forgotten she was there. "It seems that Mr. Porter may have left his Asian partner holding the bag on some bad debt. We are still sorting this out. But it appears that this partner, Joseph Cheung, saw a couple of his real estate ventures crater last month, triggering default clauses in the loan agreements. Then he disappeared. We've traced his movements to Washington on April 1. He was seen leaving the Mayflower Hotel early that morning, and we think he headed over here in a cab. We believe the bomb was on his lap in the cab in front of the garage when it detonated."

"Joseph Cheung?" Talbott maintained perfect decorum, his bearing erect as ever. "You believe Mr. Cheung was responsible for all this?"

"Yes," Hickman responded confidently, "that's where we're heading."

"Cheung, a murderer?"

"Well, it may prove to be a crime of revenge."

"Revenge?"

"Payback. We've had our sources trying to get more details out of Hong Kong this week. But frankly, the cooperation of the Hong Kong authorities comes only in fits and starts. Helpful one week, stonewalling the next. So the work has been quite challenging."

"I see."

"Mr. Hickman?" Rachel said. "May I ask a question?"

"Yes." His soft eyes held her again.

"Are you sure you understand *who* they were trying to kill? The bomb went off right outside our main offices, where Mr. Talbott and I were due to be meeting. I mean, on your recommendation, I've had police around my house twenty-four hours a day ever since."

"That's right, ma'am. We appreciate your cooperation. And I certainly understand your concern." His steady gaze calmed her. "But there's evidence that Mr. Cheung had issues only with Mr. Porter. Mr. Cheung had suffered a series of business reversals in the Hong Kong real estate market. He apparently blamed Mr. Porter and his Hightower Fund for exacerbating a run on his capital. Cheung went to Tokyo before he came to Washington. He was erratic, drinking heavily, and ranting during his meetings with his Japanese bankers. Your Mr. Porter allegedly defrauded him, then pulled the rug out from under him with their partners in Tokyo. So we think we are pretty solid on motive."

"I see."

"It's also clear that the bomb itself was targeted at personnel—there wasn't a whole lot of structural damage beyond the entrance and the offices facing the street. It was *people* he was after."

"So Alan was killed over money?" Talbott said. "What a horrid thought."

"Yes, sir."

"And . . . do you think we are safe now?" Rachel asked.

"Yes. Mr. Cheung was after just Porter, and was heading for his office. We plan to notify local jurisdictions over the course of the morning and withdraw the police protection. Sorry for the intrusion."

Mr. Hickman stayed for a while, and the three shared a coffee, Rachel drinking deeply, craving the caffeine jolt. Talbott and Hickman reviewed how they would handle the release of information regarding the investigation's wrap-up. Soon, the rest of Rachel's first morning back was gone, lost to internal PR planning and to calculating discussions about who should be told what.

They were doing what the TPB team did best. They were shaping the news, sculpting content, spinning the murder of one of their own. Their PR team would blithely explain away the violence on their own doorstep.

So this was where it all led, she thought. *This is how it would have ended for me—with a carefully massaged press release regretting my demise.*

When finally they broke just before the noon hour, Rachel found herself spent. No longer able to face her day, she felt compromised by the compulsion to flee.

She gave in. She rode the elevator down to her BMW and drove out the F Street garage, its entry covered with fresh whitewash. She turned left on Fifteenth Street, driving past the rows of Vietnamese-American tee-shirt vendors, all the way to Constitution Avenue. She drove down the Mall, past the White House and the Ellipse, rolling through the flashing yellow light at Twenty-Third, then pulling up the westbound ramp onto the Roosevelt Bridge. She hit the northbound merge onto the George Washington Parkway in a transfixed state, and drove right past her Spout Run exit.

Opening the sunroof, she saw now, for the first time, what a glorious spectacle this May day had become. Full green-leafed oaks lined a brilliant blue ribbon of water, several crews sculling in the river's center. Every neck was strained, oars cocked, awaiting a signal from a small boat alongside. As she cruised past, the stillness was abruptly broken by a signal that sent the athletic bodies churning down river in a frenzy, all arms working together.

Rachel drove on in silence. She was an electronic runaway, her Blackberry turned off and stuffed in the glove compartment. She felt wild as she opened all the windows, breathing deeply again, letting the wind whip her hair and flatten her silk blouse against her chest.

She took the McLean exit and retreated south down Kirby Road through neighborhood streets toward home. She found the driveway once again empty; the police had apparently gotten the FBI call to withdraw.

She felt relieved as she returned, the home blessedly quiet at mid-day. Barry had already been and gone over the weekend. He and Jamie had taken in the latest Harry Potter movie on Sunday before Barry headed up to New York City for the week. But the debris Jamie and Rachel had left during their frantic morning getaway remained—a Corn Flakes box on the counter, a hair brush and a milky napkin by the sink.

She found reassurance in the hum of the dishwasher. At least she'd remembered to set the timer to run their bowls and cups. She began to walk the house, her methodical patrol, double-checking the locks and dead-bolting the front door.

She was alone with her thoughts as she walked up the stairway, kicking off her shoes at the landing. In the master bedroom, she ran a bubble bath, pausing to watch the foam steadily rise. She leaned against the sink with a sigh as she took the last clips from her hair and peeled off her stockings. She finished undressing, tossed her clothes on the bed, then returned to regard herself dispassionately in the bathroom mirror. After a few moments, she shut off the water and reached for a towel, before remembering it was Monday—her big laundry day—which meant no towels.

She slipped naked down the stairs toward the dryer in the laundry room. As she passed the door to Barry's den, she stopped at his music center and impulsively reached for a Stanley Turrentine CD, some fluid saxophone to fit her flighty mood. Then she adjusted the speaker controls to throw the sound into the master bedroom suite.

She sat against the arm chair, fiddling with the dials, and then she turned and gazed about the room, feeling the chill of leather against her bare bottom. The room was all Barry, all controls and smooth surfaces. The neat-as-a-pin desk. The locked filing cabinets. The abstract graphic print hiding the wall safe. The coolness masking the infinite inaccessibility.

That was it, she realized—his infinite inaccessibility. That's what hurt her the most. All those years of trying to rediscover his heart, to comfort him in his secret retreats, to revive his ardor. All those dollars wasted on frilly underwear she'd ordered from the Victoria Secret catalogues in a fruitless search for a renewed spark.

Despite her anger, she felt mischievous. In her noon-time escape, she searched for an old tune, a recalled scent, a mood upon which to float away as she sat right there on Barry's chair. She savored the sensation for a long minute, then stood, tall and shameless, to leave. She stretched her calves, leaning jogger-like against the arm of the couch. For a moment, she felt fairly Amazonian. Men just might be dispensable.

A flicker of motion alerted her eyes. Her pupils locked on the back of a man's head, then a nose in profile outside the window glass, just turning round the shrub. A face, peering past her, expressionless.

"Aaah." It was a grunt she huffed out, lacking the volume of a scream. She darted behind the lounger, then, like a crab, scurried on hands and knees toward the stairs, her bad shoulder throbbing anew as she cursed.

She swung to her feet in the hallway, elbows to chest now, racing up the stairs as she shouted. Her arms were shaking, the image of the impassive face against the glass superimposed with all the villains she had ever feared.

She spun around at the landing just in time to see, at the louvered window in the front doorway, the silhouette of yet another figure, slightly crouched, with a gun in hand. This time she screamed, an impressive guttural scream of rage and violation. She leaped up the last few steps and raced into the bedroom, grabbing her cell phone from the dresser. Her heart was drumming as she ran into the bathroom and slammed the door.

For a second, she considered making a run back to Barry's den with the key to the pistol he insisted on keeping locked in his desk drawer. But the den was too far to risk now. *So much for all the gun safety crap*, she thought, in a fury now.

"Goddamn FBI," she muttered as she punched 911, leaning against the pathetic button lock on the bathroom door. "Got your man. Right!"

"Hello, this is Emergency Operations. What is—"

"I'm at 3631 Chesterbrook. There are two men trying to break in!"

"Calm down, ma'am."

"I *am* calm! They have guns!"

"That's 3631? What is the cross street?"

"Thirty-sixth Road. Three-six-three-one! There are men at both doors with guns!"

"Two armed men. I understand. We will get Arlington Police units on the way as we speak."

"Hurry! Please! We *had* the police here! Where the hell are they now?"

"I'm going to stay on the phone with you. Now just stay calm. Where are you in the house?"

"I'm in the damn bathroom!" Then she stopped speaking. Over the casual settling of the bath bubbles, she could hear the creaking sounds of feet steadily climbing the staircase.

"Ma'am? Is this the Lavin-Paulson home at 3631 Chesterbrook. My records show that—"

"They're *inside!*" she whispered frantically. "They're coming up the stairs."

Rachel would never be a docile victim. She set the phone on the counter and searched for a weapon, any weapon. She grabbed the hair dryer with one hand, a heavy silver brush—an antique with a formidable handle—with the other.

She stepped into the bath, leaning on the damp tiles as she crouched expectantly. Over the crackle of the 911 operator's voice coming from her cell on the counter, she could hear a distant siren. She switched off the noisy phone. Her mind was surging, searching for an escape. Her knees were moist, sweat mixing with steam.

"Touch that door and I'll blow your fucking head off!" she shouted into the silence. She could hear the floorboards squeak, then someone's footsteps scuffling away from the other side of the door. "I've got a gun in here and I know how to use it!"

The cell phone rang, startling her before she snatched it. She cradled the hair dryer under one arm, her eyes still intent on the locked door.

"Mrs. Paulson, do you hear me?" The 911 operator was shouting in her ear. "We have units in your—"

"They're in my damn bedroom!"

"Hello? You in there, Ms. Paulson?" The voice from outside was deep, and quite close. "Open up."

She stopped her breathing a moment and, ignoring the telephone, considered her options.

"Is the intruder in sight?" said the voice beyond the door.

She spit out a response: "Who are you?"

"Arlington County Police. Are you being held?"

There was another voice at the bedroom doorway now—softer and younger. There were sirens approaching fast down the street. "Got you covered, Mike. We're clear downstairs."

"Ms. Paulson. Can you open the door? Please put down your gun and show us your hands!"

Her eyes were darting about as she thought. It took another few seconds for a clear picture to emerge from her confusion, for her to comprehend.

She sank to the edge of the tub and sat, slowly setting down her chosen weapons as she began to shake. She gathered herself and spoke into the phone: "Operator, what are the names of the officers in my house?" She could make out the squawk of walkie-talkies in the foyer and her bedroom.

"Ms. Paulson! Put down your weapon." The voice behind the door was all business now. "Come out with your hands up. Please!"

"Greer and Paschetti," the operator said.

Rachel closed her eyes very tight. She could hear more shouts outside on the lawn.

"The officers are in the house with the pass key your husband gave Arlington Police." The operator was insistent now. "They were coming back over to drop off the key when they saw some suspicious activity and heard screams inside—"

"Officers?" Rachel called through the door. "What are your names?"

"Officer Paschetti and Officer Greer. Arlington Police. Now please put down your weapon and we'll secure the residence."

How much dignity could she muster? She waited as long as she could. "Guys, uh, I don't know how to say this . . ."

"Come out with your hands clear!" The voice had grown stern. "You sure you're alone?"

"Yeah," she said, trying to compose herself at the door, "and, uh, two things."

"Yes?"

"Well, first, I lied. I don't have a gun in here."

"Just come out. We've got the door covered."

"And, uh, second, the, uh, the towels are all in the laundry. So, if you'd grab me a robe from the closet, please, I'm afraid I'm buck naked." Then—what else to do?—she opened the door and strode purposefully out, palms pointed skyward.

The uniformed officers were locked in identical Police Academy firing stances, deployed about her bedroom with their guns drawn. Officer Greer, the one she suspected she had seen at the den window, stepped forward tentatively. There was a terrycloth robe in his left hand.

It was several hours later, after a couple of Coors Lights and a long Monopoly game with Jamie, before her nerves began to settle. She followed the boy around, sitting at his elbow until he finished his science homework, and shampooing his hair when he bathed.

"You sure you're OK, Mom?" the boy asked. He scrunched up his nose, his head cocked, as he searched for some clue, still suspicious after her bland reassurance.

She struggled mightily to suppress the scenes of the day—the cops, the humiliating scene in the bedroom. She labored to expunge it all, to bury it in the file of Embarrassing Moments Never to be Relived.

She was still addled later in the evening, after Jamie was asleep. She finally settled into bed after ten and began to read the morning's *Post*. *Pathetic*, she thought as she lay in an oversize tee-shirt. *Big Washington expert and I haven't even read the local section news*. It was happening more often these days. She'd begun once more to live in fear of being found out, ignorant of some crucial development, exposed for her failure to stay on top of the game. Maybe she *was* a fraud.

The ring of the bedside phone startled her. She checked Caller ID, then snatched the receiver at the second ring.

"It's Alexander."

"Hi. I know. I've been screening calls."

"I tried you a bunch of times earlier. I was a little worried."

"I wasn't picking up. Sorry, I just checked out for a bit. I'm afraid I made rather a fool of myself today."

"The office that bad?"

"Wasn't really the office, though that was tough, too. I had a little mix-up with my security detail. Long story."

"I figured when your secretary said you'd left for the day at noon ..."

"I just . . . couldn't manage the whole scene today. Heavy Monday, that's all."

"Are you OK?"

"Yeah, I guess. I'm finding it hard to get in rhythm. I just need to climb back on my horse."

"Is that Turrentine you're listening to?" Alexander asked, impressed.

"Yeah."

"So, what exactly were you running from today?"

"Running? I don't know. From work, marriage, all of it. I feel like road kill. I just can't balance it all sometimes. I mean, sometimes I feel like I'll never be good enough at anything."

"Whoa."

"And how about you? How was *your* day?"

"Rachel, I'm worried about you."

"Tell me. Surely it couldn't have been worse."

"OK, well, it went great, actually," Alexander conceded. "A little peculiar, in a way. I kind of need to fill you in on something I've been working on—it's about TPB. It may complicate your—"

"Are you writing about the bombing?"

"No. It's a China story."

"Because that's over, Alexander. They figured it out. The FBI's got their guy."

"They've arrested somebody?" Alexander pressed. "Really? There's nothing on the news yet."

"No. No," she stumbled, "he's dead. The guy who did it supposedly blew himself up."

"Who was he?"

"Alexander, you know, you can't use this. I don't even know if it's been released yet. I mean, I just walked out of the office at noon, and I've been kind of out of it ever since."

"Rachel! It's *me*. Alexander! I'm not going to file some story on this tonight. I just have a passing curiosity about somebody who damn near killed me and one of my best friends!"

"*Best friends?*"

"You are. I mean, at least." He paused. "What should I say?"

"It's OK. Best friends is OK, I guess."

"What's going on with you?"

"And what is going on with you, Mr. Reporter, and what is this China stuff you're writing about that's going to cause me such grief? Did I say something indiscreet that morning at the Willard?"

"Rachel! No, you didn't say anything indiscreet. And, yes, my story is something that will affect you. It's a piece that gets into stuff about your firm—Mickey Dooley even. But damn it, wait a minute. What's the deal with the FBI investigation? I have a right to know, don't you think?"

She waited, wanting her head to clear, wishing she was back on the parkway with the wind washing over her. Her elbows were on her knees, one hand pressed at her temple. The tee-shirt was becoming too warm, bunching at the hips.

She sighed, exhaling long and slow. "Alexander, it was just some guy, apparently. Some guy who was pissed off at Porter. It was just some business deal gone bad. He lost his millions and then just lost it. Went crazy. I guess he wanted to take Alan Porter with him."

"Apparently? You sure they're not getting pressure to close the case?"

"No. Talbott's confident they know what they're doing. The bomb was kind of amateurish, Hickman says. Crazy stuff. 'No big sin. No big virtue.'"

"Oh." Alexander waited to make sure she was done. "That's Steinbeck, by the way."

"I know."

"*Grapes of Wrath*: 'Ain't no sin. Ain't no virtue. There's just stuff people do.'"

"Just stuff some people do."

They fell silent for several moments. She realized once more how she hungered for that trust, that shared space. Even across the telephone wire, it felt as if Alexander was there in the bed with her. There was none of Barry's irritating busy-ness, his intolerance for spontaneity, his obsession with control.

In that long silence, her mind meandered from murder to motherhood, from work to home, and back to the whole weird scene beginning with her moment in the den. As she ruminated, her path ahead was suddenly clear. She decided; she would live this way no longer.

"So," she began anew, kicking the covers off her toes, "what exactly is it you've done to me?"

"I haven't done anything to you," Alexander replied. "Just doing my job."

"Out with it, Bonner. What exactly have you written? Must I treat you, too, as the enemy now?"

"Rachel, c'mon. Of course not."

"Is this the long-awaited lobbying piece? Some nasty story on all our alleged conflicts of interest? Thanks, 'best friend.'"

"No. No, this is a China piece. A piece about their trading practices. Import-export stuff. Dual use items."

"Satellites?"

"Satellites. Missiles. Computers. Your basic modern shopping list."

"You hitting my favorite client, Telstar?"

"Rachel, Telstar's *always* at the center of this kind of story."

"Just what I needed. Welcome back, girl."

"Yeah, sorry," he said. "Welcome back."

11

WHISTLING IN THE CRYPT

"**M**r. President! Mr. President!" The raspy voice of Georgia's senior senator, Harold G. Parker, startled Booth. "Staff members out of the well!"

"You're busted again," said a grinning Senator Kip Cavanaugh, needling Booth as the aide slunk away from the legislators, who were crowded before the presiding officers' desk like anxious travelers at an airline counter.

The small Senate chamber, at mid-morning roll call, was stuffy already. The TV lights felt unusually warm, as if they were drawing oxygen out of the room. Knots of tardy senators were still popping through the east doors from the banks of elevators just outside, fragments of jocular conversation carried with them from the world beyond.

"I see you've roused our good Senator Parker again," Smithson said. "Looks as if we're in for a long day."

"How," asked Booth, "am I supposed to count votes without working the well?" He was smoldering, perched now on the small armless staff chair at Smithson's elbow. "I'm just trying to do my job."

"Down, boy. Parker will be on our ass all day." Booth could sense the flinty eyes of the proud Atlanta scold, burning into his back from the row of desks behind him. "Don't take everything so damn personal."

The chairman sat beside his aide at the old mahogany desk of the majority leader, reserved for the floor manager of the measure of the day: the State Department funding bill. On a small table before them, mounds of paper were growing. Booth was responsible for juggling it all; the draft amendments, the special provisos for senators' pet projects, and the mischievous proposals designed to gut a provision with a simple verb change, the raw power of language being what it was in the legislative chamber. This was Booth's burden. He could play the role of a minor god, deciding fates, but it was a daunting task. A minor misstep could become a major screw up under the media's watchful eyes. A few words here or there might mean little at first glance, but mean everything in Peoria or Pakistan.

Smithson's teasing was interrupted as Senator Widener, the Colorado maverick, lumbered up the carpeted steps leading from the Senate well. "Mis-ter Chairman, what exactly are your intentions in having us vote at dawn?"

"Wasn't my request for a roll call," said Smithson. "Looks like Oliver's checking attendance. Making sure enough of his troops are here to table my China amendment."

"We got the votes on this China thing?"

"Maybe. You with us?"

"Well, Jake, it's kinda hard to say. I'd planned to be . . ."

"But?"

"It's just that . . . I'm getting some heavy static from back home. Industry's all riled up. Do we really have to raise this whole issue of export controls again?"

"Come on, Sam. You know we've got to do something. Big business pressures are making us too damn permissive with export licenses. Even the anti-terrorist crowd in the administration lets dangerous stuff out. Satellite launch equipment. Super high-performance computers. Sophisticated machine tools. Laser guided munitions. We can't be letting every rogue nation on the planet buy cutting-edge hardware. My amendment will help ensure we don't."

"But you know the European industry folks will sell it if we don't."

"Hey, I've got the biggest high tech constituency down here. We've got to learn to say 'no' sometimes."

"Mr. Booth," said Widener, "your boss here has a goddamn death wish." The Coloradan shook his head in bewildered admiration as he strolled away.

"How'd we score him?" Smithson demanded, pulling out an elongated tally sheet. His dog-eared vote count looked like a cash register tape, covered in +'s and -'s.

"He was an L-plus: 'leaning for.' "

"*Leaning against* sounds more accurate. I've got to be conservative on these vote counts. Guards against inevitable disappointment in my fellow man."

"What's with this *planned to be* crap?" Booth asked. "That like arguing over the definition of what *is* is?"

"Hey! A blow job is a blow job," Smithson snickered, trying to rattle his sober aide. He pursued the point as they waited for the interminable conclusion of the day's first vote. "You know what our last president said to me once? Their guys in the House had been ragging him all week in the press about 'word games.' So he says to me with that Arkansas twang, 'You know, Jake, language is like snow. It's only pure and virginal in the countryside. Come to the big city, and it gets obscured with smoke and foot traffic.' Turns out he stole the line from some Commie poet."

"Yevtuschenko," Booth offered quietly, then pressed the business at hand. "You still think we can get to fifty-one votes on export curbs?"

"Oliver's move for a bed-check roll call is a good sign. Probably thinks he needs every single body here to have a chance at winning."

"Aren't we close to being over the top?" Booth asked. "I mean, we had forty-six senators by my last count."

"Yeah. But the undecideds . . ."

"I know."

"The undecideds are going to break with the White House and industry. They always do. Even Cavanaugh's getting slippery with the double team he's getting from United Technology and the insurance folks. Your pals like Rachel Paulson over at TPB are going into overdrive on this one."

"*My* pals?" said Booth, squirming. "Aren't they on your host committee for tonight's fundraiser?"

"Sure. Old man Talbott will have half the firm there. But it's his gal Rachel who's killing us on this one. I understand from one of the senators in the cloakroom she came back on the job just for this vote. By the way, she really OK now?"

"I guess. Amy and I saw her at the hospital. She still sounds a little spaced out, though I know she's out there working the lobby."

"Such an energetic, talented lady. A lovely lady." Senator Smithson sighed wistfully. "I can't believe some bastards were trying to harm such a gorgeous creature."

"Hey, you still sure they weren't after you, Senator?"

"Hell, Martin," Smithson bristled, "I've been all over that with the authorities."

"Right. And by the way, I think you'll be able to congratulate Ms. Paulson on her labors against us when you see her at this evening's event," Booth said, "but don't take it *personal*."

"Of course not! Nothing here is personal, right? Even with a sweetheart like the"—Smithson caught himself. Senator Landle was standing before them, smoothing the sleeves of a finely tailored suit, the unctious bearing of a British butler confident in his own cleverness.

"Mr. Chairman, may I steal a moment for a word with you? Something's just come up in an Intelligence Committee briefing I want to make sure you're aware of."

"Certainly, Tom."

Landle gazed dismissively at Booth, waiting for the staff man to leave. But Smithson grasped Booth's arm. "Martin's security clearances are in order, of course."

Landle paused, clearly uncomfortable, before launching ahead. "Jake, I am concerned by the anti-China tone the upcoming debate is likely to take. You know, I and others are deeply sympathetic to many of your motives."

"Of course you are."

"But your timing here is really atrocious. We're trying to mop up in Iraq. Afghanistan still needs work. We need Chinese cooperation on the North Korea nuclear talks. We need 'em at the UN on Iran—hell, we need 'em on a bunch of issues. You're going to undermine the moderates in Beijing who want to work with us."

"Tom, with all due respect, the White House *always* complains Congress' timing is bad. Same old tune I been hearing since I came here. Folks up there still think we ought to have a king and keep Congress out of

these war and peace matters—and these guys say they're strict construc-
tionists!"

"But Mr. Chairman, the upcoming summit makes the timing critical.
The Chinese are at a crossroads. The moderates in Beijing have taken a
lot of heat for joining the World Trade Organization and opening up
the economy—even making such a big deal out of hosting the Olympics.
China is changing as quickly as any society ever has. They've doubled their
GDP in just ten years!"

"Yeah, by dumping goods on the U.S. market, Tom. A bunch of their
guys may have gone to Wharton, but they're still a Communist dictator-
ship that wants to—"

"Jake! I'm surprised at you. You know as well as I do that our intel
shows there's a factional rift running right through the Chinese government. If you punish the moderates right before the summit, if you cut off
their access to U.S. technology, the hard-liners will have every reason to
turn up the anti-American volume."

"And how the hell would we notice the difference?"

"They're holding hundreds of billions in U.S. bonds right now. Imagine the dislocation in our markets if they sat out the next few Treasury
auctions."

"Exactly my point, Tom. We let Beijing get away with stuff because
Uncle Sam is borrowing billions of dollars a week from the Chinese. You
don't want to pick a fight with the banker who's holding your mortgage.
So now the White House is going squishy soft on some basic security standards for exports. Well, it's long past time for the Senate to take a stand."

"You're going to take a hit back home, Jake. I don't have to remind
you of that. You'd be closing markets for your own guys in California.
You're going to regret it."

"C'mon, Tom. The Chinese are shoving more and more ballistic
missiles in Taiwan's face every year." Smithson barreled ahead, the commotion all about them masking their rising voices. "They're locking up
Chinese-Americans on trumped up spying charges. Torturing priests.
Arresting foreign journalists. Censoring the Internet. Having PLA soldiers
gun down unarmed fishermen and environmentalists. This is your defini-

tion of moderation?"

"It could get a whole lot worse if you—"

"They've had something like a twenty percent annual increase in their defense spending over the last five years—so they can buy every new-fangled weapon the French and Germans and Russians sell them. And they're selling everything the Iranians and the Syrians can buy."

"We need to see the big picture," Landle said.

"Tom, I *am* seeing the big picture. The big picture is what my little amendment is about. Someday, if we don't draw a line now, we're going to stumble into a goddamn war with China—a shooting war. Hell, they're working joint maneuvers with Russia on a routine basis now. If it comes to war, I just don't want Telstar's precision-guided munitions raining back on us."

"Jake, I'm warning you, you're going too far with this thing. You know, there are some really troublesome things coming over the transom about Taiwan. Signs of escalation there, too."

"Meaning what?"

"Meaning a change in Taiwan's strategic posture. New missile imports of their own. Some in the U.S. intelligence community even think the Taiwan folks may be flirting with nuclear ideas again. So it's a lousy time for you to press the China issue, just to gain some political advantage."

"Nuclear?"

"You really ought to get off the administration's back for once. Stop playing politics. Let the pros work the problem. You polarize things with a floor vote, and a whole lot of stuff may fall on your head. That's all I'm saying." Landle was off into another chattering group across the aisle.

"What the hell was that all about?" Booth asked when Landle was out of earshot.

"The China business?" Smithson responded. "Or the Taiwan stuff?"

"Both," Booth replied. "That's a pretty heavy load he's carrying."

"It's horseshit, Martin. Same old executive branch horseshit. They think they can intimidate me. Landle talks pretty. But he's just a messenger for the bully boys down at the White House. Well, Jake don't quail before bullies."

Just then, they were startled by an outburst of laughter. Senator Jennings was regaling a clutch of legislators in the well with one of his vulgar jokes. An upright Catholic, the Pennsylvanian saved his raunchiest lines for the Senate chamber. While the civics classes observed reverently from the gallery above, sophomoric Jennings would whisper about hooters and a tight snatch, squealing with the same clique of buddies.

"Want me to go check the NID?" Booth said, thinking the daily National Intelligence Digest might shed light on Landle's game. "Maybe we should hold off a couple of days."

"No, Landle's probably just messing with our heads. Longer this amendment sits out there, the more erosion there will be of our base. Let's roll the dice."

"You know, Cavanaugh was with us on the China human rights resolution last fall. We might still hold him."

"That was then, this is now," Smithson said. "Human rights resolutions are freebies. Export licenses mean real business, real jobs, real campaign donations."

"Industry has cranked up the pressure," Booth agreed. "I saw Talbott in the Senators' Dining Room at breakfast with Senator Knowlton and Senator Mueller."

"Well, it was that big Telstar satellite launch contract that triggered our amendment. I'm sure Talbott and Miss Rachel are pulling out all the stops to beat us."

"Senator, are you sure you're comfortable with this?"

Smithson pulled his head back slowly, regarding his aide with a skeptical eye. All about them, a dozen senators' conversations ran together in a burbling stream of noise.

"Comfortable?" he said, laughing. "Comfortable! You know, Martin, let me tell you something. When I went up in Apollo that first time, I sat there for hours through a launch delay. Too much cloud cover. Could have messed up recovery if we'd aborted. I'm the rookie sitting on top of the candle with two vets. Top of a gantry with a gazillion gallons of explosive fuel under my ass and I gotta take a leak so bad I don't want to wait for launch to fill my bag. My commander turns to me and asks, 'You comfortable with this?'"

"Senator, I just mean—"

"Martin, I know what you meant." They both smiled as Smithson paused. "I'm just trying to manage a State Department funding bill here. My little amendment is probably about as popular as a skunk at a garden party. I'm thinking of running for president from a state full of high tech execs who'll be pissed off about this one for months."

"Try years."

"But you know what? I'm doing the right thing for our country. That's the only goddamn reason worth coming here, except the ego trip. So if somebody doesn't see that it's a good thing, well, screw 'em."

"Senator, I didn't—"

"So, yeah, Martin. I'm very comfortable. Thanks for asking."

Booth truly loved the man. It was at moments like these that he best understood why. Yet, Booth wondered increasingly of late about his own staying power. His wife Amy joked that, had he not ended up in the Senate with Smithson, he might have drifted into the priesthood, where he could have clung to his illusory visions of righteous man.

Booth was content with the sense of public purpose that attended his every decision. He relished the sense that he labored at the heart of things, that his life's work was significant. He could stand for God and country, oppose Communism and nuclear proliferation. The choices were clear, the stakes meaningful. His father, he knew, would have been proud.

As his day unfolded, Booth worked a thirty-yard perimeter around his staff chair next to the Majority Leader's desk, keenly attuned to the odd rhythms of the yellow-walled chamber. He would drift out into the two party cloakrooms, where senators were using the phones or watching film of an Arizona factory hostage situation on Fox, occasionally crossing the hall to the Vice President's office, where the administration staff sat at a long table poring over legislative language. Then he would work his way back toward the well to buttonhole senators and warn them their speaking slot was approaching.

He faced a series of distractions, primarily senators checking in with scheduling inquiries. His hip kept vibrating, persistent efforts to reach him on his Blackberry. One number he recognized as Alexander's cell phone. Another was Charleen, his administrative assistant, summoning him yet again.

A Senate page brought him some backup files Charleen had sent over, accompanied by pink phone message slips from Smithson's secretary. Some guy named "Kwan" had called three times, insisting it was urgent. Booth tucked the slips back in his Action File with a dozen other unreturned messages.

Just after four o'clock, Alexander surprised him in the Vice President's Lobby, gesturing over the shoulder of a committee aide who'd been conferring with Booth.

"I need five minutes," said Alexander, who held up his fingers as he mouthed the request. "Alone."

Booth asked a staff colleague heading back into the Senate chamber to cover for him while Smithson disposed of some minor amendment on the floor. Then he and Alexander walked together, away from the noise.

Booth led them down two flights of stairs to the crypt under the rotunda. The small room was a favorite retreat of his; it afforded a cool refuge to share a private moment. It was here that the Union troops had baked their bread when quartered in the building during the early days of the Civil War, even as construction of the great dome proceeded.

"You need to see this," Alexander said, handing him a three-page computer printout. "It could help your vote."

"On export licenses?"

"Yeah. My story will run tomorrow. And I thought you might want to hold your roll call until after it's in the paper. Might be able to pick up some votes."

"Why, Alexander," said Booth, cocking his head mischievously, "are you playing politics?"

"No. I just thought—"

"He doth protest too much." Booth straight-armed him as he chuckled. "Mister Bonner gets down and dirty. Welcome to the fray."

Alexander shrugged as Booth began to read aloud from his draft of the next morning's story in the *Los Angeles Times*. The punch of the piece was clear from the lead:

> *Military officials of the People's Republic of China have expanded efforts to circumvent U.S. export controls and to purchase sensitive weapons technology, according to diplomatic sources. These purchases of dual-use technology have aided Chinese efforts both to deploy medium range ballistic missiles against neighboring democratic Taiwan and to aid the missile development programs of U.S. adversaries, so-called rogue nations like North Korea and Iran. Coming on the heels of increased anti-American rhetoric from Beijing officials, these new developments threaten the U.S.-PRC summit slated for this summer in Seattle.*

"I like the detail here," Booth commented before he read aloud again:

> *A second scheme involves the veiled purchase from Telstar Corporation of specially designed computer systems used for real-time battle management, which have reportedly been sold to the People's Liberation Army in contravention of U.S. export controls.*

"How'd you track down this stuff?"

"I've got my sources. Actually, I was thinking of trying to insert a Smithson quote there."

"Yeah. I could get in a plug for our vote on export controls."

"Like I said . . . "

Booth let out a low, steady whistle, the sound rolling about in the darkened crypt. "Is this Telstar stuff solid?"

"Of course it's solid. CIA is all burned up because the State Department's sitting on it. And the Congressional Relations people at State have been kept in the dark, so they won't have to lie to you. A lot of stuff I got from people sick of the promiscuous Chinese exports to Iran."

"Let me just guess—Israelis?"

"Don't go there."

"Hell, I thought that FBI sting on the Israel lobbyists put a damper on them. Better watch yourself. You may be on tape."

Booth pondered for a few moments. His Blackberry was zapping his hip again. He looked down to read the latest: Charleen with their 911 signal. "I've got to get back, Alexander. I think we can win our China amendment vote with this story."

They turned to climb the small spiral staircase, its steps polished smooth from two centuries of use, then transited the tiled hallway outside the Majority Leader's second floor suite. Before they separated, Booth had a final question.

"Hey, one more thing. Have you picked up anything on a revived Taiwan nuclear program? You know, some last-ditch deterrent against the Mainland?"

"*Nuclear* stuff?"

"Yeah, nuclear stuff. Sensitive imports of dual-use stuff."

"To *Taiwan*?" Alexander was incredulous.

"Yep."

"Holy shit. Where're you picking this up?"

"Just got a whiff of it."

"Jesus. If Taiwan is even considering getting nukes, the PRC will go nuts."

"Right you are. Anyway, let me know if you hear anything. And . . . thanks. I've got to go have the vote put over until your story comes out tomorrow."

They parted, Booth striding past two armed Capitol Police officers and entering the Senate chamber through the swinging doors on the south end.

The first thing he heard was the presiding officer's gavel, as Senator Pierpoint intoned, "Without objection, it is so ordered."

"What's up?" Booth grabbed Senator Cavanaugh, who was darting out of the cloakroom.

"Nice job with the time agreement," Cavanaugh complimented him.

"What?"

"Jake just got a unanimous consent agreement to finish the bill before five-thirty tonight."

"You're kidding! What about the amendment?"

"Next vote is on your China amendment—then we're out of here."

So much for tactical delay. It was showtime.

12

THE THOUSAND DOLLAR MARTINI

Smithson's amendment was crushed just before the cocktail hour, an ignominious 59-41 defeat.

"We were toast from day one," Smithson muttered as they filed out of the chamber. The Chairman's acknowledgment was no salve for Booth's irritation. Years in the game had done little to take the edge off his disappointment, his propensity to care too much.

"I can't believe they got every one of the undecideds," Booth groaned.

"How about my 'solid' forty-six? Evaporated like a spring snow on a sunny day. Guess our pals at TPB earned their retainer."

"Now—this just kills me—we get to drink with them," said Booth.

Because of an oddity in the Washington calendar, springtime in the nation's capital meant more than just the cherry blossoms and busloads of schoolchildren on tour. The July 1 deadline for filing cash-on-hand reports with the Federal Election Commission drove incumbents into a frenzy, working to report maximum dollars in the bank to scare off potential opponents. April 1st through June 30th, Tuesday breakfast through Thursday night receptions, was prime fundraising season.

Smithson's event of the evening would be modest by Washington, D.C. standards. Drinks, not dinner. On Capitol Hill, not downtown. Stand-up cocktails and finger food in a restaurant, not a black tie sit down dinner at tables in a ballroom, and $1,000 a head for martinis, not $4,000 per couple for rubber chicken.

Booth ambled ahead of Smithson, walking out the west front of the Capitol, restoring himself with some fresh air after a day spent in the musty Senate chamber. To his surprise, the weather had become thoroughly pleasant.

He gazed down the mall in the early evening sunshine. The commuters' tail-lights followed the lines of L'Enfant's vision, heading west over the filled-in swamp to the Potomac. The curved gold bowl atop the Natural History Museum glowed across at the red brick of the Smithsonian castle, Grecian temple acknowledging medieval fortress. He closed his eyes a moment, taking comfort in a sense of permanence as he tended his psychological wounds.

At forty-eight, Booth retained an ideological purity that was almost quaint. He could tolerate Smithson's serial dalliances with the opposite sex because the senator fought the good political fight. Smithson sailed into the wind with conviction, if not reckless abandon. But the senator's ability to balance cause-politics with hard-nosed realism did not come naturally to the righteous aide. Booth questioned once again his ability to stomach the endless compromises ahead.

They are wrong and we are right, Booth thought as he waited for the boss. *It's that simple.*

"Buck up, buddy-boy," Smithson chirped as he approached with confident strides. "Let's go make nice."

"You're really up for this?" Booth asked as they fell in step, bouncing down the long marble staircase heading west into the sunlight.

"Sure thing."

"I can't wait to hear Talbott's introduction."

"Hey! Tomorrow, he'll be helping us get funding for an AIDS prevention program, or something else."

"Meanwhile, the gang at Telstar will be raking it in from the Chinese," Booth said. "What was it Lenin said about the capitalists: 'They are stupid enough to sell us the rope with which we will hang them'?"

"Now, don't go bad-mouthing free enterprise."

"You know, fundraisers are the one thing I'll never miss when I'm gone from this town."

"A necessary evil."

"But you know what the real sin is? It's not that our most powerful elected officials become supplicants," Booth said, suddenly aware he was coming on a bit strong. "It's the *time*, Senator."

"Huh?"

"The time. When you get closer to the presidential primaries, you'll be putting in twenty hours a week on the phone just asking strangers for dough."

"At least."

"Do the American people know this? Do they know many of our leaders spend half their days closeted in some campaign office begging rich guys for contributions? It has always struck me as an almost criminal waste of talent."

"Hey, it's the mother's milk, Martin. The grease that lubricates the wheels of our fine government machinery here. Like Churchill said, democracy is the worst form of government on the planet . . . except all the others."

As they quickened their pace, Smithson was clearly enjoying himself, welcoming the brisk stroll. All those NASA years in cramped space capsule mock-ups had made him eager to hoof it—the heck with Town Cars, and security, and being on time.

Passing unnoticed among foreign tourists, they traversed the site of the next presidential inaugural stand, and Booth wondered at the contraposition. *Where will I be that day?* Despite all his misgivings about what lay ahead, he could still daydream.

They paused before jogging with the light across the six lanes of Constitution Avenue, just where it began to climb up to the Senate-side office buildings. "It'll be interesting to see how today's victory rallies our good Ms. Paulson," Smithson said.

"Yeah. First time back in circulation."

"I meant to tell you, a colleague I saw in the cloakroom—a guy who is on the Judiciary Committee—told me the FBI's about to break that case. Some Asian connection. Justice Department is starting to brief Talbott and his people about it," Smithson continued. "Weren't you at Stanford with her and that Telstar guy? What's-his-name? Dooley?"

"Mickey Dooley, yes. We were all in a club together."

"Somehow I can't picture you as a frat boy."

"Actually, it was more like a cross between a debate club and a drinking society. We lived together. Sort of an Animal House for China scholars. We'd argue all week; we were the TA's for many of the seminars. Then we'd blow off steam together on the weekends. Half of us were out to do good, the others—like Dooley—to make a buck."

"So don't be giving me such a hard time about the company I keep. And, you know, old Jonathan Talbott is a great guy. He's done a lot more good than harm in this world. He's pro-environment, pro-choice. We agree on more than we disagree about."

"Sure. He's a friend whose buddies are going to nail us at the—"

"Listen, Martin. If anybody in Silicon Valley is there for me in New Hampshire, it'll probably be because Jonathan convinces them to bury the hatchet. Jonathan fights fair. My amendment passes and his client loses a lot of business. They've got every right to try to trounce us. All's fair in love and politics."

"Senator, did you ever think maybe you're too forgiving sometimes?"

Smithson chuckled. "Nobody promised me a cakewalk when I got into this gig."

"I admire your ability to tolerate the situational ethics of others."

"*My* dad was a bricklayer, not a preacher. And maybe you're right. Maybe I mellowed out a bit staring back at the earth from one of those rockets."

They were crossing now under the aged cherry trees flanking the Capitol's northern grounds, great sturdy trunks with gnarled branches, thick with green leaves tinted by the setting sun. At the crosswalk, they joined the flow heading to Charlie Palmer's Restaurant, and "The Spring Tribute to Senator Smithson."

Charlie Palmer's was the steakhouse alternative to the Monocle or La Brasserie, the other Senate-side restaurants of choice for hosts in the lobbying business. The building was too modern and flashy. But the location was irresistible, and the owners made up for the ambience deficit by producing surprisingly good meals.

At the fundraiser, the young ladies running Smithson's finance team put on a great show, several notches above the usual cocktail hour fare. There were strolling accordion players. Waiters in gaily-striped shirts. Cleverly strung Japanese lanterns. Pseudo can-can girls in frilly skirts

worked the door, checking in guests and accepting their campaign donations. The overall effect was a sort of retro Renoir picnic: not exactly
politically correct, but it *was* springtime.

The fun part, Booth decided, was to watch them fawn over his boss.
There were limousine liberals from Georgetown—wealthy white males
with their black chauffeurs waiting outside. There were grungy environmentalists using the check of some movie star board member to purchase
their admission ticket. There were defense contractors—some of the very
same lobbyists who had opposed them that day. They rarely agreed with
Smithson, but they did too much business in his state to risk staying away.
There were "five-thousand-dollars-a-month men," the harried small-town
lobbyists who labored each year to secure modest earmarks for places like
Eureka and Oceanside.

Smithson worked the crowd, soaking in the flood of adoration. He
seemed to revel in it, like a sweaty trail dog rolling in mud at the end of
a long day. The senator was a tactile man. As he spoke, he employed an
almost Mediterranean manner of using his hands to gesture and to touch.
He seized admirers, slapping backs, posing for pictures, kissing every
woman between eighteen and eighty, drinking wine with one hand free.
Smithson needed the attention and was restored by it.

Jonathan Talbott had been among the first to greet the senator. Smithson asked after his health. Talbott congratulated him for completing the
State Department bill. Neither mentioned the China amendment. The last
Booth heard of the conversation, Talbott was recommending a play at the
new Signature Theatre facility.

Rachel Paulson came next. She was stunning, tan and tall in a low-cut
cocktail dress. Booth had expected to find her wan and wobbly. He had
called twice, and Amy had tried to get her to bring Barry and Jamie for a
family dinner. But he was chagrined to realize he had not seen her since
a hospital visit the day after the explosion. Now she looked five years
younger. It was remarkable: she had no sling or bandages, and possessed
the freshness of a high school kid. While Booth propped himself at the bar
to sip a ginger ale, Smithson chatted her up at some length. An attentive
Talbott stood by.

Alexander Bonner was there, too. Booth knew he'd see him at the little reunion dinner Rachel had plotted for Mr. K's later that evening. Alexander rarely put in an appearance at fundraisers. Yet, there he was talking with Talbott, and across him, with Rachel. It was such an animated group that Booth wanted to move close enough to listen.

Draining his soda and turning to set it back on the bar, Booth saw Mickey Dooley, of all people, taking Rachel's arm. Mickey Dooley, bald on top and trimmed short on the side, but with the same big country grin. It was quite a tableau: Alexander Bonner, avoiding Mickey, who was clinging to Rachel, who was firmly escorted by Jonathan Talbott, who was sucking up to Senator Smithson, who was gamely trying to peer down Rachel's dress.

Booth watched it all, then turned to order something stronger. As he waited on his glass of wine, he felt a beefy hand grip and spin his shoulder. It was Mickey.

"How the hell are you, buddy?" Mickey said, startling him with a hug. "I've been looking forward to seeing you!"

Mickey was all over him, joking, name-dropping, ordering a scotch, and whipping out pictures of his Chinese-American boys in their baseball uniforms. Before Booth could say much of anything, Mickey was barreling ahead, utterly ignoring the business of the day, getting personal. He began pouring out his troubles, confiding in him, imploring him to help.

"I've got to come to you on something," Mickey warned. "I'm in a real mess back home. I may need the senator to go to bat for me."

Booth, flabbergasted, was just promising Mickey they could speak privately later in the week when his secretary, Charleen, appeared at his elbow, clearly agitated. The din around them had grown and Booth had to struggle to make out her words.

"This guy Kwan has called five times on his way from Vienna," she said to Booth after smiling apologetically at Dooley. She handed the Senate aide another wad of pink phone messages.

"He'll probably be at Dulles by now. Says it's a critical matter. Something about nuclear proliferation. He's expecting your call. Tonight." She nodded for emphasis.

Vienna? Booth stared at the call slip on top of the stack she'd thrust at him. *Vienna, Virginia? Home of that FBI traitor who'd gone KGB?*

Vienna?

Then it suddenly dawned on him as he recalled Landle's oblique reference. *Vienna. As in Vienna, Austria. Headquarters of the International Atomic Energy Agency, the UN inspection group that had won the Nobel Peace Prize.*

Maybe Landle did have something solid, Booth was appalled to concede. *Maybe something was rotten in Taiwan.*

13

THE BACK ROOM AT MR. K'S

"To neutral territory!" Mickey raised his Scotch at the table in the restaurant's elegant bar, drawing sustenance from his smooth yellow juice.

"Neutral?" Alexander asked.

"Look around. It's like the demilitarized zone," Mickey continued. "It's the only place where the Taiwans and the PRC guys will tolerate eating side by side. They park their ideology at the door. Wouldn't happen in Asia."

"Testament to the food, no doubt," Alexander said as he glanced about warily.

Mickey was right. An uneasy truce was maintained by tacit consent at Mr. K's. Most of the best Chinese places in the suburbs were not so fortunate, being firmly associated either with the Mainlanders and their Washington cohorts, or Taiwan. Seven Seas in Rockville, one of Alexander's favorites, was frequented by the Taiwan independence crowd. The Yenching Palace on Connecticut Avenue was practically a lunchroom for Beijing's embassy staff. But at Mr. K's, diplomatic personnel, investors, and security men from both camps sat coolly in the pink and gold banquettes.

Alexander was looking forward to the company and a good meal. He'd found the fundraiser awkward, something forced and farcical in the mix of players. He had run by the small *Times'* office in the National Press Building to check his story on the way. He expected the others to be waiting when he made Mr. K's. In fact, only Mickey had arrived and was there at the bar, drinking alone.

"So, how the hell are you?" said Mickey, greeting him with a disarming wave.

"I'm good," Alexander said. "I guess. Busy."

"You look young," Mickey said.

"I still got my hair."

"Ouch. Getting me where I live."

"No. I mean, you look . . . " Alexander searched for the right words. "Wiser. Less hair, but more wisdom. Like the Buddha."

"Bonner, you never were a good liar. I'm just spreading out. Belly, forehead—it's all expanding. I'm growing old, far away from home."

A waiter in a sharply creased tux appeared. Alexander ordered a lite beer to join Mickey.

"So," Alexander asked, "why don't you come back home?"

"Home. Sounds so nice. Back in the land of baseball, Springsteen, and the IRS. Did you know, I still gotta pay taxes in both Beijing and New Mexico?"

"Seriously. I mean, what are you, forty-nine?"

"Yep, 'bout to go over the falls."

"When are you going to make a home you can grow old in? Bring your wife and boys over?"

"Ain't that easy," Mickey said.

"Of course it is," Alexander insisted. "You've accomplished all you need to, or want to, in China, haven't you? I mean, are you going to retire there? Just move. Telstar's got plenty of work stateside, I'm sure. They owe you."

"You know, Alexander. I'm afraid I'm about tapped out. Used up all my tricks. I'm like an old racehorse, ripe for a breakdown. But they'll have to shoot me to get me off the track."

"Jesus, Mickey."

"I ain't gonna win the big prize. Ain't gonna be chairman of the board. Ain't ever even gonna break par."

"You know, my minister says life's transitions are like little deaths."

"Deaths?"

"Resignations. You need to find a way to let go of some of your old dreams. So you won't be president. So you won't be a Wall Street mogul. Make new dreams. Besides, most rich people I know are miserable."

"Yeah, but I'd rather be rich and unhappy than poor and unhappy."

"You just need to focus on what brings you joy, on how you might give something back to the world."

Mickey regarded him oddly. "The weird thing is, despite all my travels, the one thing I do well these days is parent. At the office, I couldn't give a damn. Besides, things are getting kind of weird in Beijing."

"Really? We need to talk some business on that."

"Some crazy shit going down behind the scenes."

"Like what?"

"Still fighting over succession, I mean."

"Most analysts say that's all over—that the new team is firmly in charge," Alexander said.

"There's still lots of maneuvering going on. And there's more and more saber rattling. They're playing these elaborate mind games with Taiwan. It's weird. I always thought the next generation over there would be more pragmatic. Only Fox News even mentions the fact they're still Commies. Most Americans figure the Chinese these days just lust after new cars and houses in the 'burbs."

"We thought they'd become like us. Convergence."

"Well, the joke's on us. They've talked themselves into all this ideological crap. The younger guys in government show very little restraint. So, anyway, my dreams of doing noble deeds in China seem a little empty these days."

"Hell, Mickey, you've been very successful."

"It just seems irrelevant, sometimes. Mercenary. I just wanna come home."

"Wouldn't your boys love that?"

"Sure. Unlimited Internet access and video games. They think the US of A is one big amusement park."

"The grandparents still in Albuquerque?" Alexander asked. "Still calling every Sunday to make sure you're behaving?"

"Right." Mickey swirled his ice. "But their Chinese grandpa in Beijing is still jerking me around every day."

"No law says he can't come visit them after you move to the States."

"Like I said, ain't that easy."

"Hey, you've done Beijing for nearly thirty years. Doesn't Mei Mei understand you have your roots, too?"

"Alexander, she won't even come visit the U.S. any more."

"Even for Christmas vacation or something?"

"She *hates* Christmas. She hates America. Says we're vulgar and smelly and materialistic." Mickey sighed, throwing up his hands. "Or maybe that's just me she's talking about."

Alexander flashed back to a rainy Saturday afternoon of watching college football and drinking beers together in front of the TV, Mickey providing a running commentary on the anatomy of the female cheerleaders. Alexander missed his irreverence, the attitude he had that life was a party and they should all just try not to get caught.

"Problem is," Mickey continued, "she listened to all that crap the Party taught her in school."

"Like what?"

"You know, about the violent Americans, armed to the teeth in their gas guzzling SUV's, murdering each other in race riots."

"Race riots?"

"Well, their textbooks are a bit dated."

"Whoa."

"It's gotten so bad she tries to forbid the boys from speaking English around the house. We're talking about American citizens here!" Mickey was getting worked up. "All that jealousy comes home to roost. I mean, you can take a Chinese peasant to Paris discos and she'll lust after Chanel. But eventually, the girl falls back onto the stereotypes Mama fed her. Being modern doesn't mean they get out from under the weight of their cultural heritage. Truth is, we all revert to form."

Alexander was taken aback. He had other things to discuss with Mickey, but here was an unexpected stream of profundity. He returned to his earlier point. "So, Mickey, can't you just propose a trade? Get the boys and her here part-time. Or, if things are so bad, bring them without her."

"Do you have any idea how screwed up the immigration stuff is?"

"They're not—"

"The newspapers in Beijing are full of horror stories about how Americans abuse Chinese women—you know, those mail order brides. Guys treat 'em like chattel." Mickey was sipping his drink again. "Lady comes to the U.S., gets married, has kids. Then her husband decides he doesn't have the hots for her any more, so he divorces her. *She* gets deported because Pops won't sponsor her residency application. She never sees her kids again. So, let's just say Beijing isn't real sympathetic to American fathers who want their kids to grow up in the States."

"Things are that bad, huh?"

"No exits." Mickey looked even more disheveled. "I'm trapped like a fucking hostage. She'll string me up by the nuts if I try something to—"

"Save your nuts, old man!" The voice startled them both as they spun around.

There stood Barry Lavin, so tan his white teeth almost hurt the eyes. He was impeccable in a banker's wide-striped suit, sky blue shirt with a starched white collar. His hair was very short, almost a buzz cut, tiny lines of white barely discernible at the temples. He looked like a male fashion model from a Bachrach's catalogue.

"As I live and breathe," Mickey said, offering a big right hand that Barry took with a smile. Alexander offered his own hand, disquieted by yet another twist in his peculiar day.

It unsettled him, this awkward intersection of the personal and the professional. He still felt uncomfortable crossing lines, about the clumsy mixture of head and heart. Tipping Booth off on his China missile exclusive. Schmoozing with Smithson. Nailing Dooley's company—and Rachel's client—with the story he had just filed. Now came Barry, the absentee husband, whose wife was the object of Alexander's . . . well, he wasn't quite sure what to call it, though he had grown determined now, after so many years of wondering, to find out.

Alexander was spared. Sweeping through the door just behind them came the rest of their dinner group—Rachel shimmering in blue, Booth on one arm, and a serious looking Branko on her heels. She passed Alexander with a sly smile, a scent of elegant perfume lingering in her wake.

The seating for the Club's reunion had been Rachel's doing, an advance conspiracy with Mr. K's pliant maitre d'. Alexander's interest grew as he watched her, Mickey and Booth flanking her, Alexander and Branko on the wings, and a clearly self-conscious Barry opposite at the round table.

Rachel exuded a graceful élan, laughing gaily as she shared an inside joke. She was clever, parrying with her old pals. She provoked them playfully. She appeared entirely comfortable at a gathering that was otherwise stag, a pro who refused to relinquish any of her femininity. She was unrelenting. She had climbed the mountain, been knocked flat, then arisen and marched ahead again. To Alexander, who admired a fellow survivor, she seemed irrepressible. The more he watched her, the more his curiosity mounted, and the more he struggled to contain his long suppressed desire.

There were plenty of distractions. Alexander could cover his tracks as the jousting one-liners flew and double entendres were batted mercilessly about. Mickey seemed to find some comfort in old friends and whiskey. Occasional flashes of wit aside, he seemed to have grown morose, a caricature of his old self. Branko was reserved, but his observations grew more pithy as the evening wore on, offering biting commentary on the state of Beijing and Beltway politics. Booth played his willing foil. Yet, the more they spoke of China, the more rancorous and adversarial they seemed to become.

Then there was Barry, the duck out of water. He was not really part of their group any longer, eclipsed by Rachel, excluded in the most peculiar way even as he seemed to create his own distance. His obsession with business trends was of little interest to the others this night. He had achieved his career ambitions, yet somehow been marginalized in the process. Barry struggled to work his way into a conversation he and Mickey had seemed to dominate for so many years. Barry was like a spectator in his former life, diminished and out of place.

Appropriately, it was Rachel, the hostess du jour, who was the master of ceremonies now. She was leading the conversation, full of ideas and passions, talking about books she had read, plays she had seen. Her hand was guiding the interplay. Alexander saw it clearly—to his amazement, it had become *her* Club. After the dessert dishes were cleared away, it was Rachel who banged her glass, calling mischievously for a final round of Truth or Dare.

"The first question," she declared, "goes to . . . Alexander."

He peered cautiously across at Mickey, seeking safe ground. Alexander searched for something boringly substantive, and threw out a question about what the factional rifts in the PRC government portended for the fate of American investments.

Next, Mickey went after Branko, about his five kids and apparently robust sex life. Something about Irish twins and birth control that brought a warm smile from the gang.

Branko threw a zinger at Booth. It was a loaded question about the next war in Asia. "Cyber attacks," Booth predicted matter-of-factly. "China will bring her neighbors to their knees by mastering electronic warfare. Targeting data bases. Screwing with air traffic control. Crippling banking systems, locks, and dams. They'd all better surrender now in Taipei lest they forfeit their billions in Mainland investments." Sobering—with a message. But that was Booth. He was still too serious, smarting from his fiasco on the Senate floor earlier that day.

They worked their way around to Rachel, the hostess going last. She was gazing, too long, across the table at Barry, who seemed to have shrunk, his over-starched collar wilting at party's end. Alexander saw clearly that they no longer knew Barry, excluded now by his own choice. *When had the superstar begun to fade?* Suddenly, Alexander was anxious for him. *What the hell was she going to ask in front of all the guys?*

Rachel paused, so long and so confidently that her power seemed to mirror Barry's discomfort. There were too many witnesses to this most intimate of moments. Then she smiled tenderly, as a mother would to comfort a troubled child, before she said: "Barry, dear, don't you find it ironic that China first brought us all together, but it's this China business, and all it has wrought, that will end up splitting us apart?"

It was four days later—the Chinese Embassy's diplomatic pouch carrying the intelligence sections' audiotapes was running slow—before Lee replayed the entire conversation from Mr. K.'s.

Sitting in the privacy of his Beijing study, Lee listened with care to the disturbing chatter. Middle age was eroding his old friends' sense of purpose. They were going soft.

Mickey Dooley had grown sloppy, as Lee himself had observed of late in Beijing. Lee found Barry to be pathetic, the high-flying business-man now the weakest of the lot. With the exception of the ever-doctri-naire Branko, they had become defeatist. Most troubling to Lee, they all sounded resigned to the idea that things would only get worse. Booth's line about cyber-attacks, Lee found chilling, and yet another echo of Chen's warning. *Where were they getting this stuff?*

To a troubled Lee, eavesdropping from Beijing, it seemed that the strength of his old American friends was sapped, their convictions eroded. *Maybe the guys in the Defense Ministry are right,* he sighed as he weighed the inescapable conclusion. *When the PLA makes its move across the Taiwan Strait, maybe the Americans will just sit and watch.*

14

PASSING THE BUCK

Martin Booth had a theory about duty. He believed it offered the promise of fulfillment—the satisfaction of knowing a commitment had been met. It was a burdensome rationalization.

"Every man is guilty for the good he does not do," Voltaire had written. Booth's father had borne the notion like a stigmata, this idea that debts to society were the first that must be paid. It was an ethic handed down through the generations of Booths, from minister to minister. It was burned deep into Martin's soul, this sense of community obligation that led him to a life of service.

It took years of unanticipated happiness to erode the overarching priority he attached to his work. The more joy he found in marriage and family, the less compelled he felt to make all the world's troubles his own, to take every struggle so personally. As he matured, he began to let go. It was as if he was on an airplane about to descend from its cruising altitude—those moments just before the seat belt sign comes on for the last time. He could sense a distinct slowing of the persistent motion, an ever so gentle glide back to a welcoming terra firma.

For Booth, duty remained a certain compass, impossible to ignore. On this night, after the heady dinner with what had been such an odd mixture of old compatriots at Mr. K's, duty was undeniable. So he trudged Willy Loman-like to this last chore, his rendezvous with the irksome caller Kwan.

"It is imperative that I see you!" The voicemail was insistent as he replayed it on the brief drive over to Georgetown. The man was practically hyperventilating, running on in his heavily accented English. The anxiety, the apparent lack of professionalism, bothered Booth.

"I have landed in New York from Vienna, to arrive in Washington early this evening," Kwan had exclaimed. There was some airport announcement crackling in the background. "I have critical information about nuclear weapons developments in Asia and must see you. I will meet you at the Latham Hotel on M Street, at the bar. Ten o'clock tonight, please."

Booth had ridden an emotional roller coaster all day—from the unnerving business with Landle about Taiwan, to Alexander's story and the disastrous China vote, topped off by the weird encounters with Mickey and Barry at Mr. K's. He wished he was home in Amy's arms, with the covers over his head. He felt spent, pulled in different directions, all too conscious of the troubles of others around him. But public purpose propelled him forward over the M Street bridge to the tony hotel above Citronelle, another of his favorite eateries. They had another "live one," as Smithson liked to call such tipsters, some spook appearing out of the blue with insights into the world of clandestine nuclear developments.

It was a peculiar role Booth had come to play—a magnet for weapons proliferation tips—and the senator was unswervingly supportive. As the leading Washington critic of lax technology export controls, Chairman Smithson had developed something of a cult following among the international think tanks. There was a steady stream of visitors to the senator and his aide from obscure research institutes. Swedes. Pakistanis. Israelis. Brits. An eclectic cast of characters they were, too. "Retired" diplomats. Arms peddlers. Awkward professors.

They were spies, all of them. Plants, sent out by various foreign intelligence agencies to troll for fresh morsels, furnished with their own tidbits to offer up in trade. *Did you know Pakistan is drilling at the Baluchistan test site again? Have you heard the Iranians are importing unemployed Soviet bomb designers? How about those latest Chinese missile deliveries to Teheran?* The guests invariably asked leading questions, sprinkling their conversations with nuggets gleaned from their own digging. Teasers from their control officers. Bait for Booth.

The game was high stakes intelligence poker. Even the sober Booth got a big charge out of the play. He was good at it, usually knowing just when to call a bluff and when to bail. He relished the tips. He enjoyed the riddles waiting to be unraveled, the motives not yet ascribed, the challenge of sorting wheat from chaff and discerning who was reliable and who was just another con artist.

Most of his take he would bounce off his own intelligence sources. CIA. Pentagon. NSA and NGA. He liked to road test his haul before proposing that Smithson go public with his conclusions. Then they would make a sensation; Senator Smithson's latest warnings about weapons proliferation often made page one, leading the national news, above the fold.

The cycle was self-renewing. Publicity begat more tips, which in turn yielded still more coverage. New streams of information were brought forward from foreign adversaries, eager to link up with nuclear control advocates in the American capital. Through it all, Smithson had shone bright. The national press portrayed him as the sage uncle, much beloved for his righteous alarums, and he was always good copy. Booth, the staffer in the shadows, felt validated, gaining the satisfaction of moderating the dramas, his sense of public purpose fulfilled by the Good Works.

The challenge was before him once more as he strode into the bar at the Latham and a slim Asian gentleman with silver framed glasses motioned toward him from a table in the corner. The game was on.

"Thank you for coming, Mr. Booth." It was Kwan, anxious yet dignified as he offered a limp handshake. He beckoned Booth to sit on the chair opposite him. "It is most urgent that we speak."

Booth was squinting, his legs weighty. A headache, a real pounder, was cranking up. Kwan, playing host on Booth's turf, signaled to their waiter. On the table were remnants of a meal, the soda he was sipping, and the day's *Washington Times*.

"I used to work in this city, you might know. A detailee to the Nuclear Regulatory Commission," Kwan began. "Export Safeguards Division."

Booth put in an order for yet another cup of coffee, and nodded.

"In Bethesda. Before I joined the International Atomic Energy Agency overseas." Kwan paused, grinning nervously again. "So, you checked me out?"

"Yes, I did," Booth replied, waiting to understand the urgency.

Kwan gathered himself. "I come to you and your senator to avert a great disaster. There is a cover-up going on. I assure you, I have no need of this trouble. The job in Vienna is a—how do you say?—a plum assignment. Over one hundred thousand dollars per year, American. Tax free. Lots of travel. People line up for years to be international inspectors."

Kwan was Korean, it seemed, not American-born, judging by the over-hanging accent. *Maybe British trained. Perhaps Hong Kong.*

"I work in the most interesting section. I am an inspector for—I should say I *was* inspector for—the East Asia mission. I covered Tokai-Mura, the big Japanese plutonium recovery facility. The Indian reactors, the ones subject to international inspection. South Korea. China . . ."

He paused here for dramatic effect, milking the moment as he leaned in. "And Taiwan."

Kwan began to accelerate again, his accent growing more distinct. "I wasn't on every mission to the region, mind you. But I have access to all files. I've seen them all, Mr. Booth."

Kwan reached quickly below the table, producing a locked briefcase, which he placed on his knees. Booth shifted a bit opposite him, badly needing to take a leak, but not wanting to miss the next part of Kwan's show-and-tell.

The engineer spun the numbers and snapped open the lock. He glanced about them; they were unnoticed at their table—only a few late diners passing in the stairwell across the room. Their corner of the bar felt quite safe.

"Now, some of our IAEA inspections are better than others. We go into a place like Korea or Taiwan. We look only at facilities subject to IAEA safeguards. We check inventories of fresh uranium fuel going into the power reactors. We count spent fuel rods coming out. We verify that none of the used rods are diverted to extract plutonium to make a nuclear weapon.

"We are quite thorough, really. We also check to see that no fuel has been diverted between the reactors and the ponds where the used nuclear fuel is stored. We check seals on everything. Of course, we can't be look-ing for some 'undeclared facility' that isn't on our list. If a host country has a secret plant they haven't declared to IAEA where they are up to mischief, the Agency has no authority to inspect. But we can report our suspicions."

Kwan drew closer. At the bar, two waiters were watching the early news on Channel 5.

"Most are very routine. We are like accountants. But sometime, you pick up information. Get a peek behind the curtain, you can say." He was opening a clean manila envelope. It disgorged an impressive collection of technical papers. IAEA charts stamped "classified." Photographs with circles and arrows marked in black pen.

Kwan's tone grew triumphant. "Now, I will tell you about Taiwan."

The case he laid out was straightforward and, to Booth's horror, all too plausible. The Republic of China on Taiwan, Kwan asserted, was taking steps to develop a clandestine nuclear weapons capability. The Taiwanese were systematically siphoning small increments of plutonium from their civil power program, diverting spent fuel rods from their peaceful electrical generating program, then expertly sneaking dummy rods back into their spent fuel ponds.

Their books were square with the IAEA. But their secret plutonium source on the side gave them the critical ingredient to develop crude warheads. Presumably, a nuclear capability was envisioned as the last line of defense against their overbearing Communist Party cousins on the Mainland—a Doomsday deterrent, for revelation only during some future crisis with Beijing.

"What about the monitoring cameras?" Booth asked. He had been following the Iran situation closely and knew well the significance of cameras to the monitoring regime.

Kwan seemed delighted by the question. He produced internal IAEA reports chronicling numerous discrepancies, alleged "fogging" of cameras monitoring spent fuel rods, thus requiring frequent replacements.

"What corroborative evidence is there that Taiwan is weaponizing?" Booth said.

"That is what's most alarming!" Kwan had an annoying habit of accelerating through his sentences until his words ran together like an onrushing stream. "InterPol is getting reports of krytrons being brought in. You know, those high speed electrical switches. They are used as precision triggers in implosion warheads. Ask your Customs people about it. You'll get verification about a strange krytron export from California, you will see."

"And what is Vienna doing with this information?"

"Nothing! They just shuffle their paper. Deny that they have hard information. That is why I took my files and come to you, so somebody will expose what the Taiwan authorities are doing."

Booth felt his calf about to cramp. "But why in the hell would Taiwan risk something like this?"

"Don't you see? This is from the new independence crowd in charge there now. The separatists, native Taiwanese. They try to look reasonable, but they reject their Chinese heritage. They don't answer to the people. Their generals are out of control, secretly developing some bomb-in-the-basement."

A long silence passed between them as Booth ran through the implications in his weary mind. "Taiwan has occasionally flirted with this stuff—even before the current pro-independence government was on the ropes. But I still don't see what evidence you have that they are preparing actual weapons, what evidence that—"

"What evidence?" Kwan erupted in a violent whisper. "Mr. Booth, I ask you, please! I risk my job, my life, to bring this evidence to you, to your Senator. You have a reputation for fairness, for action. The evidence is here."

"What makes you—"

"I would like to know what you are going to do about it."

"Well, with all due respect," Booth was on the defensive and resorted to formalisms. The coffee was kicking hard at his kidneys. "What exactly do you expect Senator Smithson to do for you?"

"For *me*?" Booth was sorry he had said it, but it was too late, as Kwan hammered away. "This all is not about me, Mr. Booth. I resigned from IAEA, before they could fire me for taking these classified documents."

"But—"

"And, no, I won't be making testimony for your hearings. You won't find me tomorrow. I will go—disappear. I just want to know what *you* will do. There are some reckless separatists in Asia making nuclear weapons that can only bring big trouble. I want to know what the USA is going to do about this."

"I can't say."

"Maybe you will send them more Patriot missiles so they feel more brave to provoke China? Maybe you will hide your head in the sand and pretend you can have more business as usual in Asia. When will you see that you have a nasty little problem? When radioactive cloud floats around to California?"

Kwan stuffed the IAEA documents back into his envelope so violently that he sliced his index finger on the edge. He cursed, sucking furiously at the wound with his thin lips.

"Here!" He slid the package at Booth, a faint sheen of blood at the top. "I do my part. This is all *your* problem now."

Kwan stood abruptly, banging the table with his knee, before pivoting and walking away.

Booth simmered as he drove home up Wisconsin Avenue, trying to determine his next move. His conflict of interest could not be more acute. Sure, Senator Smithson was Mr. Nuclear Nonproliferation, and they were equal opportunity whistle-blowers. Over the years, they had ticked off the Indians *and* the Pakistanis, the Chinese—even the Israelis—with a scorched earth series of revelations on the Senate floor.

Booth could see all too clearly where these new Taiwan allegations led, however. If Smithson was to go public demanding that Taiwan's friends prove a negative, he would alienate yet another valued constituency while providing crucial ammunition to his pro-China adversaries. It was not the ground they wanted to be plowing in the weeks before Smithson launched his presidential campaign. Booth didn't need a clever campaign strategist to explain this to him.

He was less than impressed with the whole Kwan performance. True, there was an echo there of something Senator Landle had said about an item in the NID suggesting Taiwan might again be exploring a nuclear option. It would be easy enough to ferret out if Customs had something about krytrons moving to Taipei. Still, he was loathe to take it to Branko.

And both the State Department and the Pentagon were too squirrelly on Taiwan Strait stuff lately, buddying up to the Taiwan military while trying to smooth China trade deals for the Fortune 500 companies. It was a clumsy balancing act. Just look at how the administration was fudging on the whole question of the Chinese missile build-up.

Everybody is speaking with a forked tongue, Booth concluded in disgust.

It was almost midnight as he pulled into his driveway on Irving Street in Chevy Chase. He shut the motor off and sat a long moment, listening in the stillness as the engine crackled and the hood contracted. The release seemed to have its own rhythm, its own sequence for letting go of residual heat and energy.

He entered the kitchen from the side door. The breakfast table had been set, fresh flowers in a mason jar by the window bordering the nook. His oldest, Aaron, age ten, had left a science test—a "96!"—for his inspection along with a tiny Tootsie Roll. There was a new painting clipped on the busy refrigerator, a complicated piece of space equipment with "NASA" printed on the side and the signature of Sarah with a smiley face on the bottom. He touched it with his fingertips, pausing.

He sat at the table, chewing the candy, pondering his Kwan problem. He gazed at a stack of mail Amy had left. Out the window, he could see strong shafts of moonlight.

In the den, he stripped to his boxers, trying hard not to wake anyone. On tip-toe, he checked the kids, lingering over the youngest to press his hand on a dreaming forehead. The dizzying images of the day scrolled before him. He didn't need this Taiwan business now, and neither did Jake Smithson.

There, in Sarah's bedroom with the Harry Potter poster, he arrived at a solution. He would pass the buck to Alexander. Let it be *Alexander's* problem. Let Alexander use his journalist's hunting license to separate fact from fiction. Then let the chips fall where they might, without Smithson's fingerprints. Booth could justify taking a pass on this one. He was taking a State Department authorization bill to conference with the House majority. He had a bunch of campaign speeches to draft. His plate was full.

He felt relieved as he slipped into the master bedroom and sank into his pillow. On his back, he pulled the comforter over him like a calming shroud. As he closed his eyes, he held that image of sleeping children. Amy's peaceful breathing beside him triggered thoughts of domestic tranquility smoothing the rough edges of his long day until, finally, he slept.

When his dreams came, though, they were bitter and twisted. Dark apparitions leapt up in the night. He saw small Asian figures, rifles in hand, scrambling over a landscape at dusk. High foreign voices of an enemy, calling signals. He saw the bamboo hats of the Viet Cong. They had returned, back from a childhood nightmare, darting from behind one tree to the next.

Then the sky flashed phosphorescent red and yellow, a nuclear fireball. He saw faces, grotesque and deformed, their skin slumping away like ice cream drooping down a cone. The fire continued to burn, a warning beacon on the horizon, a tower silhouetted in a yellow sky like the upright of the Cross. The Great Plains of his youth were aflame, silos glowing with fire. Then he could hear the voice of his father calling out his Old Testament admonition: "Be ye a seeker of truth."

Booth was swirling and thrashing, snarled in his sheets, when Amy awoke. Wordlessly, she reached out to him, caressing him, once again the healer. Her fingers soothed his temples. She whispered to him, indistinct words that had little meaning save for the human contact.

Gently, in an old ritual, she began to rake her nails across his chest. Then she rose up and kissed him, sloppy and soft, on the lips. He was alert now, responsive to her touch. He was released from his black vision, no longer burdened by his worldly concerns. That was his blessing, finally, at the end of a tumultuous day—to find a simple kindness in the dark, to receive the unexpected pleasure of making love at home, in his own bed, with his wife, wide awake once more.

15

MICKEY'S DILEMMA

Mickey Dooley awoke at peace with God. It was a peculiar sensation, one he had not known for years. A childhood of smacking gum and telling dirty jokes with his fellow altar boys had been followed by an adulthood passed as a recovering Catholic. Today, however, he felt refreshed, the beneficiary of a visitation. He was born again to some new purpose: all was before him now.

It is Tuesday, Mickey recalled after some effort. *Tuesday in America.*

He lay quite still, admiring the finish on the crown molding, following the carpenter's lines to the smooth intersection in the corners of the ceiling. He sat up, took several slow, deep breaths in an unfamiliar hotel room painted powder blue and gray, then tried to remember where he was.

As he stretched his calves gingerly and reached to touch his toes, he recovered a piece of his calming dreams. Something about a long lunch with his kid brother and a hot fudge sundae. The morning fears of previous days had lifted, as if lifted by an unseen hand. Today, he was on a mission. It was about the boys, about escaping, about starting over. Now, with that special clarity of dawn, he had a plan.

Mickey stood and walked to the corner window. The oddball protesters who made their home in Washington's Lafayette Square amidst cardboard signage had yet to stir. The White House and its north gates were still, two uniformed guards standing in front of the high fence. The Sixteenth Street traffic was light, a Saturday-like calm that confused him until he remembered it was still before seven a.m. Across the way, he saw the warm yellow paint of Saint John's, the church of presidents.

On a whim, he considered joining the few souls who would gather there for morning services, Episcopalians all. He was feeling nondenominational today, prepared to cover his bets. He had prayed there before, one day at noon. He had spontaneously taken a pew in back and beseeched the Lord to intervene after his mom's heart attack. Mom recovered, and Mickey, not yet fully prepared to repent and reform, was glad he hadn't made any deals with God.

Mickey drank from a bottle of Perrier as he stood gazing at the church, the cool drink refreshing him. He turned about in his undershirt, half expecting to find a witness. He had pondered the problem for weeks before approaching Branko. He had wrestled with thoughts about his boys' future, the fate of his marriage, and his China business. He had scrolled through the names in his palm pilot, searching for an idea, weighing various plans for extricating himself from his dilemma.

Mickey's quandary was simple. He could no longer tolerate his bleak existence in Beijing, staggering on in a life of infinite compromise. He could neither stay in Beijing with the frosty Mei Mei, nor leave freely without the boys. His spouse had evolved into a caricature of a daddy's girl, a woman who so loved gambling she was out to all hours playing mahjong, and who, it seemed, lived also to shop. As the boys matured and came each day to more resemble Mickey, admiring his Western ways, she came to vent her fury on them as well. The children, he readily convinced himself, were better off with him in the States, where they used to live every summer. Already, she was using them as pawns in her marital war, taking them away to her father's country place, barring them from trips overseas with Mickey.

Mickey's path to hope and revival seemed open and his vision clear: *Branko would save them.* Mickey was sure of it.

Upon later reflection, it seemed inevitable that his search for a savior would lead to his longtime critic. For too long, he had feared the disdain of his old friend. Branko had been the most selfless of the Mandarins, the one who had fully led the life he had planned. Branko was the straight man. From the day of their first seminar together, Mickey had been the risk taker. Branko had every right to judge him harshly, a fact that for some time had scared Dooley off his proposition.

Mickey had floated a trial balloon with Branko before, with no success. He had been saving tidbits of information in his files, gleaned from years of double-dealing, with which to trade. Between courses at Mr. K's, he had dropped hints—even followed Branko to the men's room, muttering a few choice asides and looking for a private meeting, before Branko cut him off. Yet, there at the end of the supper was a passed note, with blunt instructions to call this morning. A name, a number, a beachhead that Mickey wanted desperately to believe could be widened.

When he called just after nine, a young woman's voice proposed a Friday evening meeting. Branko was prepared to talk. Directions for the rendezvous were simple, and encouraging. They were to meet in the minor league baseball park in Frederick, Maryland, a concession to Mickey's old sporting tastes.

Thus, at week's end, Mickey found himself sitting in the bleachers at Harry Grove Stadium, home of the Class A Frederick Keys. They were hosting the Wilmington Blue Rocks, rookies from the New York Mets' farm team in Delaware. Mickey and Branko were both in polo shirts and chinos, studiously dressed down amidst the suburban crowd.

"I'm trapped, old buddy," Mickey said when the right moment arrived. "I need an escape hatch."

"I see," Branko replied, though he didn't—yet.

"I mean it. I've worked it every way I can. I've pleaded with Mei Mei to try the U.S. I even promised a house on the hill in Sausalito. She won't budge. Now that we may be heading for divorce court, she won't even let me bring the boys to New Mexico for summer vacation."

"Have you proposed shared custody?" said Branko, sipping a soda.

"She rejects the idea out of hand. And she's got all the cards. With her father working the judge, I'm going to get slammed in court."

"I can see where that might be a very brief hearing."

"I know it sounds crazy, but when I'm in Beijing, I'm their primary caregiver, not the nanny she leaves them with. I drive them to the American School, take them to music lessons. I play ball with them—I help them do their homework. I mean, I'll get affidavits from schoolteachers, even a psychologist in Albuquerque. They all support my position that the boys need to be multicultural, to live with their dad. But the whole court process is stacked against a foreigner."

"The Chinese have not developed an appreciation for the rule of law yet," Branko observed. "But Mickey, what if you just took the boys and left?"

"God, Branko, I thought hard about it last winter in Hong Kong, even before things got so bad. We were there with her parents. I had my ticket for LAX, and I went ahead and bought two more for the kids—just in case I could see my way clear. Then she found their passports in my stuff and went ballistic on me. Now she's brainwashing them that I'm some heathen from the West."

"Sounds ugly."

"The worst thing is, it's like she's blackmailing me. The shit I'm into with Telstar, the satellite telemetry stuff, is getting hairier and hairier. I don't produce for Pops and she's all over me. She ditches the boys out at his country place, and then she flies off to some fucking fashion show."

The crowd cheered as the third baseman speared a one-hop liner headed down the line and turned a neat 5-4-3 double play from his knees, a big league ease to his side-arm toss.

As the crowd settled, Mickey pressed the issue. "Branko," he pleaded, "I need your help, man." He barreled ahead shamelessly, reaching into his wallet and passing photos of the two boys—half cowboy, half Confucius—smiling in baseball uniforms. Pre-game eye black accentuated their almond-shaped eyes, but the smiles and the teeth were unmistakably Mickey's.

For several moments, Branko was silent. The sun was falling behind the grandstand, the last rays reaching toward the ballplayers on the field, their white uniforms set off by red piping. Splotches of pure sunlight were scattered randomly about the diamond.

Branko held the photos at length before passing them back. They were alone, in their own row near the top of the bleachers, both thinking intently.

"Mickey," Branko said at last, "what exactly do you expect from me?"

"I, uh, I want to make a deal."

"A deal?"

"Yeah," Mickey answered, "like a trade. I've been saving some stuff for you. Tips that might help your work. Little insights into what they're up to. Hardware shopping lists. Some good stuff. "

"You want to make a trade to get your boys out?"

"I want you to recruit me. Put me to work. Let me do something for Uncle Sam. I mean, I got some ideas about some of the games they're playing. High tech stuff. Dirty tricks against Taiwan. You name it."

Mickey waited anxiously, popcorn in hand, beer at his feet. Branko was gazing across the field toward the sinking sun. He would not look at Mickey for the longest time, peering at some distant marker.

"Fuck you, Mickey Dooley," Branko finally said.

"What do you expect me to—"

"No, Mickey. *Don't*. Don't even try to defend yourself."

"It's just *fuck you?*"

"Yeah. Fuck you."

"For what? For asking an old friend—"

"No, Mickey! Fuck you for screwing up your life."

"Gimme a break!"

"Fuck you for making such a mess and for expecting people who live cleaner to bail your ass out."

"So what was my sin? Marrying a Chinese woman? Trying to help China join the twenty-first century? What do you expect a businessman to—"

"You're a businessman with the morals of a sewer rat. Do you have any idea what the file on your Beijing operations looks like?"

"I'm as patriotic as the next guy. I mean—" Mickey caught himself, curious. "So, what exactly do they think they have on me?"

"Let's just say your patriotism is highly suspect. Your damn Agency file is so thick I had to get two waivers just to have a meal with you. The fact is, you've screwed up, Mickey. You could have put your brilliance to a higher purpose. Now you're paying the price."

"For God's sake man, don't sit in judgment of me. It's just business. We don't sell it, the French or the Germans will."

"So you go through your life doing whatever your sleaziest neighbor will do? How exactly does your version of least common denominator ethics elevate the species? Whoring for the People's Liberation Army? Skimming off all those dual use licenses for the Chinese Defense Ministry? Your little games on the side for Telstar? Sprinkling cash around both capitals like some bagman?"

"Branko, I just am—"

"You were the cleverest of us all. What did you do with your God-given talent? Do you have any idea how the Chinese use the stuff you help them get? How it will be used against the West in a war?" Branko turned and faced him squarely now. "You've got blood on your hands, man."

"And the CIA's full of nuns? We've *all* got blood on our hands. That doesn't mean a guy can't have a second chance to do the right thing."

Branko stopped to listen.

"I figure it's like my mom used to say . . . 'it's what you're aspiring to that matters,'" Mickey said, suddenly preaching. "That is what we answer to God for, she said—our dreams, not our failings."

Branko held his silence as Mickey continued to squirm.

"Listen, Branko, I know you're pissed that I haven't done many noble things with my life. I went off to China to make some money and open doors. I thought marrying Chinese was part of the future, that my family might be some kind of bridge between the two worlds. So why is it my fault when it turns out we have nothing in common but our kids?"

"This is not about your kids."

"It is for me! Jesus, think ill of me—tell me I'll fry in Hell. But why should they suffer just because I screwed up? Look at them!" He thrust the photos at him, as if they were defense evidence at trial. "They're American kids, American citizens. They're hostages in the Commies' corrupt legal system."

Branko kicked at bits of popcorn with his toe, working them methodically down to the sticky ledge below.

The sun was gone now, settled off behind the ridge to the west. The sky above them was laced with elongated Z's of orange and purple, punctuated by the harsh light of the electric towers. The bulbs burned in a ring about the stadium.

"Will you help me?" Mickey pressed. "If not for old time's sake, then for the kids'?"

Branko was more than willing to let Mickey prostrate himself. But Branko was a professional, resigned to his purpose. He knew what he needed to do here, even as Mickey continued to pursue him.

As they sat, a line drive was hit into the gap in left-center field. The crowd responded with noise. The ball seemed headed directly at their row, until it began to fade. An arm reached up at the warning track, snatching it with leather. The two outfielders dodged a collision and circled, their legs a perfect parabola as they concluded the play with a slap of their gloves. They loped back toward the infield, matching stride for stride.

"Yes," Branko finally replied, "yes, Mickey, we will help them."

"God, thank you, Branko." Mickey grabbed his left arm with both his hands, clinging. "Thank you."

"You need to understand a few things, though." Branko was gathering himself. Mickey had seen it in the old days as his colleague prepared to skewer an undergraduate in some tutorial.

"Sure."

"Past friendship does not oblige me to take foolish risks on you. The CIA doesn't do custody disputes. This is business."

"Sure, Branko."

"You need to listen for once—really fucking listen."

"I promise."

"You must pledge not to repeat what I say. To any one. Ever."

"Right."

"We never talked. And you will never talk about it. To anyone."

"I won't."

Branko inhaled, gaining strength, reflecting on the events of an alarming week that had brought him to this crossroads. The truth was, he had wanted to say "yes" for days. But he could not justify it. Before his discussions late Wednesday with one of the CIA's key Beijing assets, he could not support the notion. After the chilling new analysis of recent Chinese actions, after confirmation that Lee was once again rebuffing any contacts from his local controller, Branko saw no better option.

"If you get sloppy with this, they will kill you. Others will suffer, too. You have to justify my blind faith in you, in your essential decency."

"You have my word. As a father, as an American. Now what the hell is it?"

Branko lit a cigarette, pulling hard for sustenance.

"Mickey, we've concluded it's not safe for you to return to Beijing."

"Not safe? What the hell do you mean?"

"Not safe now, not safe ever."

"But I've got to go back. How could I ever get the boys if . . . Wait. What is it?"

"Something new has turned up."

"Something new?"

"It changes everything. You see, there are indications that you have been targeted."

"What? But I've worked with the—"

"Can you just *listen* a moment?" Branko's voice rose, and he shot a glance about them. But the nearest fans were a good twenty yards away.

"Goddamn it, Mickey. Wake up! This is real. This isn't some grad school maneuver to bed some blonde."

"Hey, man! It's *my* sons we're talking about. I know this is real."

Branko struggled for composure. "You know the explosion on F Street? The bomb outside Talbott's firm?"

"Of course."

"Well, the forensics experts have belatedly identified fragments of a timing device. The D.C. Police contaminated some of the evidence. Mishandled it, logged it in wrong—plain incompetence. But it seems pretty clear now to the FBI and to our people."

"What seems clear?" Branko had lost him.

"A timer, Mickey."

"A timer?"

"Yes. A timer," Branko repeated. "There were fragments of a timer in the rubble."

"So?"

"It suggests that the gentleman transporting the explosive device had no intention of being a suicide bomber. It was intended as a drop off. It was not intended to blow up in his lap at 9:07 a.m. He intended to leave the bomb for subsequent detonation."

"For when?"

"For *whom* is the more appropriate question. They had a busy day planned at the Talbott firm. A lot of visitors. Senators. Ambassadors . . ."

"And me."

"Exactly. And you."

"The ten o'clock appointment! Rachel and Talbott and the guys from the Chinese Embassy. And Lee too. He was supposed to be coming—"

"This is *raw*, Mickey. Raw, unverified, inconclusive analysis."

"But who? Who would pull such a crazy-ass stunt? Two blocks from the White House! And why me? I mean, Senator Smithson was supposed to be there at noon. How do you know that—"

"No hour hand. The hour hand, it seems, had been pulled off the watch face before it was wired to the detonator. It had only the minute hand sweep, as far as forensics can tell. It would seem they intended it to go off at seven minutes past the next hour. Ten not nine."

"But who would target any of us?"

"Who indeed? That is *our* question."

"Not Taiwan—I mean, that's crazy. The U.S. would abandon them in a heartbeat if their people pulled that kind of crap."

"We don't know the answer to that. Could be the Chinese were after just one of you. Could be you. Could be part of some in-fighting in one of their intelligence branches. Could be a ruse, a set-up, misdirection. Some guys making a hit, and trying to make others take the heat for it. They've been known to pull some bizarre numbers. Do some nasty job and try to pin it on their neighbors. A two-for-one shot."

Mickey flashed on the krytrons business for a moment, but then focused closer to home. "What about Lee? Lee was—"

"Lee apparently didn't cancel his seat on that plane. Had a ticket, left for the airport. Somebody may have tipped him off, called him back. We don't know. And your message canceling with Rachel didn't get played at TPB until just before the gentleman was juggling a briefcase on his lap in that cab on F Street."

"So . . ."

"The point is, Mickey, somebody thought they stood to gain by eliminating you. You and your boys had better come on home and keep your heads down. And Lee . . ."

"Lee's in danger, too, isn't he?"

Branko nodded somberly.

"What is it you want me to do?"

"We want to ask you to take some risks. We will take some unusual risks, too, believe me. But before we commit, I need to make clear there are a few conditions."

"Whatever."

"At least three—for now."

"Anything. Just tell me what to do."

"First, when you come home to the U.S., you are home for good. You are out of the China game. Retired. No more Customs runs in Shanghai. No more Telstar sales through Hong Kong. No more dual-use license technology deals."

"OK."

"You are done with the satellite business. We will help you. I will personally stand by you. But do *not* become a problem to the Agency, or to me. Ever."

"Sure. I don't even want to see—"

"Second, when you're back, it all never happened."

"OK."

"We never talked. You will be in great danger—and others will be, too—if you can't keep your goddamn mouth shut. About our theory on the timing device. About the bomb. About possible motivations. About the Agency's intentions. All of it. I suggest you quit drinking, for starters."

"Actually, I've already been backing off the hard stuff."

Loud organ music interrupted them, the between-innings carnival rising to a crescendo. The crowd clapped in rhythm as Mickey peered disconsolately at the beer he had been nursing.

"What's third?"

Branko was all business once more. The corner of his mouth crinkled in sympathy, the recruiter's touch as he pulled Mickey in with a final condition.

"Third is . . . third is Lee."

"Lee?" Mickey asked. "You want me to bring him a message?'

"We want you to bring him to us."

"Bring Lee to the U.S.?"

"Yes. Help him escape to the U.S."

Mickey paused before he began to ramble. "You know, Lee is the twins' godfather. He asked me to keep it a secret. He and Rachel drew the godparent duty. He adores them. Taught them Tai Chi."

"We know. Actually, we hope he might, at a minimum, provide a bit of an insurance policy for our rather unusual exit plan for the boys. It's risky and will have serious consequences."

"You're asking me to *recruit* him?"

"No. We want you to convince him to leave—to come to the United States. Convince him any way you can to get out of China. *Now*. If he feels he cannot leave immediately, try to prevail on him to help us on a couple of critical issues for however long he remains in place."

"You expect him to be a mole? Branko, isn't that, like, suicide?"

"Mickey, he is already at risk. He's been at risk for years. The risk has just gotten greater. We are certain he must see that now. He is so stubborn. But he's smarter than any of us in how he plays the game."

"He's an idealist, Lee is. I said it before. He's a fucking radical."

"He's a survivor, Mickey. Now he can be a hero, if you can convince him."

"Why now?"

"We need him. There's a threat to the summit."

"You talking about the safety of the president?"

"Mickey, you really don't want to—don't need to—get into this."

"Of course I do! How am I going to convince Lee? You must have done stuff with him before. I mean, once upon a time, after Tiananmen, when those Chinese government memos were leaked to the West, all the Politburo internal debates about how to clear the students out of Tiananmen Square? I figured you already had an inside track. I kinda hoped Lee was involved."

Branko was fixated on something in the opposite grandstand now. Then he spoke. "Mickey, you really don't want to go there. Speculation is hazardous in these matters."

"But I need to understand what is past if I'm going to convince him his future interests—"

"If you are going to work with us, you have to accept some things on faith. Sometimes you know only what you need to know. We are asking you to take a message to Lee. A very specific offer."

"But if he's cooperated before—"

"Deal with the present—the present and the future. Assume that we used to have a procedure in place for getting him out if he wanted to leave. Exfiltration it's called. He's not cooperating now. We have no contact with him. The intermediary, the method we used, has been compromised. It is too dangerous for known Agency assets to approach him. We think it will attract less attention if he is just talking with an old friend in town."

"Like me."

"Exactly. Now listen. There are indications of a concerted effort over there to disrupt the summit. Dangerous developments in Beijing. We only have pieces of it. But it is the type of thing that could conceivably lead us down the road to a major confrontation."

"You mean a military confrontation?"

"I've always thought we would end up in a face-off at some point. But that's just my personal opinion. Right now, we are completely overextended in Iraq and Afghanistan. So we're a little vulnerable. We require all the eyes and ears in Beijing we can get."

"Christ."

Branko was locked in now. It was a familiar connection Mickey could sense—it harked back to some earlier time.

"There's this little cell in their Army intelligence unit." Branko laid it out just a bit further as he gazed toward the horizon. "A bunch of impatient intellectuals in love with their own rhetoric. Probably a bunch of their war college boys taking their textbooks way too literally. But they enjoy the patronage of the old generals, who love the deniability."

"Intelligence agents, or just analysts?"

"Probably both. There's nothing more dangerous than ideologues running operations. We need to get inside. We absolutely must penetrate this cell."

"Sounds like they're a bunch of Ollie Norths."

"Exactly. Think of the Byzantine Iran-contra aid schemes—who would ever have believed the NSC would be selling arms to the Ayatollah? Think Gordon Liddy and Haldeman's Plumbers running amok here at home. That's all you need to know for now. Lee will already understand the rest—better than you or I ever will." Branko sighed in resignation. "You'll just have to swallow the rest of your questions."

Mickey nodded slowly. With that assent, a bridge to his old classmate was reconstructed. Mickey Dooley was back on the team. His sins were forgiven. His dispensation had been granted.

16

AT THE DELANO

The Hotel Delano was a fantasy, equal parts Art Deco and Studio 54. It was all froth and fiction, from another world. Rachel knew this. Yet she plunged in, striding purposefully into the lobby—and back in time.

Cheerful Italian busboys in white linen shorts and desert boots fussed with her bags as she entered the Delano lounge. Before her was a long banner of gauzy muslin cloth wafting like tent flaps in a Bedouin campground. Beckoning down the breezeway were tall white columns and dark angled walls. Lining the walkway were oversized chairs painted gold and piled with overstuffed cushions.

There was the low murmur of Latin men, tie-less in black cotton suits, speaking into their cell phones. There was a constant clicking of ladies' heels, impossibly tall stilettoes, with leather straps reaching up sculpted calves. The women ignored her with brazen disdain. But she was captivated as she stood in her rumpled business dress, still bearing her convention nametag with one of those annoying smiley faces: "HI! I'M: Rachel!"

In the early evening air there were fruity scents, aftershave, and perfumed cigarettes. The smell of curried hors d'oeuvres was from the terrace ahead. She stood at the precipice now, gazing down across the whimsy of games and bungalows, and the over-spilling water that flowed down to the beach. She followed the path beckoning her into the palms.

As she proceeded through the lawn along the flagstone, she encountered an enormous pool extending a foot or two above her, elevated like some in-ground hot tub, splashing down around her while a swimmer carved laps. Two women sat perched at a metal table set in a thin pond of water at the shallow end. One smoked carefully, exhaling into the angled rays of sunlight. The other toyed at the water with chartreuse toenails. Both were defiantly bare-breasted, chatting as they sucked shrimp dipped in cocktail sauce.

Rachel, the small-town girl, began to giggle. She rolled her hand, still stiff from the long journey, in the pool. She had been gripping the wheel too tightly, for too long. Now she would let go, lolling her wet fingers in the milky tropical air.

She didn't care if she was the last one to Ian Schrager's party at Miami's South Beach, years after the tourists had rediscovered the neighborhood, long after the arrival of chain restaurants and fashion photo shoots. This weekend in May, she had finally fled the twin responsibilities of senior executive and domestic engineer, and landed at "The Coolest Hotel in America." She was determined to enjoy it.

The impulse had come quickly. She had been standing in an Orlando karaoke bar after lunchtime with a bunch of old guys in seersucker suits at the convention of the Chemical Manufacturers Association, when she reached her limit. It was frightening in its swiftness, this realization. Her sense of the absurd was making her dangerous, though she'd been drinking only cranberry juice. As she wise-cracked cynically with the guys, she felt trouble ahead. Her sense of self-preservation helped her decide to move on.

It was only Thursday. Barry had Jamie through the weekend. The boys were fine, off reliving the Civil War at Antietam and Gettysburg. Jamie probably had on a full Union Army uniform by now. She'd already done her Washington wrap-up talk for the CMA panel, and the rest of the program was light on substance.

So she'd fled, racing east in her rental car, making the Atlantic coast-line before three o'clock, rolling south down I-95, surfing through the FM dial for just the right decade of oldies.

She was chasing some moment of frivolity she had missed during all those years of expectations—hers and others'. She had grown up too soon, entering the career track and marriage at twenty-one. All those nights out with clients, heavy with obligation, juggling the soccer car pool and PTA commitments. All the times she'd put the needs and desires of somebody else first. She was escaping, off the radar screen for forty-eight hours, to be anonymous and irresponsible, a teenager once more.

"I feel like I'm time traveling," she teased Alexander over the phone when she called him later from her room. "It's 1982. I expect to find John Travolta in that white suit, Don Johnson and Tubbs in tow."

"I call it stolen time," Alexander explained. "Living outside the calendar."

"You've done this before?"

"Sure. I used to tell the bureau I was leaving Tokyo on a Friday, and be back in the States on Monday. But I'd leave Japan Wednesday night, and just fly away somewhere. Disappear. Find a place to hike, sleep, read books—you know, discuss the meaning of life with strangers."

"Where would you go?"

"Oh, someplace where I had no past. Little town called Waimea above the Kona coast of Hawaii. Phuket, before the tsunami. Anyplace where time moved with less urgency."

"Well, time has stopped here at the Hotel Delano, that's for sure. It's all Fleetwood Mac and the Bee Gees."

"Nope." He yawned. "More like the capital of Latin America."

"You sound sleepy."

"I dozed off. Just finished a big nuclear nonproliferation story, a big scoop. Resting on my laurels."

In the silence, she imagined awakening next to him. "So, what did you dream about during your nap?"

"Water. It was a great dream. I was at the seashore."

"Ocean dreams. Like mine! My mother always told me water dreams were about cleansing."

"Cleansing?"

"She was heavy into the Church, you know. Big-time Lutheran. I always thought that meant she was washing away guilt. But my analyst says water dreams are about sensuality . . . So, did you go in?"

"Go in?"

"The water. Did you take the plunge?"

"Yeah. Of course I did."

"Good for you."

"What?" Alexander sat up, turning down a suddenly too loud saxophone riff on the CD player. "You think I'm repressed?"

"Of course you are," she said, laughing. "But maybe it's just a phase."

"Who was it I confessed to the other night that I'm the only guy I know who admits to still enjoying the occasional joint?"

"Which proves my point. You get high to escape. It's a crutch."

"Actually, I get high because I enjoy it. Intensifies my insights. Helps me see beyond the mundane."

"Naughty boy. No security clearance for you."

"Very socially unacceptable, I know. It's much more politically correct to entrust our security to the martini-drinking, caffeine-swilling guys at the Pentagon. Or the dry drunk who stumbled into the Baghdad quagmire."

"We're a little defensive, aren't we? You been reading one of your whiny liberal columnists again?"

"And how many daiquiris have you had, young lady?"

"Only two. Well, maybe a third. I'm in recovery, indulging my senses. And my skin is still tingly all over. It's like I've got hives or something."

"Maybe it's the humidity."

"I'm refusing to put any clothes on. I like the breeze."

"You're flirting with me, Rachel Paulson. After all these years, what do you do to me? You flirt."

"You noticed!" said Rachel in a congratulatory tone. "I've decided that you are my summer project. Get you to shed your armor."

"You sound like Mickey Dooley. He used to say he always tried to get laid on the first date. To get the ladies to peel off all their social armor. Said it saved time."

"Right."

"No, really. He had these elaborate theories about sex. He could be very articulate on the subject. He used to say that sex was just a short-cut in relationships, to cut to the chase, to see how a potential companion gave and received."

"Mickey Dooley gave you sex tips? Now that's a frightening thought. I mean, he could sure play the Macho Man at times. Probably was all an act, come to think of it."

"Actually, if I recall, he was rather sweet on you."

"For God's sake, I'm the godmother of his boys. I was like his sister!"

"And I was like a brother."

"You *all* were like my brothers."

"You were always such a good sport."

"Such a good girl."

"I always thought you were wiser than us, Rachel—about people, I mean."

"But I was 'Barry's girl.'"

"Made things safe."

"Safe. Story of my life." Rachel sighed. The windows were open as the evening air moved by, the billowing curtains letting in shafts of neon from across the avenue.

"It's fun here," she continued. "There's great imagination in the design, all geometric. Long white lines set off by an obelisk or a triangle. They've put hammocks and chessboards and mirrors on the grass walk. Just for the hell of it. And the women! Alexander, you would be inspired!"

"They're probably all models, Rachel. Lot of silicone and bulimia there."

"They're all these incredible shapes and flavors. The food on Lincoln Road I had tonight was amazing. Some blend of Cuban and French, grilled with rich fruity sauces. And the people watching! Even *I* like looking. There are just so many different textures and colors."

"So the Wyoming girl is finally making the South Beach scene."

"I'm lying on the bed naked in an all-white room." Her voice slowed suggestively. "The only bit of color is this Granny Smith apple they put on a pedestal."

"You are *naughty*," he said with a laugh. "Where the hell is your husband?"

"Yeah. Where the hell *is* he? Oh, Alexander, I'm not good at this. There I was, watching all these men in the lobby bar. And you know what sucks? They're all looking at *each other*! Even in the little Delano gift shop, all the skin magazines have male models."

"Since when does a married woman go ogling a bunch of—"

"I'm not exactly a . . ."

"Not what?"

"Well . . . sort of."

"What do you mean, *sort of?*"

"Sort of not married. Separated. I filed for divorce. Last week. Barry's moving out."

"Rachel! Why didn't you say something?"

"I just figured it was something I had to do on my own. I've got too many things I still want to do, and I know I've been living a lie."

"I know things were screwed up. But you should have told some—"

"Don't you understand? All these years, I've felt not right, like everything was a test and I never quite made the grade. Well, I finally figured it out. It wasn't about me, about my own self-expectations. It was all about Barry. Barry never liked himself enough to be happy. It was all about Barry. It always was."

"So . . . what now?"

"So, now I'm free," she said. "And now I'm going to eat this goddamn apple."

17

ABOVE THE FOLD

Alexander felt like a voyeur. Alone at midnight, he logged onto the Internet. It was a telling conceit, this habit of his, checking the placement of his big story, viewing the *Times* homepage to weigh his competition for the attention of the reading public.

Page one, he congratulated himself as the paper's website materialized. *Above the fold.*

Before he could sleep, he scrolled once more through the story, imagining the reactions it would spark across the city and around the globe. It was a triumph:

> WASHINGTON—Military officials in Taiwan are developing capabilities associated with nuclear weapons production, according to intelligence sources. These initiatives include the import of so-called "dual-use" technology, appropriate for use in a weapons program, and the alleged diversion of modest, but significant, amounts of spent nuclear fuel, a source of weapons-grade plutonium, the *Times* has learned.

Nice pithy lead. Gets the key facts right on the table.

> State Department officials in Washington refused to confirm the reports of possible spent nuclear fuel diversion. But these officials concede that the implications of such a clandestine nuclear weapons development program on Taiwan would be profound for U.S. policymakers.

Truth is, they're scared witless over at State. The "Taiwan-is-flirting-

with-nukes-again" lead will force the U.S. to reassess positions throughout the region.

"This is an inevitable result of two decades of a pro-Beijing tilt by successive U.S. presidents: denying Taiwan the right to purchase advanced weapons," states James Liu of the pro-independence Taiwanese Association for Public Affairs. "China's build-up of ballistic missiles deployed against Taiwan requires a robust response." Liu argues that the People's Republic of China's 15 percent annual increase in defense spending for each of the last three years justifies an aggressive Taiwanese response.

Dense paragraph ... maybe I should have buried it. But it's a strong quote and readers need context.

In recent weeks, Taiwan has imported substantial quantities of krytrons, high-speed electrical switches that can be used as trigger timers in nuclear warheads. Krytrons have very limited non-military uses in electrical circuitry and special effects filming. U.S. Customs sources confirm recent shipments from California via third countries to Taipei. UN inspection agency sources confirm troubling discrepancies during recent inspections of Taiwan's nuclear power facilities.

Kwan's stuff from the IAEA was key to the piece. Wonder if he turns up again to float a follow-up story?

The issues of Taiwan's defense requirements and Taipei's renewed interest in nuclear weapons are expected to severely complicate troubled U.S.-China ties, just weeks before a summit meeting slated for July 31 in Seattle, Washington. Last night, a Chinese government press official reached for comment warned of "the most grave consequences should the ruling clique on Taiwan toy with nuclear weapons."

Love that closing. Should make for a fun morning—the phones definitely will be ringing.

Alexander slept as well as he had in days, a deep and satisfying slumber.

"You're all over the news," said Branko on the phone early the next morning. To Alexander's surprise, Branko, seemingly in good humor, had made the direct call to his home.

"I just wish you'd called me back on this," Alexander said. "I'm kinda out on a limb."

"Wish I had, too. I have been tied up on something pressing. I would have told you your limb has no strength."

"Say what?"

"Alexander, it's crap."

"What do you mean?" Alexander demanded as a wave of dread swept over him. "Which part?"

"Which part? Try all of it. It reeks."

"What are you trying to—"

"You've been set up, Alexander. It's obvious to me."

"Set up? Where? I got three sources on the krytrons. Booth has it, too. The UN stuff on spent fuel I got from documents. I got the—"

"Alexander! It's Branko here. Your sources may appear to speak the truth. They may *believe* it is the truth. However, things are not what they seem."

"Where am I off?"

"This is an open line. I'm just warning you, one professional to another. You're getting jerked around."

"Are you saying it's disinformation?"

"I can't help you with that. Just go back and work the problem." And then Branko was gone.

Alexander sat for a long time, his bare feet propped against a tidy desk.

He felt as if he was going to puke.

He remembered once, when he was a kid, butchering a Spanish dialogue in front of the whole class of fifth graders. Two cute girls up front were laughing when he looked down and saw his fly was wide open. That is how he felt now, humiliated before his peers.

He hurled his ballpoint pen against the wall and cursed. He sat still for several more minutes, his mind rolling back through the conversations of recent days. Frantically, he began to reconstruct the story, going back again to rethink the pieces.

There had been Booth's intelligence from the IAEA guy and his debrief. The confirming call with Kwan's colleague in Vienna. The Customs stuff he had cold—two different guys had seen the item in the National Intelligence Digest brief that was all over official Washington. Even the State Department guy who'd tried hard to squash the story the previous evening had known about krytrons moving to Taipei via Canada.

What did I miss? Whose game have I stumbled into? Who's messing with my head? He could only wonder as the day stretched ahead, long and miserable. He was forced to go to his managing editor for an agonizing conversation, Alexander warning that the entire foundation of their lead story was likely to collapse.

What a story it was. The diplomatic press corps was in a frenzy, with the morning briefers at both State and the Pentagon taking heated questions about Taiwan's nuclear program. The IAEA staff in Vienna went dark, with the international bureaucracy offering a terse "no comment." Kwan had vanished.

The White House knocked down the Bonner story hard, the press secretary assailing its author by name with adjectives like "irresponsible" and "sloppy." The diplomatic damage was done, however, with collateral damage to U.S. international interests. By late evening, Washington time, official Beijing was up and about, issuing ominous statements.

"The reckless splittist forces in Taipei are playing with fire," the Chinese Foreign Ministry spokesman warned. "Unless their American sponsors rein them in, there will be grave consequences for these actions, which are deeply offensive to all Chinese."

No hastily produced American reassurance would calm them. China's Ambassador to Washington was promptly recalled for consultations. He delivered a parting blast from Dulles Airport, insisting that Washington would bear "full responsibility" if Taiwan provoked military hostilities across the Taiwan Strait.

The White House responded by dispatching special emissaries to Beijing and Taipei in a desperate effort to curb tensions. In Taiwan, the stock market numbers were appalling, a twelve percent drop before all trading was suspended. The London insurance brokers doubled spot quotes for shipping that called at Taiwan's ports. The S&P 500 and the NASDAQ plummeted. Smart money fled to cash and gold.

Booth provided little help. The Senate aide had been under suspicion before for leaks. He was exceptionally cautious now. He couldn't find Kwan himself, and began dodging Alexander's follow-up calls until Amy finally took pity on him and put Booth on the line at home one evening. Booth apologized for being evasive. Senator Landle was apparently after Booth over the staffer's allegations that the State Department was dissembling—"lying" was the word Booth used—about an alleged Chinese missile build-up. Booth could offer nothing to advance the story.

A grim week of humiliation unfolded. Alexander felt like a kid chasing falling snowflakes. Just when he thought he caught something in his hands, it had evaporated. As his story was replayed, dissected, and rebuked, friends seemed to be calling to him from afar, rolling by like rubber-neckers at an accident scene.

"Do you know what it's like to get really pounded?" Alexander lamented one evening on the phone with Rachel. "To be pitching in an enemy ballpark—you reach the seventh inning and you're totally out of gas. But there's nobody in the bullpen behind you. The game is yours to finish—and you're just getting hammered?"

"You'll rally."

"My dad knew what it felt like. I saw it a few times—after he realized he'd never make the big leagues. Jesus, he'd take a beating."

"But he'd finish the game?"

"Had to."

"So finish it."

Alexander stumbled as he absorbed the rain of blows. In the newsroom, he felt like a pariah. His first effort at a clean-up story was so full of caveats that he killed the piece himself. The fact was, he didn't know what the truth was any more. Reality grew more elusive with each passing hour.

His editors were all over his case as the long Memorial Day weekend approached. He worked the phones futilely, trying to find anyone who could set him straight. By Saturday afternoon, there was nobody left in town to call. The coffee was cold. His tuna sandwich was going stale. So, when Rachel phoned with an invitation to Sunday lunch, he accepted her offer to ride out to her aunt's place in the country.

She came for him at ten the next morning. Grinning and barefoot in her BMW, she was a most welcome distraction. He felt clumsy at first, like a teenager on a first date. She offered only tough love in response to his professional disaster. "You'll get it right. But don't go and ruin a blue sky Sunday because of it," she insisted. "*That* would be a sin."

As they talked, her optimism was like a tide of good cheer, pulling him forward. He shut off his Blackberry, casting a stealthy glance at her toe-nails, painted Stanford Cardinal red. Instead of Taiwan's nuclear capabilities, he found himself wondering about whether she made love with her eyes open. The farther beyond the Beltway they drove, the more he began to mellow.

She rambled on about the old days, telling stories on Mickey Dooley and the boys. She was funny, but reflective, too, seemingly eager to question long ago incidents.

"Did you ever figure out where our stupid little Truth or Dare game came from?" she asked abruptly as they passed Chantilly on Route 50.

"What do you mean?"

"I mean, what was *that* all about?"

"It was your idea the other night," Alexander noted.

"You're right. That's why I was thinking about it, because I was self-conscious at Mr. K's. I wanted to strangle Barry that night, the way he shows up after weeks away and acts as if everything is hunky-dory."

"Didn't it start as Mickey's game?" He still felt sluggish; Rachel was moving a bit too quickly for him.

"That's the way I remembered it, too. Mickey's game. To provoke debate, to supposedly bring us closer by sharing something personal. But then I flashed back to the first time, that card game, when the boys started talking strip poker. It was *Barry*'s idea. That was Barry's game."

"Barry?"

"Yeah, a game of self-revelation for people who never really shared their secrets. It was a goddamn tease. Just like Barry. It wasn't about real intimacy."

It all came back to him—the night Barry had been winning big at cards and offered to take clothes as markers. The forced grin on Rachel's face, as she and Mickey's date played along uncomfortably with the boys. The deceit inherent in Barry's playing to the crowd. The way Barry used Mickey as the jovial pulling guard for his maneuvers. Barry held all the chips—all the power. He was the one exploiting his position of strength while the much younger Rachel followed along, all too eager to please.

"How are you doing with the whole separation thing?" Alexander asked as they rolled into open roads past Centerville.

"OK, I guess. I mean, I've tried on guilt. I've mourned—but not too long. I still feel like a failure."

"I can understand that."

"I feel out of sorts at the office, in a way I never did before. I get these flashes that being Ms. Professional with the great career is somehow, well . . . shallow."

"You should feel proud of what you've accomplished."

"I manage to fall just short in every single thing I do. Never got that Ph. D. Never had those four kids. Never had that perfect marriage. Then there's work. It all seems incredibly banal these days. Some export license. Some earmarked appropriation. Big frickin' deal."

"So what interests you most?"

"Besides parenting? Well . . . I'm embarrassed to say."

"What?"

"China. I still read everything I can get my hands on about it. One point three billion people, and we really don't have a clue how they think. Why is it so hard for us to understand them?"

"China. Goddamn China again. Why?"

She thought for a minute, gazing at the fields of corn, rising strong now after the recent rain. "Because it's so elusive, yet so alluring. Maybe I just like the pursuit—trying to solve the riddle."

"Makes sense."

"Hey, that's what my marriage was about, chasing the inaccessible. I mean, here we are, working on China more than twenty-five years. Studying it. Getting rich off it. Writing about it. Working for it. Spying on it. Building careers around it. But you know what? I think the joke's on us. China has changed us more than we've affected China."

"Whoa, you been drinking a lot of coffee?"

"Like three cups." She tapped the gas up another five miles per hour. "Watch out for me today, boy. You've been warned."

Then she continued. "I blew it somewhere. I had that perfect family feeling in Wyoming. I had it again with you guys at college—that same bond of belonging, as if we'd always find a way to cover for each other."

"Why'd you ever leave Wyoming in the first place?"

"Oh, Alexander, I was just a kid from the sticks who wanted to see the world. My first boyfriend was a wrangler, for crissake. Rode bulls at the Cody Rodeo. I wanted something bigger. I thought a guy like Barry would take me places. I probably used him, too. I just figured if the intimate stuff was awkward, it must have been my fault, that maybe I was too much of a tomboy or something."

"You're anything but. So stop beating yourself up over it already."

"You've dealt with losing Anita so remarkably well. How did you manage?"

"It's taken some time."

The silence hung between them as white rail fences flew by, cows gazing impassively. In the distance, the line of the Blue Ridge was just breaking the horizon to the west. It was several minutes before he continued.

"When Anita was first diagnosed, we went to Hawaii. We'd just sit on the beach and look at the stars. We didn't have a lot of money and we didn't have a lot of time. So we blew a wad staying at the Mauna Kea; it's a beautiful old hotel on the dry side of the Big Island. When she was healthier, we'd always done national parks—wilderness places like Glacier and Zion—and did some amateur geology stuff."

Alexander was looking off in the distance again, pausing to gather strength. "In Hawaii, we'd catch every dawn and sunset. Anita said it centered her. Made her appreciate the cyclical nature of life and death—the basics. She just turned to me one day and made me promise not to mourn too long. She dug out that old poem we'd use for our toasts—that British utopian Spender: 'Never forget those who wore their hearts at the fire's center . . .'"

"I remember . . . 'Born of the sun, they traveled a short while towards the sun.'"

"It was brutal, Rachel. We were both angry with the gods. But she said that after she died, I had to live fully, that her horrid disease wouldn't win if I defied it. She made me promise.

"I did a pretty lousy job of it at first. I was bitter. I missed having Anita to talk with, to laugh with about something stupid that happened that day. It made me crazy! I actually forgot about twenty times a day that she was gone. The agony of it would surface all over when I confronted the fact again.

"About six months after she died, I tried my first solo vacation, hiking in the Sierra desert."

"Didn't you go to Death Valley—of all places?"

"Yeah," he laughed, "Bizarre place to pick. I was staying in the Furnace Creek Inn. It was about a hundred and ten degrees each day. I'd sleep in the afternoon, and start with the beers at dusk. I stayed sober one night and hiked out to the sand dunes for a sunrise. It was unbelievably cold. The desert got down to about forty at night, even in July. But there was this remarkable glow coming over the hills. It was as if I was present at the dawn of creation. There were all these layers of geology exposed around me—an incredible, ancient, dried-up inland seabed. I was sitting on this enormous pile of sand, sobbing, when I remembered my promise to Anita, that the only way I could triumph over the forces of despair was to revere life, to live fully."

She reached over and gripped his shoulder. "You're doing pretty damn good, Alexander."

His tension was drained. When they arrived in Upperville at Rachel's aunt's place, he was refreshed by the distance they had covered. They rode horses—fast—through the woods on western saddles. They dove in the pool, Alexander feeling a bit sheepish as he checked out Rachel in her red bikini. They talked about local history and theatre with Rachel's aunt, who seemed nonplussed to have Alexander there. When it came time to leave, Alexander wished they did not have to return so quickly to the battles of the big city.

It was nearly sunset as they crossed the Beltway and headed the last few miles back into D.C.. A dread began to creep over him, a familiar Sunday evening anxiety, like the night before a big school exam. But Rachel was next to him, driving, talking, gesturing like an Italian cabbie. She would squeeze his hand to emphasize a point. Somewhere along the last few blocks, she didn't let go. When she pulled up and parked in front of his townhouse, his hand was firmly in her grip.

As they walked into the darkened entryway, Alexander went first to the living room. Out the bay window to the west was the glowing dome of the Capitol, the sun gone just beyond. As he turned, tentative in the room's grayness, there was Rachel. He reached out to her, placing his hands on her face. She looked at him brightly, greeting him. Then he kissed her, eyes open, grinning expectantly after all those years.

They moved in an unhurried dance, kissing eagerly, repeatedly, as their clothes began to peel away. They swam in their kisses, moving through the same restorative sea, washing, drinking, refreshing. Alexander's lips explored behind her neck, down the small of her back. He was strong and hungry, seeking her out with determination. Together, they reached and they sank in their lovemaking, creating a new rhythm, touching secret places, sharing simple pleasures. At some point, they settled together into Alexander's bed and fell into a deep sleep. Alexander snored. Then Rachel was whispering to him in the heart of the night, awakening him with her lips, urging him onward as they played once more.

Rachel dreamt rich dreams, filled with memories of the mountains, of hiking with the guys. Shortly before dawn, she awoke and began to pace the apartment in a rumpled button-down shirt of his. She ate an apple, then returned and began massaging his feet as she sat at the edge of the bed awaiting the sunrise.

The thump of the morning paper on the porch startled her. She headed down the stairs on tip-toe, modestly reaching an arm out the front door to collect the news. Alexander was awake when she returned to the bedroom.

"You look like a drunken sailor, kiddo," she said, greeting him with a kiss as she dropped the newspaper in his lap. "Special delivery."

"Cute paper boy."

"I'm a girl."

"I noticed," he said, craning his neck just a bit to peek through a buttonhole she had missed.

"What the hell is that?" she asked, pointing to his paper: a plain manila envelope had slipped out of the *Post*'s front section.

Alexander sat up, looking confused. He tore the envelope open. Inside was a sheaf of eight-by-ten photographs and three typewritten pages.

"What the hell is this?" Alexander whispered as he squinted at the documents, like an orthopedist evaluating an x-ray. He regarded the photos from several different angles, then began to study the written analysis.

"These are satellite photos." He looked up sharply before he was done. "Some Chinese missile base."

"And who, exactly, delivers your newspaper?"

"Well, I was going to ask you."

"Me? I'm just the paper girl. Hey—wait a minute." She was glaring as she stood over him. "What the hell are you implying?"

"I'm not implying anything. It's just, I don't know. Damn it. I'm getting a little paranoid here. I wonder if I'm getting set up all over again."

She looked at him sternly. "You actually think I'm part of the problem? Because if you—"

"No, Rachel. I didn't mean it like that. It's just . . . somebody is doing a number on me."

"Do you think your apartment is miked? Maybe they even have cameras." She eyed him warily, then leaned over to whisper. "I'd say we gave them some pretty hot stuff last night."

"These are satellite photos and intelligence analysis of that Chinese missile base in Fujian Province—the one the State Department denies the Chinese are building up. These pictures prove they're lying."

"Who in God's name gave them to you?"

"Probably somebody who wants to screw up the summit. I mean, it could be anybody from right-wingers in D.C. to some faction in Beijing that hopes to mess up ties with Washington."

"Hey, wait a minute. Aren't satellite photos rather *passé* these days? Can't some commercial outfits also shoot this kind of stuff?"

"I don't think commercial satellites can take such high-resolution stuff. These seem like the real McCoy: much more detail. Plus, they've been so kind as to give me some intelligence analyst's conclusions. It's Fujian."

"Somebody just dumps this stuff on your doorstep on Sunday mornings?"

"It's Monday, my dear."

"They probably saw me half naked picking it up. Now *that* will be interesting to explain. The summit gets screwed up, my clients get screwed—and I'm walking around using some reporter's shirt for a nightgown."

"Which clients are getting screwed?"

"Like Telstar, for starters."

"Sweetheart," said Alexander, laughing now, "you've got to savor the irony. All these pictures were probably taken with a Telstar system."

18

THE MANDARIN CLUB

They had been leaning against an enormous oak, fallen at the edge of the field, dry California brown grass thigh high before them. It was somewhere off the Bear Valley trail, halfway between the riding stables at the Point Reyes ranger station and their seaside destination of Arch Rock.

It was the long Veteran's Day weekend of 1978, and the air was surprisingly mild beneath the morning cloak of fog. The group had seen no one else since dawn. There was a deep silence all about them, broken only by the profusion of birds calling from within the forest canopy bordering the meadow.

They were in a clearing that Mickey, their designated scoutmaster, called Divine Meadow. It was right around midday, the warm overcast now frosted by a penetrating sun. Branko and Lee were walking ahead with their backpacks, the two in the lead disappearing into the fog that obscured the foot of the rise.

There was no time in this place, in this memory. Late fall, and utterly still, as if the land were on tenterhooks, waiting in the sunlight for some subterranean motion. "Earthquake weather," Mickey said the locals called it—a season when the tectonic plates were poised to shift.

"There is this African tribe, the Fantin or something," Alexander said very slowly. He was pulling the cork of a Chardonnay bottle that had spent the first night of their camping trip chilling in a creek near their tents. "They offer their guests palm wine that they tap from tree trunks."

"They sip it out of calabash gourds," Alexander continued. "But first they pour it on the ground and chant 'Come! Drink with us.' It's for their ancestors."

Alexander splashed a bit too much wine on the powdery sienna soil, staring down to watch it clump like pancake mix in the dust.

"Hey! Easy with that, man," Mickey warned as he reached over with a metal cup. "Navajos did the same thing with peyote, I think. Like a peace

178

pipe."

"You're making things up again," Alexander said, but he didn't mind. That was Mickey.

They walked on, through shaded glens. A lower layer of fern was covered by a towering forest of cypress and laurel, sequoia and eucalyptus. Rounding bends as they rolled down toward the sea, they followed a trail that opened to small clearings, where deer and rabbits would scatter at their first footfall. Hawks and seagulls angled overhead. Sounds of smaller birds drifted out from deeper in the wood, where the darkness was thicker and more forbidding.

At the end of the trail, where it opened above an amphitheater of cliffs arcing about the sea, they sat on the bluff. Hundreds of feet below was a deserted beach, the waves slamming against stacks stretching nearly a mile out into the open waters. A thick bank of fog rested far out to sea.

Closer to shore, white ocean caps splashed between the marine layer and the beach. They could see all the way up the coastline to Drake's Beach and the Pt. Reyes Lighthouse, ten miles to their west. The parkland was like an island. It was far removed from the noisy Marin County suburbs and the San Andreas Fault, which cut the land like a knife, north to south.

They had stumbled into a meandering debate about freedom, Rachel recalled, about the Vietnam War.

"What was so ignoble about helping a people fight annihilation?" Mickey said. He paced in a circle as he spoke, pontificating like some old time preacher. "Just because we lost? Look what happened to the guys we left in Saigon. Years in re-education camps. A million boat people. What was so fucking immoral about trying to help them save their country?"

"Mickey, we destroyed the country trying to save it. Remember?" Alexander continued the philosophical dispute which had raged for several years between them. Alexander was prone, Huckleberry Finn-like, a tube of straw grass in his teeth. "The Pentagon thought we could ship our tidy Eisenhower values overseas and drill them into anybody we wanted."

"We were the last hope of Saigon's freedom-loving people."

"We were foreigners, trying to impose our rules on an ancient people, a people in a civil war—with a lot more at stake than we had."

"History will prove us right. You'll see. All you bleeding heart liberals will eat your words. You ridiculed the domino theory and now, watch them fall. Vietnam, Cambodia, and Laos are already gone. Taiwan and Hong Kong will be next. Then Singapore. The Communists will take them all over in time." Mickey hurled a stone far over the cliff, its descent too steep for the eye to follow. "We shoulda stayed and won."

Alexander started to pursue the argument, then waved him off. His knees were bent high and he was lying back in the sun, his backpack a perfect pillow on the headlands. He had discarded his straw and begun to munch on a red apple.

It was Lee, propped on one elbow, who took the bait. "You should hear yourselves," he said.

"What?" Mickey said.

"Alexander's right," Lee insisted. "You Americans think you have life all figured out. You can be so very arrogant, for no good reason."

"No good reason?" Mickey was hefting another chalky stone as he stood near Lee.

"You are such a childish country," said Lee. "So very young, so self-absorbed. Your generals thought you could just beat people into submission. You had no sense of their culture or history, of what came before, of what would remain after you left."

Booth regarded them intently before joining in. "And you know what?" he said. "We'll make the exact same mistake when we finally get into China. Roaring in with all our salesmen panting after markets. Thinking we can remake their civilization if only every family buys a TV. A generation later, we'll limp out, wondering why nobody likes us."

"Asians hate individualists," Lee said. "They threaten our whole belief system, that the common good is to be exalted above all else."

"Makes for fewer identity crises," Booth said.

Lee stood, intent upon his point as he gazed at the thrashing sea below. "You always forget," he concluded. "We are not like you."

They soon made their way down a slippery wash to the beach, then settled again in a semi-circle on the sand, where they ate a snack of bread and jam. Their backpacks and gear were piled against the base of the cliff. Gargantuan tree trunks and whips of kelp were scattered at the shoreline.

The fog bank and the sea had achieved a tentative balance. The wind kicking about them began to calm.

They were quite alone, except for the distant barking of sea lions mounting the offshore stacks. The guys stripped to their boxers and T-shirts before they resumed their debate.

The subject was the Sixties this time, Mickey again leading the provocation. "Such a goddamn waste. All that potential for change, and the only legacy is bell bottoms and this new electronic disco crap."

"Better pot, too," Alexander added.

"The pill," Barry offered.

"An uplifting of the humanities," Booth said.

"Not for long," Alexander countered. "I hear the Stanford Biz School's applications are soaring. Everybody wants to get back to MBAs and law degrees and making money. The revolution's over, folks."

"Yeah," Barry agreed. "From free love to easy money."

"We get to trade the Beatles for the Bee Gees," said Alexander.

"Actually, I agree with Mickey." It was Branko this time. "The Sixties were shallow. There was something otherworldly about the obsession with higher consciousness. No realism about getting things done in the here and now."

"Yeah," said Mickey, "the *real* Cultural Revolution was in China, right, Lee? What'd they say in '58? 'Let a hundred flowers bloom.' Well, it was a set-up. They encouraged the nonconformists to stick their heads up so the authorities could mow 'em all down." Mickey was sorry he'd said it. But that was Mickey, speaking before thinking.

Lee sat up, his soft eyes squinting into the glare. "You have no clue how destructive our Cultural Revolution was. It is just some story in the textbooks for you. Some historical anecdote. We tortured ourselves, just because Mao wanted to shake things up. All that horror, then we try to pretend it never happened. Back to business as usual."

"Business as usual?" Alexander asked.

But Lee didn't hear, it seemed. "Do you know how dangerous that is? When a government comes after the creative minds, the most brilliant professors, the artists, even the university students? And then murders them? Do you know how dangerous that memory is, of a government that could do that? It breeds dissent among the young."

"You are a fucking subversive, Lee." It was Branko who saw it first, though none disputed the conclusion. "You're going to get yourself shot someday."

Rachel found that the natural power of place made her want to flee all the argumentation. She walked alone to the north, the coarse sand scouring her feet, harsh yet stimulating. Her sense of scale was thrown a-kilter on this wild peninsula, cleaved from the land like some iceberg. The driftwood, the off-shore stacks, the reaching surf—all appeared supernaturally large. Even the cliffs seemed impossibly high, like some beanstalk disappearing into the sky.

She closed her eyes and imagined Francis Drake, keelhauling his boat on this beach as he prepared to cross the Pacific for Asia, then home to England. She could envision thousands of pounds in Spanish gold ingots stacked among sails and ropes, all the detritus of a year at sea. She imagined the faces of Miwok Indians, their teeth brown from acorn mush, peering anxiously from the brush at the hairy white men.

She lay down in her own cove now, sheltered by a beached whale of a tree. The trunk was white, its bark carved away by exposure. She felt some odd sense of closure in this seaside pilgrimage, as if the countless ocean dreams of her Wyoming youth were somehow fulfilled as she sat by the water. She recalled the T.S. Eliot poem: she'd arrived here at this tide-line, back at some beginning, and knew the place for the first time.

She thought of the guys dozing in the sun down the beach. The previous night, she and Barry had made love silently in their tent, set just away from the rest. But she still felt a yearning, a wildness, as if she wanted to holler into the wind. She slid out of her shorts and shirt, reaching back to unclasp her bra. Her nipples were erect in the moist air, and she stood, unobserved, toeing the sand, her mind flooding with images. She jogged the first few steps, then ran the last yards, issuing a primal shout as she plunged into the water, stumbling, then crashing hip-and-shoulder-first into the surf.

The shock of the frigid Pacific was beyond invigorating. She ran back across the sand, shivering uncontrollably. She could hear a distant cheer go up from the boys. Then they were stripping and streaking down toward the water, their calls echoing eerily off the cliffs. The boys thrashed naked in the waves for the few seconds they could endure the chill current.

Rachel dressed quickly, using her T-shirt as a towel, and then strode back toward the rest. They were assembling their gear when she came upon them.

"You missed the shooters we drank!" Mickey said.

"Didn't need one."

"Think you're better than us?" Barry asked.

"We insist!" Mickey said, pulling out a flask of Southern Comfort. He poured a shot into the oversized cap and thrust it towards Rachel. His hair was swept long and mangy about his face, spilling out of a red kerchief. In his maroon shirt and jeans, standing tall with bare feet, Mickey looked like a celebrating pirate.

Rachel took the whiskey as the boys paused in their re-packing.

"Right." She nodded, confident now, looking about to catch their eyes, acknowledging each in turn. "Live fully. Seek the sun. Never forget."

"To The Mandarin Club!" They all said it together.

It was a grainy picture, formed in her memory, that remained with Rachel still. The smells of the glen. The moment of perfect equilibrium between sun and fog. The purgative plunge into the sea. The grinning guys gathered about, playing the Merry Men as they watched her drink. She tossed the shot back smoothly, its searing after-burn punctuating that time of perfect escape. ☀

JUNE

19

INSIDE THE WAR ROOM

The winds that whip south over the Gobi desert each spring breach the Great Wall just north of Beijing, coating the capital with a yellow film. The Mongolian dust cloud can beat for days, the stinging air driving the elderly and infirm indoors. Schoolchildren wear masks. Exposed surfaces are left with a crunchy layer of dirt.

The nagging breeze had lingered for weeks this season, making Lee's Saturday afternoon drive more unpleasant. He had always detested traffic, and rarely drove to work. He was very much a city boy—Beijing born and raised—and preferred walking, or riding a bike, to sitting in his confining Honda. The bachelor apartment where he had moved eight years ago was close enough to the Foreign Ministry that he could usually get there in less than twenty minutes on foot. To avoid the traffic, he often took the subway to the Chao Yang Men Station next to the ministry. So he used the car mostly on weekends, as he had that day to join his father for supper at his retirement compound far out in the suburbs.

Lee had been cranky all that first week of June, feeling harassed and surrounded at work. The sharp escalation in tensions with the Americans had pinned him to his desk into Saturday afternoon. Now he lit a cigarette, cursing the fact that when the Chinese provoked trouble, they rarely had in hand a consensus plan for settling it. *An old revolutionary mentality*, he reflected: *weak on the end game.*

There was an urgency to Lee's visits now as death approached. He was going every weekend to take supper together with his father and his pleasant nurse, Xu An. The old Army engineer had been a tall man. But age, and the advance of Parkinson's disease, had shriveled him, shortening his stride to a shuffle. Ironically, with the progression of the infirmity, his moodiness had lifted. A severe man in his youth, the senior Lee was more amiable in his old age. Lee was humbled by how his father gracefully accepted his fate, chuckling when he dropped the backgammon dice, smiling appreciatively when Xu An or Lee helped him into his shoes.

Lee came to collaborate in an easy domestic partnership with Xu An. His father, now in a new way, was his one true hero. With each week's visit, the old man slipped further behind the clouds of dementia. Already, Lee began to miss him and his matter-of-fact questions, the old aphorisms about duty to country.

Lee brought fresh flowers and fruit from the market when he arrived that Saturday, wearing a clean shirt and toting an overnight bag. Xu An received the flowers wordlessly in the small kitchen, arranging them in a vase before placing the fruit on the sideboard. The one bedroom apartment was tidy, order everywhere. Lee noticed again the subtle changes from another week with Xu An, a young widow who lived nearby with her mother and aunt. Now she guided the weekly reunion of father and son.

As they spoke of the weather, Lee watched her gently feed his father. Lee regarded her hands carefully as she tended to the elderly man, still quite proper as she went about her tasks. But her movements seemed softer at this hour. He saw how the evening light captured the glint of her eyes and her flowing movements as she straightened his father's hair. She was enjoying the adult company at week's end.

They lingered over the meal, long after Lee had come to relieve Xu An for twenty-four hours and to pay her. As the light began to die, two candles on the table illuminated a warm spring evening, the window open now that the dust clouds had abated with the sunset. Lee relished their conversation; he was eager for the human contact and acutely aware of their peculiar triangle. When Xu An at last said she would prepare his father for bed, Lee stacked the dishes, then settled into the chair in the sitting room by the window, enjoying a cigarette, gazing out at nearby apartment towers.

They were the parents, it seemed. Li, the elder, had become the infant. In his father's waning hours, the son was the master of this tiny home. Xu An played daughter-in-law cum matriarch. *Was life merely a string of character plays?* Lee remembered voicing the same thought when he and Mickey had sat, overlooking the ocean, more than two decades ago.

Mickey had agreed, rejecting Catholic theology for the omniscience of the Greek myths. *Surely the human dramas amused the gods.*

"I will make you a bed now," Xu An said, leaning slightly against the door frame, a blanket and pillows in her hands. "Come, you look weary."

Lee began to protest. She shushed him and smoothed the sofa as he sat back and finished his cigarette. She tucked in a single sheet, then folded back a wool coverlet, hands moving swiftly to fluff two pillows and finish with a professional pat. Then she turned to him to say good night.

She saw. All those years of spy-craft Lee had practiced, the burying of self, the stone-faced denials, were undermined. Xu An saw the truth of this moment, the repressed desire, the exhaustion and fear, the yearning to share the genuine presence of a fellow human being.

She crossed the room and licked her thumb and forefinger. She pinched the two candle wicks and became a silhouette. A single shaft of city light gave an outline to her face as she came toward his seat in silence. She began to massage his neck with both hands, pulling him closer to her chest with each stroke, until he closed his eyes and buried his face in her breasts. She drew him in, working her way down his back, then up to his temples, rhythmically soothing his scalp with strong fingers.

After a few minutes, she stepped back, opening her blouse buttons one by one. She sat in a simple cotton slip on the sofa, patting the pillows again. She took off his shoes as he sat next to her. Then she lay back and welcomed him, enveloping his body in sweet safety as they held each other.

Xu An departed some time during the night. Lee had slept soundly after they made love and was not aware she had left. But she returned promptly at six the next evening.

Again they had supper. Lee was more conversational this time, almost clumsy as he affected some false bravado, playing the gregarious host. He began to confide in her, desperate to prolong the hours.

This night, it was Lee who lingered close to the dawn as they confirmed their new ritual. Xu An made up the sofa again and extinguished the candles. Lee awaited her eagerly and they made love with great energy while his father's snores could be heard through the bedroom wall. They spoke in whispers deep into the night until, finally, Xu An slept and Lee crept out. He was confused—confused and uplifted as he made his way down the stairwell to begin the long Monday morning march through Beijing traffic.

The dawn arrived gray and ugly, an eclipse-like gloom in the sky long after daybreak. The traffic backed up on the capital's second ring road, moving at an airport-counter crawl. Lee rode the brakes in the fast lane, stop and go at seven a.m. The closer he got to the office, the more the oasis of the weekend dissipated.

His arrival at the Ministry found his staff none the better. Lee sat at his desk, poring through his morning intelligence summary, attempting to calm himself with the deferred gratification of his second Camel of the day as he contemplated his next move. Things were going way too fast.

He had to hand it to the guys in the intelligence bureau of the PLA. They rarely showed their face at the Foreign Ministry, virtually boycotting the tense quarrels that plagued interdepartmental meetings. But the fear of their mounting power existed among the moderates in the inner councils. Increasingly, Lee and his colleagues recognized that the hard-liners were gaining the upper hand.

Once again, they were pounding Taiwan in the psychological-warfare department. They had grown quite adept at this lately. Indeed, there was a government-wide commitment in Beijing to "fighting local wars under high tech conditions." That was the new mantra, the doctrine of the day. Jamming radar of surveillance aircraft. Hacking into Taiwan's military computer network. Sprinkling false data throughout the region. Playing their own masterful brand of dirty tricks.

As Lee observed the flowering of these new techniques, he developed his own doubts about the veracity of Alexander Bonner's sensational "Taiwan-is-going-nuclear" story. He saw threads in the peculiar tale that led him to question its sources. *The Bad Boys over at the PLA? If this latest ruse was entirely a Second Directorate operation, it had yielded one killer disinformation campaign.*

The intelligence bureau's "active measures" made the Foreign Ministry team very nervous—a bit of not-invented-here jealousy combined with the diplomats' innate caution and preference for the status quo. Lee's worst suspicions were confirmed that Monday noon when he met his Defense Ministry counterpart Chen for a quick lunchtime prep session before their bosses convened in the war room. Lee had to fence and probe before Chen finally acknowledged the ruse: the Taiwan nuclear flirtation story was an intelligence set-up, a brilliant gambit with only a few kernels of truth. Score one for the PLA provocateurs.

Remarkably, Chen's own access to his colleagues' doings was quite limited. Over at the Second Directorate—he conceded to Lee—they had developed a rogue group within a rogue group. They ran their operations on a level that somehow floated above the factionalism that divided recent internal debates in China. Chen had only ferreted out their role in the latest ploy through an inadvertent slip-up from a colleague in the gym.

PLA operatives had planted the krytron story—sure to throw Taiwan on the defensive—then sat back, ready to pounce when the international press inevitably rose to the bait. The story had ensured maximum media coverage—and provided justification for a firm Chinese response.

Now the American officials were on the defensive—right where the Chinese wanted them on the eve of the summit. The tit-for-tat diplomatic escalation that ensued was swifter than Beijing had anticipated, though. China's recall of its ambassador had Washington stumbling. The White House was already pressing for yet another kiss-and-make-up mission to Beijing.

"There is a limit to how much you can manipulate the Americans," Lee warned Chen as they walked off their lunch.

"They're not like the Russians, though," Chen dismissed him. "The Americans try so hard not to lose their tempers. Bad for business."

Lee regarded him coldly, lighting a cigarette. "We are playing a dangerous game."

"Yes. But it is a rough world we live in."

"So what is the plan if the Americans cancel the summit?"

"We're still in good shape," Chen said.

"Good shape for the Party Congress?" Lee pressed. "Nice way to frame things, to be butting heads with the American superpower. Have our relations go to shit and watch trade cutbacks slow down our economy. We'll set back the whole modernization effort."

"America is not the only superpower."

"Right. In another thirty years, our economy will catch theirs. In the meantime, is the People's Liberation Army going to march across the Pacific and take Los Angeles? Or maybe have a new Cold War alliance with Moscow?"

Chen glared back. "You Foreign Ministry boys are out of touch—behind the times."

"Why must you mistake reason for weakness?" Lee countered as he gazed at the civil servants on parade. "Where will this game end?"

"End? What do you mean? The krytron business?"

"Beyond that. America and China?"

"When?" Chen asked, regarding him skeptically. "In one hundred years? Two hundred years?"

"I mean sooner. In our lifetimes. We have two global powers with nuclear weapons and a lot of military hardware buzzing each other. Is it inevitable the two systems will collide?"

"Of course. America is corrupt, immature, never satisfied," Chen said. "Americans always wants more. To push others around. To bend us to their will. Well, the Chinese will never submit. We are a great country. Ours is a superior civilization."

"So, you really believe that confrontation is unavoidable? That reclaiming Taiwan is the only way China can get respect?" Lee asked, pulling furiously on his cigarette between questions. "You believe that is the fate of your children, and your children's children?"

"You don't get it, my friend," Chen replied. "We may never even have to attack Taiwan with conventional arms. The Chinese on Taiwan worship money. They have sunk so much capital into the Mainland that they will make Taipei's politicians bow before us. They have sold their own independence dream just to keep their production costs low. Typical of the capitalists!"

"Who in China really gives a damn about Taiwan, except the old generals and weak politicians?" Lee asked as they began to walk more briskly, throwing out his heresy as a simple aside.

"Come again?"

"Some of my friends say we should get real about this obsession with Taiwan. For centuries, the place was mostly aborigines and smugglers. After the Japanese occupied it in 1895, the Mainland never really controlled Taiwan. And the people's government, the PRC, never did. Never. The Taiwanese are like a different tribe. We are more than one billion people. They live on a tiny polluted island of less than twenty-five million. Why don't we just ignore them?"

"I am sure you have corrected your friends' thinking," Chen said.

"Yes, I am very reliable when it comes to reminding them of the Party line," Lee snapped.

"You like to live dangerously, don't you? You like having dangerous friends." Chen was shaking his head. "You know what the guys at Defense call your office?"

"Sure."

"The Traitor's Ministry."

"We know."

"If it weren't for your father," Chen warned, "they might lift your Party membership for such thinking."

"Maybe they'll have to send us all to the countryside for re-education."

"What is your problem, Lee?" Chen was seething now. "Do you *want* to see us fail? Do you think China is some second-rate civilization? That five thousand years of superior culture should bow before the American dollar?"

"What kind of victory is it to swerve from confrontation to confrontation? To squander billions on buying weapons? We've got millions of unemployed people crowding into the cities because our corrupt Party bosses are closing industries and cutting deals with foreign investors. We've got tens of millions of men without brides, and no hope of a family, because the Party's one child policy has produced lots of dead baby girls. Couldn't we just meet the people's needs first?"

"So you want the Defense Ministry importing brides? You are abandoning your senses, Lee."

"No, I am just tired of these pathetic little military diversions. I see them for what they are."

"Maybe you need a long vacation."

"You know, the device is so transparent. Like when the American president who couldn't keep his pants on kept bombing Iraq whenever he feared impeachment. It's an old trick, not worthy of the Chinese."

"Lee, you are hopelessly bourgeois. The decadence of the West will lead ultimately to their ruin."

"It is not about ideology."

"No, it is about cultural supremacy," Chen said. "America will fall like the Roman Empire someday, in an ocean of debt, one big Disneyland in ruins, infested with stray cats like the Colosseum."

They had pulled up by a small fence encircling a duck pond. There was a squawking at the center as two females fought over a tidbit. Chen and Lee waited to see who would strike the last blow. They watched the ducks' tussle as first one bird, then the other seemed to get the better of it. The morsel frayed and fell back into the water, where the ducks snatched at the remains.

As they observed the thrashing ducks, Chen spoke somberly. "I need to remind you that individuals serve the people. We're all expendable."

"What are you trying to say?" Lee asked, working hard to read his face.

Chen would not give him his eyes. "You are at risk," he said after a time, muttering it softly, as if offered in apology.

Lee sighed, gazing into the distance. "Yes. Thank you, old friend. Actually, I have been at risk since the day I first went off to America. I was always suspect of having been contaminated by Western thought."

"Don't be a fool!" Chen pleaded. "You mustn't grow comfortable with your peril. You will fly too close to the flame, like Icarus in the Greek myths. Your wings will not hold."

"I love my country as much as the next man. Maybe more. The zealots have no monopoly on patriotism."

"I know that. *They* don't."

"They? Who? The wild boys in the PLA who want to spark a fire?"

"Comrade Lee, I've always admired your father. You have his guts, too. But you have become reckless, full of false bravado. There are some who will try to make an example of you."

"I won't let them silence voices of reason just because we—"

"Choose your own path. I'll say no more. But you'd better do so without illusion. Actions have consequences." Then Chen turned away a last time.

The two men walked slowly back to work, a silence fallen between them. Over the course of the tense afternoon, they would eye each other warily as they sat reviewing the plans for the upcoming Taiwan maneuvers. Their tense lunchtime conversation lingered within, burning like the aftertaste of a bitter stew.

20

SIN AND REDEMPTION

Mickey Dooley would make a great spy. His capacity for compartmentalizing his affairs had long ago convinced him of the proposition.

As the years went by, he grew ever vigilant in his deceits. His skill at dissembling enabled a whole series of contradictions to co-exist. Where the occasional rough edge protruded, there was always Scotch and his gift for blarney to smooth things over.

With Telstar, Mickey was the omnicompetent wheeler-dealer, the go-to guy for all things Chinese. His Beijing customers liked him, too. His confident attitude, combined with his father-in-law's connections, ensured reliability. At home with his children, Mickey was the model dad. Fatherhood provided a sound anchor in a life otherwise adrift. Toward Mei Mei, he was unfailingly correct, yet always cautious. She had become the enemy and he labored to dodge her frequent rages.

The secrets of his complicated life would be mercilessly laid bare by the lie detector. The polygraph was a Langley pre-condition to his assignment. Mickey knew it that June morning as he sat, focused and sober, in a holding room in Langley. He felt like a guy who'd messed up the interview at St. Peter's Gate, then been referred Down Below for a follow-up interrogation.

The room was small and windowless, on the third floor of the main building on the CIA campus. The Agency personnel were curt, exuding all the warmth of harried medical lab technicians. There was no immediate sign of Branko, though it was unclear who lurked behind the smoked glass in the fluttering room. The hardware experts resembled the IT guys at Telstar, earnest young men with pocket pens and beepers, more interested in machines than people. Nobody seemed to engage Mickey as they tinkered with the wires and the dials that would measure his veracity.

He grew anxious, though he knew it was his heart, not his brain, they were testing. He had only to tell the truth to pass; they knew most of the bad stuff already.

The pre-examination began innocently enough, with a lot of legal waivers to execute. At an elementary school desk, the kind with the right-handed arm rest used when you get stuck with a needle at the doctor's office, he sat and signed away his rights.

"I'm not giving blood, am I?" Mickey said.

"Depends," the technician dead-panned as he tightened a velcro wrap onto Mickey's right bicep. Then they signaled to him that they were ready to begin, to explore his various transgressions against God and country.

As they moved along, he found it oddly liberating, this business of telling only the truth. The farther they went, and the more tired he grew, the easier it became to unburden himself, to let go and watch all those balls he had juggled for so long come crashing down.

Some of the questions were uncomplicated. *Drug habits?* No, actually. Like most of the guys from college days, he had given up pot for whiskey shortly after leaving campus—the quest for respectability in vices outweighed possible liver damage.

Tax fraud? Clean there, too. He'd always been careful with his book-keeping, not wanting to jeopardize his perks and his company-subsidized travel. Besides, he always told himself, his taxes paid veterans benefits, and his dad had earned every nickel of his pension the hard way.

Marital infidelity? That one required substantial detail, taxing his memory. His story was straightforward; there had been no blackmail attempts or foreign agents involved, at least any he was aware of, though he sometimes wondered about his dear Jin in Hong Kong, and was relieved to have finally had the guts to end it with her.

Mickey's relations with foreign intelligence services were also of interest. Yes, he ran errands for the Defense Ministry guys in Beijing, Telstar's best customers. Yes, he knew some of his contacts were in the espionage business. In fact, he assumed most everybody he dealt with was, in one fashion or another—it made things easier for him. To Mickey, it had all just been business—favor-banking to bring in more Telstar sales.

No, he had not trafficked in classified documents with intelligence sources. Yes, he had helped run some disinformation games on Taiwan, though often unwittingly. He told how he had greased some side sales for his Beijing pals on stuff like krytron buys and electronic countermeasures sales, the significance of which he never fully understood. He had learned not to ask too many questions.

They spent almost an hour on his relations with his now retired father-in-law, and then, on Lee. He tried to help them as much as he could, willingly speculating on connections and subplots. He stumbled to explain who had orchestrated the planting of the krytron deal story with its Taipei nuclear angle—a story it took him some time to figure out himself. He gave up everything he had on his smuggler buddy Rashid with an ease he thought would make him uncomfortable. It didn't.

In the end, he found a way to get back to basics, even when the confessional was not called for by the question at hand.

Yes, he freely entered into his new commitment with the Agency. He loved his boys. He loved his country. He repeated the pledges he had made to Branko at the ballpark. By now, he sensed his friend was certainly behind the one-way mirror. No more drinking. No more foreign sales. Success or failure, no mention ever to anyone about the mission. *I can do this*, he thought.

When they finally unstrapped him, it felt like being unwrapped from a dive suit. He could breathe freely once more. He flexed his arm and smiled up weakly at Branko, who joined him, appearing very much the parent come to collect his charge from Day Care.

They walked in silence down the hallway, then up an elevator to the top floor. Mickey followed Branko down a short corridor until they entered another stuffy room, this one lit by a skylight and recessed track lighting. At its center, a small table was set for lunch.

"So . . . ?" Mickey asked.

"So?"

"So, how'd I do? Like, did I pass?"

"Did you pass? Sure," Branko said, "you did fine. Answered all their questions, for today. No lies. Even gave us some stuff on the krytron business that confirmed some of our suspicions."

"So, we're on? The mission, I mean?"

"Yes, we've been granted authority to proceed. For now."

"I thought you had the last word on that."

"I'm in charge of Asia analysis for the intelligence community. I don't run agents. That's Operations."

"Does that mean we need some kind of congressional finding? Those damn Hill committees leak like a sieve."

"Relax, Mickey. We've made this a special case, and there's ample precedent. I got a waiver to be directly involved in this one since it is not exactly standard operating procedure."

"It's not going to get out that, that—"

"You've had a long morning. Eat some lunch."

Mickey found he was famished—and the food surprisingly good. As they ate, Branko began a methodical exposition, walking him through the mission, the contact methods, and the fallbacks. He was clear on the decision points, both for the boys and for Lee. Branko was brutally direct on the consequences of failure. The more explicit he was on the assignment—to get to Lee and convince him to defect—the more anxious Mickey became about the details.

"What's the evidence there's an imminent threat to the summit?" Mickey pressed.

"Some conversations we've been picking up. People over there talking as if they assume it will be cancelled. Or end in some fiasco."

"Like what?"

"Unclear."

"Wouldn't an incident make it harder to get Lee out later?"

"Of course it would." Branko was reluctant to indulge him, pausing to choose his words carefully. "But that is a choice we cannot make for him."

"But where is the threat coming from?"

"I can't say."

"Can't say? Or don't know?"

"Mickey . . ." Branko was shaking his head now, "we really don't know."

"What? You're the fucking CIA, Branko. I thought you guys had a solid read on this kind of stuff."

"The truth is, there are lots of things we don't know. Sometimes, the best we can do—all we can do, in fact—is ask the right questions, then make some calculated speculations. Get used to it."

Their table had been cleared, and it was nearly two o'clock when Branko began to wrap up. "I am having an escort come up to take you back through the gate in a van."

"You don't want to be seen with me?"

"Standard op. You were never here. No need to take a chance you're recognized by somebody waiting in Reception."

"So, this is goodbye?"

"Goodbye? Yes, I suppose. But only for awhile, hopefully."

But now, fatigued as he was, Mickey needed to say more. He felt an urgent desire to defend himself, to justify his choices—to sum up.

"Branko," he began haltingly, "I haven't really thanked you properly."

"I haven't done anything yet—except get you strapped to a polygraph."

"No. I mean, thanks for taking a chance on me. Thanks for sticking your neck out here."

Branko fiddled with the buttons on his coat. Then he mumbled something Mickey thought he might have misheard. "It's just business."

Branko looked up again, lecturing him now. "This summit is going to play a critical role in the ongoing Chinese succession struggle. They have a new guy in charge, but he still has significant internal challenges. They've got a big Party Congress soon and they're facing a lot of popular discontent. They're at a fork in the road. If guys like the Red Dragons prevail, things could get real ugly. So, we're willing to take some chances."

"Just business, huh?"

"It has to be."

"Jesus, Branko. It's me! Mickey. Remember? The Oasis? The road trips? Shots at the beach? 'All for one and one for all'?"

Branko grimaced, his stern gaze eroding as he considered. Then he spoke softly again. "Of course, I remember the promises we made. We were young—very young and very naïve."

"We promised. You can't deny the prom—"

"I've denied nothing! But don't labor under a false impression. I can't do this as a favor to an old friend. I'm a professional intelligence officer pursuing the national interest. I'm taking a chance, a very big chance. If you screw up, it's on me, on my watch."

"I know that."

"Have you any idea what the hell 'professional intelligence' means?" Branko said, letting out a pained sigh. "Because if you don't, I cannot in good conscience permit you to go forward."

"I can do this."

"Mickey, your whole life has been some frat boy game, racing your car at night without the headlights on. This game is real. If you fuck up, I will still get to go home and hug my kids and sleep in my wife's arms. *You*'re the one who is gonna rot behind enemy lines."

"I know."

"They could be very rough on you in Beijing. Just for sport. You'll be powerless, and we will not be able to help when they throw you in some shit-hole prison. There will be no Rambo flying in to get you, no Blackhawk helicopters coming to the rescue."

"Branko, I know."

"I think you do know, and really do understand, the fundamental choice you have made. I respect you for that."

"Despite all my fuck-ups?"

"Despite all your fuck-ups."

Branko averted his gaze for a moment as the light in the room was altered, as if by an invisible hand. Through the skylight overhead, puffy June clouds floated by, cotton white and disembodied.

"If you want to get personal," Branko continued, "I should be honest with you. You do have a right to request a favor of an old friend. Just as I have a professional obligation to refuse if it is unwise, no matter what we promised in all those toasts we made. You know, Mickey, you gave me energy in the old days. I was envious of your ability to live life outside the lines."

Mickey stared glumly.

"But I mistook your lack of restraint for creative genius. You got sloppy with your life, lived with no discipline," Branko said with a scowl. "You want to . . . to redeem yourself now? I can't help you with that."

"I don't—"

"The CIA does not offer absolution for sins. And I am not your parish priest."

"I know, Branko," Mickey said, deflated now. He thought they were finished, but Branko did not relent.

"I suppose, if you must know, that there *is* something personal coloring my judgment. I was a refugee from tyrants once. If I have any personal agenda here, it's that I'll always take chances for people who are powerless, but who have guts. It's for your kids, so they have a chance to grow up without a dictator's boot heel on their neck."

Mickey nodded.

"So, my friend, I admire your courage. You and your boys will be at great risk. May God protect you."

Branko spread his arms wide and placed both hands on Mickey's broad shoulders. Then, finally, he hugged Mickey powerfully, holding him a long time in a fraternal embrace.

21

HONORING THE PROCESS

It was stinking hot in Washington that first week in June. Waves of tropical moisture drifted up from the Gulf of Mexico, the sultry air camping over the city, limp and polluted. A tourist from Kentucky nearly drowned seeking relief in a waterfall at the FDR Memorial. School groups on government class pilgrimages lined up five-deep for iced sodas at the Constitution Avenue concessionaires alongside the Smithsonian Museums.

Each broiling day of the late spring heat wave, Alexander worked his story, double-checking every fact. He was obsessed, determined to get it right this time. He dissected the pieces of the Chinese missiles puzzle, carefully reassembling them as he went. He even used an old *Stanford Daily* technique they'd taught in Journalism 101, laying out the subtopics on note cards spread across his dining room table like a movie storyboard. He was rarely in the Washington bureau office, instead working the phones from home or interviewing sources in person. He already knew the headline he'd request for the new exclusive: "New Chinese Missile Build-Up Threatens Taiwan; White House Misrepresents Implications."

The static between Beijing and Washington was just beginning to quiet down after a hastily arranged meeting of their respective foreign ministers at the UN. The Seattle Summit was still on. Alexander knew his second major Asia story of the season would again lead the news. If he didn't get this one right, there might not be a third chance.

Working the trail was a rush, his instincts for self-preservation kicking in. He developed a prodigious appetite for protein—steaks for dinner, burgers for lunch, bacon and eggs for breakfast. He began to carry a pocketful of M&M's and peanut butter crackers—between-meals fuel to keep him surging ahead. He dreamt rich dreams, and awoke flush, thinking of Rachel. Great things seemed attainable.

Rachel had also dug into work more deeply, again finding a rhythm of her own, pulling herself back into the center of the frenetic legislative dance. She was amused by the illusion of control she recovered as she worked with her clients, pressing their points with Congress, working the hallways of the executive branch, advancing their agendas. Her voice sounded authoritative as she set forth strategy and tactics. Her staff listened attentively. Her interns took copious notes. Her analysis seemed sound—she still knew how to get things done in a town that mystified those unfamiliar with its Byzantine pathways.

She called Alexander several times the first week after Memorial Day. It was mostly to buck him up, to encourage him in his effort to nail down his story. She relished feeling needed. She liked knowing that her presence in his life gave him strength.

Pieces of their conversations over so many years came floating back to Alexander as he worked. They reordered themselves in his reflections, providing insights, offering a suggested direction. He pondered observations she had made during their drive in the country, things she had remarked about during her call from the Delano, whispered words during their first night in bed together.

By Wednesday morning, they were reaching again for each other's embrace. Rachel had seen Jamie off at the bus stop, then raced across the Fourteenth Street Bridge, curled under the Capitol, past the congressional commuters, and bounded up the steps of Alexander's townhouse, informing her office with a quick call that she had to drop by a Hill fundraising breakfast. Alexander set aside his note cards and they barely spoke before making love on the couch. Then she was off, in a hurry, to the office with an extra bit of blush.

Alexander felt renewed by the simplicity of their lovemaking. It was the perfect complement to their years of rich conversation. He felt shy, yet he liked to watch, to see her face change under his ministrations. She made him feel puckish and nimble. He felt honored by her trust as she shared lascivious desires. Their sex became equal parts rehabilitation and religion, a transforming experience more satisfying than the richest of meals. They were enraptured.

He was on the phone to her again Thursday morning, and they met for lunch at her place in Arlington. They had sex in the shower, quite clumsily. She was convulsed with laughter as she sat in the steam on the edge of the tub and finally confessed details of her gallant last stand against the Arlington Police. Then they were off again in a rush—both had much work to do.

Mid-day Friday, it was her initiative. She Blackberried him in a meeting with a virtual summons. She awaited his return from a Pentagon appointment at one, standing in her front hallway in a blue ensemble—negligee, stockings, and a garter belt—with two glasses of chilled champagne in her hands, a wicked smile on her face. They made love urgently, then were back out the door again within the hour.

They were clueless about where this all led. Yet, neither was anxious. By tacit consent, they ignored the question of where they were headed. Alexander wasn't sure he was doing her any favors by pursuing her after all these years. But then, he conveniently concluded, she *was* a grown-up. She didn't need him making decisions for her.

Alexander felt rejuvenated as he pursued his professional inquiries. He began with the photos left at his doorstep. *What about the commercial angle?* If there were militarily significant activities underway in the PRC's Fujian Province, could they be detected by some weather satellite or news organization? He satisfied himself with two calls to a source at NASA and an old Stanford buddy now with the Geological Service doing land mapping. The quality of the pixels on the photos he had in his possession far exceeded commercial capabilities.

Next up was the textual analysis. The narrative accompanying the satellite photos artfully mimicked the jargon of the intelligence analysts—with their dry references to "a concentration of launch assets."

Alexander decided he'd approach the CIA *last* this time, and then stay on Branko until he received a clear confirmation or denial. He held off on any direct questions to Langley. But he did have his research assistant pull off the Internet some declassified materials the CIA had released during the recent Iraq-WMD investigation. They bore a striking resemblance, both in narrative tone and the accompanying photo spread, to what he had in hand. It was inconclusive, but anecdotally corroborative.

The Taiwan angle he worked next. If China was doubling its medium range missile launch capacity in Fujian, it would be a violation of private assurances made to the White House. But Alexander's Taipei sources had gone cold after he ran with the bogus information about an alleged Taiwan nuclear program. Congressional contacts proved equally unproductive.

Finally, Alexander scored with sourcing from a renegade Pentagon consultant. The former Assistant Secretary of Defense was a member of the anti-China Blue Team whose members often fed reporters sensitive material on the China threat. This source was able to confirm each of the key facts in the documents—even said he had read a highly classified version at the Pentagon. It took a full week before Alexander felt confident enough to lay his draft article before his editor. Once he did, he knew the lead three paragraphs would be explosive:

> *The People's Republic of China has systematically increased ballistic missile deployments opposite Taiwan, threatening to spark a confrontation along the Taiwan Strait, the* Times *has learned. The new deployments of CSS-6 short range ballistic missiles (SRBMs) include more than one hundred being added this spring at the Nanping base in Fujian Province, upsetting the tenuous balance of forces in the region, U.S. and foreign intelligence sources confirm. These new additions bring to more than 500 the total number of SRBM's targeted at Taiwan, sufficient to overwhelm its limited defense capabilities, according to recent U.S. intelligence agency reports.*

> *The new Chinese actions violate private assurances made in Beijing last year to U.S. officials regarding future restraint on missile deployments. In return, the White House reportedly decided to withhold exports to Taiwan of sophisticated Aegis battle management systems sought by that island nation. The PRC's move increases the possibility of a military conflict in East Asia.*

The new Chinese commitments to their Nanping base, approximately one hundred twenty-five miles west of Taiwan, add to an existing force of CSS-7's and CSS-6's already at Lizhou and Yongan. The missiles were apparently manufactured west of Lizhou, at the PRC's Yunnan Province facility, and were delivered in recent weeks. According to Jane's Defense Weekly, *China has recently tested its new Russian-made AA-12 Adder air-to-air missile, and deployed new submarines and a Russian-built Sovremenny destroyer at its fleet facilities in Zhanjiang, near Hainan Island.*

The balance of Alexander's text proceeded with similar detail. No confirming quotes were provided by the executive branch, and there was no direct comment from Taiwan. Nevertheless, Alexander was elated with his exclusive. This time, he had nailed it.

The story broke in waves. The *Los Angeles Times* web site had it up by eleven p.m., the Sunday night before the newspaper hit the stands. The *Post* and *New York Times* played catch-up in their late editions, both with brief stories grudgingly crediting Alexander and the *LA Times*. By mid-morning Monday, his efforts to assemble a follow-up story were overwhelmed by the steady stream of phone calls coming in from the networks. A tacit confirmation of many of his facts came through a non-denial at the State Department's eleven a.m. briefing, and that produced yet another round of calls, including a request to comment on PBS's evening news program, *The News Hour with Jim Lehrer*, and a slot on a Fox News panel. He was on top of his game again, riding the crest of media interest.

The Chinese government was thrown on the defensive, and its Foreign Ministry clammed up. On Capitol Hill, key legislators were in a tizzy. The anti-China legislators had a field day before the cameras, demagoging the issue and pouring on gratuitous complaints about the latest PRC human rights violations. The pro-China voices—especially senators from grain exporting states—struggled to focus their comments on the bigger issues at stake in U.S.-China ties, including cooperation in containing the North

Koreans' nuclear ambitions.

Alexander's exclusive put Senator Smithson in a peculiar bind. The senator was making final preparations to lead his Foreign Relations Committee colleagues on a trade mission to East Asia. The late June trip was to focus mostly on Japan and Korea, and Smithson would have several leading California high tech executives in tow. But the delegation's last stop, ending on the Fourth of July, was to be in Beijing. The agenda here would be mixed. Some of the senators from the committee, pushed by Landle, wanted to press grain sales. For Smithson, the China leg was an opportunity for a bit of posturing—"speaking truth to power" on some human rights issues. It was likely to be his last foreign travel before his presidential bid rolled out in earnest. Politics was on everyone's mind, including that of his old adversary from Iowa. Indeed, it was Senator Landle who brought him another unwelcome headache, when he came to see him in his Senate hideaway office the day Alexander's story broke.

"This is an outrage, Jake," Landle said as they drank coffee in Smithson's hideaway office off the Senate floor. The Iowan was wearing a seersucker suit on another oppressively hot June day.

"Well, I'm outraged, too," Smithson agreed. "The Chinese lied to us. And so did the State Department."

"Jake, it's the *leak* I'm talking about. How can we expect to do business with the administration if somebody's going to give raw CIA analyses to the newspapers?"

"Isn't this about the Chinese?"

"Jake, it's about *the process*," Landle said. "Congress can't earn White House respect—we won't deserve any—if material they share ends up in the paper the next week."

"What are you getting at, Tom?" Smithson sipped from his mug as he sat at his old roll top desk.

"The committee staff was briefed on the CIA analysis of this issue not ten days ago. Then, boom, it shows up in the newspapers. We look like complete amateurs. It's grandstanding, pure and simple—some smart aleck trying to embarrass the White House before the summit."

"Oh c'mon, Tom. Most of the leaks in this town come from executive branch dissenters. You know that. So let's not jump all over ourselves—"

"That can't justify violating the law."

"Besides, talking about 'the process' like it's some kind of Vatican ritual is just another way of changing the subject. It's an old trick around here. The fact is, State has consistently denied there was any conclusive evidence on new missiles. And China's been lying about how they've allegedly shown restraint. I can think of worse things than having both of them called on it."

"So you condone this leaking?"

"Of course not."

"You don't think the Taiwan nuclear buildup might justify some of this Chinese response? Isn't that just what the U.S. did in 1962, when Castro brought Russian nukes into Cuba?"

Smithson held him in his gaze a long time. "You're serious, aren't you?"

"Darn right, I am, Jake. I won't tolerate this kind of reckless leaking of classified material. I've already called the Ethics Committee. They've agreed to an immediate investigation. I want staff taking polygraphs—everybody who handled this material."

"And senators?" Smithson added.

"What do you mean, *senators?*"

"Don't you want to include our elected colleagues in your little inquisition, since we're most often the ones who leak stuff from the Hill? I mean, why single out the poor staff professionals?"

"You want to wire up senators?" said Landle, incredulous. "You and me, too? That is out of the—"

"If you're going to try to bully the staff, sure," Smithson said, fiddling with his phone now, avoiding Landle's eyes. "What's good for the goose ought to suit the gander."

"Mr. Chairman!" Landle fumed. "That's a non-starter and you know it. Surely you're bluffing."

"Fine then. Go ahead with your FBI interviews. But I won't sign off on polygraphs for staff unless you've got probable cause in each and every case."

"Then how can we get the job done?"

"It ain't fair," said Smithson, setting down his mug and folding his hands. "And I, for one, won't be party to it."

Landle glared at him for a long time, before he shook his head in disdain, stood, and walked out.

22

No good deed goes unpunished

The FBI got to Booth in just three days.

It was during the preceding hours, however, that his torment was most intense. *How did I fall into this crazy game?* He lay awake at night, wondering, pondering his future, reconsidering his past.

Layers of idealism were shed as he questioned his purpose, waiting to meet with the investigators. He had been manipulated by events—he saw that now. His righteousness boiled to rage, then was reduced, upon reflection, to cool resolve. This series of little deaths, one piled upon another, made his future course seem, in retrospect, almost inevitable. There could be no turning back.

He did not speak of the issue with Smithson. If the chairman suspected him—or if his boss believed Booth was suspicious of him—it remained unsaid. When they did communicate during those three long days of waiting, it was about such basic concerns as the logistics for the upcoming Asia trip. They hid in the routine, choosing to leave unacknowledged the danger closing in upon them both.

Booth's staff colleagues were full of flip comments as they trudged back, one by one, from their interviews with the FBI inquisitors.

"Good cop, bad cop," a Democratic colleague volunteered, "except the good cop's got great legs."

"Retreads from security clearance interviews," a Republican friend offered at a lunch table in the Dirksen cafeteria. "Not exactly CSI caliber. They're at a complete loss—they figure *everybody* up here leaks."

"Watch out, Booth," another warned. "I got a hunch they're looking to nail the chairman-who-would-be-president."

Booth could not sleep. He took to patrolling the house in the blackness, looking in on the children, dozing off on the sofa to anxious dreams before dawn, his father there again, the old man's voice insisting on distinguishing right from wrong.

Finally, the hour he dreaded was upon him. He was summoned for his FBI interrogation at two p.m. on the 16th, eight days before wheels up for Asia.

The room the FBI had set up—on the House side, of all places—was in the decrepit staff annex across the freeway off-ramps from the Rayburn Building. The suite was cramped and windowless. A large, round man named Albertson, bald on top and wearing a short-sleeve white shirt, sat at an old metal desk. Beside him, a demure Ms. Tedesco was perched on a leather chair, feeding the questions. Booth sat opposite, in a metal folding chair too close to the questioners for his taste.

The first few questions were for the record. Name, title, phone number. Then basics such as: how long had he worked for the committee? Level of security clearance? Office procedures for handling classified documents? Booth remained on guard; he knew these were just warm-ups, questions for the record to which they already knew the answers.

"Robert, we forgot to swear him in," the lady interrogator said.

"Dang, not again." Albertson snapped his fingers. "Just a formality you know."

The man's eyes betrayed the ploy, Booth thought, as he noted the coolness with which the FBI agent regarded him. Booth raised his right hand and swore to "tell the truth, the whole truth, and nothing but the truth, so help me God."

"So you've worked with Senator Smithson more than twenty years?"

"Twenty-six, actually. With time off for good behavior."

"Twenty-six?"

"That includes a couple of years on sabbatical."

"You guys get sabbaticals in Congress? Nice deal."

"Actually, it was an informal arrangement. I consulted with the Committee while I went back to finish my doctorate at Stanford."

"An informal arrangement?"

"Yeah. I still got paid."

"You had access to all the classified stuff while you were in grad school?"

"Sure."

"Weren't there a bunch of Chinese students in that Stanford program? Foreign Ministry people?" Albertson began throwing out more of the questions now, the prim Ms. Tedesco—and she did have quite shapely legs—taking notes.

"There were several PRC citizens there over the years, yes. The program is considered one of the best for figuring out what goes on in China. But I only accessed classified documents when in Washington."

"If I might ask," Tedesco said, "what procedures are in place for when you convey classified information to the senator?"

"What exactly do you mean?"

"How do you brief the senator?"

"Well, I read the National Intelligence Digest at the Intelligence Committee or Foreign Relations. And I give him a daily 'NID sweep'—that's what we call it—whenever he's in town."

"Where?"

"In his personal office. Or in the committee chambers."

"How do you prevent exposure to foreign intelligence?"

"Detective Albertson—"

"It's *Agent* Albertson, actually. We're not the police."

"Yeah," Booth conceded. "Agent Albertson, the Senate offices are swept regularly for bugs. Besides, I'm just giving him the headlines, not details or photos."

"Photos. Right. That's why we're here. Just where would you show him photos?"

"Photos?'

"Say the Intelligence Committee was briefed on something hot, like some new nuclear facility in Iran. Just where would you show him the evidence?"

"Well, that type of stuff would require Codeword level clearance. It's all kept in the committee safe in S-407, the secure committee room up in the attic of the Capitol."

"It *never* leaves?"

"Only a few people can check it out. Senators. Staff directors. Leadership staff."

"Right. Guys like you."

"Sure. I, uh, usually bring it down to him in the hideaway."

"Hideaway?"

"It's a small private office the chairman has in the Capitol, a perk for the senior members. And yes, we have that swept for bugs regularly, too."

"So, let me see," said Albertson, looking at some notes, "after you checked out the CIA briefing materials the committee requested on the alleged Chinese missile build-up, where did you take them?"

"Let me think. That was right before the Memorial Day recess?"

"May the twenty-fourth."

"I took them to Senator Smithson. He was in his hideaway."

"Alone?"

"Yes."

"And did you take calls from anyone?"

"What do you mean?"

"Were you present for a call from any reporters while you and the documents were with Chairman Smithson?"

"I don't think I stayed."

"You didn't stay to brief him on this sensitive new information that might make a great headline?"

"There was a bill I was tracking for him on the floor . . ."

"Defense appropriations," said Ms. Tedesco, referring to notes. *Impressive.*

"Right. But wait a minute. What exactly are you getting at with this business about headlines?" Booth wasn't going to let the insinuation hang.

Albertson stood, walking to where a window might have been— should have been—if they weren't in some leftover storage room in the House staff annex. "Senator Smithson has something of a reputation for making public speeches about sensitive international military matters—"

"Never using classified materials as the source."

"The fact is, there was a phone call from one Alexander Bonner to the senator's private line in that office that very afternoon. A twelve-minute phone call."

"So what? Senator Smithson talks to Bonner all the time."

"All the time?"

"Sure. He's a Washington correspondent from the state's number one paper. He covers Capitol Hill and the diplomatic beat—especially big Asia stories. I bet he called half the committee members that same day."

"He's your old classmate, if I'm not mistaken," Tedesco said, again being helpful.

"Right."

"Weren't you in some kind of fraternity together?" Albertson asked, flipping far back in his notebook. "With a bunch of other folks in this town now?"

"It was actually more like an extended family."

"Family?"

"We were housemates . . . it wasn't only guys."

"Well," Albertson said with a smirk, "I suppose it *was* the Sixties—and in California."

"It was the Seventies, actually."

"So, you had some little commune—and what was your organizing principle?"

"We stayed in a house together, and were just real good friends."

"The Mandarin Club, it was supposedly called," Albertson said, again studying his notes. "What was *that* all about?"

"We stuck together."

"Why call yourselves 'The Mandarins'?" Albertson still didn't get it.

"It was just a play on words," Booth said, letting out a sigh. "We were in this obscure field of language study. Even in a campus full of specialists, there weren't many people studying Chinese then. Most of us had aspirations to positions of leadership . . . like the Mandarins who used to rule over the Chinese bureaucracy."

"So, what became of your little Club?" Albertson said.

"We've stayed in touch."

"And looked out for each other—'stuck together,' didn't you say?"

"Yeah."

"And covered for each other?"

Booth just shook his head. His inquisitors stole a glance at each other, and another long silence ensued. It was the silences Booth had come to dread. They afforded him too much time to reflect on the consequences of his every word.

"What's your point, if I might ask?" said Booth. He felt better posing the questions than answering them.

"Our point?" Tedesco replied this time.

"I mean, if you think Smithson tipped Bonner, why don't you ask the senator?"

"You're the senator's top aide."

"But if you want to accuse the chairman of leaking something, have the decency to confront him directly. Don't drag others into some partisan witch hunt."

"So you think this is a 'partisan witch hunt'?"

"That's what he said, Agent Albertson," said Tedesco.

"Sure," Booth shot back, "stuff gets leaked all the time. Bonner is a nationally renowned reporter. The FBI only gets called in when somebody's out to smear someone. It's the same old shoot-the-messenger stuff they use all the time. I mean, look at the Wilson thing. Buncha White House guys blow a CIA agent's cover to punish her husband—and you know who gets sent to jail? A reporter!"

"You're getting way off the point—"

"That's the way I see it, though."

They stared at each other a while, Albertson sipping from a Coke can, Ms. Tedesco gripping her notes. There was very little air in the room. Booth could hear the ancient air conditioning unit straining to function.

"So, if we asked whether you spoke directly with Alexander Bonner on May the twenty-fourth, your answer would be no?"

"Yes. It would be 'no.'"

"And did you ever discuss the CIA report regarding the Chinese missile build-up with him?"

"Yes."

"Yes?" Both the FBI agents leaned forward now, looking for a crack in the wall.

"He called me looking for confirmation. Some time in early June. You've got his phone records, so you can probably tell me exactly what day and time. I told him I couldn't help him. Probably you got that on tape, too."

"Let me disabuse you, sir," Albertson said. "Federal judges don't like us to tap reporters' phones, even phones of guys who like to harm U.S. security by passing around classified stuff."

They fenced on, parry and riposte. Booth got better at it as he went. The FBI couple became increasingly terse; both agents seemed convinced Booth was trying to cover up a politically charged matter for his boss. He was determined not to give them anything that might embarrass Smithson. Situational ethics, or no, he owed it to the senator to keep mum.

Booth cruised to the finish, breathing strong with his second wind, even as he grew more and more disgusted with himself. But then, just at the threshold of a successful exit, he was leveled by one final blow.

"Dr. Booth, that's all we have for you today," Agent Albertson said as he snapped his notebook closed. He looked up, eyes seeking their target. "At least, that is until we receive the final Committee authorization on fluttering."

"Fluttering?" Booth did not understand at first.

"Polygraphs," he elaborated. "Lie detector tests. Senator Landle has requested them for all interviewees in the second round. I'm going to recommend we start with you. Then maybe we'll learn a little more about which reporters Senator Smithson has been unburdening himself to."

Booth's affected smile flattened. Struggling to suppress his horror, he got out of there as quickly as he could.

He walked in a daze back up the Hill toward the Capitol plaza. Throngs of tourists were suffering in the mid-afternoon heat, shuffling slowly up the incline towards the towering white dome. The sky was heavy with dark gray cumulus clouds, thickening for a thunder and lightning strike.

Booth turned left just before he passed the Senate steps, skirting under the marble stairs to the VIP entrance, then strode down the hallway in search of Jake Smithson.

Sure enough, he found the senator in his hideaway. Smithson would sit in the small room—just down the hall from the Committee's ceremonial meeting space in the Capitol—puttering about with old family photos, and fiddling with the velvet, ceiling-to-floor drapes. It was, Booth believed, one of Smithson's safer sources of relaxation.

The office seemed ageless, an intensely personal clubhouse suspended somewhere in another time. Smithson had filled the musty room with memories of family, not politics. It was almost devoid of the typical Washington-wallpaper that consisted of old head shots of grand personages. The exception was an autographed NASA photo of Smithson with Richard Nixon, of all people. The balance of the frames contained decades-old candids of his relatives. Smithson would walk about the room, tinkering with mementos as he meditated on the issues of the day. He might even sit at his desk, feet up, and take a power nap—a skill, he claimed, he learned in flight school.

"Yes?" said the senator with a hint of irritation at Booth's knock. "Oh, it's you, Martin. What's up?"

Booth did not immediately respond, instead sitting without being asked. He eyed a can of Sprite on the Senator's desk and suddenly felt parched.

"You OK?" the senator asked. "You look shook up."

Booth still didn't know how to begin. He didn't have any plan here, any grand design.

"I, uh, I guess I'm having trouble living with contradictions."

"Contradictions?"

"Yeah. Not sure what to do when competing values clash."

"Whose values?" The phone rang, but Smithson ignored it, continuing the conversation. "You're speaking in riddles, my friend. Who've you been talking with, the White House?"

"No," Booth said, looking up to catch the concerned Chairman's eye this time. "The FBI."

"Oh. OK. So, you got 'contradictions'?"

"Yeah."

"They can be a pain in the ass."

"But you're better at them. Always were."

"What do you mean by that?"

"You're better at balancing—dodging—whatever is the polite way to put it."

"What the hell are you talking about? Why were you 'dodging' with the FBI?"

"I mean, maybe it comes with the territory, being a politician in the public eye and all." Booth was stumbling. "I . . . I just don't understand how you do it."

"Do what?"

"Juggle the ethical conflicts. Professional. Personal. Marital, whatever. I don't know how you balance it all and walk about day and night as if you're all there, one coherent whole."

Smithson observed with horror the strange transformation affecting his aide.

"It's the *contradictions*, Jake. I just don't understand how you balance them."

Smithson stared at his aide, then slowly began to shake his head in bewilderment. "I really don't know what to say. I mean, *you* go see the FBI, and now you want *me* to defend myself? Were they quizzing you about my private life?"

"No. But by the way, what *are* you going to do when the subject comes up in the primaries?"

"I'll cross that bridge when I have to. I mean, a man's got to live the life he's made. God doesn't expect us to walk around miserable if we're trying to do His works."

"Sorry, senator. They weren't asking about your private life. See, the thing is, the FBI thinks you're the one who leaked the satellite photos to the newspapers, to Alexander Bonner."

"Me? Well, with all due respect, fuck 'em. Let 'em come after me with their lie detector crap. I just want to see them wire up Tom Landle and his boys, too. I'll pay the price of admission for that."

"You still don't see it, do you?" Booth said, shaking his head slowly.

The phone rang again, but Smithson was intent upon him. "You still don't get it."

"About my personal life?" the senator asked.

"No, Jake." He'd never called him Jake twice in a day. "I mean about the FBI. The satellite photos. The leak."

"Screw the FBI. It's just some partisan crap the White House has put Landle up to. To have me slimed as a guy who can't be trusted with sensitive stuff. Well, you know what? They can't pin this one on ol' Jake."

"It's not you."

"I know it's not me."

"It's *me*, Jake. *I* gave Alexander Bonner the stuff."

Senator Smithson took a last swallow of the soda as he sized up his long-time aide, seeing him now in a new light. "*You?*"

"Me."

"Oh-kaaaaay. So . . ."

"So?"

"So, what *exactly* is the problem? How can they ever prove it was you? I mean, did they catch you doing it on tape?" said Smithson. "Did you say anything stupid to them today?"

"Sir, I'm afraid I did a very good job of dodging," said Booth, who stood and began to pace, touching a photo here and there as he gathered himself in an unconscious mimic of his mentor.

"Afraid?"

"I looked two agents of the Federal Bureau of Investigation in the eye and lied under oath for over an hour. It's a felony, I believe."

"*Really?*" Smithson followed Booth closely with his eyes. "Can I . . . I mean . . . Martin, do you mind if I ask why?"

"Oh, man, that's what I don't know." Booth's shoulders were sagging. "At first, I thought—I convinced myself—I was covering for you. I owe you that, at least. To not get you in hot water for something I did."

"I see. I appreciate that."

"But in retrospect," Booth continued, "I see more clearly. I see a lot of things more clearly. It was about *me*, about my own attraction to power. I perjured myself to save my own neck, to save my own career."

"Actually, I meant, why did you leak the photos?"

"Because they're lying to us—the Chinese, the State Department, the White House. They're all goddamn liars. If we tolerate it, it subverts our whole system of government."

"So you got back at them. Shit," Smithson said, heaving a sigh of disgust. "No good deed goes unpunished."

"Don't you *see*? I got back at them by stooping to their level. By lying right back."

"Damn it, Martin, you can't put it that way. *They* are the bad guys here. You can't give in to bullies like that."

Booth had a vacant look.

"They'll own you," said Smithson. "You know, I grew up in a pretty tough neighborhood. Navy docks down on the Oakland waterfront. Guys would come after you and shake you down all the time, just for your lunch money. You had to fight 'em—you just had to—even if you took a beating. Try to hurt 'em back. Make 'em bleed, too. That's the only way they'd know to respect you and know not to mess with you next time."

"Right."

"This ain't Debate Club. This isn't a Stanford tutorial with some honor code you gotta sign."

"Senator, I'm sorry. It's just . . . that's how I was brought up. Don't go into the gutter with your enemies. Try to make this a kinder, gentler world."

"Robert Kennedy?"

"Yep. The night Martin Luther King was killed. Speech in Indianapolis."

"Great speech."

"Made me cry when my dad read it to me—and I was just a kid then, a kid whose heroes were dying."

No words passed between them for a time. Booth had always admired Smithson's tolerance for silence—a politician who actually liked to think.

"What now?" the senator finally asked.

"It's not fair, you know."

"No. It's not."

"They lie to us, but we feel the heat."

"Martin, if Reverend Booth were here, I'm sure he would remind you that God didn't promise perfect justice on earth. Can't you see there's no moral equivalence here? Their wrongs are far more egregious than yours. 'Fight injustice,' he'd say. 'And remember, God helps those who help themselves.'"

"It's not that simple, Senator. I can't compartmentalize things like you. I get sick of the endless compromises of basic principle that politics requires you to—"

"Will you *stop* being so hard on me?" said Smithson, almost shouting now. "And on yourself, for that matter."

"Senator, it's just that—"

They were interrupted again by buzzers, loud as a fire drill. They waited through a series of five rings—a vote on the Senate floor.

Just as Smithson began to speak again, there was a firm knocking at the hideaway door.

"Jesus Christ," Smithson grumbled before barking: "Yes?!"

"Mr. Chairman, I tried to call you, but—"

It was Senator Landle bursting in. He stalled mid-sentence when he saw Smithson was not alone.

"Oh, sorry. Mr. Chairman, I, uh, just wanted—I felt obliged to inform you that I have an Ethics Committee letter. It was signed just now. For subpoenas on the leak inquiry. It authorizes lie detectors."

Smithson's brows narrowed as he took the papers Landle handed him.

"We'll put it to a vote in the full Senate, if necessary. But Mr. Chairman, I, uh . . . we'd prefer to have your support."

"You work quick," Smithson snapped.

"Well, we have to protect the integrity of the institution," Landle replied. "Even if this is uncomfortable."

Smithson looked at the committee letter casually, perusing the signatures. "We've been pals a long time, Tom. I really kinda like you, you should know."

"Thanks, Mr. Chairman. I feel the same way about you."

"It's not just good politics. You always used to disagree agreeably. I never felt better than when we were on the same side." Smithson turned his head now, rising in his seat as he jabbed at the papers in his fist. "But *this*, this is the lowest piece of—"

"This is different, Mr. Chairman!"

"It *isn't* different! It's the same bullshit your caucus has been putting out for thirty years—ever since we brought Nixon down. The partisan cheap shots just get nastier and nastier—on both sides, I'll grant you. I mean, we block poor old Judge Bork, then you guys spend the last eight years of the twentieth century—a hundred million bucks—going through the fucking president's garbage because you couldn't knock him off in a fair election. No, Tom, this isn't different. It's the exact same bullshit you've—"

"I'm not going to stand here and listen to a stream of your barnyard obscenities, Jake. I'm really very sorry you make it come to that."

"You're the one who marches into my office with some asinine subpoena. But you know what really pisses me off, Tom? It's that you don't see how they're using you."

"Nobody uses me!"

"Of course, they are. China lies to Washington. The White House and State Department lie to Congress. And who do you go after? The Senate staff! You want us to have an orgy of self-flagellation up here over some newspaper story? Well, sorry, friend. I'm not going to be a party to it."

"I totally reject your characterization of—"

"Tom! You're too smart not to see it!"

"It's about defending the integrity of the process, Jake. If you have something to hide, it's your own darn fault."

The two men glared at each other, calculating next moves until Landle's discomfort became so great, he snatched back the committee letter and turned to leave.

"That won't be necessary, Senator," Booth heard himself remark, as if he was watching from afar.

"What?"

They had almost forgotten about Booth. The staff man had remained seated, observing as the scene played itself out like a familiar Greek trag-edy. He already knew the inevitable denouement.

"The subpoenas." The two legislators stared at him, uncomprehending, even as he continued, "They won't be necessary."

"What?"

Calmly, Booth stepped off the cliff. "It was me," he said.

"Huh?"

"Senator Smithson didn't leak the missile story to the newspaper," Booth explained, turning to Landle now. "*I* did."

"You?! Jake!" Landle's eyes darted back and forth between Booth and Smithson, who were regarding each other intently. "Did you know about this?"

"*I* leaked it," Booth said matter-of-factly as he stood and began to walk toward the door. "I leaked the photos because I thought it was the right thing to do. Because we shouldn't let them lie to us. Because we shouldn't let the Chinese and the White House get away with it."

His confession silenced the senators. They waited, confused as to what they should say, as Booth concluded: "I just came over to tell all this to Chairman Smithson. And to submit my resignation."

Booth regarded them both for a moment longer as he stood at the threshold. They were cringing as they watched him depart.

Booth turned the brass knob and opened the hideaway door. He gen-tly pushed it shut until it clicked behind him, then headed down the tiled Capitol hallway one last time. He walked out through the heavy revolving door under the Senate steps, stepping into a warm spring rain. The first thick drops splotched his gray suit. Soon, they began to penetrate.

He was surprised to notice that, as the moisture soaked through to his skin, he felt cleansed.

JULY

23

THE DEPARTURE LOUNGE

Mickey Dooley discovered the comfort of prayer late in life. The free fall of faith yielded a wondrous consolation. As he let go, trusting in the Lord to cushion him, he conjured visions of deliverance. He could see himself surviving the gauntlet ahead, breaking loose, back home in America with his children.

Faith was the perfect antidote to overcome years of swaggering bravado, the false empowerment of the playboy's hustle. Things would work out, he grew confident, because an omniscient God intended them to. Huckster Mickey could no longer will them to.

The prospect of failure was too grim to imagine, and he preferred the idea of some glorious death—martyrdom in the streets of Beijing—to the repugnant alternatives he tried to bar from his mind. As he flew into China on this final trip, he was full of hope. He could pull this off. He could rescue both his children and Lee from a bleak future and redeem himself in the doing.

It seemed too easy at first. The U.S. Air Force plane ferrying the official delegation into the Communist capital took a smooth glide path, cumulus clouds parting over the Pacific shore. Quite soon, the road-ringed capital loomed ahead, arid mountains barely discernible on the far northwest horizon. After all the recent tensions between Washington and Beijing, Mickey found the placid scene unnerving. *Could this be a tease?*

It was just a twenty minute descent from the coastline to the capital as the Smithson delegation savored the steak and Merlot served en route by the pursers on the plane they called "Air Force Three." Up front, many of the senators on board were dozing, an odd bipartisan mixture of legislators whom Smithson had roped in for cover or comfort. The corporate hitchhikers rode in the rear.

After the comforts of Tokyo and Seoul, China promised to be tense.

The furor over the Chinese missile build-up had almost led Smithson to bail on the Beijing leg. As they had left Andrews Air Force Base in suburban Maryland, the Chinese leadership and the White House were still deep into the media spin cycle, suspicious of each other's every move and looking to exact revenge. It was an odd game of diplomatic chicken; neither side wanted to take the blame for axing the summit. So with the pretense of business as usual, the Congressional delegation anxiously proceeded with the China portion of their itinerary.

The Smithson entourage had an agenda as internally contradictory as it was familiar. The chairman was eager to lecture the Chinese about human rights and nuclear nonproliferation, to debate the responsibilities of a twenty-first century superpower. At the same time, he would encourage them, thank you very much, to buy American—commercial aircraft, computer software, bridges, and dams. As always, there was no consensus among his senior colleagues on how to deal with China. Some wanted to talk grain and citrus sales. Others were more interested in arguing about the missiles deployed against Taiwan, proselytizing about religious freedom, or encouraging uncensored Internet access.

Rachel had joked with Mickey that the delegation's mixed message was the perfect metaphor for two centuries of Washington's contradictory impulses towards all things Asian. They would preach democracy while lusting for commercial opportunity. They would come to do good and stay to seek profit—Mickey had called it right years before.

As they prepared to land, Rachel sat next to Mickey in the plane's rear. She worried about the ground logistics like a den mother. Mickey was fretting yet again, she noticed, as he had all week, working over his nails as he gazed into space, anxious as a cat looking to sprint across traffic. *Suddenly a white-knuckle flier? Couldn't be.*

Rachel was struggling to stay focused on her pending business with Telstar and others on board. With Booth missing in action—rumors had him accepting a position with Smithson's nascent presidential campaign or even taking another teaching sabbatical—the care and feeding of her clients, and their legislative champions on the plane, fell largely upon her. The opportunities facing her and her clients in China were sufficiently important that she was along to make sure everything went smoothly—and to lobby Smithson and his colleagues for help on the margins.

She was in a disembodied state as she ruminated. She sat with Mickey, babysitting Smithson, wondering about Booth. But it was Alexander whose presence she sensed all around her—Alexander's words, his smell, his touch.

Barry was so far away, already the forgotten man. Jamie seemed terribly distant, too. On the phone, he was quiet and obedient, the little boy's small voice sounding tentative. Still, she saw his drawings in the clouds, and she heard his voice playing air traffic controller in the chatter on her headphones. She envisioned him tinkering with his spaceship models, arcing them through the sky with his small hands, orbiting in the imaginary world of an only child.

"This has got to be my last road trip for a while," she confided to Mickey as the wheels touched down.

The arrival of Smithson delegation's was a breeze. The Chinese seemed to have become downright civil about customs and passports, allowing an easy transit to the exclusive VIP lounge, where the American ambassador was waiting with a Foreign Ministry protocol team. Their bags were loaded swiftly into a couple of trailing Dodge vans, and the entourage barreled into town with a minimum of fuss.

The afternoon afforded time for a provocative session at one of the government-run think tanks, where earnest scholars posing as the freest of academics spouted the government line. It was clear that the recent leadership campaign to undermine intellectuals had restored orthodoxy.

A second meeting with carefully selected students at Beijing University confirmed the outline of their stateside intelligence briefing—China's recent flirtations with openness to the West had spawned a virulent nationalism. The campuses, the city markets, and the local media were devoid of any other ideological glue. The young men spouted a version of "China right or wrong" that would have left Rachel feeling more comfortable if accompanied by empty Leninist rhetoric. The kids, it seemed, were growing up hating America, but liking Americans. Economic flexibility had not brought much change to the rigidity of the masses.

Perversely, the first spontaneous confrontation in China for the Smithson delegation came at the hands of their own countrymen. The expatriates were more than willing to rail against Washington policies at an American Chamber of Commerce reception. A bullet-headed aerospace executive named Bernhardt was particularly pointed with the senators, complaining that they were losing sales, right and left, to the Europeans. Chairman Smithson held his ground, though, and the delegation made it through the session, and the balance of two busy days, with few incidents.

Down time for Rachel and Mickey finally arrived that Friday afternoon. With Smithson attending a formal meeting at the Foreign Ministry—elected officials only—the two of them peeled off, unaccompanied, for a walk in the park.

They were letting off steam in a meandering conversation, Mickey preoccupied by his concern for the Lee meeting that night, when Rachel finally began to pursue her jumpy companion.

"You've been spaced out all week. What gives?"

"Nothing," Mickey said, grinning evasively.

"Bullshit, Mr. Dooley. I've known you since you were practically a teenager. Fess up."

"All right," said Mickey, scrambling for misdirection. "You want confession?"

"Yeah."

"I'm about to go over the falls; I turn fifty later this year." He gazed past her. "I need to make some things right in my life—I might as well admit it."

"What?"

"Oh, I don't know . . . " He was wringing his hands again. "I feel like I've been dancin' with the devil. I shoulda lived my life differently, shoulda said some things years ago."

"Like what?" She was peering at him with penetrating eyes.

"Like, well, for starters, I had a wicked crush on you at Stanford."

"What are you talking about?"

"I'm serious," he replied, pleased at how easily he had sidetracked her inquiries. "I had this fixation on you. At first, I felt like a jerk for it because

Barry was a friend and I was all for women's liberation and respect for—"

"Liberated? You? Ha!"

"I thought it would be ganging up to make a pass at you—you know, tacky."

"And why didn't you ever reveal your sentiments?"

"I never really was very good at sharing personal confidences. Maybe it was the Army brat thing."

"You had plenty of girlfriends, for God's sakes. I was probably just terra incognita—unknown territory for potential conquest. Must have been a guy thing."

"I was curious. You led with your chin, the whole tough cowgirl shtick. I just knew there was more under there for whoever knew the magic password."

"You thought you could seduce me with a password?" She stopped and crossed him now, arms akimbo. They were in the middle of an expansive gravel walk in Ritan Park, which sits in the middle of the embassy district, and not far from Rachel's hotel. Mothers were queued up with their children to pay for ice creams opposite a messy duck pond.

"That's not what I mean. I was seeing a lot of girls from the Business School, hard-bitten types. I felt as if I was just a notch in their belt on a Saturday night. I was, like, a workout for them, some fling they would fit carefully into their over-programmed schedule."

"Which you vigorously resisted, no doubt."

"What can I say? I was a horny grad student looking for fun. It was like fast food, though. Unfulfilling. Not exactly romantic. I ended up wanting more—and you were obviously deeper than the rest. But you were my roomie's girl."

"'Story of my life."

"You know, guys always try to make decisions for women they like. You probably think that's sexist. It's innate, though—a male thing to protect those we care for. Take it as a compliment."

"Mickey, I'm actually rather flattered. You were a bit of a hero figure to me then. Larger than life."

"A hero? C'mon."

"Sure. You were the one I figured would accomplish great things. You were the real risk-taker, the one I figured I'd be hearing about in the news someday."

"Ya never know," Mickey muttered, privately amused by her unintended irony.

"I'm developing this theory about life," Rachel continued. "I think where our generation went wrong was to confuse adrenaline surges with some higher consciousness. We thought cliff diving and smoking dope were so very deep. But they didn't yield any vital human experience. They were just a cheap rush."

"I always thought you were sweet on Alexander," Mickey said, abruptly returning to the previous subject. "All those long talks, those walks in the rain. I thought you were the other night too, come to think of it—at Mr. K's."

"It showed?" said Rachel, laughing. "Actually, Mickey, if this is the day for grand confessions, I should admit it. It seems I've quite recently fallen hard for Mr. Bonner."

"Are you serious?"

"I think it may actually be quite serious."

"You *were* sweet on him! I love it! So, how come you never acted on your impulses before?"

"Good question." She picked at a thread in her madras shirt. Trim and short sleeved, she looked like a Junior Leaguer abroad. "I never was particularly good at acting on impulses. And then motherhood rather limits one's spontaneity."

"I mean, back then."

"Guess I was afraid of where it might lead. Even before Stanford, I wouldn't let myself be wild, like the other kids in school. They dropped acid for kicks. I drank Coca-Cola."

Mickey waited again. His struggle to listen amused Rachel; she felt as if she was watching a middle-aged man learning to ride a bike.

"I suppressed a lot in those days," Rachel continued. "I really did care for Alexander, that deeper vein of his character. But you were dangerous."

"So, why did you choose Barry?"

"Barry chose me. It always just seemed inevitable. He was kind—kind and clever. He seemed safe. The Eagle Scout, the banker's boy."

"You make it sound like a trip to the dentist. You jumped into it with your eyes open, didn't you?"

"Yeah, barefoot and pregnant."

"What?"

"As I said, I kind of rushed to do the expected. Didn't seem like a lot of options at the time."

"Really? That quickie ceremony in the garden at Serra House? I thought . . . " Mickey began to realize how many things might not have been as they had appeared. *How much of the past was a lie?*

He regarded Rachel in a new light. "What happened?" he asked.

"Oh, Mickey, you know it seems like another century now. I was twenty years old. All you guys were much older. You forget—you were all catapulted into these jobs you could only dream of. Happened overnight. Remember the Last Dance? Your visions were already realized. You were celebrating. I was scared. The morning after, I was still an undergraduate, five years away from a doctorate in history. Barry was commuting to Shanghai, and I was . . . well, I was 'in a delicate way.'"

Mickey had no idea what to say, and was grateful when Rachel continued after a time.

"I lost the baby. About three weeks after the wedding. Miscarried one day in Shanghai. My first trip to China. Barry had already gone up to Beijing for a meeting. I was alone in this hotel bathroom when it happened."

"God, Rachel. How horrible."

"It *was* horrible. Took almost fifteen years for us to manage to start a family again. And, I really think something in the anxiety, the sense of loss, the pressure to perform, made Barry nuts. I was not blameless there, either."

"I had no idea."

"Nobody did. Our little bedroom secret. But you know, we make our own choices in life. I always seemed to be following somebody else's idea of where I was supposed to be."

"And your idea would have been . . . ?"

"Not sure I ever let myself figure that out. Just felt I was missing something everybody else had enjoyed. I always felt like I was a little too late to the party."

"We did have a good time. But then, I was always playing at being the class clown. Least that's what Branko tells me lately."

"Branko? What have you been talking with him about?" She turned to confront him.

"Oh, he's been all over my case—become my new Father Confessor."

Mickey was biting his nails again, his cuticles pink from the self-inflicted wounds. "Rachel, it's like I said—I shoulda lived my life different."

She squinted at him, studying him carefully, disconcerted by his stumbling introspection.

They walked in silence for a bit, drifting away from the crowds of mothers and baby strollers around the pond. The humidity matched that of Washington's Tidal Basin. Rachel spotted an ice cream cart and bought a Summer Shower popsicle—red, white, and blue. Mickey declined, but watched her enjoy it, amused, as her lips changed color.

He was carrying some oppressive burden, Rachel could now see. She was determined to ferret it out.

"Do you ever ask yourself what exactly you're doing with your life?" She had not meant to sound so accusatory.

"What do you mean?"

"I mean, what's your mission here on the planet? How are you contributing to the advancement of the species?"

"I'm just trying to get through the week."

"Do you intend to stay in China doing the Telstar thing forever? Are the boys going to go to college here? Where the hell are you going to be in ten years?"

"Shoot," he said, foundering under a tide of self-doubt, "I don't even know what I'm going to be doing next month. A buddy of mine in Beijing has this theory. 'We make our own little Hell,' he says. 'We reconstruct some of the dysfunction from our own childhood.'"

"Are things that far gone for you?"

"Rachel, you have no idea."

"You want a beer?"

"No. I'm trying to stay on the wagon. Except for ceremonial stuff, like toasts."

"Mickey Dooley sworn off the hard stuff? What in God's name is that about?"

"Over thirty days now."

"Mickey!" She halted abruptly, putting a firm hand on his shoulder. "What the hell is going on? You got a girlfriend somewhere doing a make-over on you?"

He shook his head and gave her a tight smile. The sun's glow softened his baldness. In the angled light, she could see now a reflection of his former glory—his manic smile, the frenzied energy of the college years. There was still an intensity about him, although only a fraction of his old power remained.

"What *is* it?" she repeated.

"Rachel, it's like this," he began, turning to walk again at her side, an arm holding her at the shoulder. "It's about the boys."

Mickey squinted into the distance, doubling back in his mind, looking to dissemble. He had promised Branko he'd keep his mouth shut. *This was different, though. This was Rachel.* She'd been in danger, too, he rationalized. She could still be in danger, for all he knew, though Branko had doubted she was the primary target.

Conflicting emotions washed over him. Rachel's strength, her familiarity, her reassuring presence beckoned like a snug lifeboat. She had confided in him, shared her most intimate secrets. His mind veered this way and that, flipping and flopping, until it settled once again, as it had so often of late, upon the graceful comfort of confession.

He told her.

Like an idiot, he told her most all of it in a rush, surprised at the equanimity with which she heard him out. He told her about his custody fight, about his efforts to change his life, to cut his ties to China. Ultimately, he told her about the elaborate Fourth of July plans to leave with his boys.

"There's no other way?" she asked with concern when he finally paused.

"All or nothing," he said, hands trembling. "I gotta leave. If I leave the boys behind, or if I get busted trying to get out with them, they have a damn bleak future—kids of a run-away American businessman. Children of divorce raised by a maid because their mother is a mean drunk. But if they make it home safe, their whole life is in front of them. We can live happily ever after."

"Mickey!"

"I know. It's too fucking horrible. It's like Sophie's choice. I have no good options. I can't stay, and I can't leave without them."

"What about Lee? Can't he help you with the authorities to—"

"Lee can't intervene without drawing attention to himself. He's in danger all the time already."

Mickey watched as Rachel began to understand that which remained unsaid. It was a godmother's intuition, he figured. But then again, it seemed she had always been able to read him.

"Branko." She saw it. "Branko's doing this for you, isn't he?"

He just nodded.

"So the old gang is rallying round one last time?" She smiled, pleased at the notion. "Jesus, I can't believe this is what things have come to."

He shrugged, turning with that sheepish grin of his. On impulse, he kissed her on both cheeks as she laughed and hugged him. Then once, after all the years, she kissed him right back, full on the lips, and they spoke no more of his troubles.

Mickey had told her everything—everything except the effort to bring in Lee. With Lee, in the end, it was so very personal. Mickey had waited until the last evening, hoping that, once persuaded, Lee would not change his mind. They had promised to meet each other some time that Friday night, after the Smithson delegation wrapped up their official activities. Few senior Chinese were going to the U.S. Ambassador's small July 4 gathering, relations still being too touchy to celebrate publicly with the Americans. Friday's informal hotel supper was going to serve as the delegation's send-off, except for the routine diplomatic niceties planned the next day for the airport's VIP lounge. This would be Mickey's last chance with Lee.

There were five round tables of six at the St. Regis Hotel's meal. They were in a conference room that had few of the decorative touches of a formal dining setting, with senators and staff from both sides drifting in and out with the waiters. The room opened onto a patio and a gravel walkway it shared with a much larger banquet hall, nightclub, and series of shops ringing the courtyard. Several other parties were going on in other meeting rooms and at the outdoor bar. Even with the doors closed, the delegation could detect the distinctive notes of an overzealous wedding band playing some disco tunes across the way.

Inside, Mickey took a seat next to Lee. He had promised his old colleague a few minutes with Smithson, who was on Lee's right. After the senator and Lee exchanged a series of pleasantries, Lee turned back to his left and began a sidebar discussion with Mickey. Lee was drinking Tsingtao beer, but then the waiter brought *bai jui* for the two men to toast each other's work. Three times they raised a glass in a private *ganbei*. Mickey kept sober by limiting himself to a polite sip. But he was hurting for something stronger as he steeled himself for the crucial ask.

The pitch itself Mickey saved for the coffee. He and Lee had slipped away when the others shifted tables during dessert, small groups milling about, drifting out for a cigarette or to use the facilities. The two of them had headed out into the courtyard for a smoke, Mickey steering away from the dining area that was surely wired for sound. They ambled across the plaza and found a bench under the trees, near the dance hall where a Donna Summer tune was pulsing. Amidst the cacophony of sounds and the crowds milling about, it seemed a surprisingly safe spot. The noise and bustle provided perfect cover for what Mickey needed to say.

He was clear-headed as the moment approached, there on a bench under a canopy of lantern-lit trees, small insects darting through the shafts of light. They spoke briefly of sports and road trips, various pleasures they had once shared, common ground from campus days. Then, very deliberately, Mickey backed once more into the subject that had hung over them for years. China and America. Beijing and Washington. Duty and country, again.

"Dangerous times," Mickey said.

"Yes, dangerous times," Lee repeated.

"How long will you stick this out?"

"What do you mean?

"The Foreign Ministry, your career. If the hard-liners gain the upper hand, there won't be much of a future here for voices of reason. Your way may be suspect."

"*My way?* And what is 'my way,' Mickey?"

"Oh, that's right, Lee. I forgot. You Chinese aren't allowed to have an individual conscience. It's only about collective will and all that crap."

Mickey hadn't meant to bait him. It wasn't in the script they'd rehearsed at Langley. But the hour for improvisation had arrived.

"I have taken my stand." Lee steadied himself as he pulled on his Camel.

"I know. I respect you for that."

"You know? What exactly do you know, old friend? That we're just little pieces somebody else pushes around the chessboard? That we're each being used, even as we try to do good?"

"*Try to do good?*" Mickey seized it. "That's what I said we'd do! Remember? That last night; I said we'd be do-gooders!"

Lee was sobering now, struggling to find firmer ground, eyeing Mickey cautiously in the dim light.

"We did good, damn it," Mickey continued. "We helped build bridges between our countries. We opened trade. China is a better country for it. But now there are people who want to take you back to the days of the Opium Wars. "

"Don't lecture me, Mickey," Lee said, rolling his stiff neck. "I'm getting too old for it. I fight them every day."

"I'm sorry, I just—"

"What you don't understand is that even as we become more modern, the young people are more fanatically nationalist. They see modernization as simply a means to renew ideological struggle. The new regime believes it deeply. They saw what happened to the Soviets. They're way too smart to ever allow it to happen here. That's why they are purging elites for political correctness. That's why they've lately been pouring billions into the security services, buying them whatever they want. It looks like more wealth means more repression, not less. We are victims of our own success."

"I understand that, Lee. But you've done a lot. You've fought the good fight. Couldn't you do more if you, if—"

"Don't, Mickey. Please don't. I've made my place."

"You've had guts. We know your actions took incredible courage. We know all that you've done to try to help the situation."

"What is this *we* crap?" Lee said without looking at him. "It's just you and me on this bench."

"You're in great danger here. You've risked your life for a cause—trying to help your country progress without being dominated by a new bunch of Cold Warriors."

"Please, old friend. I ask you to stop this talk." Lee kicked at the gravel with the toe of his shoe. Mickey could barely hear him now, right at his side. "You are such an innocent."

"*Innocent*? After all the shit I've done? All the little errands for the Ministry, for my father-in-law, for Telstar? My innocence died long ago."

"Don't get involved."

"I'm *already* involved. I got involved the first time I made a deal. And I sure as hell got involved after somebody tried to blow us up in Washington." Lee was growing more agitated, but Mickey ignored him, barreling ahead in a rush. "It's me asking!"

"Asking what?" Lee countered.

"Asking you to help us understand what the hell is going on. So nobody does something stupid and we blow up half the planet in a dispute over some goddamn little island."

"It's Branko, isn't it?" said Lee, aghast. "Branko put you up to this."

"We need to stick together." Mickey was making it up now, freelancing, in way over his head. "We need to stick together. For our kids' sake."

"I have no children."

"This whole country is full of children who share your vision of a more open society. They're all our responsibility."

Lee studied the paper lanterns overhead a long time, squinting, as if to measure the distance between lights. Bursts of conversation rang out from the wedding revelers. Groups from the party ambled by, oblivious to their heated quarrel, as the disco band played on.

"I am touched by your concern," Lee said. "But let me be clear, so I don't leave wondering. What exactly are you asking of me?"

"I'm leaving tomorrow." Mickey blurted it out.

"I know. I'm supposed to see your delegation off at the airport."

"I mean *leaving*."

"What?"

"I'm not coming back—ever." Mickey gestured about them. "I'm leaving this whole world behind."

"Huh?"

"I'm taking my boys home—home to America. Branko's arranged it."

"And what exactly do you expect me to do?"

Mickey said it is baldly as he could. "Just *leave*."

"I am Chinese, Mickey . . ."

"I'm authorized to make whatever arrangements you want to get you out of the country, or even slip you onto our plane tomorrow. Lee, it's the best way—"

"I am *Chinese*. I don't wish to play any more of your American games. I am sick of it all." Lee sighed. "Our guys, your guys. Our military, your military. You arm our enemies to the teeth. You buzz us with spy planes. Then you act surprised when we take offense. I don't want some stupid war over Taiwan. Why can't you just leave us alone?"

"Some of your people are trying to sabotage the summit. We need to figure it out *now*, before it risks sparking something larger."

"You want me to abandon my country? To go sit in Langley and educate your spies while they feed me Happy Meals?"

"Not just that—"

"It's a great life a traitor lives."

"What good can you do dead? Stop deluding yourself, Lee. That bomb at Rachel's firm was meant for us. Somebody wants you out of the picture in the worst way. You want to be a fucking martyr? Well, that wasn't the deal. That's not what we promised each other years ago. We were going to *live* life."

Lee fell silent. They seemed quite alone, even amidst the noise and the passing crowds. After a long while, he asked again: "What precisely do they want to know?"

"Have you heard of the 'Red Dragons'?"

Lee nodded.

"In the Second Directorate over at the Defense Ministry, they tell me," Mickey said. "Supposedly a buncha hard-liners with powerful allies in the bureaucracy, a buncha guys who spend their days coming up with novel ways to screw up U.S.-China relations."

"Yes, Mickey," he said. "I have to deal with their little games every day."

"We figured. Well, Langley is desperate to get some greater kind of transparency on their operations, to find out how they exploit divisions between political factions. And they've got to know more about this threat to the summit."

"Meaning what?"

"They need a roadmap. They have some sense *what* these guys are up to. They don't really know the who, and where, and how it's being done."

"So you want me to infiltrate this PLA cell just so your president can secure his little photo opportunity at the summit?"

"Lee, we need you to help identify them. Maybe help avert some disaster."

"And after that? Would you try to eliminate them? A dozen more will rise in their place, like weeds."

"No. They just need to track them. Listen in. Whatever the hell our intelligence community does for a living. Target assets. Intercept cell phones. Capture e-mail."

Lee was shaking his head, burying his face in his hands. "I'm tired, Mickey. I'm so tired of the game."

"Listen. You've got two options as I see it. And this is me talking, not some professional spook. One, you can try to get out now, while you can still do some good. Before they pull another crazy stunt and try to take you down, just for sport. Or, two, if you want to be a stubborn asshole, do it your way. Stay, if you insist. But try to get inside and share some insight with our people here. Maybe we can help counter their plans, cover your backside some way. But you gotta maintain contact with us. Branko's complaining that you've rebuffed every approach for months. You're at greater risk each day."

Lee regarded him intently, his eyes full of sorrow, the noise of the band pulsing through the courtyard. "Yes, Mickey, I *am* in danger here. And if the CIA is involving amateurs like you, I am in greater danger than even I suspected."

"Lee, I would *never* betray you," Mickey whispered.

Lee regarded him carefully before he replied. "You know, I lied to you once."

"What?"

"I was drunk. At that hamburger bar. The Oasis? I was drunk and scared."

"You lied to me?"

"I lied, yeah. When I said that someday I would betray you all."

"You lied?"

"I won't. Maybe I thought I would have, could have, years ago. Maybe I would have done it out of some wrong-headed sense of patriotism. Like my father."

"That was a long time ago."

"Experience has changed me. Tiananmen changed me. I won't."

"I remember the night. You scared the shit outta me."

"I won't betray you. But how can I do what you ask? To stay and spy on my own people?" Lee said. "I am Chinese, part of a great and ancient civilization."

"I understand."

"Without that, I am nothing. If that means I must leave, then let it be so. Maybe that is my duty."

"We will always honor you."

"Honor?" Lee scoffed. "What do we think that really means these days?"

"It's the right thing to do."

"To flee?"

"It may be the one truly patriotic act you can perform."

"Sure," Lee muttered, his shoulders sagging. He seemed broken, and Mickey feared little could be done to repair him. So Mickey buried himself in the details, hurriedly explaining Branko's audacious plan to get Lee and Mickey's boys onto the delegation's plane. So simple, yet so remarkably bold.

They sat a while longer in the shadows of a few leafy trees, the passersby quite oblivious as sound cascaded all about them. In the end, Lee seemed to give up. He consented to the exit strategy Mickey detailed for the very next day.

They would leave the U.S. Embassy together. A diversion would be created at the airport, and the ploy would unfold right there in the departure lounge, Lee's absence going unnoticed until after the U.S. Air Force plane and Senate delegation were heading east in international airspace across the Pacific.

Lee was fatalistic, though, as if someone had died. Mickey could see it, recognizing the grave danger inherent in this final resignation. So, when they said good-bye some minutes later after rejoining stray members of their party, Mickey found no comfort in their resolution. Mickey sensed that this was the last time for them, that they would not speak again—that this was an end, a despairing end to a quarter century of friendship across a great divide.

The next morning, the Beijing dawn broke stale and gray; it was the fourth of July. A thick layer of formless clouds obscured any possibility of sunshine. At home in his apartment, Mickey was ashen. He'd slept only in brief patches, staring at the alarm from the couch in the den. He had packed and repacked the one bag he would bring, taking great care not to include anything that might trigger suspicion if it was searched.

Old songs floated through his head, haunting melodies about leaving home—Joan Baez, John Lennon. He *was* leaving, forever. The lyrics had made it real to him in the heart of that last night in China. He had awoken around four a.m with a sudden need. Photographs—he wanted some baby pictures, and went silently into the master bedroom in search of an album. Mei Mei was sleeping soundly. He lingered for several minutes, watching her, feeling guilty now for the first time, despite years of weathering her contempt.

He felt sorry—sorry for the failure of their long-ago dreams. He felt ashamed of his calculation, even as he stood at the threshold, preparing to spirit their two sons away. He could justify it all. He could justify fleeing with the boys to give them a more promising future. It was the best move for them, he had convinced himself, even as he questioned the enormity of the act.

How in God's name do you just walk away from your life? He gazed about the room, taking it all in once more. Then he slipped away.

He got the boys up early, had them dressed and out the door before Mei Mei awoke. They were off to the pancake breakfast at the American Embassy. After seeing their father off at the airport, the boys were ostensibly going to return to the apartment with a family friend from the Embassy staff. Mickey had reconfirmed everything the night before with Mr. Peck, his Embassy control officer, who was elated by his apparent success in re-enlisting Lee. It would be a coup, the man reassured him—a major breakthrough for U.S. intelligence. "Pull it off and you're a hero, pal."

Mickey wondered, though. In the flat light of the morning, he felt anything but heroic.

Saturday was still a workday in the city, and the streets were crowded as their taxi angled its way through traffic, his boys chattering away in the back seat. They wore matching blue pants, red and white shirts, and baseball caps. A normal Saturday it seemed, as Mickey tried desperately to calm himself. His every sense was alert. Street smells of diesel fuel and cooking oil seemed intense. Sharp sounds made him jumpy, even the tooting of traffic horns. He searched every face, sizing up passing drivers.

The Embassy gathering was desultory. The delegation members were exhausted after a week on the road. The Ambassador's decision to low-key the affair, and the absence of most of the Chinese officialdom, drained all energy from the event. Rachel and a man from Protocol had gone ahead to the airport to clear passports and bags. The rest were left to chat listlessly, peering at their watches as they waited for departure hour to arrive. The boys played a game of catch with a tennis ball in the garden while Mickey sought out Mr. Peck for a few last words.

The man was staring grimly at Mickey as they milled about, motioning for him to follow. Mickey saw only his back as they strode into the residence and followed into a washroom. Peck walked forward and flushed the noisy toilet, then wheeled upon him.

"We're fucked," Peck whispered.

"What?" Mickey was stunned. "Where's—"

"Wait." Peck held up a hand as he motioned to the listening walls about them, then whipped out a small note pad and began to scrawl.

"No Lee," he wrote.

"Where?" Mickey just mouthed the word, feeling helpless. Somehow, he had known the night before that Lee would not show.

"No sign of him."

Mickey grabbed the pen. "What now?"

Peck's eyes narrowed as he read.

"You GO," he wrote. "GO with the boys."

Mickey stared at the paper. He had tried to prepare himself for this eventuality. But now he was sagging, knees weak.

He watched as Peck added: "You get out. Today. Langley's orders." He even underlined it for Mickey, before adding "Lee's on his own."

It was Peck's last note before he tore the paper in pieces and threw them in the toilet. He then urinated and flushed, before walking out, a touch of professional disgust in his brusqueness.

Now Mickey's life shifted into slow motion. The droning voices of the Embassy party mixed with the pedantic conversations of the few Chinese diplomats present—so many words of so little interest. He craned his neck about, looking anxiously for Lee to join the rest of the Protocol guys who comprised the small Foreign Ministry escort. He took to patrolling the grounds, checking the driveway, peering beyond the Marine guards at the gated entrance, hoping against hope.

Where the hell was Lee? Mickey tried to contact Lee on his cell phone, then made inquiries, struggling to mask his concern. But neither the Americans nor the Chinese had word of him. Mickey wanted to call. He wanted to send Peck's people again to Lee's residence and to his office.

Time was up, though. Mickey had to choose: to stay and try to help his friend, to stay and sleep in the messy bed he'd made of his life? Or to make a final all-or-nothing dash, to accept Branko's offer and abandon Lee to his fate? As the entourage shuffled their way to the three mini-buses taking them out to the airport, Mickey had to decide all over again.

Lee was lost. Mickey was beyond caring for himself now, for his own life, for his own bleak future. It was only about the boys. They were American more than Chinese. Their future in China would forever be tainted, sons of an American barred as a spy. The boys would be scorned, raised by a cranky mother who'd openly voice the anger she felt toward their father. To his horror, it seemed quite clear. It was all about his children now—nothing more. Lee would agree. Mickey had to make a run for it.

He felt sick as they drove through the mid-morning traffic, his stomach in revolt. He slid open a window against the waves of nausea, muttering only a few words while his boys played with their Game-boys amid continued sirens. They were slowed by road construction. Then, at last, the airport complex was before them.

Mickey gripped his boys' hands firmly as the group was escorted through the main terminal. The voices buzzing about him were disorienting. He heard German and Russian and Korean, guttural voices quarrelling about bags and tickets. Soldiers strutted by, seeming to eye them all with suspicion. The crackling of the loudspeakers began to penetrate his skull, and he grew dizzy. The harsh tones of Asian authoritarianism seemed to press in on him once more as the disembodied voices echoed off the great hall.

"*Come to Chamber Three now, Yankee dog,*" they could just as well have been taunting. "*Time for your noon beating.*"

He fought for composure as the delegation skirted the lines of international travelers. They were escorted by a Foreign Ministry man whom Mickey recognized from Lee's department, past the smoked glass of Passport Control, past the armed soldiers through the VIP area, and into the small departure lounge. Mickey was cleared in. He had an exit visa to hitch a ride back to Washington with the delegation on the Air Force plane. The boys and the rest of the Embassy staff proceeded unchallenged, with the American ambassador and the Senate delegation. They had made it that far.

Rachel was there, and Mickey wanted to go to her, for strength, for comfort. She was deliberately ignoring him, though, as she fussed over little things, playing the staffer role again, fetching an *International Herald Tribune* for a senator and chatting with one of her clients, a Silicon Valley CEO. Before them was a tray of lemonade and Coke, a stack of newspapers, and pans full of hot hors d'oeuvres warmed by little Sterno cans underneath.

The twins buried themselves in the box scores, checking on baseball statistics, as their father had taught them. Mickey was at the window, nose pressed against the glass, gazing at the Air Force plane near the special VIP runway. He half expected to see Lee come sprinting across the tarmac, making an insane dash for freedom. Mickey still clung to the hope that he would appear, absurdly, suitcase in hand.

How can I leave him now? Lee had been his bridge here—master and mentor in one, his first true Chinese friend. They had swung a dozen deals together. They had played the game, sharing secret hopes and fears.

The Chinese would kill Lee. When Mickey's boys did not return, and Mei Mei's father went into a rage—when Mickey's actions sparked a security review—a witch-hunt would ensue. They would choose their time and place carefully. Then they would come for Lee and make an example of him.

A sharp commotion broke out at the door. An Interior Ministry policeman was arguing with a Foreign Ministry assistant about some paperwork. Branko's colleague from the Embassy, Peck, loitered not far to the side. Mickey was transfixed. He strained to catch Mandarin words like "papers . . . delays . . . engine." The argument grew heated as he leaned forward in an attempt to hear more.

Then Rachel was before him, interposing her body and blocking Mickey's view of the unfolding scene. She gave him a casual morning kiss on the cheek as she whispered. "Lee couldn't make it. Needed to be with his father. Now, get on the damn plane." She smiled brightly at him as she patted his cheek for emphasis, then moved on to greet Smithson before Mickey could respond.

So many eyes were watching. So little he could say now, halfway across a field of mines, lights on, snipers firing. He tried to concentrate on Michael and Henry, on bringing them home to America.

"Ladies and gentlemen," an American voice called out after a time—it was Branko's guy—"I have a brief announcement. We've got clearance for take-off. But there appears to be a brief delay. Captain Browner has powered up and found a couple of maintenance items to tend to in the cockpit. Doesn't look serious. While he attends to this little glitch, the captain invites you all to come on board and have some ice cream in celebration of Independence Day."

The senators and spouses went first, followed by the business travelers. Rachel was directly behind as they stood and walked toward the jet-way, a firm hand on Mickey's back.

"Here. It's from Lee," she whispered again, pressing into his hand an old silver medallion, a vintage Saint Christopher, patron saint of voyagers. "Booth's father gave it to him the day Lee flew home from Stanford." Then she was smiling at the guy behind her as she chatted up some computer company executive. Mickey rubbed the silver furiously between his thumb and forefinger as his boys began to walk casually down the jet-way.

Shouting erupted from behind them. Mickey could see an Interior Ministry official berating the man from Lee's department. Something about papers and access to the secure area. His troops had pea green uniforms, crisp with black pistols tightly holstered. Now he was glaring toward Mickey and the boys, a pointed finger stabbing the sheet of paper before him. His eyes were dark and challenging. The soldiers began to push forward.

A command came from behind them, and the soldiers halted just as quickly. A path parted. Another group of grim-faced officials appeared, led by a haggard looking man calmly calling the Interior Ministry official's name. And there was Lee.

Had he come to join them? Impossible; it was too late, too overt. *Was his appearance to provide some last minute insurance for the success of the plan?*

Mickey fought the impulse to call out to him, to plead with him again, to pull him across the line that seemed to divide the Americans from the Chinese at the plane's threshold.

Lee's distant eyes told him "no," however. They were puffy and defeated—as if Lee's heart was long gone, fighting some other war already. It was best for Mickey to let go of hope for his friend.

Focus. Gently, he nudged his boys forward, a hand on each of their shoulders. They walked ahead, cheerful and innocent, oblivious to the determined contest of wills underway.

Just keep walking. Branko's people had been very clear. He and the kids continued unchallenged across the threshold and down the aisles of the plane, the angry voices beginning to dissipate behind them.

There was animated conversation now among the American delegation even as some began to store their carry-on bags in the overhead bins and find their seats. Mickey grabbed a bowl of ice cream from the galley in the plane's rear. He began to spoon-feed his boys like infants as they sat in the last row, reaching across as if trying to shield them with his body from the fracas beyond.

He started to pray in silence, afraid to look back up the aisles or out the windows into the lounge. The chatter about them seemed very slowly to settle in upon itself, like waves in the sea softening after sunset. Few noticed as the ambassador and other Beijing-based staff stepped off the plane and drifted back into the waiting area. The oxygen flowing into the cabin shot out more forcefully as the captain again powered up the engines for a test.

Then the call of frightened voices came surging down through the jetway from back in the lounge area, American and Chinese voices shouting past each other. White smoke was billowing up from the center of the VIP lounge. People were rushing about.

Mickey witnessed it all, viewing the bizarre spectacle through the windows of the plane as it sat in its spot on the tarmac just yards away. Flames erupted quickly in the departure lounge, bits of newspaper sailing about and the Sterno stoves overturned. Automatic sprinklers shot water from the ceiling. A soldier wrestled with a fire extinguisher as more men rushed into the lounge and alarms rang. From the cockpit, Captain Browner barked orders to seal the plane. Almost immediately, they began to roll away toward safety.

Out his window, Mickey could see a fire crew race into the secure area, spraying the buffet table and couches with foam. Through the smoke, Mickey could just make out the stoic face of Lee standing by, stamping calmly on the ashes. Lee peered up one final time to watch them pull away, looking for all the world like Zhivago's brother, the aging revolutionary from Pasternak's last scene, gazing wistfully at a future that had just passed him by.

There was animated chatter onboard the swiftly rolling plane now as it sped away from the fire danger, dozens of voices talking all at once. Over the intercom, the "Star Spangled Banner" was blaring. The aircraft raced forward down its dedicated runway, then was airborne to the music. In minutes, the Air Force plane was out over the East Pacific, safely into international airspace. The boys were giggling with excitement. Mickey was shaking as he tried to cover himself with nervous laughter.

"I have a holiday surprise for you," he said sheepishly as Michael and Henry looked at each other, confused but grinning. "They said I could take you for a special ride—maybe all the way to Alaska."

Then he held them tight, tears of joy mingling with tears of sorrow.

24

NIGHTCAP

By the time Mickey Dooley and his boys landed at Elmendorf Air Force Base in Alaska, the carefully woven fabric of U.S.-China relations had begun to shred. Official Beijing was full of super-charged rhetoric. But inside their airborne cocoon, as they waited on the runway for refueling, the American travelers were, for the most part, blissfully ignorant of global developments.

With his groggy boys, Mickey slipped away from the delegation and disembarked at the military facility just outside of Anchorage. They rode in a car Branko had sent, heading straight to the international airport and a United flight to San Francisco. Albuquerque, Branko had concluded, would become too hot, the media likely to turn the grandparents' neighborhood into a replay of the Elian Gonzalez circus once played out in Miami. They even had a passing concern about Mei Mei's father sending agents to pull some wild stunt on U.S. soil, though few in Langley took that threat seriously.

Mickey was sobered by the need to further debrief his Agency escort about his on again-off again efforts to recruit Lee. He employed some code names and phrases about the fruitless attempt to bring Lee in, lest the serious talk in front of the kids concern them. He remained horrified by what might befall Lee, marooned in his homeland. But Mickey stuck to the facts and focused on getting through with the boys. The Agency officers then brought them through a secure entrance to the terminal, giving Dooley two overnight bags with some underwear, socks, and a clean change of clothes for his sons. There would be more in California, he was assured.

Mickey postponed a more serious reckoning with the boys, devising an elaborate tale on the plane about a surprise visit to the grandparents and a major league baseball game. He fervently hoped it would be his last lie. It would not be easy for the boys to endure the separation to come, with their mother in a fury back in Beijing.

For now, the boys took it all as a lark as they arrived back in the USA. During those first hours of flight, the strangest thing for Michael and Henry turned out to be the fact that, having crossed the international dateline, it was July 4th all over again in Anchorage. They were giggling about the "Groundhog Day" movie with Bill Murray they had seen on video—clamoring for a holiday do-over. But they were hurried away and pre-boarded, First Class, on the domestic flight. They were asleep again before they took off, bound for California. Mickey was still in a state of shock, worrying about Lee and awaiting an uncertain future.

Rachel flew on toward Washington with Smithson's entourage. Out her window, the jagged peaks of the Canadian Rockies gave way to the great flat northern plains. There had been little cell phone traffic from Alaska because everyone but Mickey and the boys had stayed on board. Gossip from those who had called home nevertheless began to fill the fliers in on the drama unfolding about them.

They had become part of an international incident, the full significance of which was as yet unclear. The only overt sign on board was when Senator Smithson huddled with military liaison in the cockpit, on what Rachel later learned was some special Pentagon hook-up.

It was very late Saturday night—again—when the plane finally rolled to a halt at Andrews Air Force Base near Washington. The fireworks on the Mall were long past done, dissipated into the tons of garbage that patriotic revelers left in their wake. The exhausted travelers gathered their carry-on bags and peered onto the tarmac. Just outside the modest military arrival terminal, a full press stakeout awaited them, complete with live cameras and bug-attracting klieg lights penetrating the heavy air. There, too, to Rachel's great relief, was Alexander.

"Welcome back to the land of the free!" said Alexander, greeting her with a chaste peck and immediately taking her carry-on bag. "You guys OK?"

"Bless you for being here," Rachel said, clutching his arm as she waved away a couple of reporters headed her way. "I haven't become work for you again, have I?"

"I came for *you*, not for this circus."

"What the hell!" An elongated boom mike was hanging just above Alexander's head, and Rachel swatted at it as if it was some grotesque insect. It seemed to bob and weave, guided by its own manic design, before veering off toward another target.

A few minutes later, they were safe in Alexander's car, motoring across the still-busy Beltway and around the weary city.

"I'm afraid I'm not quite all here," Rachel apologized, breaking the silence.

"It's always a killer flight. Even with Air Force wheels."

"Eighteen hours—and through about four civilizations, it feels like. Major culture shock."

"And I thought we were converging." Alexander chuckled before putting the question to her: "So, what exactly happened at the Beijing airport? Did you see how he did it?"

"Did what?"

"The, uh, 'kidnapping' I believe is what the Chinese Foreign Ministry is calling it."

"Kidnapping! You're serious?"

"Really. It's all over the news. They're making a really big stink about it. And it's the perfect cover because the PRC is rolling out their annual Taiwan war game exercise early. So it's part of a much bigger story. Was it really Mickey and his boys?"

Rachel buried her eyes in her palms, rubbing in a vain search for clarity. "Yes, Alexander, it really was. And Cowboy Mickey pulled it off." Then she slumped back, her thoughts on Jamie and the coming dawn.

There was an awkward scene when they first arrived at Rachel's home. Barry was up, pacing in the hallway. Having tucked Jamie in, he was there for the night, evidently, and had opened up the sofa-bed in the den. Several of his bags were packed in the front hallway for his morning departure.

An opera was playing in hidden speakers—Pavarotti—too boisterous for midnight. Rachel set her bags in the front hall and Barry hugged her, told her he was relieved she was back safe and sound. She lingered a long moment while Alexander busied himself with her bags in the entry, then she headed up to give Jamie a kiss and collapse in her bed.

Barry and Alexander made small talk, non-sequiturs trailing into meaningless generalities—the weather, the Nationals' playoff hopes, whatever. Alexander went to use the toilet before hitting the road. But when he came back, Barry had two Amarettos in his hand, standing expectantly.

"Nightcap?" The question hung in the air, part demand, part peace offering.

"Sure," Alexander said. "I guess I could use one."

He followed Barry through an immaculate kitchen, where only the stove light illuminated glistening counters. He waited as Barry fiddled with the lock to the sliding glass door, and then they walked together onto the deck, side by side. A fattened moon rode between waves of rolling clouds. The air was thick with crickets and humidity; it seemed too bright for the depths of the night.

They sipped the almond liquor, and leaned against the railing, peering into the distance. "So, I'm off for a few weeks," Barry said matter-of-factly, leaving his itinerary typically vague.

"Jamie will miss having you twenty-four/seven, I'm sure."

"We had a great two weeks."

Alexander was staring down, averting his eyes even in the dark.

"You know, there's something I always meant to ask you, Bonner."

Something in Barry's tone made Alexander want to leave. He regretted accepting the drink. He felt guilty; he didn't really want to be there with Barry, for whatever it was that needed to be said.

"I mean, I don't necessarily have any right," Barry said, stumbling. Alexander could hear now that this wasn't his first drink of the evening. "But, then, what the hell."

"Barry," Alexander began, turning to face him, "you don't need to—"

"For old times' sake. You can ask your own question first."

Barry had squared up at him, taller and more formidable than Alexander had remembered. Alexander saw the strength in his shoulders, the old swimmer's bulk looming above him in a streak of moonlight.

"C'mon, I'm not really up for—"

"Just do this with me. Ask me whatever the hell comes to mind. I get one question for you. And no bullshit."

"Sheesh." Alexander felt his head droop.

He could hear Barry breathing, too close, an intimidating presence. They stayed like that for several moments, Alexander waiting.

"OK . . ."

"Shoot."

"OK," Alexander began again, "I guess I always did wonder . . ."

"What?"

"What's the deal with all the safes?"

Barry did not answer immediately. After several moments, he just repeated "the safes."

"Yeah. Like the wall safe, the combo safe on the filing cabinets—your whole inner sanctum thing with all your stuff."

"What do you mean?"

"You don't need all that security just to bring your Wall Street business home. Can't be that many corporate secrets you carry around on weekends."

There was a stillness about them now as the clouds streamed noiselessly before the flush moon.

"So," Barry finally responded, "what if I told you it was none of your business?"

"Hey, the game was *your* idea," Alexander noted, then set his glass down and stood to leave. "This is dumb."

"No," Barry said, catching him firmly by the wrist. "Stay a minute."

Alexander first tried to eye him in the dark, then spoke. "You know, I always had this theory . . ."

"What's that?"

"Well, I'd make up my own story for you. Like when you're waiting at an airport, killing time, watching people, and you make up secret lives for them, detailed biographies. You ever do that?"

"Sure."

"After Stanford, once we all scattered, I never really felt I knew you. I never really knew Barry any more. None of us did. The years went by and the rest of us managed to stay connected. You became an enigma. You seemed more and more remote. I wondered where you had gone."

"So . . ."

"So, I made up a story. I had it all figured out."

"Right."

"I figured you were some secret agent, a regular James Bond type."

"That's a reach!" Barry laughed, too loud, shattering the evening air. A frog scampered through the bushes near the birdbath.

"I figured Lee had recruited you, made you a Chinese spy. Sold you on the idea he could land you some mammoth business deal if you helped him look good with all the Party higher-ups. That was my theory, anyway."

"That would also enrich me, no doubt. What was Mickey's old line about coming to do good, and staying to do well?"

"Sure. Then I figured maybe the CIA found you out—had Branko flip you as a double agent."

"Thus the need for two safes."

"Exactly! A double agent must keep his files straight. Anyway, the absurdity is what gave the theory color."

"Bonner, you always were meant to write fiction."

"I wish."

"It's your overactive imagination."

Alexander finished his drink and, with a swirling movement, launched the ice in the general direction of the woods. They both stared at the moon. They were slowing now, like a carousel after the music stopped.

"Anyway . . ." Alexander began again tentatively.

Barry was still lost in a private thought.

"So, man . . ." Alexander stood and offered a hand.

Barry did not move as he muttered, "I never asked you *my* question."

"No," said Alexander, halting. There was some perfect balance to this moment, some equilibrium he was loath to upset. Gently, he placed his hand on Barry's shoulder. "And you never answered mine."

"I'm not sure you really want an answer," Barry said, his voice so soft Alexander could not quite make out the words.

"Huh?"

"I'm not sure you really want the truth," Barry continued, purposeful now. Alexander noticed the light go out upstairs in the master bedroom. "Sometimes, people *don't*, you know. They just pretend to. But then, despite the awkwardness of our situation, I respect you too much to lie."

"Suit yourself," Alexander said, again fighting the impulse to leave.

There was some reckoning that needed to be achieved here, Alexander knew, something to be said before either of them could move on, though Alexander was clueless where they were heading.

Barry turned now. Their eyes were not two feet apart. A breeze rustled the trees. Leaves, still laden from the afternoon thunderstorms, were shedding splashes of water with a shudder.

"It's funny," Barry began, "it's hard to have all that many secrets from a man who's screwing your wife."

Alexander winced but held his ground, listening.

"It's very difficult," Barry continued. "You know, I remembered the strangest thing the other day. I was sitting at the playground, watching Jamie. Just sitting with my Starbucks, watching his pure joy in his fantasy world. Then I remembered. It hit me out of the blue, like some connected moment from another life, from twenty-five years ago at Stanford. It must have been some kind of premonition. I was jealous of you back then. As if I knew, already. As if I could see it coming."

"Barry, don't be paranoid. There wasn't much to know."

"I *saw* it, Alexander. I don't hold that against you. I saw it. I was performing harder, even then, whenever you were around. It was like I was performing, to hold Rachel's interest, to be the big man on campus. Working at it. Filling the silences with happy talk. Trying so damn hard to impress her—even then."

"You were several years older than Ra—"

"No. You still don't get it. You would just *sit* there. Sit and watch and listen. Remember the line Mickey and I used? To provoke you? 'Step right up. Pay five dollars and make the mute man speak!'"

"I wasn't competing with you—"

"Chicks dug it. Thought you were *very* deep. They always wanted to draw you out of your shell, to mother you."

Alexander regarded his glass, still empty. Before he could speak, Barry bolted for the kitchen. "I'll get you another," he called over his shoulder.

Barry was back soon, ice cubes in one bare fist, the liquor bottle held by the neck in the other.

"What?" Barry asked, his arm unsteady as he poured.

"Nothing."

"No, what were you thinking?" Barry said as he gestured accusingly with the bottle.

Alexander was on autopilot now. But Barry, it seemed, could detect his emotions.

"I was thinking that you still never answered the question."

"You're right," Barry said as he sat on the edge of a deck chair. He sipped slowly at his drink. "But this time, I'm going to."

"There was a man named Alan Wallingford . . ." That was all Barry said for a while, as Alexander waited. "He lived with his wife and two daughters in New Canaan, Connecticut. Great kids. One is up at Hampshire College, at that great film program there. Lovely girl. The other, a soccer player, is on her way to Sarah Lawrence next year.

"Alan was a wonderful man. You would have enjoyed each other if you'd ever met. Did deals on Wall Street all day. Loved the theatre at night. Loved to hike, to swim. Did the Matterhorn. Pike's Peak. Mount Rainier. Played the horn. Wrote sonnets. A remarkably multi-dimensional guy—a true renaissance man."

Alexander watched as Barry began to reach, then to coil, as if in pain, pulling his knees to his chest.

"Alan died on February ninth. Pneumonia and 'other complications.' Nice obituary in the *New York Times*.

"I loved him, Alexander. I loved him for seven years. Shared a space on this planet with him. Shared a fantasy that we could openly be together, some way, somehow. That someday we could stop compromising, stop maintaining pretenses. You, of all people, Alexander, understand what it's like to lose someone you love. But you'll never know how hard it is to love someone, to live with your secret, but then to have to watch from a safe distance while they die, denying it all."

"My God, Barry—"

"You know what was the hardest?" Barry demanded. "The very last lie, the last one. That goddamn obituary."

"You should have said some—"

"So proper. So fucking proper. It made me nuts! In the end, I became irrational after all those years of calculation. I loved the man for seven years, and I wanted to think *I* could be some small part of that last story. I wanted to read my name there. I wanted it to read, 'Barry Lavin also loved him.' I didn't want to be excluded just because our love was inconvenient, that seventy-three percent of Americans think it's some socially aberrant behavior. It was *real*. Anyway, it was a stupid need, a stupid desire."

"No."

"Stupid!" Barry was shouting now, flinging the arm that held the Amaretto bottle, splashing the deck. "He lied to his wife, almost to the very end. He lied to his daughters about his disease. The lies were the means to an end, to our times together. We deserved that time, we cherished it, lived for it. I didn't mind all the lies so much when he was living. But with his death, I just couldn't tolerate them all any more. It was like a goddamn sacrilege, denying my life. I'll never live that lie again."

"Barry, you should have said something."

"Like what?"

"I mean—"

"What the fuck *could* I have said? People want you to stay in your box. You contradict the caricature—the archetype they've pegged you for—and, well, that gets real uncomfortable."

"I just wish you hadn't felt like you had to shut everyone out," Alexander said. "You should have had someone there for you."

Alexander set his glass on the railing and waited, staring at the moon.

"Branko was the only one who knew," Barry said.

"You told *Branko*?"

"I never *told* him. I never volunteered my little secret to anybody. Didn't even tell my mom—even when I was afraid for my own health, that maybe I was a danger to Rachel. I just told Rachel recently—and you, now."

"How did Branko find out?"

"It was the weirdest thing," said Barry, wiping his face on the back of his hand and straightening. "Some crazy deal about some Chinese agent he was running. Apparently, the CIA was tipped by a source in Beijing that there were a couple of guys from the Chinese mission at the UN tailing me. I was doing some big transaction with Shanghai, and the Chinese were trolling for guys they might be able to blackmail, to help them get some deals for prohibited satellite technology or something."

"And Branko?"

"Branko warned me."

"What'd he say?"

"Said it was his professional duty. Specifically said he wasn't telling me out of friendship. Just wanted me to know that if the little Commie buggers ever threatened to out me, I should tell them to fuck off, and then tell Rachel everything so they couldn't use it as leverage to blackmail me."

"Sounds like Branko." Alexander shook his head. His limbs felt heavy as he peered at his watch. "Hey, you know, I should get going."

"Not fair, man."

"What?"

"I get my question."

"Barry, c'mon. Haven't we covered enough ground for one night?"

"No. I get mine, too."

"It's late."

"It was *my* goddamn idea, Alexander. Now it's my turn. It's an obvious question."

"Shit."

"When did you fall in love with my wife?"

"Do you really want to go over all the—"

"Because I love her, too, you know. I loved her first. I didn't stop loving her just because . . . it was awkward."

"No, I know you didn't." Alexander felt like a jerk. He was speaking in almost a whisper now. "She knows that, too."

"She was in denial for so long. She didn't want to accept failure, but she didn't want to live a lie any more than I did. It was so unbelievably hard for us both. She felt abandoned. She deserved better. It wasn't her fault.

Wasn't anybody's *fault*."

"Jesus, man."

Barry punched him on the shoulder, not that lightly. "So answer the damn question."

"I don't know . . ." Alexander saw no alternative. "I always was attracted to her, Barry. She was honest and mischievous and full of life, even when she seemed so vulnerable. She was better with people than I was, so much more engaging. I admired her. But there was nothing romantic then. She was like a kid sister. You two were a couple before I got to know her well. It always felt safe, our friendship. Like loving her *that* way would be some kind of sacrilege. It wasn't until after she was wounded this spring. The whole bombing thing seemed to change her outlook so much. She seemed more sure of what she wanted, like she finally wanted to live her truth."

"But at Stanford?"

"I never even kissed her," he said, lying now to console Barry, to ease the man's loss.

"So I was jealous for nothing?"

Alexander put his hand on Barry's shoulder again. "Maybe it *was* a premonition."

They walked together down the steps, around the house, and through the damp grass, their soft footfalls feeling like the careful steps of conspiratorial teenagers, creeping home long past curfew.

As they crossed the darkened drive, Alexander turned once more to Barry. "Thanks," he said.

"Yeah, sure." Barry stiffened and stepped back, remembering something.

"Oh," Barry added, almost as an afterthought, "about the safes?"

"Yeah?"

"Poems."

"Poems?"

"Alan used to write these incredible poems. And photographs. He would take lots of photos, too. Landscapes from our hikes together. Portraits." Barry took a deep breath and exhaled.

"Towards the end, I kept *everything*. It helped keep me sane. Somehow, the stuff I kept in there became a kind of memory chest. They were like artifacts, each with a story to tell. I needed to keep them, to have some tangible evidence it had all been real. I needed to know it hadn't just been a dream I'd lived alone in my head for all those years."

25

THINGS FALL APART

"**G**entlemen don't tell tales," said Alexander, determined to resist Rachel's inquiries.

"No, really!" Rachel demanded. "What the hell were you guys talking about for so long? It was as if Barry knew everything before we even came in the door together. I was upstairs drifting into dreamland and there you two were, yammering on like the old days, talking about God-knows-what."

It was almost noon, and Rachel's call found Alexander at his office.

"We were talking about the good old days."

"Sure."

"It was, well, private."

"But I would like to—"

"Rachel, trust me on this one. And—hey, you need to get caught up. Unbelievable things are happening. The planet never rests."

"What do you mean?" She was still groggy with jet lag, struggling to clear her head after two Tylenol PM's and nine hours of deep sleep in her own bed. "Actually, I had these bizarre dreams about Wyoming and World War II."

"That seems appropriate. The surreal is upon us."

"What the hell's going on?"

"With?"

"With the real world. What's the word out of Beijing?"

"Oh, they're playing it for all it's worth. "Kidnapping . . . CIA plot." They've been running stock footage of the Air Force plane and Smithson for hours. They're kicking out Ambassador Davis. Gave him twenty-four hours to leave."

"Davis?"

"Yeah."

"He didn't even know . . . Actually, I'm really not sure any more."

"They're using some weird war crimes language. Trying to make it an issue at the UN."

"War crimes!?" Rachel was incredulous. "They're *American* kids, they've got American passports, an American dad. Mickey was getting screwed on custody in the Chinese courts. They violate their own laws. He couldn't even take them home for the summer."

She stopped. She was lying barefoot on the couch in her living room, thinking of Jamie again—Jamie, with his mournful eyes, looking anxiously at her as she saw him off to summer camp that morning.

"Rachel, it's OK. You don't need to justify yourself."

"I feel like we've got to justify everything. Me. Mickey. You. Everybody."

"Relax. You've just come straight through twelve time zones."

"Sure."

"I mean, you haven't heard the worst of it yet."

"The worst of what?"

"The annual war games the Chinese have launched against Taiwan are bigger than ever. That's probably what the Chinese over-reaction is about in the first place. It's just for cover. They aren't going to start a war over a custody dispute."

"Great frickin' timing. They roll out the big war games the day we leave."

"Could be they were waiting for something to distract people, to use as a smokescreen. They always have their 'summer games.' They're called the 'Jiefang Live Fire Combined Services Training Drill.' But they're usually later, in July or August."

"Right."

"My sources say this year it's different. Appears they've cooked up something major, building on the joint maneuvers they've been doing with the Russians. They're using all the new hardware their military's been importing—the destroyers, the new Russian Sovremenny. Testing their amphibious assault groups. The whole works. They've even announced a test firing of their new Ju Lang missiles, the submarine launched ones. They could trigger something much, much bigger here."

She stood now, bouncing nervously on her toes. Alexander's report was sobering, and she wanted to get the blood flowing again—anything to jump start her foggy brain.

"Hey, since we've been talking, there's an MSNBC crawler saying the U.S. has just expelled three Chinese diplomats in retaliation."

"Unbelievable," she mumbled.

"It's all BS. They've had this war game stuff planned for months. The Chinese *always* like to say they're provoked. Goes back to the Opium Wars and their nineteenth century blame-the-foreigners game. The Pentagon correspondent says the Chinese are announcing live fire missile tests on targets in the Pacific east of Taiwan. That's clear across the island!"

"There goes the summit."

"You're probably right. They must've wanted an excuse. This stuff they're doing is so *calculated*, like it was sitting on the shelf ready to go."

Rachel was gazing out the window, sliding open the curtains with the back of her hand. The sunlight was brilliant, and the scene she viewed was impossibly green, almost jungle-like, compared to the barren urban landscapes of Beijing. The impatiens were tucked into their shaded beds, none the worse for the oppressive July heat. The Japanese maple was stretched out full, leaves covered with a soft sheen. Geraniums stood in pots lining the back porch. Barry had kept the yard well watered. She'd meant to thank him for it.

"Beijing seems like some apparition to me now," she said. "As if we just made it up that there's this big country far away that wants to go to war over some sixty-year-old misunderstanding."

"Right."

"Do you really believe we're going to get into a military confrontation over where Mickey's kids spend their summer vacation?"

"I think you need some breakfast," said Alexander, laughing, and she welcomed the sound.

"And a bath. I need a bubble bath. I want to wash it all away."

Monday morning proved equally sobering. There were reporters in the TPB lobby. Talbott had closed the curtains to his rebuilt, behind-the-reception-area office, and laid on extra security. The boss awaited her in the boardroom.

"Jonathan, why on earth is all the press here?" she began, feeling confused after nearly two weeks away from the office.

"Sit down, my dear." Even in his worried state, he was formal, pulling at his fingers. "I'm afraid we have a bit of a situation."

"A situation? You mean the stakeout? Is that for you—or for me?"

"Actually, it's for our client, Mr. Dooley. That's who they're looking for."

"Mickey? He got off the plane in Alaska." She was watching Talbott now, as if he knew something she didn't. She sat and sighed. "Why do I feel like a spectator again? I mean, *is* he? Is Mickey here in Washington?"

"We don't know. I have sought clarification from some of our friends in the State Department. It's just that Mr. Dooley has been a very prominent client of our firm, and our role appears to some to be quite suspicious."

"Telstar is our client. Mickey is just—wait a minute. What are you implying about 'our role?' That getting his kids out of China was some TPB operation?"

"Actually, that is what the Chinese press has been reporting this morning."

"Really?" Rachel was shaking her head, bewildered.

Talbott waited for the information to sink in. "There is something I need to ask you, Rachel. Man to woman, partner to partner, or however one should put it."

He was patronizing her again, but she didn't mind. She could hear the enormous grandfather clock ticking in the corner.

"Rachel, the question I must ask you is this . . . " Talbott paused, earnest to the point of awkwardness. "Did you have knowledge of this planned activity *in advance?*"

She felt like mush. She hadn't read a newspaper in several days. Her brain was still somewhere over the Pacific, and her feet were not yet settled in her heels.

"Oh, Mr. Talbott," she replied, "I suppose so."

"You 'suppose'?" He folded his hands, his displeasure evident. "And did you ever consider the consequences of this planned activity, for your colleagues here at TPB?"

"Well, to be honest, no. But I knew about it only because Mickey and

I have been friends since I was in college. He just sort of spilled it out. It was personal stuff he was sharing, out of friendship."

"I see."

"Oh, I'm not sure you do, Jonathan. It was just a fluke. Mickey was scared, he was troubled, and he just blurted it out. He said some things he shouldn't have. Now that I think about it, I suppose Senator Smithson knew, too. I don't think they could take that sort of risk without his permission."

She paused, straightening herself, then continued. "But I . . . I really have no idea who they had arranged it with, Jonathan. I don't want to know. It was just a family issue as far as I was concerned."

"Do you have any idea what this so-called 'family issue' has unleashed, Rachel? Its impact on us? The expulsion of an ambassador? The accelerated military maneuvers. The—"

"Jonathan, with all due respect, that's just bull. The Chinese are playing with our heads. It's just for show. They have these war games every year. They're still trying to punish Taiwan for having the temerity to hold free elections. First, the voters elected a native Taiwanese, then they elected a human rights lawyer who favors independence. The PRC is just using this latest incident as an excuse. They have another agenda here."

"It appears quite grave this time. And our business has suffered."

"It's just a *game*."

"Hardly."

"It's just a game of chicken. Like when they rammed our spy plane, and tried to make us apologize."

"Rachel, I don't think you can compare—"

"Beijing and Taipei have been playing this game for sixty years. Don't you see? *They* know the rules. China does. Taiwan does. We're the only ones who don't."

"But *we* are the ones to suffer, here at TPB. Rachel, I must tell you that Telstar terminated their contract with us."

"*What?*"

"Right after they fired Mickey Dooley, that is. O'Neill Aerospace is also balking at their scheduled renewal. Those are two of our biggest retainers."

"Why did they cancel the—"

"I don't need to tell you, the team leader on both accounts, that this constitutes a very substantial revenue loss for which you must bear considerable responsibility."

"Why did they cancel?" Rachel was thoroughly confused. She couldn't keep up, though she could already see how the office would be buzzing with gossip. She had stumbled again.

"They both do considerable business with China. The Chinese maintain that TPB employees and clients helped 'kidnap'—their word—and—"

Talbott was interrupted by a sharp knocking on the boardroom door. His secretary appeared, looking stern, a folded note held at arm's length for the boss. Through the open doorway, Rachel could hear commotion from the press gaggle out in the reception area.

"Thank you, Marian," Talbott said, folding the note neatly and placing it in his coat pocket as the heavy door clicked shut.

He walked toward the wall and pressed a button, sliding a paneled section back to reveal an enormous flat screen TV. The firm gathered here to watch major congressional votes upon which they had all worked. They had watched the impeachment speeches here, once upon a time, as well as the ghastly developments of 9/11. Otherwise, the screen stood dormant, used only for the occasional sports playoff game over an evening session, with pizza and beer.

"What is it?" she asked.

Talbott had his back to her. He was fumbling under the console for the remote control gadgets. He held the two clickers, cradling them gingerly, as if they were live grenades, while he tried in vain to coordinate their functions.

"'Things fall apart . . .'" he began to recite, "'the center cannot hold.'"

"Yeats."

"You're well read."

"Stanford does that."

He managed finally to click the TV on, but got only some cartoons on the local Fox station. "Damn. Here, can you get CNN for us, please?"

Talbott waited as Rachel pointed the VCR remote, then continued matter-of-factly. "Marian says the networks are reporting missile strikes against Taipei."

Rachel found Channel 12. As usual, Marian was correct.

There was a voiceover from the Pentagon correspondent, and live footage from the Taipei nighttime sky, smoke spiraling up from a distant hilltop.

"Yes, Dave, we've lost our audio connection with Taiwan right now, and have just this picture. But U.S. intelligence sources are reporting that the likely target was the Yangmingshin Mountain facility of the Taiwan Ministry of Defense—excuse me, that's Yangming*shan*. It's a major signals intelligence facility said to be operated jointly by Taiwan's MOD, the super-secret U.S. National Security Agency, and the CIA."

"And what would be the purpose for targeting this facility?" the studio anchor was asking now. "It's in the suburbs, outside the capital, is it not?"

"Yes, Dave, it's outside the capital city of Taipei. A big military compound in the foothills, quite noticeable for its many giant satellite signal-receiving disks. It's called a 'data processing facility' because supposedly the U.S. doesn't have military personnel in Taiwan—that might upset Beijing. But actually, it's known to be a giant signals intelligence center, a spying facility where the U.S. and Taiwan cooperate in sifting through intelligence captured from the Communist-led government in Beijing."

"And the Chinese justification for such a strike?"

"Well . . ."

"I mean, so many issues are out there now . . ."

"To be sure. The allegations by some that Taiwan is developing nuclear weapons capability—the so-called krytron smuggling case."

"Yes, and more immediately, the bizarre allegations they have made that the CIA allegedly 'kidnapped' two Chinese-American boys. The unrelenting Chinese missile buildup, and their provocative military maneuvers. The expulsion of the U.S. ambassador, the refusal by Taiwan to agree to a timetable for reunification talks. There's quite a list of grievances."

"Yes, Dave. It certainly calls into question the Seattle summit."

"Or if the summit will even take place."

"It has certainly been a long and tortured road that has brought us to this juncture, to a military confrontation. What we are picking up here from our sources at the Pentagon is speculation that recent events caused the Chinese to ramp up their annual military exercises opposite Taiwan. But with the new military hardware the Americans have provided Taiwan—the Kidd destroyers in particular—Taiwan's radar systems may have been 'locking on' Chinese fighters. These radar locks are quite readily mistaken for a preparation to fire on—"

"Oh my!" Both of the TV voices shouted as there was a flash of light on the screen so bright it seemed to penetrate even the darkest corners of the TPB boardroom. Then the screen went blank for a moment, punctuated by the disembodied voices of American reporters talking excitedly over each other.

Rachel stood as several colleagues raced in.

"The market's frozen!" Wally Ashburn, a senior partner exclaimed. "What the hell's going on, Rach? You startin' World War III?"

Braden Sechrest was with them now, too, a tall woman in a lilac suit with a ream of papers in hand. "Lloyd's has pulled insurance on all shipping in East Asia. NASDAQ suspended trading—off ten percent already. The Tokyo markets are going to go bananas."

"Uh, Dave, that was quite a strike!" Now they had a live picture of the Pentagon correspondent standing before a podium in a briefing room in Virginia. 'We are getting speculation here of EMP weapons being used."

"EMP?"

"Electro Magnetic Pulse bombs. Kind of like the old neutron bombs designed to kill people, but leave the buildings standing. These EMP weapons are likely designed to knock out all the communications systems—the electronics and avionics the Taiwanese are using for battle management."

Soon enough, the TV news whip-around came to the North Lawn of the White House, where the CNN correspondent was speaking grimly of possible American losses at the intelligence-gathering facility in Taipei. Most of the senior members of the TPB firm crowded in to watch it all on the big screen TV.

After a time, Rachel slipped out of the board room, feeling like the walking dead. Everything seemed to be happening on her watch. Somebody sets off a bomb beneath their lobby—naturally, *she* gets hit. Mickey causes an international incident—and *she* gets blamed. She felt like a modern day Typhoid Mary.

She retreated back to her private office, viewing the space as if through some distant lens. Her routine day was waiting in front of her. Her desk was covered with neatly piled papers, the Washington detritus from two weeks away. Her dutiful assistant had opened all the mail and sorted the folders. Her "Action" files were neatly stacked. The one marked "Fundraising Invitations" was thick—no doubt in anticipation of the fall rush, trying to get Rachel and TPB calendared well in advance. "Client Correspondence" was thinner—the volume of e-mail traffic and voicemail would be far greater than the snail mail here. The bulging travel file full of business expense receipts from her Asia trip was waiting to be processed.

Rachel, her routine shattered, sat regarding it all. Her hip was vibrating, the Blackberry gone mad again, with the zapping of yet another someone trying to reach her. Her phone lights were flashing. Her voice mail light was illuminated, with a red indicator on: it was full. The computer was beeping, hailing incoming e-mail behind her. Outside, below a cerulean sky, a jackhammer was pounding staccato-like on F Street.

She walked slowly to her door and closed it. Then she sat back at her desk and began, for the first time since April, to cry, the salty tears flowing freely. She wanted to let go with one great wail. She could not find the voice to call out, however—not here, not now.

How have I come to this place? She wondered at it all, at the long journey from her Wyoming childhood. The work started out as a challenge, a cause to pursue, an intellectual frontier to conquer, a climb up the economic ladder. Too soon, the career became its own end. Then, as if in the third step of grieving, the job became a definition of self. You *were* your job. It defined you—she realized now—especially in this city where status and access meant everything. Your vocation became your entire identity. You clung to it, terrified of the day when they would have to pry the desk from your desperate hands.

She had seen it. She had seen the utter defeat on the faces of aging TPB officers—the ones let go quietly after lunch on Fridays. Their building access keys were seized. Their computer network passwords were suddenly denied. Some escort from Personnel loomed close by to practically frog walk them off the premises.

She struggled in vain to rally, to climb beyond the chaos breaking all about her, to make sense of the world events and to figure out her proper role in them. There was a knock at her door; then her secretary's head appeared.

"Oh, there you are, Rachel," she said, relieved. "It's Alexander Bonner. He's holding on line one. Say, are you feeling OK?"

"Sure," Rachel said, "thanks, I'm just kind of spaced out again today, I'm afraid."

"You need some coffee or something?"

"Maybe something stronger."

Rachel stared a moment longer, even after the door was closed, then found Alexander on her private line.

"So, I guess maybe the summit is off," Alexander began.

"No kidding."

"Are you watching?"

"I was. I mean, it's kind of buzzing all around me, like Sensurround. The TV, Internet, the phones. I can't really process it all. "

"I know," he said.

"I mean, I've already *done* this. My goddamn office got bombed to start this season—and I'm still not sure we know the who and why of that."

"Hey, believe it, girl."

"But a war? With China?"

"You think all those RAND studies were just academic exercises?"

"It's just so . . . so surreal. It feels like a stupid video game. The news stations have all become Entertainment Channels. Except today, they keep playing some new horror film."

"Welcome to the twenty-first century."

26

THE E-WAR

The war unfolded very much the way Booth and Branko had fore-seen: cyber warriors ruled the field. It was all over in less than thirty-six hours. But the repercussions of Beijing's technological blitzkreig promised to be felt for generations to come. The Communist goliath humiliated the nettlesome island democracy with remarkable ease, while a confused world watched on satellite TV.

From the very outset, Alexander was embarrassed to find that the conflict was tailor-made for his coverage. It was a perverse reward for years of developing unique China sources. He had cell and home phone numbers for virtually every Western policy-maker responsible for managing the conflict—from Langley to the Pentagon, from the White House to Honolulu's Pacific Command. Even amidst the electronic chaff hurtling about, he managed to get direct calls through to a number of key players in Beijing and Taipei, yielding some brutally blunt on-the-record quotes.

Alexander was appalled. He could sit at his desk and witness devastation raining down on familiar avenues twelve thousand miles away. Yet, he could not suppress his fascination. It was like that horrible September morning, watching those damn planes sail into the Twin Towers over and over again—only this time, it fell to *him* to explain it all to the reading public. This was his story; he felt like the assigned witness to the macabre.

Branko had long ago warned that the financial markets were the West's most vulnerable point. That is precisely where the Chinese military had wittingly designed their early blows to strike. The prospect of the U.S. being drawn into a shooting war with China provoked panic among global investors. In its earliest hours, the conflict halted commercial shipping throughout the East Asia region. The possibility of losses drove insurance rates through the roof, effectively shutting down trade in the region, halting ships at sea. Critical communications with many Fortune 500 companies' overseas production facilities—especially the legions of chipmakers on both sides of the Taiwan Strait—were crippled. Capital investments froze. Share prices plummeted around the globe.

Once the shooting stopped, Branko explained to Alexander just how the Chinese government could credibly allege that *Taiwan* had initiated the hostilities. "Planes go up and troll for targets every day. That is what they're *supposed* to do. The problem comes when adversaries detect a 'radar lock,' even from fighters on routine patrol. It appears like the headlights of an onrushing train; a pilot has only seconds to react, or risks losing the plane and being killed. When that happens, orders are to shoot first and ask questions later."

The Chinese accusation that Taiwan had started it all was thus difficult to refute, especially amidst the chaos of the ensuing conflict. The reality was that such radar-lock incidents happened all too frequently. Alexander's analytical stories accurately noted that the justification was the same used after the first Gulf War by the Americans, when they continued to assault random Iraqi targets throughout the 1990's. Perhaps Taiwan's fighters *had* provoked Beijing by using radar in a hostile fashion. If so, Taipei was guilty of escalating above a clear threshold—an indisputable provocation.

Responding to these incidents, the Chinese methodically assailed the spine of Taiwan's electronic infrastructure, crippling the island nation. The PRC forces began with a missile attack on the Yangmingshan listening post, a traditional military target. China's missiles knocked out Taiwan's intelligence nerve center, blinding Taipei from the outset of the crisis. Then Beijing escalated with a series of ingeniously targeted follow-up strikes. The Pulitzer committee would ultimately credit Alexander with the phrase that best captured the novel nature of the ensuing contest. It was, Alexander had explained to his readers, "The First E-War."

Branko's department had long been criticized for its hard-line views about the Chinese military build-up. The events in the Taiwan Strait offered some unwelcome vindication. For more than a decade, the People's Liberation Army had been preparing for just such a high tech conflict. Alexander's *LA Times* had even run stories about the nearly one hundred thousand Chinese cyber attacks on U.S. security software. "Titan Rain," the Pentagon called these assaults on the five million DOD computers—many of the attacks emanated from the more than one hundred million PC's in China. And like the old ABM debates about Soviet missile threats, U.S. planners were chagrined to discover that cyber war *offense* was much cheaper—and far more effective—than defense.

The PRC had learned from watching Desert Storm and the "no contact" wars like Kosovo and Afghanistan. Overconfident Western war gamers had assumed that Taiwan would use its technology to advantage in such a showdown. Two days in July proved them wrong. Taiwan, it turned out, had spent too many years futilely pleading with Washington to buy traditional 1980's military hardware—ships, planes, missiles, and ammunition. But Taiwan had purchased the wrong goods. Driven by an imaginative procurement team in the PLA's central command, the Chinese had leapfrogged a generation of technology, rolling out a computer-driven war that incapacitated much of Taiwan's antiquated military hardware while hitting the West in its pocketbook.

The E-War was fought on a new battlefield. It rewarded ingenuity and freelancing within the Chinese military, and the general populace as well. "It mushroomed into a uniquely populist assault," Alexander wrote, "a thoroughly modern conflict which enabled even armchair Chinese patriots to become involved. Every hacker on the mainland became a modern day Minuteman."

It was true. PRC citizens were poised to join in from home, with every personal computer becoming a potential weapon. The new PLA dogma held that citizens could help seize the initiative to establish "electromagnetic dominance" early in any high tech conflict. The plans were put in action this time: computer viruses were exported wholesale, polluting Internet access in Taiwan. Trojan horse viruses were planted in Taiwan's networks, unleashing destruction. Alexander stayed with his analogy of the Redcoats' 1775 retreat at Lexington and Concord, a vivid image that captured the spirit of this element of the assault plan.

Both military and civilian air traffic control—and even Taipei's subway trains—were frozen by the deft cyber-attacks. TV broadcast towers and electrical plants were targeted with extremely accurate missile strikes.

Financial data banks were penetrated and compromised. Market records of stock trading were dumped. Commerce above the level of cash-in-the-fruit-market virtually halted throughout the country.

Dummy radio broadcasts and junk e-mail full of disinformation were tossed into the mix by the Second Directorate in a kitchen sink-load of techno-warfare. Electro-magnetic pulse bursts were detonated, disrupting the electronics of scores of Taiwan's weapon systems, creating electrical shock waves akin to that of a nuclear blast. The information warfare assaults and the electronic weapons eroded Taiwan's command and control, freezing many of their defensive weapons platforms. Even Branko's command post in Langley, Virginia found communications with Taiwan a challenge, and solid data hard to come by.

Life in Taipei regressed decades in a matter of hours as fire crews rushed to rescue thousands trapped underground in subway cars. Civilian aircraft were frantically rerouted to Tokyo and Manila. One Taipei-bound plane full of tourists from Australia ran low on fuel and limped into Shanghai, making a forced landing.

Alexander's articles in the *Times* chronicled the ensuing escalation in great detail. Taiwan scrambled its F-16 aircraft out of Jia-shan and flew them off from nearby Hualien Air Force Base. Emerging from hangars carved from caves in the side of the hills, the jets were a terrific sight, straight out of *Battlestar Galactica*. Taiwan's military had few inviting targets for retaliation, however. An instinct for self-preservation made Taiwan's leaders reluctant to respond to the initial Chinese attacks with any substantial targeting of the Mainland. There was little future for a Lilliputian island nation assaulting the territory of a nuclear-armed power, a Gulliver possessing an army that outnumbered Taiwan's ten to one. Most of Taipei's ripostes were against Chinese jet fighters and ships at sea. Here Taiwan's military scored their greatest successes. The air-to-air and air-to-ground missiles sold to Taipei over the years by Washington proved effective, and the Chinese lost several fighter planes.

The second wave of Chinese strikes hammered more traditional Taiwanese military targets, beginning with Chiang Chuan Kang Air Base. In the 1960's, the old U.S. Strategic Command facility had been used to launch B-52 sorties over North Vietnam. Once upon a time, the base had housed scores of American nuclear weapons to deter an Asia conflict. Now, it proved to be ground zero for a Chinese direct assault. The airfield's defenders expected the Chinese to start up with short-range ballistic missile attacks, then after that softening-up, launch waves of F-8 fighters and Su-27 jets against the facility. War-gamers assumed it was here that Beijing would try to first seize a base to be used as a staging area for incoming airborne troops.

The Chinese pounded the base as expected. But then they stopped abruptly. The anticipated wave of paratroopers never materialized. An invasion was unnecessary. The Chinese military, Alexander later explained, could accomplish virtually all conflict objectives without landing a single solider on Taiwan's soil. It was quite remarkable. All Taipei's preparations to defend against amphibious troop landings or paratroop assaults against Taiwan's airfields went for naught.

Taiwan did undertake a couple of half-hearted missile strikes against the Fujian Province launch facilities. In turn, the Chinese briefly moved to expand their targeting of missiles against Taiwan's ports and energy facilities. But the PRC chose to limit destruction of the valuable economic assets they would soon possess. PRC post-war planners were not eager to have Taiwan emerge from the conflict with a nineteenth century economy.

American military might proved to be of minimal consequence to PRC's plans. U.S. naval forces in the region were drained by Persian Gulf actions, and only a handful of U.S. warships arrived before the fighting stopped. U.S. planes out of Okinawa eventually circled the region, but found few attractive targets to engage. U.S. military capabilities were spread far too thin by the twin engagements in Iraq and Afghanistan. Overnight polls showed American voters opposing by a more than three-to-one margin any direct military involvement in the Taiwan Strait conflict.

Congressional voices proved strident. A faction of members had long clamored for greater interoperability between U.S. and Taiwan military forces—these legislators now assailed the Chinese and the Pentagon alike for the fiasco. They were especially irate about friendly fire casualties. In their confusion, Taiwan inadvertently hit American and Taiwanese assets.

Accidental casualties among the limited U.S. military personnel in the region proved predictable, though regrettable, collateral damage. Before the shooting stopped, American pilots had inadvertently killed more than a dozen Taiwanese, and vice versa. An American carrier force did not even reach the Taiwan Strait until after the shooting had been halted and the United Nations was in full debate mode.

The swift Chinese escalation had forced geo-strategists and financiers to plead with the United Nations to propose an immediate cease-fire. Global markets had tanked. Wall Street suspended trading for hours, and the Treasury Department's deficit-financing bond sales were cancelled for the week once it was clear China—and many other nations—would take a pass.

From their Security Council perch, Beijing insisted that they would brook no interference in what the Chinese maintained was an internal affair. They had been provoked, they argued, by renegades in denial—the last remnants of a seventy-year-old civil war. Most General Assembly nations subscribed to the PRC's assessment.

The wording of the subsequent UN resolution was quite clear. The authorities on the island of Taiwan were invited forthwith to meet with Chinese officials to discuss a broad agenda. It included not just an enduring cease-fire, but also, quite ominously, "issues unresolved since 1949 relating to unification of China." In other words, as Alexander summed it up, "Taiwan's democratically elected officials were now welcome to negotiate with Communist Party authorities in Beijing the terms of their own surrender."

The Beijing leadership had much to point to in the way of "progress" on the long troublesome Taiwan issue. As with China's tough stance in previous negotiations to return Hong Kong and Macao to Communist control, the hard-liners had convinced their colleagues to gamble in assailing Taiwan. The People's Republic of China had won the battle, and they had won the lightning-quick war. Taiwan's days of political autonomy and de facto independence were over. It was left only for the diplomats to sort out and confirm the new status quo on the ground, and for journalists like Alexander to explain how it all had come to pass.

Even as he filed his stories, Alexander was haunted. A line had been crossed. Like that day he had slipped Booth an advance copy of his missile export exclusive, he was complicit. His emotional distance—that journalistic reserve his profession so revered—was gone. His politics, and his personal prejudices, all became part of the story.

As he worked his sources, Alexander's days were frantic. His nights were restless, his body supercharged with adrenaline and slow to calm. His friends seemed distant. That first week, Branko was stuck at his Langley command post around the clock. Rachel was withdrawn, viewing the events from a safe distance the way a mortified rubber-necker would maneuver around a bloody car wreck. Mickey was incommunicado.

For Alexander, the gruesome story was the culmination of his life's work. He poured himself into his pieces with great passion, sharing all his accumulated insight and expertise. But late at night, when he reflected upon the experience, he wondered at the consequences. Was his entire career as a journalist on the Asian diplomatic beat really just a preparation for *this*? He felt soiled for having witnessed the slaughter. In his darkest moments he was, he concluded, a modern day vulture, just another media voyeur.

AUGUST

27

LOST AT SEA

"In the end, nobody at the State Department gave a rat's ass about Taiwan," one senior legislator told his Senate colleagues. "Having a tiny democratic island out there in a Communist sea became an enormous historical inconvenience."

Jake Smithson was the cooperative—if chagrined—source of that anonymous quote, which became Alexander's lead for one of his stories. The observation perfectly framed his five part post-mortem series on the E-War. Smithson had leaked the vignette from a meeting inside the Majority Leader's office: all the Senate's senior leaders had gathered to consult over the wording of a Congressional resolution deploring the Chinese assault.

At the height of the crisis, Smithson had pressed his colleagues for a vigorous response to China's perfidy. The California senator assailed the weakness of the consensus approach—it was "nothing but a wordy resolution full of gobbledygook," he argued, imploring legislators to adopt a stronger stance. But his fellow committee chairs demurred. Abraham Gubin of New Hampshire ended the private debate with the colorful line Alexander cited. It ably summarized the hard realities confronting the Taiwanese. They were simply outnumbered. American legislators could give their outraged speeches. But there was a new reality on the ground; Taiwan was left largely to its own devices. Its capital fled and its people anxiously awaited the outcome of negotiations over some type of coerced "confederation" with Beijing.

Alexander's articles dissecting Washington decision-making were immediately embraced by his editors. They gave the series page one treatment daily, with an unlimited space budget for those who could follow the *Times*' endless jump pages beyond the computer and automobile ads.

Rachel read Alexander's pieces with the same detachment that had infected her since her return from China. As a professional woman, she had been paddling against the tide for months, ever since the April day she had awoken in an ambulance. After two of her largest clients walked, the knives were out around the office. Her efforts to share her management responsibilities with some of her colleagues were met with suspicion, particularly by some of the more aggressive career climbers amongst the office sisterhood. The Taiwan conflict stunned her and she couldn't help taking it all personally.

Rachel was further discombobulated when Barry announced shortly after her return from Beijing that he was moving to New York. Whatever her many suspicions about their estrangement over the years—his distance, his incessant travels, his resistance to intimacy—their revealing conversation preceding his departure completely unnerved her. *What next?*

She would sit in her office and stare at the growing mounds of paper, trying to figure out what really mattered. She was off the Beijing beat, what with the contract cancellations and U.S.-China relations in a deep freeze. Her disengagement from the events swirling around her was thoroughly disconcerting. She glanced at the TV news with disinterest, as if it were reporting events from an imaginary world. Unread issues of the *Post* began to pile up alongside unopened mail. Sorting through the stack one Sunday, she found a notice for past due property taxes, the utility bill, and a copy of the final divorce agreement awaiting her signature. She was ready to pack her and Jamie's bags and head out of town for an extended holiday.

The last Friday before they set out for her August vacation, she sat for a full hour on the back porch of her Arlington home, breathing slowly and sipping iced tea. She felt like a traveler at a border crossing, lightening her load, now aware she needed only a fraction of the baggage she had been carrying. The rest could be shed—left at the roadside, never to be missed.

Returning to her Wyoming roots, she found renewed pleasures in the natural world. She and Jamie became great hikers, walking the ridges of the Absaroka Range east of Yellowstone. Setting out early from her parents' cabin in Sunlight Basin, they would pick wildflowers and watch in wonder as impressive cloud formations overpowered the blue ceiling overhead. They could go an entire morning without seeing another soul. They could go an hour without speaking, the communication of mother and son often subsisting on a simple gesture.

Jamie was naturally contemplative. He flourished in the silences away from the video games and televised blather that often mesmerized his contemporaries. He would track small animals, humming little ditties as he walked. He kept a careful longhand journal of his sightings: one day, a moose, another, an eagle in soaring flight near Dead Indian Pass.

Rachel would ponder, building her reserves like an animal fattening against winter's coming storms. She was healing a second time, taking inventory of her resources once more. She was completing a process of renewal she had failed to finish after the tragic events that spring. Her body had mended, her strength was returning.

Back in the Washington area near the end of the month, they continued their natural explorations, walking in the Blue Ridge Mountains above the Shenandoah, and along the Potomac River cliffs at Great Falls. Soon, it would be time to empty the poncho and compass out of Jamie's backpack and reload it with sharp pencils and a binder. Rachel often used Meg Greenfield's line, the one about Washington being just like high school. The boys and girls would soon be back in session on Capitol Hill, with their new clothes and summer stories, as surely as Jamie's fifth grade would reconvene at Jefferson Elementary.

The Taiwan Strait war was over, the financial markets had calmed, and Rachel was going through the motions of the season, determined to meet her obligations. Back at her TPB desk, she began to work again at inserting her clients' requests into the end-of-the-fiscal year House-Senate conference reports. She made the rounds with Congress, and set her calendar for the fall schedule of fundraisers and charity galas. She collected gossip from congressional leadership aides, getting an early edge on the office betting pool to pick the exact date and time of final adjournment. She still had the occasional noble cause to pursue for her clients, the Head Start pro bono work, the breast cancer earmark in the Defense Department appropriations bill. Operating on autopilot, she tried to help drive the TPB business, ignoring the hallway whispers that she had lost her edge.

Rachel began working out at dawn, jogging along the leafy avenues of north Arlington. She would finish with a sprint, gasping for air. Her pores were open; her senses were alive again. After two seasons of pummeling by the vicissitudes of life, she felt wiser.

Deep in the night, her dreams grew ever richer. They brought vivid images of nature's power, Wyoming thunderheads, pounding California surf. She developed a voracious appetite for books, staying up late with a stack of fiction. She also read psychology, even some religious philosophy, studiously ignoring the temporal concerns of newsmagazines and network television. She cut off the cable TV premium service. She cancelled her subscription to *People*.

There was also the matter of Alexander. She kept him at a bit of a distance after her Wyoming trip, eager to center herself before she went too far, still wary of the rebound effect. He was conveniently absent for weeks. He had worked straight through to mid-August, producing his landmark pieces on the China-Taiwan conflict. Then he went off on his own vacation with a bunch of high school fishing buddies in the Sierra Nevada Mountains.

At month's end, Alexander was back, bronzed and mosquito-bitten. He appeared on Rachel's doorstep one afternoon, sporting a salt and pepper beard he had yet to shave. They sat on the porch and talked for hours, floating along in a meandering conversation as the light angled across the top of the oak trees.

There was a confidence about him once more, an openness to life, that she found utterly compelling. His ego was restored, his skepticism tempered. He had a wise heart and he listened—*a man who actually listened!* In his hearing, her self-analysis, which had tended over the years to become whiny and sophomoric, began to mature. She found herself climbing steadily again toward solid ground. It was then that Rachel, once again in the comfortable glow of his presence, began to suspect he was her guardian angel.

On Friday morning, the week before the Congress returned, she called him at his office on a whim.

"Are you working hard?" she asked.

"Hardly working, actually. Just plodding through some Asia Society conference papers for a Sunday *Current* piece."

"Is it terribly interesting stuff?"

"Of course. I found some documents tracking cash flows in and out of East Asia after the E-War. Did you know the Taiwan market is still off thirty-one percent, but Shanghai and Hong Kong have had a net *increase* in European investment?"

"Fascinating," she deadpanned.

Alexander laughed. "I knew you'd agree."

"Is there any possibility I might corrupt you?"

"Well, I have certain standards. But then, what exactly did you have in mind?"

"I was thinking of playing hooky—a picnic maybe? It's about eighty degrees and crystal clear. Seems like a mortal sin to waste one of these last summer days indoors. Can you take a long lunch?"

"Best offer I've had all week."

"Great. By the way, what are you wearing?"

"Is this one of those phone sex questions?" He chuckled again. "I thought you needed a really husky voice for those. But, since you asked, I'm clothed in journalists' business casual: chinos and topsiders."

"Excellent."

"Why? Where are you taking me?"

"Out to sea."

She picked him up forty-five minutes later with two salami sandwiches and special sauce from the Italian Store, and drove to Jack's Boathouse, under the girders of Key Bridge at the foot of Georgetown. There was Jack himself, taking the sun in a weathered lawn chair, chatting with a couple of off-duty cabbies, who drank beer as they fished. A long line of green metal canoes lay on the pier in the sunshine.

They sat on some moldy boat cushions in their rented canoe and launched into the gentle river flow. Rachel paddled strong in the prow, while from the stern, Alexander guided them with an almost imperceptible turn of the blade.

She talked a steady stream into the breeze, Alexander urging her on, or steering her with a question. There was a rhythm to their work together, aided by a friendly current, which lulled her.

"So, I've been thinking about going back to get my Ph.D," she offered.

"Really?"

"Finally finishing something for once. I could teach some undergraduates American history as I go. I want to make sure the next generation knows what came before al-Quaida and the Internet. Remember the past—Santayana and all that."

"Remind me again how in the hell you ended up a lobbyist instead of a professor."

"I was the youngest," she laughed easily. "Equal parts mediator and manipulator. Beneath the smart-ass act, I was actually incredibly insecure. I always wanted to make sure I figured out the process. That way, I could make peace, I could help everybody get what they wanted, and I could be their advocate. I never wanted to just watch and analyze things. That's why I always balked at pure academics."

They floated through the narrows between Roosevelt Island and the Virginia shore. The Lincoln Memorial and its back porch were just coming into view around the southern tip of the thickly wooded island. The water lapped lazily at the marble steps.

"I've been too damn busy for years," she said. "I kind of had my head down, barreling ahead—probably welcomed all the distractions. All the background noise of modern life getting in the way; too busy to see things. I mean, Jamie will be gone in eight years, away to college and his own life."

"Makes a lot of sense," he said, following her carefully from the stern. "Getting back to your history thing, you were such a happy student once upon a time."

"I just feel burnt out. I wish I could achieve something that'll last beyond the next pay check. Something with some enduring value beyond the next election cycle. I mean, it could be just building a house for Habitat for Humanity. You know, one real roof over the heads of one needy family. Or help save an acre of rain forest off in Costa Rica."

"You're not burnt out."

"I wonder sometimes." She stopped paddling for a bit, then turned in the boat to catch a glimpse of him. He was wearing a blue Nationals cap that clashed awkwardly with his maroon polo shirt. "I'm just feeling so damn restless."

"Restless is good. Lotta great things spring from restless minds."

"How you figure?"

"Lewis and Clark. Bill Gates. Teddy Roosevelt—they were all restless guys. I mean, Winston Churchill was an insomniac. Wrote volumes of history all night."

"He was well-lubricated, if memory serves me correctly. Gin, wasn't it?"

"He stayed up late scheming to outlast the Nazis. The gin must have helped; he pulled it off. So, yeah, restless is good."

He shifted their course, circling back to the north along the eastern shoreline of Roosevelt Island. The park was deserted—no joggers out with their retrievers in the midday heat.

"So you think I'm driven?" she asked. "I feel as if I've been direction-less for months."

"Rachel, you've been one of the most driven people I've known since the day I first met you in Palo Alto. You used to intimidate grad students much older than you. You'd take on anybody, anytime. But after what you've been through lately, my God, if you hadn't become a little reflec-tive, you'd be pretty twisted."

"You've been through a few changes, too, lately," she said, smiling weakly as she observed the water dripping from the end of her rutted paddle. The drops formed circles pulsing away from the canoe. "You're starting to show some signs of life, Bonner."

"You lectured me on the subject, if I recall. That day in Upperville. Challenged me to come out of hibernation, or something."

"And you finally have. Don't you see?"

"What do you mean?"

"You were feeling so sorry for yourself. Especially after you screwed up that krytron story and got pounded. You were in danger of becoming a little pathetic. Now, you give a damn again. About the China story. About doing your best. You care about me. You take risks." She turned her head to look at him again. "You're driven, too."

"Well, I care about my work, about getting it right. I actually believe that line about newspapers being the first draft of history. I feel like only the good writing gets preserved. The rest of the garbage—the McPaper junk—will just get used for kitty litter. But, hey, I'm not like you. You seem obsessed sometimes. Like you've got to be the perfect super-woman."

"Sure, or else they're all going to find out I'm some kind of fraud, some kid from Cody just playing grown-up."

"It's another reason I don't envy women at all. You have these incredibly contradictory role models you're supposed to fulfill. Look at the crap on the newsstands. I mean, how can you live up to *Ms.*, *Good Housekeeping*, and *Oprah*, all at the same time?"

"Not to mention *Playboy* and all that soft porn on the drug store magazine racks."

"It's no surprise to me that women stress out when they can't be all things at once. It's impossible."

"Goddamn Madison Avenue. They make us all feel like failures."

"You shouldn't work at it so hard, Rachel. Sometimes with your stuff—with Barry, with your job, hell, even back in the Stanford days—it seems like you're dancing to someone else's tune."

"Guilty as charged."

"Well, maybe it's time to find your own music. Find your own inspiration. I'd love you, whatever that was."

Rachel considered this last declaration for some time before she spoke. "You know, that's probably the answer to about a thousand women's group questions. The one they all try to figure out."

"Say what?"

"The 'what do women really want?' one."

"Oh. Sorry, didn't mean to pontificate."

"Don't apologize, silly. It *is*. Women just want to be appreciated for who they truly are. Not for some performance they pull off. At the office. Or in the kitchen. Or in the sack, for that matter."

Alexander was studying her from behind, wishing he could read her eyes. Her arms swung wide in oversized gestures as she paddled, carving the air in big circles. Across the water, the few faces along the Georgetown waterfront were too distant to discern. Beyond the Whitehurst Freeway and the Watergate Towers, the city loomed, all glass and steel and silence. Inside, work was grinding on, churning out the memos and e-mails that passed for the city's natural product.

"You got me all figured out, wise guy," she said after a time. Then she set her paddle across the bow and they began to drift. "So, what the hell do I do now?"

"Now?"

"I mean, next."

"Right. Well, I guess I'm afraid you'll move out west somewhere. You and Jamie. Head for the ranch, get closer to his uncles, or something."

"And you'll stay here chasing that damn Pulitzer until you're eighty?"

"Unless I actually win sometime. Probably wouldn't know what to do with myself if I did."

"You're like a dog chasing a car," she laughed. "What the hell *would* you do if you caught it? By the way, are you really worried we'll leave town?"

"Of course I am," he admitted. "With Barry gone and your work stuff sounding kind of shaky, I'm not sure what holds you to this city on a swamp."

"So, do you have an alternative plan?"

"I suppose I could come up with one . . . if pressed."

"Try me."

He didn't speak at first, yet she could feel his eyes on her back. "I think you should stay right here in town. Find something meaningful to do, like you said. Something enduring."

"Such as?"

"Oh, all kinds of things." She could hear his breathing now, anxious as he paused. "Work for some non-profit—I'm sure they'd love your expertise—getting money for housing. You could teach history at Georgetown. Take some real chances . . . "

He paused, watching a jet climbing north from the airport, before he added, as if an afterthought. "Maybe have another baby."

"A baby?" She spun her shoulders full around in the canoe and stared. "I'm well past forty. Soon to be divorced. Potentially unemployed . . . and you think I should have another baby?"

"Well, I mean . . . sure. *That's* enduring."

She was shaking her head slowly now, an incredulous grin spreading. "You're quite a piece of work, Bonner. You really think an old man like you is up to it?"

He splashed her once. It was just a reflex, just a quick flick of the paddle. He was joshing, but it was a critical miscalculation. Her back was hit by the sudden spray, soaking into her red T-shirt.

She came back strong, two hands full of river water across his face. He retaliated with the paddle again, soaking her front this time. She came after him now with an open can of beer. As she reached and he dodged, she lurched over the edge and fell into the river.

She surfaced quickly, grasping the edge and flipping the canoe, tossing Alexander into the shallows alongside her. Alexander was gasping when he came up, hip deep in the water, somehow grabbing the cooler with their sandwiches. He hollered as she pointlessly splashed his face again, the last residues of tension washing away.

They struggled to right the canoe, then finally pushed it, stumbling in the muck on the uneven river bottom, until they beached it on a deserted strip of sand on the eastern side of Roosevelt Island. Somehow, two beers and the sandwiches were salvaged.

They made their picnic right there on the shore. They sat unobserved in their own secluded cove, waiting for their clothes to dry. Everything around them was stillness, save the river flowing smoothly past, unheard. Awkwardly at first, they began to kiss. In the silence, they began to caress each other, fingers tracing lines as they lay at the edge of the sand on their private island. Their eyes were open and their bodies warm, absorbing the simple touches.

"What are you thinking?" he asked, his eyes on the sky.

"I was thinking that at this moment, after all these years, we are finally breathing the same air," she replied, her certainty growing. "I love this air."

They laughed together and kissed some more, eyes closed now. Then they were entwined, enveloping each other, and they made love in the gentle heat, oblivious to the busy city all around them.

SEPTEMBER

28

PENANCE AND LIBERATION

Mickey Dooley found the irony quite delicious. The CIA recruiters for Asia work now preferred UC Berkeley's graduates to those from Stanford.

In the old days, the Agency fed off the preppier grads, the more reliably Establishment students from the sylvan haven down on the "Farm" in Palo Alto. Berkeley was then considered suspect: too close to the People's Park crowd, Telegraph Avenue, and the Viet Cong sympathizers on the radical fringe. Since the Mandarin Club's campus days, however, Serra House had drawn considerable resources from the local high tech companies most eager to promote U.S.-China trade. Silicon Valley satellite vendors, software designers, high performance computer execs—they were the Serra House champions now. Power politics and analysis of China's byzantine bureaucratic factions had become a Berkeley specialty. So the CIA talent scouts increasingly targeted the Chinese-American linguists and expatriates at Cal.

It was in post-Cold War Berkeley that Langley had placed considerable assets. These included a modest new investment in Mickey, whose first consulting job back in the States was there on the fringe of the sprawling UC campus.

It was a gorgeous fall—dry days and cool nights—in the Berkeley hills above the noise and smog on Interstate 80. Branko had been good to him, more than fulfilling his every commitment. He had taken the heat from within the administration and the congressional oversight committees for the messy exfiltration effort on July 4. He had also promised to use all available assets on the ground in Beijing to watch Lee's back, though he gave Mickey no operational details. In the wake of the E-war and the bitterness produced by the cancellation of the Seattle summit, U.S.-China relations remained moribund. Branko had apparently failed to make contact with Lee through back channels, and Mickey had no news of their old friend in the PRC's Foreign Ministry.

Branko arranged for the Agency to fly Mickey east a couple of times. He sat on an ad hoc committee with some of Branko's staff reviewing China analysis, providing alternative views, testing old assumptions. While China issues were hot, it nevertheless seemed like make-work. It was as if Langley was just keeping tabs on him or holding him in reserve for some future effort. Mickey knew he wasn't seeing anything particularly fresh or sensitive, nor was he apprised of any detail on the desperate effort to penetrate the Red Dragons. The riddle of the cowboys deep inside the Second Directorate was too raw for Mickey to see any of the good stuff.

Branko did let down his reserve for an unusual dinner invitation, welcoming Mickey into his home for a family meal. Just seeing Branko calmly serving up plates to his four youngsters, and watching his wife Erika and the new baby, made Mickey ever more reverential. Branko was so purposeful, but such a decent guy for a spook. That was the Branko he had known back in college. That was the man Branko had grown to be. Over the course of that simple meal—Branko had even asked Mickey to say the grace—Mickey felt years of chill between them melt. Lost respect was restored, suspicion replaced by touches of the camaraderie of old. This restoration alone brought Mickey contentment, as if, amongst so many of his failures, here was one mission where success remained at least a possibility.

Mostly, Mickey found himself on the sidelines as events marched onward. He awaited the arrival of some of his clothes and papers a family friend had retrieved from his Beijing closets. He spent some time with a RAND affiliate, doing a long-range study, funded by the CIA, on Chinese technology policy.

Having been terminated by Telstar, he was persona non grata in Beijing, and any overt cooperation Mickey might have offered the company could only have harmed their sales. The Chinese had long memories. So it was a very quick goodbye, a slice of Telstar stock tossed into his abrupt severance package, and Mickey was floating free.

It was a gift from the gods—this isolation that afforded him so many hours with the boys. He would meet their school bus each afternoon, sitting on the curb chatting amiably with the waiting au pairs and mothers, flirting in his jocular manner.

It was a fantasy world for him, a voyage back to some wondrous childhood. He'd stay with the boys after school, playing catch, sipping lemonade and eating cookies. The boys, who were shy and quiet at school, would roll about and wrestle at home in the afternoon. Then they would do homework around the kitchen table. Mickey let them have "TV dinners" consisting of decent, mostly Italian food Mickey cooked up fresh and served up as they watched the baseball pennant race games together.

They talked a lot when the sound was off, rambling conversations about California history and Spanish verb conjugations. For some time, Mickey felt guilty that the boys rarely spoke of their mother. He had taken them to a counselor, worried about the psychological toll their flight had exacted. The boys were remarkably unfazed by the new arrangements. They readily accepted Mickey's declaration that this was the only way he could secure them a solid American education. He never interfered with Mei Mei's letters or phone calls, which had already become less frequent. The one time they spoke directly on the phone, he promised her access whenever she decided to visit the States.

She rejected the offer once more. She hated America. She hated Mickey for his audacity and for the powerlessness he made her feel ten thousand miles away. She spoke coldly, as if the boys were property in dispute, or that they were complicit somehow, that father and sons were in cahoots. She threatened him clumsily, promising to use her father to ruin his business affairs, ignorant of the fact that Mickey had already been fired by Telstar. She seemed, in the end, resigned to the reality that Mickey and the boys were beyond her reach.

As the weeks passed, Mickey felt the enormous gratification of release. He was lost in a suburban reverie. *Virtual irrelevance—that's my penance.* Mickey saw it now; *my penance and my liberation.*

He surprised himself with his latent domesticity. He became a compulsive house-father, running laundry, packing nourishing school lunches at midnight, careful to set the breakfast table before he turned in. He rose ahead of the boys' alarm, taking great pleasure in making pancakes with fresh strawberries and bacon. He relished the domestic routine and the sense of accomplishment it afforded.

He went to the office late and left early. He had no day-to-day boss, and his local Agency contact brought him little work those first weeks. He settled in, determined to enjoy each day. He found himself as contented as he could ever remember being. He'd pay eventually. He knew it in his lapsed Catholic gut.

Once the second wave of news stories from Asia passed and the Albuquerque court granted him custody, he began to dream again—great dreams, satisfying and complete. He would dream of sports and of women. In his nighttime thoughts, his amours were friends from long past. Sometimes, they were women with whom he had shared just one dance or a single furtive kiss. His curious mind now played out the scenes in vivid detail. He dreamed of sports conquest as well, of hitting the last-second basket in a high school game, of sinking a long putt at junior golf. It was typical jock stuff. But Mickey awoke feeling renewed and triumphant.

He saw a good deal of Booth his first couple of months back. They would take a weekday afternoon in San Francisco, meeting at the Giants' glorious ballpark in China Basin. Mickey would ride over from Oakland on the ferry, a cheerful pedestrian with his windbreaker and newspapers. They would sit high above the bleacher wall, soaking up the rays in left field on September afternoons when most responsible adults were at work and kids were in school. Mickey would drink a Diet Coke, Booth would nurse a Sprite as they munched peanuts and rooted heartily.

Booth had settled in at Serra House, already launched on a solid second career at Stanford. Mickey teased him unmercifully for doubling back to the scholarly world—if only to mask his envy. Beyond his temporary Agency gig, Mickey had no long-term job plans of his own.

"Twenty-seven years it took you to worm your way into that faculty office!" Mickey taunted. "Asia's a mess. Smithson's heading to New Hampshire. Where's Booth? Drinking lattés down on the Farm."

Booth wouldn't rise to the bait. He waved off Mickey's jabs with an easy smile.

"I've come full circle," he acknowledged, his relief evident. "Once upon a time, I promised myself I would balance action and reflection. Live life in the center of the ring, but step outside for contemplation now and again."

"Corporate America never rests," said Mickey. "Commerce doesn't take a sabbatical."

"And look what happens to them," Booth observed. "Seems like a lot of big businessmen are heading to prison lately."

"I suppose they'll have plenty of time to reflect on the meaning of life," Mickey conceded.

"'The unexamined life is hardly worth living.'"

"Socrates?" Mickey guessed, delighted to wear the anti-intellectual hat once more.

"Try Plato."

"That scrawny guy who plays second base for the Tigers?"

"Yeah," said Booth, going along with their old gag. "Batted only .198 and got sent down to Scranton."

They played hooky together, using the time to decompress. They had one particular discussion of baseball cards, Mickey's lifelong obsession that resonated with Booth for days.

"The boys just don't get it," Mickey lamented. "I got a bunch of my best cards out of the folks' attic back home. The memories, the cards, the sense of time and place they brought back—well, it was just overwhelming."

"What do you mean?"

"I spent hours going through the old cards. Looking at the teams, the statistics, the cartoons on the back, the faces. I had this intense reconnection with the day I'd opened each pack. I could look at a 1964 Topps Dick Ellsworth and remember exactly where I'd been, on the steps of the PX at Fort Ord."

"Cool."

"I always thought having a baseball card of yourself was like ensuring your immortality. Remember that guy Ken Hubbs?"

"Cubs' National League Rookie of the Year. Died in a plane crash that next winter."

"Right. But Topps had already put out that card of him with the gold trophy on the front. So, no matter what happens, you have a baseball card of yourself that a bunch of kids keep in a shoebox, and some part of you lives on."

Mickey tried to explain the experience to Amy and their kids—Mickey and the boys visited for supper more than once. The Booth family merely smiled and passed the peas—*crazy Mickey was rambling again*. They welcomed him, though, and Amy in particular gave him some gentle but firm instruction on drawing his boys out about the tumult they had endured.

Booth had recreated a cozy nuclear unit there in their rented home in San Francisco's gentrified Haight-Ashbury district. He didn't mind the reverse commute south to Palo Alto, and casually ignored the financial uncertainties of signing a lease.

Booth's departure had been handled smoothly. Smithson—and even Senator Landle—proved remarkably gracious. After Booth's resignation, the committee's leak investigation was quietly halted, and the FBI was taken off the case without any confirmation of their suspicions. Having chosen good etiquette over partisan advantage, Senator Landle helped ensure that the matter ended there. Booth thought it was mighty decent of the man.

Booth slid easily into a Senior Associate's slot at Serra House, with two Poly Sci 101 sections to work as a teaching assistant, and a book contract from a scholarly publishing house. He was a natural pick-up for the renowned China Studies Program. Stanford welcomed his California industry connections and his ties to the Senate Foreign Relations Committee.

Booth would sit calmly at the small window, looking onto the Serra House quadrangle, with its rock garden and burbling fountain. The work went slowly, but the campus tranquility lent some prescience to his prose as he wrote about the transnational security challenges of the new century.

Mickey pressed him only once about the choice he had made. "How could you just walk away?" he asked.

"I'd ask how could *you*, Mickey, but the boys make your choice rather clear."

"Don't you itch to jump back in some days?" Mickey said. "To be out on the campaign trail with the senator?"

"No. I'm surprised, actually. Leaving was a lot easier than I ever suspected." Booth grew pensive and gazed over Mickey's shoulder. "Some weird stuff went down those last months—some things that made clear what the right thing was for me to do."

"Hell, I don't even have a real job, yet," Mickey said. "Been thinking about going for a realtor's license or something. But, hey, what about the campaign? Doesn't Smithson call and try to rope you back in?"

"I can still make my contributions. Been ghosting a speech or two. Trying to articulate grand visions I'm sure the pollsters and the message mavens will just delete. But, you know, after all those years of politics on the Hill, I needed the clean break."

"Funny, I had no idea I was ready to turn on a dime until it just came to me one morning in a hotel room," Mickey said. "I was so goddamn tired of waking up in a strange bed, of trying to keep all my stories straight, of having to keep my adversaries at bay. I was just ready to surrender. I figured the best revenge on them all was to find a way to be happy."

"That's a lousy way to live, Mickey. You can't pursue happiness out of vengeance."

Mickey had to ponder this unwelcome notion for a moment. "I guess I should just say I was ready for a radical change."

"Hey, 'the universe is change . . . our lives are what our thoughts make it . . .'"

"Plato again?"

"Nope. A guy my new book club's been reading, Marcus Aurelius Antonius."

"Shortstop?"

"Right. Cleveland Indians. Hits with power to all fields."

Mickey did find an opportunity to thank Senator Smithson in person for the risks he had tolerated that harrowing mid-summer day in Beijing. The senator was riding the pre-presidential campaign circuit, doing county picnics in Iowa and New Hampshire, but stopping in California to hit up long-time supporters for campaign cash. After addressing a policy luncheon at the Commonwealth Club in San Francisco, Smithson found time for coffee, making Mickey and Booth feel like players once more, however briefly.

Jake Smithson could not have been kinder. He was a regular guy, deflecting Mickey's gushing appreciation. The senator asked after Michael and Henry, then shared some Senate gossip until an anxious campaign aide came to hustle Smithson along. Booth and Mickey walked him to the elevator. Once the doors closed, the frenetic road show moved on without them. They were relieved to see it pass.

Mostly, Mickey's days were spent in a state of suspended animation.

He cut back on the lattés. He started swimming in the morning, and lifting a bit at the gym. He read books at lunch, sitting on the campus grass, taking the sun, watching without a care in the world as the co-eds strolled by.

What good deed have I done? Mickey wondered, feeling undeserving. *Why have the gods smiled upon me?*

He felt like a kid alone in a candy store. He could help himself with glee to all the pleasures about him, untroubled by the inevitable prospect of discovery. He would enjoy himself until his day of reckoning arrived. His punishment would come soon enough.

It was an oblique note in the National Intelligence Digest that shattered his idyll. It surfaced one morning during a seminar with some visiting CIA analysts, held this time on the Stanford campus, and hosted by a couple of the hard-liners at the Hoover Institute. They had been reviewing some analysis of the Chinese satellite launch program, then had broken for coffee. The senior man in town from Langley, a short fellow named Kent, pulled Mickey aside as they walked out the door.

"What do you make of that Chinese guy gone missing?"

"Who's that?" It seemed to Mickey as if China were some miniature world under glass, as if they were museum curators studying it from afar. For him, it was a world inhabited now only by ghosts and forgotten voices. Still, he didn't like the sound of "missing."

"In Singapore," Kent said. "I guess he used to be some kind of asset."

"Where'd you pick that up?"

"Something in the NID."

"I'm not cleared to get the NID."

"The guys were talking about it on the ride down from the airport. This guy was pretty senior over in the Foreign Ministry."

"A Foreign Ministry guy?"

"You didn't know? Damn, I tried to check with the NIO, with Branko. But he's out on some special assignment or something," Kent said, his voice growing edgy. "I just thought since he was someone you . . ."

"*Who* are you talking about?"

"It's like they offed one of their top guys at some international conference. Left a bloody mess. Supposedly, CNN is about to go with a story about the local Chinese Embassy covering it up—paid off the Singapore cops. There's something about no body that has them all stumped."

"What is his *name*?" said Mickey, who was nearly shouting. But then, it all became too clear, and Mickey answered his own question.

"Oh, Christ!" Mickey said. "It's Lee, isn't it?"

"Lee?"

"Li Jianjun."

"Yeah, that was the name."

Mickey felt sick. He veered from the foot-path, staggering toward a bench under a tree behind the Hoover Building.

A group of undergraduates passed by lugging backpacks, talking animatedly about a physics lab. Mickey's mind raced. He barely saw Kent standing awkwardly nearby, pulling out a cigarette.

"They killed him," Mickey said, mouthing the observation pointlessly. "Those assholes killed him."

He conjured up visions of Lee's last moments. Some honey pot bullshit, most likely. A woman at the bar slips something into his drink. Some muscle boys shove him out a high-rise window. A clever ruse by the Second Directorate. It would be just like them to make the killing messy enough to blame on some random act of violence, yet blunt enough to send a message, a warning to all in the know. He flashed on that old Richard Gere movie, where the American businessman is set up in his Beijing hotel room.

Where did I screw up? Mickey remembered the courtyard where they had talked, recalling Lee's words of resignation beneath the syrupy disco tunes. *Who betrayed us?*

Lee had seen it coming. Mickey knew that much. Lee had warned of the dangers when amateurs got involved.

They should have known Lee would not leave. His sense of duty would not permit it—his obligations to father and country, his eternal stubbornness. Goddamn bull-headed Lee, staggering like a boxer bloodied in the ring, waiting to take their last shot. What for?

Mickey stared angrily into space as he sat on the bench. *Had Lee died just so Langley could steal a glimpse into the Red Dragons' game? Just to salvage a summit photo op the Chinese were already going to sabotage? It was all a fucking game.*

Next came the guilt. *The Interior boys must have fingered Lee for the Departure Lounge ruse. Lee died so my boys could grow up free. It was that simple,* Mickey concluded.

Somehow this last thought offered Mickey consolation in his torment. The boys' freedom. That was Lee's legacy, the final sacrifice of the godfather. It was a proposition—a gift—Mickey could live with. He touched the St. Christopher encircling his neck, rubbing its smooth surfaces for comfort.

Mickey sat by himself long after the Hoover session resumed. He tried with his cell phone to get Branko, but he was indeed away on some special assignment, and Mickey ended up leaving a garbled message with a secretary. An urgent call to Alexander Bonner proved similarly fruitless.

Then Mickey began to walk, moving very slowly at first, as if he had planned the route before, retracing an altogether familiar path back to Serra House. He nodded at Ginny Clark—same den mother receptionist at the same desk, twenty-seven years after he had left the place. Time seemed to have advanced little here in the musty academic corridors, where dissertation footnotes were still being reworked by earnest scholars. Ginny gazed absent-mindedly as she greeted him, and he walked down past the

China Studies Library in search of Booth.

Booth was out. So Mickey sat at Booth's desk and logged onto the Internet, scrolling through CNN, the *Times*, and Reuters' web sites. He found nothing—no word of any missing Chinese diplomats. He stared at the lined legal pad he was toting. He briefly caressed the paper, like a father rubbing a baby's tummy to calm him.

Then he began to scribble notes, beginning some kind of private eulogy. He felt a desperate need to write something, to somehow find a way to memorialize the significance of Lee's deeds. He needed to honor Lee's life in words, if only for the boys to read some day, to ensure they would never forget his name.

Mickey was scrawling the old Spender lines, when, abruptly, he stopped. He set the pen down and steepled his fingers, drumming them against each other for several moments of thought.

Then he leapt up, banging Booth's chair back against the window ledge, and raced down the hallway. Exiting the building, he took off on a brisk jog, long strides heading up Galvez Street towards the Hoover building. His hamstrings were pulling tight. His pace grew more rapid, his breathing labored, yet improved, because of the recent workouts. He caught Kent chatting in a cluster by the door with a couple of guys from Hewlett-Packard.

"Mr. Kent, I need a word, if I might," Mickey said, out of breath. The man from Langley excused himself, and the two of them walked down the sidewalk.

After they had gone only a few steps, Mickey blurted it out. "Did you say that the report you had was that there was 'no body'?" He was practically on top of Kent. "They didn't find a body?"

"That's right."

"And you said Singapore, right?" Mickey demanded. "Not Hong Kong? Not in the PRC?"

"Right."

That was all the hope Mickey needed. The hope carried him up Highway 101 and back across the Bay Bridge. Somehow, he didn't require the cryptic voicemail from Branko, which he found on his answering machine when he returned to Berkeley. He didn't need to ask for details on an open line. He could see now why Branko could not reach out to him earlier, and the silence cheered him.

For several days, Mickey awaited a signal. He waited for some confirmation that—to his great surprise—he fervently prayed for. He went about his domestic routines. He remained expectant, though, sleeping lightly, his animal senses aroused.

It came less than a week later, in the form of a note in an unfamiliar hand, passed by an attractive young lady wearing a blue and gold Cal sweatshirt at the end of a seminar he had been auditing. She was gone before he could open the blank white envelope she had handed him. The plain paper inside read simply "Road Trip. Come alone. Golden Hinde Inn. 11:00 AM, tomorrow."

Then, he knew.

29

OUT THE BEAR VALLEY TRAIL

By nine-thirty the next morning, Mickey was driving west toward the Pacific. He'd seen the kids onto the school bus, gassed up his car, then taken the Richmond-San Rafael Bridge over the placid bay. He rolled past the mustard-colored prison walls at San Quentin, and snaked out Sir Francis Drake Boulevard below the slopes of Mount Tamalpais. Over White's Hill he sped, past the golf club at San Geronimo, then plunging into the redwoods of Samuel P. Taylor Park, looping back and forth on the S curves bordering the dry creek bed. The one-stop-light towns of Lagunitas and Olema slowed him little. After more than an hour, he crested the last hill and pulled up by the boat harbor of Inverness, on Tomales Bay.

The town was quite still. It was a school-day morning, with few signs of life on the one thoroughfare. A solitary man in a red-checked shirt hosed down the pavement in front of the grocery store. The spray and the sound of tires being installed in the service bay of the gas station were the only noises. It felt as if he was hundreds of miles from the big city. Warm fog overhead flattened the light, and Mickey creaked a bit as he emerged, stiff jointed, from his Ford.

The lobby of the Inn was also deserted. A haunt for bed and breakfasters heading out from the Bay Area for weekends, it was empty on this early fall day. Mickey peered about, feeling awkward and out of place.

A soft, dull voice called from a den behind the lobby counter, startling him a bit. "Would you be Mr. Dooley?"

"Yes, that's me," Mickey said as the man emerged. Midwestern. Conservative. A tad formal. He didn't seem like an Inverness kind of guy.

"A gentleman left this for you." He handed Mickey a business-size white envelope.

Mickey nodded curtly at the man, walking outside before he opened the envelope. Inside was a simple printed sheet: "Thanks for coming," it read. "Better to talk in Divine Meadow. See you at noon."

Mickey ducked into the grocery to grab some snacks and water for the hike ahead, then drove the two miles to the ranger station at the Point Reyes trailhead. He parked his car at the stables and headed down the path toward the woods.

Clutching his paper sack, he paused for a drink before the trail entered the shade. Soon, ferns were all about him, lazily uncurling to reach toward shafts of light penetrating the darkened canopy. A small creek gurgled on his left, rolling through banks of needles and pinecones. Sequoias towered overhead. He could taste the air, with its pungent mix of laurel, eucalyptus, and redwood all about him.

Out the Bear Valley Trail he strode once more, out where they all had played in that time of youthful dreams more than a quarter century before. He could hear the leaves crunch underfoot as he climbed steadily up the grade, deeper into the forest.

After a couple of miles, the trail crested before a familiar clearing. At the top of the meadow was a rough-hewn log bench. Mickey sat there, sipping water, watching, still fifteen minutes early. Slices of fog were spilling up the field of dry grass, two feet high and straw yellow. Fingers of gray would reach up the incline, only to expire in the strengthening sun, just cresting above. Wave after wispy wave tumbled forward, only to disappear in an evanescent dance. The diffuse light accentuated the contrast between the deep greens of the well-moistened ferns and the pale field that lay open before him.

In the stillness, he reflected upon the road he had tread from Stanford to China and back. He reflected upon time spent and time lost, upon life yet to live. He closed his eyes for several moments, half meditation, half prayer, as if waiting for a sign.

He sensed movement nearby, a flicker in the tall grass. Midway down the field, about a quarter mile in length, he saw a white deer, its coat flecked with brown. The doe was standing, ears prone, observing him. A fawn was close behind her, ambling carelessly. It was a vision—ever so brief—of innocence. The mother held Mickey with her stare. Then she was startled by some footfall Mickey could not detect. She fled abruptly, leaping through the sea of downy grass, the fawn scurrying after.

At the foot of the field now, there was a puff of dust. Two figures emerged from the grass, walking deliberately toward him, two purposeful-looking men, military in bearing, in windbreakers and dark glasses.

Mickey flashed back to the Interior Ministry goons at the Beijing departure lounge, like sergeants on some old black-and-white cop show. The figures continued to stride directly toward him, the two men approaching up the quiet field.

He was alone, utterly alone in this wild place. He felt naive and vulnerable. *How stupid can I be?* His stolen time was ended; he knew it. His bill had come due.

"Mickey Dooley?" said the first man, the breeze outlining a shoulder holster beneath the flattened nylon jacket.

"Yeah?" Mickey said tentatively, his heart racing, his head cocked at an uncomfortable angle.

"You come by yourself?"

"You sure you weren't tailed?" asked the second man before Mickey could answer.

"Sure," he said, glancing over his shoulder, peering anxiously behind him. "As far as I know."

The first man reached for a walkie-talkie. "Good to go, Jack. Bring him on."

The men began to back down the path. Only then did Mickey's final fears dissipate like the lifting fog. He began to calm, recognizing the security escort now, there as protectors, not executioners. As he turned, ashamed for his momentary fright, a familiar face was walking towards him, not twenty yards away.

It was Lee. Grimacing shyly, looking wan and thin in jeans and a hiking shirt, it was unmistakably Lee. There was a rumpled canvas fishing hat on his head, pulled forward almost to his brow.

"By God, you did it!" Mickey rushed forward to envelop him in a bear hug. Lee felt limp in his arms before Mickey released him. "You pulled it off!"

"Yes, I'm afraid I did."

"When did you make it here, to the States?"

"Oh, about three days ago, I guess it was." Lee sounded weary.

"How did they get you out?"

"Probably best not to discuss," he said.

"But, Branko . . . Branko did it! Well, let me look at you!" Mickey stood back regarding Lee as if he were an apparition. Mickey noticed again how lifeless he stood, shrunken in pants that were too large. "Where are they keeping you, man?"

"Some safe house out in the suburbs. I am a captive of Middle America."

"You're *free*, Lee! I was so worried that day you didn't take the plane. I didn't want to leave without you. Thank God you made it out of all that craziness!"

Lee was unresponsive as he gazed down the field to where the two security men were lingering, shades on in the drifting fog. Mickey noticed a third agent with a walkie-talkie now, on the trail back toward the ranger station.

"You should feel great! I'm so proud of you for having the balls to pull it off."

"Sure. Big balls."

"To break free of their clutches—"

"Mickey," Lee interrupted sternly as he faced him, "I am not free. I am like a prisoner."

"Hey! They probably just have to debrief you for a while," Mickey said. "Do you have any idea whatsoever how valuable your contributions can be? To stability? To peace? You can help figure out what the hell's going on back in Beijing. You're a goddamn hero."

"Heroes act selflessly for others. Bravado is for those who like to show off. I'm not sure what that makes me."

"You're a genuine patriot."

"I'm a patriot without a nation."

"You've got a window into their game. It's like cracking the code for the Red Dragons. You can help us stay out of some idiotic war. It's all I'd asked from you that last night."

"And after?"

"What do you mean?"

"And after they are done with me? I will still be a prisoner in a foreign land."

"It won't be that way forever. I mean—" Mickey caught himself as he began to pace. "Is it your father?"

Lee gazed into the fog again. It was some time before he replied. "My father is dead."

"Oh, God," Mickey could only mumble, "I'm so sorry."

"Yes. You see, I had promised him, Mickey. His nurse did, too. Before he sank into that faraway place, we both promised him we wouldn't leave him to die alone." Lee's eyes were dry and pinched as he spoke, self-reproach in his tone. "I felt we both had to stay, to honor that promise. So I stayed that day you left."

Mickey could think of nothing he could say to comfort him.

"He fell into a coma in early September. Then he passed in peace," Lee continued. "I did not let him die alone. And now I will be the one who dies alone in a foreign land. That is not the way of a Chinese hero."

"You won't be alone! They just need to protect you. For a while. For your own good."

"It's one thing in theory and another in reality—all the interrogations and the isolation. I can never be free here."

"But they—"

"I am a non-person. A man with no name, like the forgotten dead."

"We won't ever forget the—"

"Don't you see the irony, Mickey? It is so very Western. The individual makes a difference. But, then, it is so very Chinese. The individual is sacrificed for the greater good."

"Well, shit. I'm just going to call Branko and see if we can't break you out of this box. Sounds like they're going way overboard with all this security."

"You still don't understand," said Lee, stopping him with a firm hand. "I *chose* this path. It is my own free will. Now I must walk the path I have chosen."

"But you knew when you decided to help—"

"I knew only that I could not stay, even if I had wanted to." Lee thought of Xu An, and the choice pierced him yet again, even as he held onto his hope—to Branko's promise and to Xu An's. "I was suspect. They believed I had become the enemy, an enemy who questioned all their empty nationalist slogans."

"They were so wrong."

"No, Mickey. They were right."

"What?"

"They were absolutely right with their suspicions. I *was* contaminated. I became Western in my thinking."

"The Chinese have sent five hundred thousand students to the U.S. in the last thirty years. They don't all become a threat because—"

"I became a foreigner in my own land! My country left me before I left my country. China is run by a corrupt clique driven by a dead ideology. They're men who believe their own rhetoric. They will do anything to cling to power—even turn on their own."

Mickey was watching him cautiously as Lee seemed to shrink under the weight of his burdens. "So, you *knew*?"

"Knew what?" Lee asked.

"You knew all along, didn't you?"

"What?

"That someone had tried to kill us. That someone had tried to eliminate us, to screw things up, to play dirty tricks on Washington and Taiwan."

"I was very slow to see it. It took some time to accept that anybody would really go that far. But those hotheads are without adult supervision in their work. Everybody likes the deniability."

"Those guys are crazy."

"No, they are clever—very clever and calculating. They are zealots, neo-Maoists. They are the spoiled children of the Red Guards. They combine the worst of both countries' modern generations, yours and mine. The impatience, the hunger for instant gratification, the fascination with high tech violence of the West. The rhetorical fury, the chip-on-the-shoulder jealousy of their Asian contemporaries."

"Couldn't you see where they were headed with—"

"I didn't want to believe it. I was distracted by my father, my worries, my hopes for a new relationship. By the time I accepted the reality of my situation—of what the Red Dragons' game is about—it was almost too late. *Branko* understands. Branko sees it all. He always did."

"But Branko promised we would try to protect you."

"Branko has kept his promises from the first day. He always has, Mickey. Your people learned that I was only permitted to join the delegation in Singapore so they could liquidate me there. Make an example of me while blaming it on somebody else—same as the incident outside Rachel's firm. Branko's people were just one step ahead."

"Only because you helped them penetrate the cell."

"Who really knows how our fates are decided?"

"Well, now you're free," Mickey said, repeating himself.

"As you say."

"You're a godsend for us, for any hope of stabilizing the relationship."

"I will always be a traitor in China."

"No! You betrayed no one." Mickey grabbed Lee so hard that one of the security men started toward them. "You'll help us all to live on the same planet without incinerating each other."

"You flatter me, Mickey." Lee smoothed his jacket and flexed his arm a bit. "You called me a subversive once."

"You always were."

"Maybe it's true. I warned you before I left America that first time. I admired you all then, for your loyalty to each other, for your promises to never forget. I never had such a family. But I tried to serve China when I returned. I tried."

"You *did* serve China."

"I tried to believe. At first, it was not so hard to respect my leaders."

"Hey, we all respect China, your history, your future."

"It was not so hard at first because your government was so arrogant—all those belligerent fantasies about Star Wars machines, all those inflated fears about the Sandinistas invading Texas, your obsession with pathetic little Fidel Castro."

"C'mon, Lee. Let's not open old arguments."

"Your government had no appreciation for the history of other cultures, none of that 'decent respect for the opinion of mankind' that your founding fathers had promised. It was easy for me to disrespect America. Then, when the Soviet empire collapsed, you thought you could rule the world on your own. I made a career of explaining America to my people."

"You seemed settled in once upon a time," Mickey said, determined to change the subject.

"Yes. I married. But things didn't work out. I was lonely. I divorced. I missed my American days, and the freedom I felt with all of you. Then I allowed myself to dream. All those intoxicating ideas I had been exposed to. Thoreau. Jefferson. My ability to conform was undermined by my search for a more enduring truth. I grew to hate bureaucrats."

"They are just careerists," Mickey said as they sat on the log bench. Mickey burrowed into his paper bag now. He was famished and began to peel an orange. "Just like bureaucrats anywhere—they try to perpetuate themselves in power."

Lee ignored him as he continued. "Worse yet, I secretly encouraged this belief among the young. Their dreams were crushed under Li Peng's tanks at Tiananmen Square. And the new group of ideological suck-ups running the show now were the lead cheerleaders back then—the very ones urging the Army on against the people. For me, Tiananmen changed everything."

"But you stayed."

"I admired the students so very much. The democracy activists who were killed at Tiananmen—they had big dreams for the future." He took a section of fruit from Mickey. "You know, they would have fit right into our little club at Stanford. They were just a bunch of Martin Booths with noble visions."

"Sounds like you were quite a help to Branko."

"I merely provided some insights from our internal debates. That is what I offered, from time to time. When I chose to. We spied on you. I helped *you* listen to us."

"Amazing."

"Transparency—that was my policy. There was a mischievous symmetry to my approach. I was determined to reduce the chances of miscalculation on either side. I helped you understand us by letting you hear our internal debates."

"But you were playing with fire."

"I was playing God," Lee said. "It was easy to rationalize. I sat on a precipice, viewing two worlds and the chasm that separates them. I told myself that, if in one hour a few American and Chinese generals can incinerate the planet—and any memory of our existence—there could be nothing more important for me to do. Spies tell themselves these things."

Mickey was struggling to fit together old pieces, wondering about the future. Lee was moving too fast. After a time, Mickey spoke cautiously. "So what about this 'relationship' you mentioned?"

"What about it?"

"I mean, who is she?"

"Her name is Xu An. She is a healer. She was my father's nurse. She became family, my friend, my confidant. I trusted her in all things these last weeks. Maybe I am just being a fool, Mickey. I do her no favor sharing these burdens. But it is nice to have hopes." Lee paused, before adding, "I stayed for Father as well—for my father and the game."

"Did the CIA pressure you?"

"Not really. I was always the one in control. That was the illusion. I could choose what to give the Americans. Sometimes, I would go months, a year even, without passing anything on. Sometimes, I would pass on something false, or take some hard line at home—just to allay suspicion."

Mickey regarded Lee in a new light, impressed by the risks with which he had lived for decades. Mickey's own life of compartmentalization seemed easy by comparison.

"I developed a fantasy about my final act," Lee said. "To return to the U.S.-China Relations Program at Serra House. To go public with everything at some Stanford policy conference. To tell all the little secrets of the game—with a bunch of Chinese diplomats there to be shocked. To speak truth to power."

"Do it!" said Mickey, embracing the idea immediately. "I mean, Booth is already there. I hear Rachel may come out and finally finish her doctorate. Alexander may even be coming. This is something you need to do!"

"It is a fantasy, Mickey," Lee said, shaking his head. "It is not a serious proposition."

"But it would be great. We could get all the old gang together and just blow everybody's minds. Come full circle."

"Mickey, how can you still be so naïve?"

"What?"

"They would kill me. If I ever surfaced, the Chinese security guys would hunt me down like an animal and kill me. "

"No."

"Of course they would," Lee insisted. "Just to make an example of me."

"Not on American soil."

"Sure, if only to save face. Heck, even Taiwan killed a critic on U.S. soil. That's why we were so careful about getting together today. The Chinese will watch you—for years—to see if you come to me."

"I figured that—"

"Besides, I wouldn't do that to Stanford. Stanford was always good to me. China would never let their students come again; they would cut off all contact with Serra House. And my sponsors in Washington—even Branko—would not welcome the attention."

"Branko probably has wanted to do it himself for years."

"Too provocative." Lee was still enjoying the idea even as he dismissed it. "Such work is best done in the shadows."

"Too *provocative*? After the Chinese ram our planes out of the sky, hold our airmen for ransom, and send the plane home in pieces? After they push hundreds of missiles against Taiwan and violate their pledges of restraint? After their renegade outfit pulls shit like the F Street number? After the whole E-War disaster? *That's* provocation."

"It is simply not how Washington will want to use me."

They were sitting now, sharing the bottled water. As they pondered their next move, Mickey peeled the last sections of orange. The juice ran down his fingers as he handed pieces to Lee, who took them appreciatively and tucked them in his mouth. It was several minutes before Lee spoke. "Some things in life you must accept, Mickey."

"But it's like you have a second chance. It's like you came back from the dead."

"Li Jianjun *is* dead—gone to dust." He was stoic once more. "Let him rest."

"We will make a new life for you."

"It is resurrection I will hope for, yes. They say they will find me some new identity, like in your FBI's Witness Protection Program."

"But China needs you to—"

"China is a great country. We have survived and flourished over the many centuries. But I am done with all this rancor. I prefer to just write a bit, to live quietly with the knowledge and company of a few friends."

"Maybe we can go back someday," Mickey said. "You and I, together."

"No, Mickey," said Lee. "I will never go back."

"You need to have some hope for the future."

"I *have* hope. I have hope for many things. For knowledge. For understanding. For human love."

"Let us help. Let Branko help—with Xu An, I mean. Can they get her out?"

"We don't know if that will be possible. You know, I don't even have a picture of her—just in my head. But maybe you will be able to meet her someday."

Mickey was silent, watching Lee work through these things. Then Mickey reached for his coat pocket. "I almost forgot. I was in a similar situation that day I left. Couldn't bring anything of my past with me. So . . . I brought you some pictures." Mickey opened the small envelope and pulled out three small color prints, handing the stack to his friend.

The first two were of the boys, Michael and Henry. They were copies Mickey had gone back into the master bedroom for on his last night in

Beijing. The children were grinning conspiratorially in Yankee pinstripes, their first Litttle League uniforms.

The last was a photograph from long ago. It was a snapshot from that New Year's Eve party, the night they called the Last Dance. The camera had framed their tableau as they solemnly toasted from the couch, packing boxes on the margins—Booth and Barry, Rachel and Alexander, Branko, Mickey, and Lee, each peering anxiously into their future.

"It started then, you know," Lee said as he examined the old photo.

"What?"

"It began that night."

"*What* began?"

Lee was focused on something far distant now, examining the past, reconsidering his life as he watched the wind sweep through the towering trees far down the meadow.

"He asked me that night. Branko did."

"He asked you what?"

"He recruited me . . . on the night of that last party."

"No!"

"That is the remarkable thing about Branko. He *knew*. He knew even before I did. He could see it all then. To him, it was like a chess board; he was preparing for the end-game decades in advance. He knew the contradictions we would encounter, the choices we would have to make. He foresaw the paths we would take. He somehow saw it would come to this." Lee was chuckling in admiration. "Mickey, he recruited me from the very beginning."

"He recruited you to do what?"

"He was a talent scout from the very first day. He anticipated future needs. He enlisted me to share information, to provide extra eyes and ears, to help in any way I chose. He recruited me to be his spy."

"Jesus."

Finished the thought, Lee sat in silence, resolving an old memory. Then he turned back to Mickey, tapping the photos. "And you must know, friend, these photos do help me have hope. For me, yes, but mostly for another generation."

"For the boys . . ."

"Of course. I hope they can move freely back and forth across the bridges we tried to build. It is not about us any more. It is about Michael and Henry. About the world they can make."

"Like I said, Lee, you're a goddamn hero."

"Enough with this hero talk."

"It's *true*. You've done a great service. To me, to my boys, to Branko, to us all. You've upheld everything we ever pledged to believe in, every toast we ever made."

"We toasted to many things," Lee said, gazing again at the photos. Then he cleared his throat, before adding quietly: "We were so very young."

"To 'wearing our hearts at the fire's center.' To never forgetting. You've taken risks, made a difference. What could possibly have more enduring a meaning?"

"Mickey, you credit me too much."

"Because of you, I have my boys."

"That was you. I hardly did—"

"No!" Mickey was shouting now, hopping about as he circled in front of Lee, crumpling the bag of trash in his spreading palms. He was full of pulsing energy once again. "I don't even know exactly what you did that day at the airport with the soldiers, the fire. I don't need to know. All I know is that my boys are free. We are together. Without you, it never would have happened." Lee stood now as Mickey halted his pacing. "And I . . . we . . . we will honor you for it always."

They were quite close, facing each other. The fruit was finished. The water was gone. The fog was lifting.

"So, what now?"

"Yes, Mickey. What now?"

"Where to?"

"To work," Lee said. "I will see if I can help Branko and his people, help to buy some time until wiser voices can prevail."

Mickey nodded before Lee continued. "Then I will go sit on the mountaintop. Somewhere near this place, I hope, where I can dream again. Perhaps I will not be alone for so long."

"Someday, the realities may change," Mickey offered. "Maybe then you could hope to go home."

"No. Not in my lifetime. In the boys', perhaps." Lee was still grimacing. But this last thought pleased him and, as he placed the photos in his breast pocket, his visage began finally to brighten. "You must learn patience, my friend. These things take time."

"I'm trying, Lee," Mickey promised. "I'm really trying."

Now, at last, they could smile together, their confessions honored, their memories complete. They were redeemed and at peace.

Mickey laid a heavy arm around Lee's shoulders. Tentatively, at first, then purposefully, they began to retrace the path into the sunlight before them, two old school friends heading back up the trail together.

ACKNOWLEDGEMENTS

The Mandarin Club, while a work of the imagination, is fiction that echoes many true events. Also genuine are several of the current challenges in U.S.-China relations it explores.

Any parallels between the novel's characters and actual living persons are, however, coincidental. It is true that the author once drank with idealistic Stanford scholars at a sketchy bar on El Camino Real. But the characters introduced at The Oasis are made up. So, too, are the lobbyists, journalists, senators, and spies they come to meet.

Fables are enriched by fact. Similarly, the weaving of a story about modern China—and the Americans who have chosen to engage that great civilization—has benefited from the guidance of experienced hands. Some of the assistance extended to the author was witting and deliberate. For this, special thanks go to friends such as Richard Bush, a former U.S ambassador to Taiwan who's currently at the Brookings Institute; Michele de Nevers of the World Bank; and Frank Hawke. Their knowledge of things Chinese is remarkable. A word of respect is also due democracy activists on both sides of the Taiwan Strait with whom the author has been privileged to work. Their often anonymous voices have shown great courage and patriotism; their labors helped inspire the story at hand.

To fellow polishers of prose, the author is deeply indebted as well. Joe Kanon, Joe Tanner, Florence Ladd, Leonard Wolf, Jason Warburg, Demaris Brinton, Liza von Rosenstiel, Colleen Sechrest, Kim Armstrong Strumwasser, Gordon Kerr, Ron Goldfarb, and the indefatigable Bruce Bortz deserve special thanks. Bruce leads by example while bringing wisdom and style to all he touches.

Power in Washington is exercised in the most peculiar ways. Learning to savor this combat while upholding essential values can prove to be a challenge, one that is aided considerably by the knowledge and candor of friends. Having a day-job populated by the likes of Carl Ford, Amos Hochstein, Jerry Schecter, Paul Behrends, Richard Dennington, Larry Barrett, Ken Wollack, Paul Leventhal, Jody Powell, P.X. Kelley, Kathy Gest, Cindy Brown, Lien Fu Huang, and Gerry Cassidy has been a source of countless insights. Each of their unique contributions is much appreciated. Many were unwitting accomplices in the work at hand. None bear any responsibility for indiscretions or literary excess.

Standing out in this crowd is my friend Kathleen Anne McCloskey, who has consistently encouraged the work as a member of our extended family.

At home, Jennifer, Joy, and Dylan enriched the story with humor, tolerance, and unconditional affection. Special appreciation goes to our in-house Chairman of I.T., Mr. Zachary Arthur Warburg, who stands as a heroic bridge across the chasm dividing parents who grew up without computers from kids who can save them—and their manuscripts—from getting lost in cyberspace.

ABOUT THE AUTHOR

Gerald Felix Warburg has worked in Washington on trade, intelligence, and international security matters since the Ford Administration. He has served on the staff of leadership in both the United States Senate and House of Representatives, where he was a principal draftsman of the Nuclear Nonproliferation Act and other U.S. foreign policy initiatives. In addition, he has provided counsel to several American presidential campaigns and to the U.S. Nuclear Regulatory Commission.

As a visiting lecturer, he has taught history and government courses at Hampshire College in Amherst, Massachusetts, and for Stanford and Georgetown university programs. The author of *Conflict and Consensus: The Struggle Between the President and Congress to Shape U.S. Foreign Policy* (HarperCollins), he is currently Executive Vice President for a Washington government relations firm.

A native of Marin County, California, Mr. Warburg holds an undergraduate degree from Hampshire College, and an advanced degree from Stanford University. He and his family reside in Virginia.

The Mandarin Club is his first novel.